WHERE THERE'S FIRE, THERE'S SMOKE

WHERE THERE'S FIRE, THERE'S SMOKE

WILLIAM W. JOHNSTONE

P

PINNACLE BOOKS
Kensington Publishing Corp.
www.kensingtonbooks.com

Kensington Publishing Corp.
119 West 40th Street
New York, NY 10018

All Kensington titles, imprints, and distributed lines are available at special quantity discounts for bulk purchases for sales promotions, premiums, fund-raising, educational, or institutional use. Special book excerpts or customized printings can also be created to fit specific needs. For details, write or phone the office of the Kensington sales manager: Kensington Publishing Corp., 119 West 40th Street, New York, NY 10018, attn: Sales Department; phone 1-800-221-2647.

PINNACLE BOOKS and the Pinnacle logo are Reg. U.S. Pat. & TM Off.

ISBN-13: 978-0-7860-4492-4
ISBN-10: 0-7860-4492-6

First printing: September 2016

12 11 10 9 8 7 6 5 4

Printed in the United States of America

Electronic edition:

978-0-7860-4562-4 (e-book)
0-7860-4562-0 (e-book)

CONTENTS

TRAIL OF THE MOUNTAIN MAN

Dedicated to Caroline Gehman. Have a nice day— or night—whatever.

BOOK ONE

This will remain the land of the free only so long as it is the home of the brave.
—Elmer Davis

I seen my duty and I done it.
—Anonymous

1

As gold strikes go, this particular strike was nothing to really shout about. Oh, a lot of the precious metal was dug out, chipped free, and blasted from the earth and rock, but the mines would play out in just over a year. The town of Fontana would wither and fade from the Western scene a couple of years later.

But with the discovery of gold, a great many lives would be forever changed. Livelihoods and relationships were altered; fortunes were made and lost; lives were snuffed out and families split, with the only motive greed.

Thus Fontana was conceived only to die an unnatural death.

Dawn was breaking as the man stepped out of the cabin. He held a steaming cup of coffee in one large, callused hand. He was tall, with wide shoulders and the lean hips of the horseman. His hair was ash-blond, cropped short, and his eyes were a cold brown, rarely giving away any inner thought.

The cabin had been built well, of stone and logs. The floor was wood. The windows held real glass. The cabin had been built to last, with a hand pump in the kitchen to bring up the water. There were curtains on the windows. The table and chairs and benches were hand-made and carved; done with patience and love.

And all about the house, inside and out, were the signs of a woman's touch.

Flowers and blooming shrubs were in colored profusion. The area around the house was trimmed and swept. Neat.

It was a high-up and lonely place, many miles from the nearest town. Below the cabin lay a valley, five miles wide and as many miles long. The land was filed on and claimed and legal with the government. It belonged to the man and his wife.

They had lived here for three years, hacking a home out of the high, lonesome wilderness. Building a future. In another year they planned on building a family. If all stayed according to plan, that is.

The man and wife had a couple hundred head of cattle, a respectable herd of horses. They worked a large garden, canning much of what they raised for the hard winters that lashed the high country.

The man and woman stayed to themselves, socializing very little. When they did visit, it was not to the home of the kingpin who claimed to run the entire area, Tilden Franklin. Rather it was to the small farmers and ranchers who dotted the country that lay beneath the high lonesome where the man and woman lived.

There was a no-name town that was exclusively owned by Tilden Franklin. The town held a large general store, two saloons, a livery stable, and a gunsmith.

But all that was about to change.

Abruptly.

This was a land of towering mountains and lush, green

valleys, sparsely populated, and it took a special breed of men and women to endure.

Many could not cope with the harshness, and they either moved on or went back to where they came from.

Those that stayed were the hardy breed.

Like Matt and Sally.

Matt was not his real name. He had not been called by his real name for so many years he never thought of it. There were those who could look at him and tell what he had once been; but this was the West, and what a man had once been did not matter. What mattered was what he was now. And all who knew Matt knew him to be a man you could ride the river with.

He had been a gunfighter. But now he rarely buckled on a short gun. Matt was not yet thirty years old and could not tell you how many men he had killed. Fifty, seventy-five, a hundred. He didn't know. And neither did anyone else.

He had been a gunfighter, and yet had never hired out his gun. Had never killed for pleasure. His reputation had come to him as naturally as his snake-like swiftness with a short gun.

He had come West with his father, and they had teamed up with an old Mountain Man named Preacher. And the Mountain Man had taken the boy in tow and begun teaching him the way of the mountains: how to survive, how to be a man, how to live where others would die.

Preacher had been present when the boy killed his first man during an Indian attack. The old Mountain Man had seen to the boy after the boy's dying father had left his son in his care. Preacher had seen to the boy's last formative years. And the old Mountain Man had known that he rode with a natural gunslick.*

It was Preacher who gave the boy the name that would

*The Last Mountain Man

become legend throughout the West; the name that would be whispered around ten thousand campfires and spoken of in a thousand saloons; the name that would be spoken with the same awe as that of Bat Masterson, Ben Thompson, the Earp boys, Curly Bill.

Smoke.

Smoke's first wife had been raped and murdered, their baby son killed. Smoke had killed them all, then ridden into the town owned by the men who had sent the outlaws out and killed those men and wiped the town from the face of Idaho history.*

Smoke Jensen then did two things, one of them voluntarily. He became the most feared man in all the West, and he dropped out of sight. And then, shortly after dropping out of sight, he married Sally.

But his disappearance did nothing to slow the rumors about him; indeed, if anything, the rumors built in flavor and fever.

Smoke had been seen in Northern California. Smoke had gunned down five outlaws in Oregon. Smoke had cleaned up a town in Nevada. Since his disappearance, Smoke, so the rumors went, had done this and that and the other thing.

In reality, Smoke had not fired a gun in anger in three years.

But all that was about to change.

A dark-haired, hazel-eyed, shapely woman stepped out of the cabin to stand by her man's side. Something was troubling him, and she did not know what. But he would tell her in time.

This man and wife kept no secrets from each other. Their lives were shared in all things. No decisions were made by one without consulting the other.

Return of the Mountain Man

"More coffee?" she asked.

"No, thank you. Trouble coming," he said abruptly. "I feel it in my gut."

A touch of panic washed over her. "Will we have to leave here?"

Smoke tossed the dregs of his coffee to the ground. "When hell freezes over. This is our land, our home. We built it, and we're staying."

"How do the others feel?"

"Haven't talked to them. Think I might do that today. You need anything from town?"

"No."

"You want to come along?"

She smiled and shook her head. "I have so much to do around the house. You go."

"It'll be noon tomorrow before I can get back," he reminded her.

"I'll be all right."

He was known as Matt in this part of Colorado, but at home Sally always called him Smoke. "I'll pack you some food, Smoke."

He nodded his head. "I'll saddle up."

He saddled an appaloosa, a tough mountain horse, sired by his old appaloosa, Seven, who now ran wild and free on the range in the valley Smoke and Sally claimed.

Back in the snug cabin, Smoke pulled a trunk out of a closet and opened the lid. He was conscious of Sally's eyes on him as he removed his matched .44s and laid them to one side. He removed the rubbed and oiled gun belts and laid them beside the deadly Colts.

"It's come to that, Smoke?" she asked.

He sighed, squatting before the trunk. He removed several boxes of .44 ammo. "I don't know." His words were softly spoken. "But Franklin is throwing a big loop nowadays. And wants it bigger still. I was up on the

Cimarron the other day—I didn't tell you 'cause I didn't want you to worry. I made sign with some Indians. Sally, it's gold."

She closed the trunk lid and sat down, facing her husband. "Here? In this area?"

"Yes. Hook Nose, the buck that spoke English, told me that many whites are coming. Like ants toward honey was his words. If it's true, Sally, it's trouble. You know Franklin claims more than a hundred and fifty thousand acres as his own. And he's always wanted this valley of ours. It's surprising to me that he hasn't made a move to take it."

Money did not impress Sally. She was a young, high-spirited woman with wealth of her own. Old money, from back in New Hampshire. In all probability, she could have bought out Tilden Franklin's holdings and still had money.

"You knew about the gold all along, didn't you, Smoke?"

"Yes," he told her. "But I don't think it's a big vein. I found part of the broken vein first year we were here. I don't want it."

"We certainly don't need the money," she reminded him.

Smoke gave her one of his rare smiles, the smile softening his face and mellowing his eyes, taking years from the young man's face. "That's right. I keep forgetting I married me a rich lady."

Together, they laughed.

Her laughter sobered as he began filling the cartridge loops with .44 rounds.

"Does part of it run through our land, Smoke?"

"Yes."

"I'll pack you extra food. I think you're going to be gone longer than you think."

"I think you're probably right. Sally? You know you have nothing to fear from the Indians. They knew Preacher and know he helped raise me. It's the white men you have to be careful of. It would take a very foolish man to bother a woman out here, but it's happened. Stay close to the house. The horses will warn you if anyone's coming. Go armed at all times. Hear me?"

"Yes, Smoke."

He leaned forward and kissed her mouth. "I taught you to shoot, and know you can. Don't hesitate to do so. The pot is boiling, Sally. We're going to have gold-hunters coming up against Franklin's gunhands. When Franklin learns of the gold, he's going to want it all. Our little no-name town is going to boom. For a time. Trouble is riding our way on a horse out of Hell. You've never seen a boom town, Sally. I have. They're rough and mean and totally violent. They attract the good and the bad. Especially the bad. Gamblers and gunhawks and thieves and whores. We're all going to be in for a rough time of it for a while."

"We've been through some rough times before, Smoke," she said quietly.

"Not like this." He stood up, belted the familiar Colts around his lean waist, and began loading the .44s.

"Matt just died, didn't he?" she asked.

"Yes. I'm afraid so. When Smoke steps out of the shadows, Sally—and it's time, for I'm tired of being someone else—bounty hunters and kids with dreams of being the man who killed Smoke Jensen will be coming in with the rest of the trash and troublemakers. Sally, I've never been ashamed of what I was. I hunted down and destroyed those who ripped my life to shreds. I did what the law could not or would not do. I did what any real man would have done. I'm a Mountain Man, Sally. Perhaps the last of the breed. But that's what I am.

"I'm not running anymore, Sally. I want to live in peace. But if I have to fight to attain that peace . . . so be it. And," he said with a sigh, "I might as well level with you. Peyton told me last month that Franklin has made his boast about running us out of this valley."

"His wife told me, Smoke."

The young man with the hard eyes smiled. "I might have known."

She drew herself up on tiptoes and kissed him. "See you in two or three days, Smoke."

2

"Word is out, boss," Tilden's foreman said. "It's gold, all right. And lots of it."

Tilden leaned back in his chair and looked at his foreman. "Is it fact or rumor, Clint?"

"Fact, boss. The assay office says it's rich. Real rich."

"The Sugarloaf?"

Clint shrugged his heavy shoulders. "It's a broken vein, boss. Juts out all over the place, so I was told. Spotty. But one thing's for sure: all them piss-ant nesters and small spreads around the Sugarloaf is gonna have some gold on the land."

The Sugarloaf was Smoke's valley.

Tilden nodded his handsome head. "Send some of the crew into town, start stakin' out lots. Folks gonna be foggin' in here pretty quick."

"What are you gonna call the town, boss?"

"I knew me a Mex gal years back, down along the Animas. Her last name was Fontana. I always did like that name. We'll call 'er Fontana."

* * *

Tilden Franklin sat alone in his office, making plans. Grand plans, for Tilden never thought small. A big bear of a man, Tilden stood well over six feet and weighed a good two hundred and forty pounds, little of it fat. He was forty years old and in the peak of health.

He had come into this part of Colorado when he was twenty-five years old. He had carved his empire out of the wilderness. He had fought Indians and outlaws and the elements . . . and won.

And he thought of himself as king.

He had fifty hands on his spread, many of them hired as much for their ability with a gun as with a rope. And he paid his men well, both in greenbacks and in a comfortable style of living. His men rode for the brand, doing anything that Tilden asked of them, or they got out. It was that simple.

His brand was the Circle TF.

Tilden rose from his chair and paced the study of his fine home—the finest in all the area. When that Matt What's-His-Name had ridden into this part of the country—back three or four years ago—Tilden had taken an immediate dislike to the young man.

And he didn't believe Matt *was* the man's name. But Tilden didn't hold that against anyone. Man had a right to change his own name.

Still, Tilden had always had the ability to bully and intimidate other men. He had always bulled and bullied his way through any situation. Men respected and feared him.

All but that damned Matt.

Tilden remembered the first day he'd come face-to-face with Matt. The young man had looked at him through the coldest eyes Tilden had ever seen—a rattler's. And even though the young man had not been wearing a short gun, there had been no backup in him. None at all. He had looked right at Tilden, nodded his head, and walked on.

Tilden Franklin had had the uncomfortable and unaccustomed sensation that he had just been graded and found wanting. That, and the feeling that he had just been summarily dismissed.

By a goddamned saddle-bum, of all people!

No, Tilden corrected himself, not a saddle-bum. Matt might be many things, but he was no saddle-bum. He had to have access to money, for he had bought that whole damned valley free and clear. Bought most of it, filed on the rest of it.

And that woman of his, Sally. Just thinking of her caused Tilden to breathe short. He knew from the first day he'd seen her that he had to have her. One way or the other—and she was never far from his thoughts.

She was far and above any other woman in the area. She was a woman fit to be a king's queen. And since Tilden thought of himself as a king, it was only natural he possess a woman with queen-like qualities.

And possess her he would. It was just a matter of time.

Whether she liked it, or not. Her feelings were not important.

Three hours after leaving his cabin, Smoke rode up to the Colby spread. He halloed the house from the gate and Colby stepped out, giving him a friendly wave to come on in.

Colby's spread was a combination cattle ranch and farm, something purists in the cattle business frowned on. Colby and his family were just more of them "goddamned nesters" as far as the bigger spreads in the area were concerned. Colby had moved into the area a couple of years before Smoke and Sally, with his wife Belle, and their three kids, a girl and two boys. From Missouri, Colby was a hardworking man in his early forties. A veteran of the War Between the States, he was no stranger to guns, but was not a gunhand.

"Matt," he greeted the rider. His eyes narrowed at the sight of the twin Colts belted around Smoke's waist and tied down. "First time I ever seen you wearin' a pistol, much less two of them."

"Times change, Colby. You heard the gold news?"

"Last week. People already movin' in. You wanna come in and talk?"

"Let's do it out here. You ever seen a boom town, Colby?"

"Can't say as I have, Matt." The man was having a difficult time keeping his eyes off the twin Colts. "Why do you ask?"

"There's gold running through this area. Not much of it—a lot of it is iron and copper pyrites—but there's enough gold to bring out the worst in men."

"I ain't no miner, Matt. What's them pyrites you said?"

"Fool's gold. But that isn't the point, Colby. When Tilden Franklin learns of the gold—if he doesn't already know—he'll move against us."

"You can't know that for sure, Matt. 'Sides, this is our land. We filed on it right with the government. He can't just come in and run us off."

The younger man looked at Colby through hard, wise eyes. "You want to risk your family's lives on that statement, Colby?"

"Who are you, Matt?" Colby asked, evading the question.

"A man who wants to be left alone. A man who has been over the mountain and across the river. And I won't be pushed off my land."

"That don't tell me what I asked, Matt. You really know how to use them guns?"

"What do you think?"

Colby's wife and kids had joined them. The two boys were well into manhood. Fifteen and sixteen years old.

The girl was thirteen, but mature for her age, built up right well. Sticking out in all the right places. Adam, Bob, Velvet.

The three young people stared at the Colts. Even a fool could see that the pistols were used but well taken care of.

"I don't see no marks on them handles, Mister Matt," Adam said. "That must mean you ain't never killed no one."

"Adam!" his mother said.

"Tinhorn trick, Adam," Smoke said. "No one with any sand to them cuts their kills for everyone to see."

"I bet you wouldn't say that to none of Mister Franklin's men," Velvet said.

Smoke smiled at the girl. He lifted his eyes to Colby. "I've told you what I know, Colby. You know where to find me." He swung into the saddle.

"I didn't mean no offense, Matt," the farmer-rancher said.

"None taken." Smoke reined his horse around and headed west.

Colby watched Smoke until horse and rider had disappeared from view. "Thing is," he said, as much to himself as to his family, "Matt's right. I just don't know what to do about it."

Bob said, "Them guns look . . . well, *right* on Mister Matt, Dad. I wonder who he really is."

"I don't know. But I got me a hunch we're all gonna find out sooner than we want to," he said sourly.

"This is our land," Belle said. "And no one has the right to take it from us."

Colby put his arm around her waist. "Is it worth dyin' for, Ma?"

"Yes," she said quickly.

* * *

On his ride to Steve Matlock's spread, Smoke cut the trail of dozens of riders and others on foot, all heading for Franklin's town. He could tell from the hoofprints and footprints that horses and men were heavily loaded.

Gold-hunters.

Steve met him several miles from his modest cabin in the high-up country. "Matt," the man said. "What's going on around here?"

"Trouble, I'm thinking. I just left Colby's place. I couldn't get through to him."

"He's got to think on it a spell. But I don't have to be convinced. I come from the store yesterday. Heard the rumors. Tilden wants our land, and most of all, he wants the Sugarloaf."

"Among other things," Smoke said, a dry note to the statement.

"I figured you knew he had his eyes on Sally. Risky to leave her alone, Matt. Or whatever your name is," he added, acknowledging the Colts in a roundabout manner.

"Tilden won't try to take Sally by force this early in the game, Steve. He'll have me out of the way first. There's some gold on your land, by the way."

"A little bit. Most of it's fool's gold. The big vein cuts north at Nolan's place, then heads straight into the mountains. Take a lot of machinery to get it out, and there ain't no way to get the equipment up there."

"People aren't going to think about that, Steve. All they'll be thinking of is gold. And they'll stomp on anyone who gets in their way."

"I stocked up on ammo. Count on me, Matt."

"I knew I could."

Smoke rode on, slowly winding downward. On his way down to No-Name Town, he stopped and talked with Peyton and Nolan. Both of them ran small herds and farmed for extra money while their herds matured.

"Yeah," Peyton said. "I heard about the gold. God-damnit, that's all we need."

Nolan said, "Franklin has made his boast that if he can run you out, the rest of us will be easy."

Smoke's smile was not pleasant, and both the men came close to backing up. "I don't run," Smoke said.

"First time I ever seen you armed with a short gun," Peyton said. "You look . . . well, don't take this the wrong way, Matt . . . *natural* with them."

"Matt," Nolan said. "I've known you for three years and some months. I've never seen you upset. But today, you've got a burr under your blanket."

"This vein of gold is narrow and shallow, boys," Smoke said, even though both men were older than he. "Best thing could happen is if it was just left alone. But that's not going to happen." He told them about boom towns. "There's going to be a war," he added, "and those of us who only wanted to live in peace are going to be caught up in the middle of it. And there is something else. If we don't band together, the only man who'll come out on top will be Tilden Franklin."

"He sure wants to tan your hide and tack it to his barn door, Matt," Peyton said.

"I was raised by an old Mountain Man, boys. He used to say I was born with the bark on. I reckon he was right. The last twelve, fifteen years of my life, I've only had three peaceful years, and those were spent right in this area. And if I want to continue my peaceful way of life, it looks like I'm gonna have to fight for them. And fight I will, boys. Don't make no bets against me doing that."

Nolan looked uncomfortable. "I know it ain't none of my business, Matt, and you can tell me to go to hell if you want to. But I gotta ask. Who are you?"

"My Christian name is Jensen. An old Mountain Man named Preacher hung a nickname on me years back. Smoke."

Smoke wheeled his horse and trotted off without looking back.

Peyton grabbed his hat and flung it on the ground. "Holy Christ!" he yelled. "Smoke Jensen!"

Both men ran for their horses, to get home, tell their families that the most famous gun in the entire West had been their neighbor all this time. And more importantly, that Smoke Jensen was on *their* side.

3

When Smoke reached the main road, running east to west before being forced to cut due south at a place called Feather Falls, he ran into a rolling, riding, walking stream of humanity. Sitting astride his horse, whom he had named Horse, Smoke cursed softly. The line must have been five hundred strong. And he knew, in two weeks, there would probably be ten times that number converging on No-Name.

"Wonderful," he muttered. Horse cocked his ears and looked back at Smoke. "Yeah, Horse. I don't like it either."

With a gentle touch of his spurs, Smoke and Horse moved out, riding at an easy trot for town.

Before he reached the crest of the hill overlooking the town, the sounds of hammering reached his ears. Reining up on the crest, Smoke sat and watched the men below, racing about, driving stakes all over the place, marking out building locations. Lines of wagons were in a row, the wagons loaded with lumber. Canvas tents were already in place, and the whiskey peddlers were dipping their homemade concoction out of barrels. Smoke knew there would be everything in that whiskey from horse-droppings to snakeheads.

He rode slowly down the hill and tied up at the railing in front of the general store. He stood on the boardwalk for a moment, looking at the organized madness taking place all around him.

Smoke recognized several men from out of the shouting, shoving, cursing crush.

There was Utah Slim, the gunhand from down Escalante way. The gambler Louis Longmont was busy setting up his big tent. Over there, by the big saloon tent, was Big Mamma O'Neil. Smoke knew her girls would not be far away. Big Mamma had a stable of whores and sold bad booze and ran crooked games. Smoke had seen other faces that he recognized but could not immediately put names to. They would come to him.

He turned and walked into the large general store. The owner, Beeker, was behind the counter, grinning like a cream-fed cat. No doubt he was doing a lot of business and no doubt he had jacked up his prices.

Beeker's smile changed to a frown when he noticed the low-slung Colts on Smoke. "Something, Matt?"

"Ten boxes of .44s, Beeker. That'll do for a start. I'll just look around a bit."

"I don't know if I can spare that many, Matt," Beeker said, his voice whiny.

"You can spare them." Smoke walked around the store, picking up several other items, including several pairs of britches that looked like they'd fit Sally. In all likelihood, she was going to have to do some hard riding before all this was said and done, and while it wasn't lady-like to wear men's britches and ride astride, it was something she was going to have to do.

He moved swiftly past the glass-enclosed showcase filled with women's underthings and completed his swing back to the main counter, laying his purchases on the counter. "That'll do it, Beeker."

The store owner added it up and Smoke paid the bill.

"Mighty fancy guns you wearin', Matt. Never seen you wear a short gun before. Something the matter?"

"You might say that."

"Don't let none of Tilden's boys see you with them things on. They might take 'em off you 'less you know how to use them."

Beeker did not like Smoke, and the feeling was shared. Beeker kowtowed to Tilden; Smoke did not. Beeker thought Tilden was a mighty fine man; Smoke thought Tilden to be a very obnoxious SOB.

Smoke lifted his eyes and stared at Beeker. Beeker took a step backward, those emotionless, cold brown eyes chilling him, touching the coward's heart that beat in his chest.

Smoke picked up his purchases and walked out into the spring sunlight. He stowed the gear in his saddlebags and walked across the street to the better of the two saloons. In a week there would be fifty saloons, all working twenty-four hours a day.

As he walked across the wide dirt street, his spurs jingling and his heels kicking up little dust pockets, Smoke was conscious of eyes on him. Unfriendly eyes. He stepped up onto the boardwalk and pushed through the swinging doors. Stepping to one side, giving his eyes time to adjust to the murky interior of the saloon, Smoke sized up the crowd.

The place was filled with ranchers and punchers. Some of those present were friends and friendly with Smoke. Others were sworn to the side of Tilden Franklin. Smoke walked to the end of the bar.

Smoke was dressed in black pants, red and white checkered shirt, and a low-crowned hat. Behind his left-hand Colt, he carried a long-bladed Bowie knife. He laid a coin on the bar and ordered a beer.

The place had grown very quiet.

Normally not a drinking man, Smoke did occasionally enjoy a drink of whiskey or a beer. On this day, he simply wanted to check out the mood of the people.

He nodded at a couple of ranchers. They returned the silent greeting. Smoke sipped his beer.

Across the room, seated around a poker table, were half a dozen of Tilden's men. They had ceased their game and now sat staring at Smoke. None of those present had ever seen the young man go armed before—other than carrying a rifle in his saddle boot.

The outside din was softened somewhat, but still managed to push through the walls of the saloon.

"Big doings around the area," Smoke said to no one in particular.

One of Tilden's men laughed.

Smoke looked at the man; he knew him only as Red. Red fancied himself a gunhand. Smoke knew the man had killed a drunken Mexican some years back, and had ridden the hoot-owl trail on more than one occasion. But Smoke doubted the man was as fast with a gun as he imagined.

"Private joke?" Smoke asked.

"Yeah," Red said. "And the joke is standin' at the bar, drinkin' a beer."

Smoke smiled and looked at a rancher. "Must be talking about you, Jackson."

Jackson flushed and shook his head. A Tilden man all the way, Jackson did all he could to stay out of the way of Tilden's ire.

"Oh?" Smoke said, lifting his beer mug with his left hand. "Well, then. Maybe Red's talking about you, Beaconfield."

Another Tilden man who shook in his boots at the mere mention of Tilden's name.

Beaconfield shook his head.

"I'm talkin' to you, Two-Gun!" Red shouted at Smoke.

Left and right of Smoke, the bar area quickly cleared of men.

"You'd better be real sure, Red," Smoke said softly, his words carrying through the silent saloon. "And very good."

"What the hell's that supposed to mean, nester?" Red almost yelled the question.

"It means, Red, that I didn't come in here hunting trouble. But if it comes my way, I'll handle it."

"You got a big mouth, nester."

"Back off, Matt!" a friendly rancher said hoarsely. "He'll kill you!"

Smoke's only reply was a small smile. It did not touch his eyes.

Smoke had slipped the hammer thong off his right-hand Colt before stepping into the saloon. He placed his beer mug on the bar and slowly turned to face Red.

Red stood up.

Smoke slipped the hammer thong off his left-hand gun. So confident were Red's friends that they did not move from the table.

"I'm saying it now," Smoke said. "And those of you still left alive when the smoke clears can take it back to Tilden. The Sugarloaf belongs to me. I'll kill any Circle TF rider I find on my land. Your boss has made his boast that he'll run me off my land. He's said he'll take my wife. Those words alone give me justification to kill him. But he won't face me alone. He'll send his riders to do the job. So if any of you have a mind to open the dance, let's strike up the band, boys."

Red jerked out his pistol. Smoke let him clear leather

before he drew his right-hand Colt. He drew, cocked, and fired in one blindingly fast motion. The .44 slug hit Red square between his eyes and blew out the back of his head, the force of the .44 slug slamming the TF rider backward to land in a sprawl of dead, cooling meat some distance away from the table.

The other TF riders sat very still at the table, being very careful not to move their hands.

Smoke holstered his .44 in a move almost as fast as his draw. "Anybody else want to dance?"

No one did.

"Then I'll finish my beer, and I'd appreciate it if I could do so in peace."

No one had moved in the saloon. The bartender was so scared he looked like he wanted to wet his long handles.

"Pass me that bowl of eggs down here, will you, Beaconfield?" Smoke asked.

The rancher scooted the bowl of hard-boiled eggs down the bar. Smoke looked at the bartender. "Crack it and peel it for me."

The bartender dropped one egg and made a mess out of the second before he got the third one right.

"A little salt and pepper on it, please," Smoke requested.

Gas escaped from Red's cooling body.

Smoke ate his egg and finished his beer. He wiped his mouth with the back of his hand and deliberately turned his back to the table of TF riders. "Any backshooters in the bunch?" he asked.

"First man reaches for a gun, I drop them," a rancher friendly to Smoke said.

"Thanks, Mike," Smoke said.

He walked to the batwing doors, his spurs jingling. A TF rider named Singer spoke, his voice stopping Smoke. "You could have backed off, Matt."

"Not much backup in me, Singer." Smoke turned around to once more face the crowded saloon.

"I reckon not," Singer acknowledged. "But you got to know what this means."

"All it means is I killed a loud-mouthed tinhorn. Your boss wants to make something else out of it, that's his concern."

"Man ought to have it on his marker who killed him." Singer didn't let up. "Matt your first or last name?"

"Neither one. The name is Jensen. Smoke Jensen."

Singer's jaw dropped so far down Smoke thought it might hit the card table. He turned around and pushed open the doors, walking across the street to his horse. As he swung into the saddle, he was thinking. Should get real interesting around No-Name . . . real quick.

4

As Smoke was riding out of the town, one of Tilden's men, who had been in the bar around the card table, was fogging it toward the Circle TF, lathering a good horse to get the news to Tilden Franklin.

Tilden sat on his front porch and received the news of the gunfight, a look of pure disbelief on his face. "Matt killed Red? What'd he do, shoot him in the back?"

"Stand-up, face-to-face fight, boss," the puncher said. "But Matt ain't his real name. It's Smoke Jensen."

Tilden dropped his coffee cup, the cup shattering on the porch floor. "Smoke Jensen!" he finally managed to blurt out. "He's got to be lyin'!"

The puncher shook his head. "You'd have to have been there, boss. Smoke is everything his rep says he is. I ain't never seen nobody that fast in all my life."

"Did he let Red clear leather before he drew?" Tilden's voice was hoarse as he asked the question.

"Yessir."

"Jensen," Tilden whispered. "That's one of his trademarks. Okay, Donnie. Thanks. You better cool down that horse of yours."

The bowlegged cowboy swaggered off to see to his horse. Tilden leaned back in his porch chair, a sour sensation in his stomach and a bad taste in his mouth. Smoke Jensen . . . *here*! Crap!

What to do?

Tilden seemed to recall that there was a murder warrant out for Smoke Jensen, from years back. But that was way to hell and gone over to Walsenburg; and the men Smoke had killed had murdered his brother and stolen some Confederate gold back during the war.*

Anyway, Tilden suddenly remembered, that warrant had been dropped.

No doubt about it, Tilden mused, with Smoke Jensen owner of the Sugarloaf, it sure as hell changed things around some. Smoke Jensen was pure hell with a gun. Probably the best gun west of the Mississippi.

And that rankled Tilden too. For Tilden had always fancied himself a gunslick. He had never been bested in a gunfight. He wondered, as he sat on the porch: Was he better than Smoke Jensen?

Well, there was sure one way to find out.

Tilden rejected that idea almost as soon as it popped into his mind.

He did not reject it because of fear. The big man had no fear of Smoke. It was just that there were easier ways to accomplish what he had in mind. Tilden had never lost a fight. Never. Not a fistfight, not a gunfight. He didn't believe any man could beat him with his fists, and damn few were better than Tilden with a short gun.

He called for his Mexican houseboy to come clean up the mess made by the broken cup and to bring him another cup of coffee.

The mess cleaned up, a fresh cup of steaming coffee at

The Last Mountain Man

hand, Tilden looked out over just a part of his vast holdings. Some small voice, heretofore unheard or unnoticed, deep within him, told him that all this was enough. More than enough for one man. You're a rich man, it said. Stop while you're ahead.

Tilden pushed that annoying and stupid thought from his mind. No way he would stop his advance. That was too foolish to even merit consideration.

No, there were other ways to deal with a gunhawk like Jensen. And a plan was forming in Tilden's mind.

The news of the saloon shooting would soon be all over the area. And the small nester-ranchers like Nolan and Peyton and Matlock and Colby would throw in with Smoke Jensen. Maybe Ray and Mike as well. That was fine with Tilden.

He would just take them out one at a time, saving Jensen for last.

He smiled and sipped his coffee. A good plan, he thought. A very good plan. He had an idea that most of the gold lay beneath the Sugarloaf. And he'd have the Sugarloaf. And the mistress of Sugarloaf too.

Sally.

Sally had dressed in boys' jeans and a work shirt. Her friends and family back in New Hampshire would be horrified to see her dressed in male clothing but there came a time when practicality must take precedence over fashion. And she felt that time was here.

She looked out the window. Late afternoon. She did not expect Smoke to return for another day—perhaps two more days. She was not afraid. Whenever Smoke rode in for supplies it was a two- or three-day trek—sometimes longer. But those prior trips had been in easier times. Now, one did not know what to expect.

Or from which direction.

As soon as Smoke had gone, she had saddled her pony, a gentle, sure-footed mare, and ridden out into the valley. She had driven two of Smoke's stallions, Seven and Drifter, back to the house, putting them in the corral. The mountain horses were better than any watchdog she had ever seen. If anyone even came close to the house, they would let her know. And, if turned loose, the stallion Drifter would kill an intruder.

He had done so before.

The midnight-black, yellow-eyed Drifter had a look of Hell about him, and was totally loyal to Smoke and Sally. Sally had belted a pistol around her waist, leaned a rifle against the wall, next to the door, and laid a double-barreled express gun on the table. She knew how to use all the weapons at hand, and would not hesitate to do so.

The horses and chickens fed, the cow milked, all the other chores done, Sally went back into the house and pulled the heavy shutters closed and secured them. The shutters had gun slits cut into them, which could be opened or closed. She stirred the stew bubbling in the blackened pot and checked her bread in the oven. She sat down on the couch, picked up a book, and began her lonely wait for her man.

Smoke put No-Name Town far behind him and began his long trip back to Sugarloaf. He would stop at the Ray ranch in the morning, talk to him. The fat was surely in the fire by now, and the grease would soon be flaming.

Some eight high-up and winding miles from the town, just as purple shadows were gathering in the mountain country, Smoke picked a spot for the night and began making his lonely camp. He did not have to picket Horse, for Horse would stay close, acting as watcher and guard.

Smoke built a small fire for coffee, and ate from what Sally had fixed for him. Some cold beef, some bread with a bit of homemade jam on it. He drank his coffee, put out the fire, and settled into his blankets, using his saddle for a pillow. In a very short time, he was deep in sleep.

In the still unnamed town, Utah Slim sat in a saloon and sipped a beer. Even though hours had passed since the shooting of Red, the saloon still hummed with conversation about Smoke Jensen. Utah Slim did not join in the conversations around the bar and the tables. So far, few knew who he was. And that was the way he liked it—for a time. When it was time for Utah Slim to announce his intentions, he'd do so.

He was under no illusions; he'd seen Smoke glance his way riding into town. Smoke recognized him. Now it was just a waiting game.

And waiting was something Utah was good at. Something any hired gun had better be good at, or he wouldn't last long in this business.

Louis Longmont stepped out of his canvas bar and game room and glanced up and down the street. A lean, hawk-faced man, with strong, slender hands and long fingers, the nails carefully manicured, the hands clean, Louis had jet-black hair and a black pencil-thin mustache. He was dressed in a black suit, with white shirt and dark ascot—the ascot something he'd picked up on a trip to England some years back. He wore low-heeled boots. A pistol hung in tied-down leather on his right side; it was not for show alone. For Louis was snake quick with a short gun. A feared, deadly gunhand when pushed.

Louis was not an evil man. He had never hired his gun out for money. And while he could make a deck of cards do almost anything except stand up and sing "God Save the Queen," Louis did not cheat at poker. He did not have to cheat. A man possessed of a phenomenal memory, Louis could tell you the odds of filling any type of poker hand; and he was also a card-counter. He did not consider that cheating, and most agreed with him that it was not.

Louis was just past forty years of age. He had come to the West as a mere slip of a boy, with his parents, arriving from Louisiana. His parents had died in a shantytown fire, leaving the boy to cope the best he could.

Louis had coped quite well, thank you.

Louis had been in boom towns all over the West, seeing them come and go. He had a feeling in his guts that this town was going to be a raw bitch-kitty. He knew all about Tilden Franklin, and liked none of what he'd heard. The man was power-mad, and obviously lower class. White trash.

And now Smoke Jensen had made his presence known. Louis wondered why. Why this soon in the power game? An unanswered question.

For a moment, Louis thought of packing up and pulling out. Just saying the hell with it! For he knew this was not going to be an ordinary gold-rush town. Powerful factions were at work here. Tilden Franklin wanted the entire region as his own. Smoke Jensen stood in his way.

Louis made up his mind. Should be a very interesting confrontation, he thought.

He'd stay.

Big Mamma O'Neil was an evil person. If one could find her heart, it would be as black as sin itself. Big Mamma stepped out in front of her gaming room and love-for-sale tent to look up and down the street. She nodded at Louis. He returned the nod and stepped back inside his tent.

Goddamned stuck-up card-slick! she fumed. Thought he was better than most everyone else. Dressed like a dandy. Talked like some highfalutin' professor—not that Big Mamma had ever known any professor; she just imagined that was how one would sound.

Big Mamma swung her big head around, once more looking over the town. A massive woman, she was strong as an ox and had killed more than one man with her huge, hard fists. And had killed for money as well as pleasure; one served her interests as much as the other.

Big Mamma was a crack shot with rifle or pistol, having grown up in the raw, wild West, fighting Indians and hooligans and her brothers. She had killed her father with an axe, then taken his guns and his horse and left for Texas. She had never been back.

She had brothers and sisters, but had no idea what had ever become of any of them. She really didn't care. The only thing she cared about was money and other women. She hated men.

She had seen Smoke Jensen ride in, looking like the arrogant bastard she had always thought he would be. So he had killed some puncher named Red—big deal! A nothing rider who fancied himself a gunhand. She'd heard all the stories about Jensen, and discounted most of them as pure road apples. The rumors were that he had been a Mountain Man. But he was far too young to have been a part of that wild breed.

As far as she was concerned, Smoke Jensen was just another overrated punk.

As the purple shadows melted into darkness over the no-name town that would soon become Fontana, Monte Carson stepped out of the best of the two permanent saloons and looked up and down the wide, dusty street. He hitched at the twin Colts belted around his waist and tied down low.

This town, he thought, was shaping up real nice for a hired gun. And that's what Monte was. He had hired his guns out in Montana, in the cattle wars out in California, and had fought the sheep farmers and nesters up in Wyoming. And, as he'd fought, his reputation had grown. Monte felt that Tilden Franklin would soon be contacting him. He could wait.

On the now-well-traveled road beneath where Smoke slept peacefully, wagons continued to roll and rumble along, carrying their human cargo toward No-Name Town. The line of wagons and buggies and riders and walkers was now several miles long. Gamblers and would-be shop-owners and whores and gunfighters and snake-oil salesmen and pimps and troublemakers and murderers and good solid family people . . . all of them heading for No-Name with but one thought in their minds. Gold.

At the end of the line of gold-seekers, not a part of them but yet with the same destination if not sharing the same motives, rattled a half a dozen wagons. Ed Jackson was new to the raw West—a shopkeeper from Illinois with his wife Peg. They were both young and very idealistic, and had no working knowledge of the real West. They were looking for a place to settle. This no-name town sounded good to them. Ed's brother Paul drove the heavily laden supply wagon, containing part of what they just knew would make them respected and secure citizens. Paul was as naive as his brother and sister-in-law concerning the West.

In the third wagon came Ralph Morrow and his wife Bountiful. They were missionaries, sent into the godless West by their Church, to save souls and soothe the sinful spirits of those who had not yet accepted Christ into their lives. They had been looking for a place to settle when they had hooked up with Ed and Peg and Paul. This was the first time Ralph and Bountiful had been west of Eastern Ohio. It was exciting. A challenge.

They thought.

In the fourth wagon rode another young couple, married only a few years, Hunt and Willow Brook. Hunt was a lawyer, looking for a place to practice all he'd just been taught back East. This new gold rush town seemed just the place to start.

In the fifth wagon rode Colton and Mona Spalding. A doctor and nurse, respectively. They had both graduated from their schools only last year, mulled matters over, and decided to head West. They were young and handsome and pretty. And, like the others in their little caravan, they had absolutely no idea what they were riding into.

In the last wagon, a huge, solidly built vehicle with six mules pulling it, came Haywood and Dana Arden. Like the others, they were young and full of grand ideas. Haywood had inherited a failing newspaper from his father back in Pennsylvania and decided to pull out and head West to seek their fortunes.

"Oh Haywood!" Dana said, her eyes shining with excitement. "It's all so wonderful."

"Yes," Haywood agreed, just as the right rear wheel of their wagon fell off.

5

Smoke was up long before dawn spread her shimmering rays of light over the land. He slipped out of his blankets and put his hat on, then pulled on his boots and strapped on his guns. He checked to see how Horse was doing, then washed his face with water from his canteen. He built a small, hand-sized fire and boiled coffee. He munched on a thick piece of bread and sipped his coffee, sitting with his back to a tree, his eyes taking in the first silver streaks of a new day in the high-up country of Colorado.

He had spotted a fire far down below him, near the winding road. A very large fire. Much too large unless those who built it were roasting an entire deer—head, horns, and all. He finished the small, blackened pot of coffee, carefully doused his fire, and saddled Horse, stowing his gear in the saddle bags.

He swung into the saddle. "Steady now, Horse," he said in a low voice. "Let's see how quiet we can be back-tracking."

Horse and rider made their way slowly and quietly down from the high terrain toward the road miles away using the twisting, winding trails. Smoke uncased U.S. Army binoculars he'd picked up years back, while traveling with his mentor, the old Mountain Man Preacher, and studied the situation.

Five, no—six wagons. One of them down with a busted back wheel. Six men, five women. All young, in their early twenties, Smoke guessed. The women were all very pretty, the men all handsome and apparently—at least to Smoke, at least at this distance—helpless.

He used his knees to signal Horse, and the animal moved out, taking its head, picking the route. Stopping after a few hundred twisting yards, Smoke once more surveyed the situation. His binoculars picked up movement coming from the direction of No-Name. Four riders. He studied the men, watching them approach the wagons. Drifters, from the look of them. Probably spent the night in No-Name gambling and whoring and were heading out to stake a gold claim. They looked like trouble.

Staying in the deep and lush timber, Smoke edged closer still. Several hundred yards from the wagon, Smoke halted and held back, wanting to see how these pilgrims would handle the approach of the riders.

He could not hear all that was said, but he could get most of it from his hidden location.

He had pegged the riders accurately. They were trouble. They reined up and sat their horses, grinning at the men and women. Especially the women.

"You folks look like you got a mite of trouble," one rider said.

"A bit," a friendly looking man responded. "We're just getting ready to fulcrum the wagon."

"You're gonna do *what* to it?" another rider blurted.

"Raise it up," a pilgrim said.

"Oh. You folks headin' to Fontana?"

The wagon people looked at each other.

Fontana! Smoke thought. Where in the hell is Fontana?

"I'm sorry," one of the women said. "We're not familiar with that place."

"That's what they just named the town up yonder," a rider said, jerking his thumb in the direction of No-Name. "Stuck up a big sign last night."

So No-Name has a name, Smoke thought. Wonder whose idea that was.

But he thought he knew. Tilden Franklin.

Smoke looked at the women of the wagons. They were, to a woman, all very pretty and built-up nice. Very shapely. The men with them didn't look like much to Smoke; but then, he thought, they were Easterners. Probably good men back there. But out here, they were out of their element.

And Smoke didn't like the look in the eyes of the riders. One kept glancing up and down the road. As yet, no traffic had appeared. But Smoke knew the stream of gold-hunters would soon appear. If the drifters were going to start something—the women being what they wanted, he was sure—they would make their move pretty quick.

At some unspoken signal, the riders dismounted.

"Oh, say!" the weakest-jawed pilgrim said. "It's good of you men to help."

"Huh?" a rider said, then he grinned. "Oh, yeah. We're regular do-gooders. You folks nesters?"

"I beg your pardon, sir?"

"Farmers." He ended that and summed up his feelings concerning farmers by spitting a stream of brown tobacco juice onto the ground, just missing the pilgrim's feet.

The pilgrim laughed and said, "Oh, no. My name is Ed Jackson, this is my wife Peg. We plan to open a store in the gold town."

"Ain't that nice," the rider mumbled.

Smoke kneed Horse a bit closer.

"My name is Ralph Morrow," another pilgrim said.

"I'm a minister. This is my wife Bountiful. We plan to start a church in the gold town."

The rider looked at Bountiful and licked his lips.

Ralph said, "And this is Paul Jackson, Ed's brother. Over there is Hunt and Willow Brook. Hunt is a lawyer. That's Colton and Mona Spalding. Colton is a physician. And last, but certainly not least, is Haywood and Dana Arden. Haywood is planning to start a newspaper in the town. Now you know us."

"Not as much as I'd like to," a rider said, speaking for the first time. He was looking at Bountiful.

To complicate matters, Bountiful was looking square at the rider.

The woman is flirting with him, Smoke noticed. He silently cursed. This Bountiful might be a preacher's wife, but what she really was was a hot handful of trouble. The preacher was not taking care of business at home.

Bountiful was blonde with hot blue eyes. She stared at the rider.

All the newcomers to the West began to sense something was not as it should be. But none knew what, and if they did, Smoke thought, they wouldn't know how to handle it. For none of the men were armed.

One of the drifters, the one who had been staring at Bountiful, brushed past the preacher. He walked by Bountiful, his right arm brushing the woman's jutting breasts. She did not back up. The rider stopped and grinned at her.

The newspaperman's wife stepped in just in time, stepping between the rider and the woman. She glared at Bountiful. "Let's you and I start breakfast, Bountiful," she suggested. "While the men fix the wheel."

"What you got in your wagon, shopkeeper?" a drifter asked. "Anything in there we might like?"

Ed narrowed his eyes. "I'll set up shop very soon. Feel free to browse when we're open for business."

The rider laughed. "Talks real nice, don't he, boys?"

His friends laughed.

The riders were big men, tough-looking and seemingly very capable. Smoke had no doubts but what they were all that and more. The more being troublemakers.

Always something, Smoke thought with a silent sigh. People wander into an unknown territory without first checking out all the ramifications. He edged Horse forward.

A rider jerked at a tie-rope over the bed of one wagon. "I don't wanna wait to browse none. I wanna see what you got now."

"Now see here!" Ed protested, stepping toward the man.

Ed's head exploded in pain as the rider's big fist hit the shopkeeper's jaw. Ed's butt hit the ground. Still, Smoke waited.

None of the drifters had drawn a gun. No law, written or otherwise, had as yet been broken. These pilgrims were in the process of learning a hard lesson of the West: you broke your own horses and killed your own snakes. And Smoke recalled a sentiment from some book he had slowly and laboriously studied. When you are in Rome live in the Roman style; when you are elsewhere live as they live elsewhere.

He couldn't remember who wrote it, but it was pretty fair advice.

The riders laughed at the ineptness of the newcomers to the West. One jerked Bountiful to him and began fondling her breasts.

Bountiful finally got it through her head that this was deadly serious, not a mild flirtation.

She began struggling just as the other pilgrims surged forward. Their butts hit the ground as quickly and as hard as Ed's had.

Smoke put the spurs to Horse and the big horse broke

out of the timber. Smoke was out of the saddle before Horse was still. He dropped the reins to the ground and faced the group.

"That's it!" Smoke said quietly. He slipped the thongs from the hammers of his .44s.

Smoke glanced at Bountiful. Her bodice was torn, exposing the creamy skin of her breasts. "Cover yourself," Smoke told her.

She pulled away from the rider and ran, sobbing, to Dana.

A rider said, "I don't know who you are, boy. But I'm gonna teach you a hard lesson."

"Oh? And what might that be?"

"To keep your goddamned nose out of other folks' business."

"If the woman had been willing," Smoke said, "I would not have interfered. Even though it takes a low-life bastard to steal another man's woman."

"Why, you . . . *pup!*" the rider shouted. "You callin' me a bastard?"

"Are you deaf?"

"I'll kill you!"

"I doubt it."

Bountiful was crying. Her husband was holding a handkerchief to a bloody nose, his eyes staring in disbelief at what was taking place.

Hunt Brook was sitting on the ground, his mouth bloody. Colton's head was ringing and his ear hurt where he'd been struck. Haywood was wondering if his eye was going to turn black. Paul was holding a hurting stomach, the hurt caused by a hard fist. The preacher looked as if he wished his wife would cover herself.

One drifter shoved Dana and Bountiful out of the way, stepping over to join his friend, facing Smoke. The other two drifters hung back, being careful to keep their hands away from their guns. The two who hung back were older, and wiser to the ways of gunslicks. And they did not like the looks of this young man with the twin Colts. There was something very familiar about him. Something calm and cold and very deadly.

"Back off, Ford," one finally spoke. "Let's ride."

"Hell with you!" the rider named Ford said, not taking his eyes from Smoke. "I'm gonna kill this punk!"

"Something tells me you ain't neither," his friend said.

"Better listen to him," Smoke advised Ford.

"Now see here, gentlemen!" Hunt said.

"Shut your gawddamned mouth!" Ford told him.

Hunt closed his mouth. Heavens! he thought. This just simply was not done back in Boston.

"You gonna draw, punk?" Ford said.

"After you," Smoke said quietly.

"Jesus, Ford!" the rider who hung back said. "I know who that is."

"He's dead, that's who he is," Ford said, and reached for his gun.

His friend drew at the same time.

Smoke let them clear leather before he began his lightning draw. His Colts belched fire and smoke, the slugs taking them in the chest, flinging them backward. They had not gotten off a shot.

"Smoke Jensen!" the drifter said.

"Right," Smoke said. "Now ride!"

6

The two drifters who had wisely elected not to take part in facing Smoke leaped for their horses and were gone in a cloud of galloping dust. They had not given a second glance at their dead friends.

Smoke reloaded his Colts and holstered them. Then he looked at the wagon people. The Easterners were clearly in a mild state of shock. Bountiful still had not taken the few seconds needed to repair her torn bodice. Smoke summed her up quickly and needed only one word to do so: trouble.

"My word!" Colton Spalding finally said. "You are very quick with those guns, sir."

"I'm alive," Smoke said.

"You *killed* those men!" Hunt Brook said, getting up off the ground and brushing the dust from the seat of his britches.

"What did you want me to do?" Smoke asked, knowing where this was leading. "Kiss them?"

Hunt wiped his bloody mouth with a handkerchief. "You shall certainly need representation at the hearing. Consider me as your attorney."

Smoke looked at the man and smiled slowly. He shook his head in disbelief. "Lawyer, the nearest lawman is about three days' ride from here. And I'm not even sure this area is in his jurisdiction. There won't be any hearing, Mister. It's all been settled and over and done with."

Haywood Arden was looking at Smoke through cool eyes. Smoke met the man's steady gaze.

This one will do, Smoke thought. This one doesn't have his head in the clouds. "So you're going to start up a newspaper, huh?" Smoke said.

"Yes. But how did you know that?"

"Me and Horse been sitting over there," Smoke said, jerking his head in the direction of the timber. "Listening."

"You move very quietly, sir," Mona Spalding said.

"I learned to do that. Helps in staying alive." Smoke wished Bountiful would cover up. It was mildly distracting.

"One of those ruffians called you Smoke, I believe," Hunt said. "I don't believe I ever met a man named Smoke."

Ruffians, Smoke thought. He hid his smile. Interesting choice of words to describe the drifters. "I was halfway raised by an old Mountain Man named Preacher. He hung that name on me."

The drifter called Ford broke wind in death. The shopkeeper's wife, Peg, thought as though she might faint any second. "Could someone please do something about those poor dead men?" she asked.

Dawn had given way to a bright clear mountain day. A stream of humanity had begun riding and walking toward Fontana. A tough-looking pair of miners riding mules reined up. Their eyes dismissed the Easterners and settled on Smoke. "Trouble?" one asked.

"Nothing I couldn't handle," Smoke told him.

"'Pears that way," the second miner said drily. "Ford

Beechan was a good hand with a short gun." He cut his eyes toward the sprawled body of Ford.

"He wasn't as good as he thought," Smoke replied.

"'Pears that's the truth. We'll plant 'em for four bits apiece."

"Deal."

"And their pockets," the other miner spoke.

"Have at it," Smoke told them. "The pilgrims will pay."

"Now see here!" Ed said, starting to protest.

"Shut up, Ed," Haywood told him. He looked at the miners. "You gentlemen may proceed with the digging."

"Talks funny," one miner remarked, getting down and tying his mule. He got a shovel from his pack animal and his partner followed suit.

"You live and work in this area, Mister Smoke?" Mona asked.

One miner dropped his shovel and his partner froze still as stone. The miner who dropped his shovel picked it up and slowly turned to face Smoke. "Smoke Jensen?"

"Yes."

"Lord God Almighty! Ford shore enuff bit off more than he could chew. Smoke Jensen. My brother was over to Uncompahgre, Smoke. Back when you cleaned it up. He said that shore was a sight to see."*

Smoke nodded his head and the miners walked off a short distance to begin their digging. "How deep?" one called.

"Respectable," Smoke told them.

They nodded and began spading the earth.

"Are you a gunfighter, Mister Smoke?" Willow asked.

"I'm a rancher and farmer, Ma'am. But I once had the reputation of being a gunhawk, yes."

"You seem so young," she observed. "Yet you talk as

*The Last Mountain Man

if it was years ago. How old were you when you became a . . . gunhawk?"

"Fourteen. Or thereabouts. I disremember at times." Smoke usually spoke acceptable English, thanks to Sally; but at times he reverted back to Preacher's dialect.

"He's kilt more'un a hundred men!" one of the miners called.

The wagon people fell silent at that news. They looked at Smoke with a mixture of horror, fascination, and revulsion in their eyes.

It was nothing new to Smoke. He had experienced that look many times in his young life. He kept his face as expressionless as his cold eyes.

Smoke cut his eyes to Bountiful. "Lady," he said, exasperation in his voice, his tone hard. "Will you please cover your tits!"

Smoke had seen the remainder of the rancher-farmers in the mountain area and then headed for home. He almost never took the same trail back to his cabin. A habit he had picked up from Preacher. A habit that had saved his life on more than one occasion.

Even though he was less than five miles from his cabin when dark slipped into the mountains, he decided not to chance the ride in. He elected to make camp and head home at first light.

He caught several small fish from a mountain stream and broiled them over a small fire. That and the remainder of Sally's bread were his supper.

Twice during the night Smoke came fully awake, certain he had heard gunshots. He knew they were far away, but he wondered about it. The last shot he heard before he drifted back to sleep came from the south, far away from Sally and the cabin.

He was up and moving out before full dawn broke. Re-

lief filled him when he caught a glimpse of the cabin,
Sally in the front yard. Smoke broke into a grin when he
saw how she was dressed . . . in men's britches. His eyes
mirrored approval when he noted Seven and Drifter in the
corral. As he rode closer, he saw the pistol belted around
her waist, and the express gun leaning against the door
frame, on the outside of the cabin.

Man and wife embraced, each loving the touch and
feel of the other. With their mouths barely apart, she saw
the darkness in his eyes and asked, "Trouble?"

"Some. A hell of a lot more coming, though. I'll tell
you about it. You?"

"Didn't see a soul."

They kissed their love and she pushed him away, mis-
chief in her hazel eyes. "I missed you."

"Oh? How much?"

"By the time you see to Horse and get in the house, I'll
be ready to show you how much."

Fastest unsaddling and rub-down in the history of the
West.

Passions cooled and sated, she lay with her head on
Smoke's muscular shoulder. She listened as he told her
all that had happened since he had ridden from the ranch.
He left nothing out.

"See anyone that you knew in town? Any newcomers,
I mean?"

"Some. Utah Slim. I'm sure it was him."

"I've heard you talk of him. He's good?"

"One of the best."

"Better than you?"

"No," Smoke said softly.

"Anyone else?"

"Monte Carson. He's a backshooter. Big Mamma

O'Neil. Louis Longmont. Louis is all right. Just as long as no one pushes him."

"And now we have Fontana."

"For as long as it lasts, yes. The town will probably die out when the gold plays out. I hope it's soon."

"You're holding just a little something back from me, Smoke."

He hesitated. "Tilden Franklin wants you for his woman."

"I've known that for a long time. Has he made his desires public?"

"Apparently so. From now on, you're going to have to be very careful."

She lay still for a moment, silent. "We could always leave, honey."

He knew she did not wish to leave, but was only voicing their options. "I know. And we'd be running for the rest of our lives. Once you start, it's hard to stop."

In the corral, Seven nickered, the sound carrying to the house. Smoke was up and dressed in a moment, strapping on his guns and picking up a rifle. He and Sally could hear the sounds of hooves, coming hard.

"One horse," Sally noted.

"Stay inside."

Smoke stepped out the door, relaxing when he saw who it was. It was Colby's oldest boy, and he was fogging up the trail, lathering his horse.

Bob slid his horse to stop amid the dust and leaped off. "Mister Smoke," he panted. So the news had spread very fast as to Smoke's real identity.

"Bob. What's the problem?"

"Pa sent me. It's started, Mister Smoke. Some of Tilden's riders done burned out Wilbur Mason's place, over on the western ridge. Burned him flat. There ain't nothing left nowhere."

"Anybody hurt over there?"

"No, sir. Not bad, leastways. Mister Wilbur got burned by a bullet, but it ain't bad."

"Where are they now?"

"Mister Matlock took the kids. Pa and Ma took in Mister Wilbur and his missus."

"Where's your brother?"

"Pa sent him off to warn the others."

"Go on in the house. Sally will fix you something to eat. I'll see to your horse."

Smoke looked toward the faraway Circle TF spread. "All right, Franklin," he muttered. "If that's how you want it, get ready for it."

7

Leaving Bob Colby with Sally, Smoke saddled Drifter, the midnight-black, wolf-eyed stallion. Sally fixed him a poke of food and he stashed that in the saddlebags. He stuffed extra cartridges into a pocket of his saddlebags, and made sure his belt loops were filled. He checked his Henry repeating rifle and returned it to the saddle boot.

He kissed Sally and swung up into the saddle, thinking that it had certainly been a short homecoming. He looked at Bob, standing tall and very young beside Sally.

"You stay with Sally, Bob. Don't leave her. I'll square that with your Pa."

"Yes, sir, Mister Smoke," the boy replied.

"Can you shoot a short gun, Bob?"

"Yes, sir. But I'm better with a rifle."

"Sally will loan you a spare pistol. Wear it at all times."

"Yes, sir. What are you gonna do, Mister Smoke?"

"Try to organize the small farmers and ranchers, Bob. If we don't band together, none of us will have a chance of coming out of this alive."

Smoke wheeled Drifter and rode into the timber without looking back.

He headed across the country, taking the shortest route to Colby's spread. During his ride, Smoke spotted men staking out claims on land that had been filed on by small farmers and ranchers.

Finally he had enough of that and reined up. He stared hard at a group of men. "You have permission to dig on this land?"

"This is open land," a man challenged him.

"Wrong, mister. You're on Colby land. Filed on legally and worked. Don't be here when I get back."

But the miners and would-be miners were not going to be that easy to run off. "They told us in Fontana that this here land was open and ready for the takin'."

"Who told you that?"

"The man at Beeker's store. Some others at a saloon. They said all you folks up here were squattin' illegal-like, that if we wanted to dig, we could; and that's what we're all aimin' to do."

So that was Tilden's plan. Or at least part of it, Smoke thought. He could not fault the men seeking gold. They were greedy, but not land-greedy. Dig the gold, and get out. And if a miner, usually unarmed, was hurt, shot in any attempt to run them off, marshals would probably be called in.

Or . . . Smoke pondered, gazing from Drifter to the miners, Tilden might try to name a marshal for Fontana, hold a mock election for a sheriff. Colorado had only been a state for a little over two years, and things were still a bit confused. This county had had a sheriff, Smoke recalled, but somebody had shot him and elections had not yet been held to replace the man. And even an illegally elected sheriff would still be the law until commissioners could be sent in and matters were straightened out.

Smoke felt that was the way Tilden was probably leaning. That's the way *he* would play it if Smoke was as amoral as Tilden Franklin.

"You men have been warned," he told the miners. "This is private property. And I don't give a damn what you were told in town. And don't think the men who own the land won't fight to keep it, for you'll be wrong if you do. You've been warned."

"We got the law on our side!" a miner said, considerable heat in his voice.

"What law?"

"Hell, man!" another miner said. "They's an election in town comin' up tomorrow. Gonna be a sheriff for a brand-new town. You won't talk so goddamned tough with the law lookin' over your shoulder, I betcha."

Smoke gazed at the men. "You're all greedy fools," he said softly. "And a lot of you are going to get hurt if you continue with this trespassing. Like I said, you've been warned."

Smoke rode on, putting his back to the men, showing them his contempt.

An hour later, he was in Colby's front yard. Wilbur Mason had joined Colby by the corral at the sound of Drifter's hooves. A bloody bandage was tied around Wilbur's left arm, high up, close to the shoulder. But Smoke could tell by looking at the man that Wilbur was far from giving up. The man was angry and it showed.

"Boys," Smoke said. "You save anything, Wilbur?"

"Nothing, Matt . . . Smoke. You really the gun-fighter?"

"Yes." He swung down and dropped Drifter's reins on the ground. "Do any of you know anything about an election coming up tomorrow in town?"

"No," they said together. Colby added, "What kind of election, Smoke?"

"Sheriff's election. Tilden may be a greedy bastard,

but he's no fool. At the most, there is maybe twenty-five of us out here in the high country. There is probably two or three thousand men in Fontana by now. Our votes would be meaningless. And for sure, there will be Tilden men everywhere, ready to prod some of you into a fight if you show up by yourselves in town. So stay out until we can ride in in groups."

"Who's runnin' for sheriff?" Wilbur asked.

"I don't know. A TF man for sure, though. I'll check it out. Bob is staying with Sally, Colby. That all right with you?"

"Sure. He's a good boy, Smoke. And he'll stand fast facin' trouble. He's young, but he's solid."

"I know that. He said Adam was riding out to check the others . . . what's the word so far?"

"They're stayin', Smoke. Boy's asleep in the house now. He's wore out."

"I can imagine." His eyes caught movement near the house. Velvet. "Keep the women close by, Colby. This situation is shaping up to be a bad one."

"Velvet's just a kid, Smoke!" her father protested. "You don't think . . ." He refused to even speak the terrible words.

"She looks older than her years, Colby. And a lot of very rough people are moving into this area. Tilden Franklin will, I'm thinking, do anything to prod us all into something rash. He's made his intentions toward my wife public. So he's pulling out all the stops now."

Both Colby and Wilbur cursed Tilden Franklin.

Smoke waited until the men wound down. "How's your ammo situation?"

"Enough for a war," Colby said.

"Watch your backs." Smoke swung into the saddle and looked at the men. "A war? Well, that's what we've got, boys. And it's going to be a bad one. Some of us are not going to make it. I don't know about you boys, but I'm not running."

"We'll all stand," Wilbur said.

Smoke nodded. "The Indians have a saying." His eyes swept the land. "It's a good place to die."

8

Smoke touched base with as many small ranchers and farmers as he could that day, then slowly turned Drifter's head toward the town of Fontana. There was no bravado in what he was about to do, no sense of being a martyr. The area had to be checked out, and Smoke was the most likely candidate to do that.

But even he was not prepared for the sight that greeted him.

Long before he topped the crest overlooking the town of Fontana, he could see the lights. Long before the rip-roaring town came into view he could hear the noise. Smoke topped the crest and sat, looking with amazement at the sight that lay beneath and before him.

Fontana had burst at the seams, growing in all directions within three days. From where he sat, Smoke could count fifty new saloons, most no more than hurriedly erected wooden frames covered with canvas. The town had spread a half mile out in any direction, and the streets were packed with shoulder-to-shoulder humanity.

Smoke spoke to Drifter softly and the big, mean-eyed stallion moved out. Smoke stabled Drifter in the oldest of the corrals—a dozen had suddenly burst forth around the area—and filled the trough with corn.

"Stay away from him," he warned the stable boy. "If anyone but me goes into that stall, he'll kill them."

"Yes, sir," the boy said. He gazed at Smoke with adoration-filled eyes. "You really the gunfighter Smoke Jensen?"

"Yes."

"I'm on your side, Mister Smoke. Name's Billy."

Smoke extended his hand and the boy gravely shook it. Smoke studied the boy in the dim lantern-light of the stable. Ragged clothes, shoes with the soles tied so that they would not flop.

"How old are you, Billy?"

"Eleven, sir."

"Where are your folks?"

"Dead for more years than I can remember."

"I don't recall seeing you before. You been here long?"

"No, sir. I come in a couple weeks ago. I been stayin' down south of here, workin' in a stable. But the man who owned it married him a grass widow and her kids took over my job. I drifted. Ol' grump that owns this place gimme a job. I sleep here."

Smoke grinned at the "ol' grump" bit. He handed the boy a double eagle. "Come light, you get yourself some clothes and shoes."

Billy looked at the twenty-dollar gold piece. "Wow!" he said.

Smoke led the boy to Drifter's stall and opened the gate, stepping inside. He motioned the boy in after him. "Pet him, Billy."

Billy cautiously petted the midnight-black stallion. Drifter stopped eating for a moment and swung his big head, looking at him through those yellow, killer-cold, wolf-like eyes. Then he resumed munching at the corn.

"He likes you," Smoke told the boy. "You'll be all right with him. Anyone comes in here and tries to hurt you, just get in the stall with Drifter. You won't be harmed."

The boy nodded and stepped back out with Smoke. "You be careful, Mister Smoke," he warned. "I don't say much to people, but I listen real good. I hear things."

They walked to the wide doors at the front of the stable. "What do you hear, Billy?"

Several gunshots split the torch- and lantern-lit night air of Fontana. A woman's shrill and artificial-sounding laughter drifted to man and boy. A dozen pianos, all playing different tunes, created a confusing, discordant cacophony in the soft air of summer in the high-up country.

"Some guy name of Monte Carson is gonna be elected the sheriff. Ain't no one runnin' agin him"

"I've heard of him. He's a good hand with a gun."

"Better than you?" There was doubt in Billy's voice at that.

"No," Smoke said.

"The boss of this area, that Mister Tilden Franklin, is supposed to have a bunch of gunhands comin' to be deputies."

"Who are they?"

"I ain't heard."

"What have you heard about me?"

"I heard two punchers talkin' yesterday afternoon, over by a tent saloon. Circle TF punchers. But I think they're more than just cowboys. They wore their guns low and tied down."

Very observant boy, Smoke thought.

"If they can angle you in for a backshoot, they'd do it. Talk is, though, this Mister Franklin is gonna let the law handle you. Legal-like, you know?"

"Yeah." Smoke patted the boy's shoulder. "You take good care of Drifter, Billy. And keep your ears clean and open. I'll check you later."

"Yes, sir, Mister Smoke."

Smoke stepped out of the stable and turned to his left. His right hand slipped the thong off the Colt's hammer. Smoke was dressed in black whipcord trousers, black shirt, and dark hat. His spurs jingled as he walked, his boots kicking up little pockets of dust as he headed for the short boardwalk that ran in front of Beeker's General Store, a saloon, and the gunsmith's shop. Smoke's eyes were in constant motion, noting and retaining everything he spotted. Night seemed to color into day as he approached the boom-town area.

A drunk lurched out from between two tents, almost colliding with Smoke.

"Watch where you're goin,' boy," the miner mush-mouthed at him.

Smoke ignored him and walked on.

"A good time comes reasonable," a heavily rouged and slightly overweight woman said, offering her charms to Smoke.

"I'm sure," Smoke told her. "But I'm married."

"Ain't you the lucky one?" she said, and stepped back into the shadows of her darkened tent.

He grinned and walked on.

Smoke walked past Beeker's store and glanced in. The man had hired more help and was doing a land office business, a fixed smile on his greedy, weasel face. His hatchet-faced wife was in constant motion, moving around the brightly lighted store, her sharp eyes darting left and right, looking for thieving hands.

Other than her own, Smoke mentally noted.

He walked on, coming to the swinging doors of the saloon. Wild laughter and hammering piano music greeted his ears. It was not an altogether offensive sound. The miners, as a whole, were not bad people. They were here to dig and chip and blast and hammer the rock, looking for gold.

In their free time, most would drink and gamble and whore the night away.

Smoke almost stepped inside the saloon, changing his mind just at the very last moment. He stepped back away from the doors and walked on.

He crossed the street and stepped into Louis Longmont's place. The faro and monte and draw and stud poker tables were filled; dice clicked and wheels spun, while those with money in their hands stared and waited for Lady Luck to smile on them.

Most of the time she did not.

Smoke walked to the bar, shoved his way through, and ordered a beer.

He took his beer and crossed the room, dodging drunks as they staggered past. He leaned against a bracing and watched the action.

"Smoke." The voice came from his left.

Smoke turned and looked into the face of Louis Longmont. "Louis," he acknowledged. "Another year, another boom town, hey?"

"They never change. I don't know why I stay with it. I certainly don't need the money."

Smoke knew that was no exaggeration on the gambler's part. The gambler owned a large ranch up in Wyoming Territory. He owned several businesses in San Francisco, and he owned a hefty chunk of a railroad. It was a mystery to many why Louis stayed with the hard life he had chosen.

"Then get out of it, Louis," Smoke suggested.

"But of course," Louis responded with a smile. His eyes drifted to Smoke's twin Colts. "Just as you got out of gunfighting."

Smoke smiled. "I put them away for several years, Louis. Had gold not been found, or had I chosen a different part of the country to settle, I probably would never have picked them up again."

"Lying to others is bad enough, my young friend, But lying to oneself is unconscionable. Can you look at me and tell me you never, during those stale years, missed the dry-mouthed moment before the draw? The challenge of facing and besting those miscreants who would kill you or others who seek a better and more peaceful way? The so-called loneliness of the hoot-owl trail? I think not, Mister Jensen. I think not."

There was nothing for Smoke to say, for Louis was right. He had missed those death-close moments. And Sally knew it too. Smoke had often caught her watching him, silently looking at him as he would stand and gaze toward the mountains, or as his eyes would follow the high flight of an eagle.

"Your silence tells all, my friend," Louis said. "I know only too well."

"Yeah," Smoke said, looking down into his beer mug. "I guess I'd better finish my beer and ride. I don't want to be the cause of any trouble in your place, Louis."

"Trouble, my friend, is something I have never shied away from. You're safer here than in any other place in this woebegotten town. If I can help it, you will not be backshot in my place."

And again, Smoke knew the gambler was telling the truth. Smoke and Louis had crossed trails a dozen times over the years. The man had taken a liking to the boy when Smoke was riding with the Mountain Man Preacher. In the quieter moments of his profession, Louis had shown Smoke the tricks of his gambler's trade. Louis had realized that Smoke possessed a keen intelligence, and Louis liked those people who tried to better themselves, as Smoke had always done.

They had become friends.

Hard hoofbeats sounded on the dirt street outside the gambling tent. Smoke looked at Louis.

"About a dozen riders," Smoke said.

"Probably the 'deputies' Tilden Franklin called in from down Durango way. They'll be hardcases, Smoke."

"Is this election legal?"

"Of course not. But it will be months before the state can send anyone in to verify it or void it. By then, Franklin will have gotten his way. Initial reports show the gold, what there is of it, assays high. But the lode is a narrow one. I suspect you already knew that."

"I've known about the vein for a long time, Louis. I never wanted gold."

A quick flash of irritation crossed Louis's face. "It is well and good to shun wealth while one is young, Smoke. But one had best not grow old without some wealth."

"One can have wealth without riches, Louis," Smoke countered.

The gambler smiled. "I believe Preacher's influence was strong on you, young man."

"There could have been no finer teacher in all the world, Louis."

"Is he alive, Smoke?"

"I don't know. If so, he'd be in his eighties. I like to think he's still alive. But I just don't know."

Louis knew, but he elected to remain silent on the subject. At least for the time being.

Boots and jangling spurs sounded on the raw boards in front of Louis's place. And both Louis and Smoke knew the time for idle conversation had passed.

They knew before either man sighted the wearers of those boots and spurs.

The first rider burst into the large tent.

"I don't know him," Louis said. "You?"

"Unfortunately. He's one of Tilden's gunhands. Calls himself Tay. I ran into him when I was riding with Preacher. Back then he was known as Carter. I heard he was wanted for murder back in Arkansas."

"Sounds like a delightful fellow," Louis said drily.

"He's a bully. But don't sell him short. He's hell with a short gun."

Louis smiled. "Better than you, Smoke?" he asked, a touch of humor in the question.

"No one is better than me, Louis," Smoke said, in one of his rare moments of what some would call arrogance; others would call it merely stating a proven fact.

Louis's chuckle held no mirth. "I believe I am better, my friend."

"I hope we never have to test that out of anger, Louis."

"We won't," Louis replied. "But let's do set up some cans and make a small wager someday."

"You're on."

The gunfighter Tay turned slowly, his eyes drifting first to Louis, then to Smoke.

"Hello, punk!" Tay said, his voice silencing the piano player and hushing the hubbub of voices in the gaming tent.

"Are you speaking to me, you unshaven lout?" Louis asked.

"Naw," Tay said. The leather thongs that secured his guns were off, left and right. "Pretty boy there."

"You're a fool," Smoke said softly, his voice carrying to Tay, overheard by all in the gaming room.

"I'm gonna kill you for that!" Tay said.

Those men and women seated between Tay and Smoke cleared out, moving left and right.

"I hope you have enough in your pockets to bury you," Smoke said.

Tay's face flushed, both hands hovering over the butt of his guns.

He snarled at Smoke.

Smoke laughed at him.

"A hundred dollars on the Circle TF rider," a man seated at a table said.

"You're on," Louis said, taking the wager. "Gentlemen," he said to Smoke and Tay. "Bets are down."

Tay's eyes were shiny, but his hands were steady over his guns.

Smoke held his beer mug in his left hand.

"Draw, goddamn you!" Tay shouted.

"After you," Smoke replied. "I always give a sucker a break whenever possible."

Tay grabbed for his guns.

9

"Your behavior the other day was disgusting!" Ralph Morrow would not let up on his wife. "Those men are dead because of you. You do realize that, don't you?"

Bountiful tossed her head, her blond curls bouncing around her beautiful face. Her lips were set in a pout. "I did nothing," she said, defending her actions.

"My God, I married an animal!" Ralph said, disgust in his voice. "Can't you see you're a minister's wife?"

"I'm beginning to see a lot of things, Ralph. One of which is I made a mistake."

"In coming out West? Did we have a choice, Bountiful? After your disgraceful behavior in Ohio, I'm very lucky the Church even gave me another chance."

She waved that off. "No, Ralph, not that. In my marrying such a pompous wee-wee!"

Ralph flushed and balled his fists. "You take that back!" he yelled at her.

"You take that back!" she repeated, mimicking him scornfully. "My God, Ralph! You're such a lummox!"

Man and wife were several miles from the town of Fontana. They were on the banks of a small creek. Ralph sat down on the bank and refused to look at her. A short distance away at their camp, the others tried without much success not to listen to their friends quarrel.

"They certainly are engaged in a plethora of flap-doodle," Haywood observed.

"I feel sorry for him," Dana said.

"I don't," Ed said. "It's his own fault he's such a sissy-pants."

All present looked at Ed in the dancing flames of the fire. If there was a wimp among them, it was Ed. Ed had found a June bug in his blankets on the way West and, from his behavior one might have thought he'd discovered a nest of rattlers. It had taken his wife a full fifteen minutes to calm him down.

Haywood sat on a log and puffed his Meerschaum. Of them all, Haywood was the only person who knew the true story about Ralph Morrow. And if the others wanted to think him a sissy-pants . . . well, that was their mistake. But Haywood had to admit that, from all indications, when Ralph had fully accepted Christ into his life, he had gone a tad overboard.

If anyone had taken the time to just look at Ralph, they would have noticed the rippling boxer's muscles; the broad, hard, flat-knuckled fists; the slightly crooked nose. It had always amazed Haywood how so many people could look at something, but never see it.

Haywood suppressed a giggle. Come to think of it, he mused, Ralph *did* sort of act a big milquetoast.

But it should be interesting when Ralph finally got a belly full of it.

Smoke cleared leather before Tay got his pistols free of their holsters. Smoke drew with such blinding speed, drawing, cocking, firing, not one human eye in the huge tent could follow the motion.

The single slug struck Tay in the center of the chest and knocked him backward. He struggled up on one elbow and looked at Smoke through eyes that were already glazing over. He tried to lift his free empty hand; the hand was so heavy he thought his gun was in it. He began squeezing his trigger finger. He was curious about the lack of noise and recoil.

Then he fell back onto the raw. rough-hewn board floor and was curious no more.

"Maybe we won't set up those tin cans," Louis muttered, just loud enough for Smoke to hear it.

"Tie him across a saddle and take him back to Tilden Franklin," Smoke said, his voice husky due to the low-hanging cigarette and cigar smoke in the crowded gaming tent. "Unless some of you boys want to pick up where Tay left off."

The riders appeared to be in a mild state of shock. They were all, to a man, used to violence; that was their chosen way of life. They had all, to a man, been either witnesses to or participants in stand-up gunfights, backshoots, and ambushes. And they had all heard of the young gunslick Smoke Jensen. But since none had ever seen the man in action, they had tended to dismiss much of what they had heard as so much pumped-up hoopla.

Until this early evening in the boom town of Fontana, in Louis Longmont's gaming tent.

"Yes, sir, Mister Jensen," one young TF rider said. "I mean," he quickly corrected himself, "I'll sure tie him across his saddle."

Until this evening, the young TF rider had fancied himself a gunhawk. Now he just wanted to get on his pony and ride clear out of the area. But he was afraid the others would laugh at him if he did that.

Smoke eased the hammer down with his thumb. A very audible sigh went up inside the tent with that action.

There was visible relaxing of stomach muscles when Smoke holstered the deadly Colt.

Smoke looked at the young puncher who had spoken. "Come here," he said.

The young man, perhaps twenty at the most, quickly crossed the room to face Smoke. He was scared, and looked it.

"What's your name?" Smoke asked.

"Pearlie."

"You're on the wrong side, Pearlie. You know that?"

"Mister Smoke," Pearlie said in a low tone, so only Smoke and Louis could hear. "The TF brand can throw two hundred or more men at you. And I ain't kiddin'. Now, you're tough as hell and snake-quick, but even you can't fight that many men."

"You want to bet your life, Pearlie?" Louis asked him. The man's voice was low-pitched and his lips appeared not to move at all.

Pearlie cut his eyes at the gambler. "I ain't got no choice, Mister Longmont."

"Yes, you do," Smoke said.

"I'm listenin'."

"I need a hand I can trust. I think that's you, Pearlie."

The young man's jaw dropped open. "But I been ridin' for the TF brand!"

"How much is he paying you?"

"Sixty a month."

"I'll give you thirty and found."

Pearlie smiled. "You're serious!"

"Yes, I am. Have you the sand in you to make a turn-around in your life?"

"Give me a chance, Mister Smoke."

"You've got it. Are you quick with that Colt?"

"Yes, sir. But I ain't nearabouts as quick as you."

"Have you ever used it before?"

"Yes, sir."

"Would you stand by me and my wife and friends, Pearlie?"

"'Til I soak up so much lead I can't stand, Mister Smoke."

Smoke cut his eyes at Louis. The man smiled and nodded his head slightly.

"You're hired, Pearlie."

"Pearlie did *what*?" Tilden screamed.

Clint repeated his statement, standing firm in front of the boss. Clint was no gunhawk. He was as good as or better than most men with a short gun, but had never fancied himself a gunfighter. He knew horses, he knew cattle, and he could work and manage men. There was no backup in Clint. He had fought Indians, outlaws, nesters, and other ranchers during his years with Tilden Franklin, and while he didn't always approve of everything Tilden did, Clint rode for the brand. And that was that.

"Goddamned, no-good little pup!" Tilden spat out the words. He lifted his eyes and stared into his foreman's eyes. "This can't be tolerated, Clint."

Clint felt a slight sick feeling in his stomach. He knew what was coming next. "No, sir. You're right."

"Drag him!" Tilden spat the horrible words.

"Yes, sir." Clint turned away and walked out of the room. He stood on the porch for a long moment, breathing deeply. He appeared to be deep in thought.

Louis shut the gaming room down early that evening. And with Louis Longmont, no one uttered any words of protest. They simply got up and left. And neither did anyone take any undue umbrage, for all knew Louis's games were straight-arrow honest.

He closed the wooden door to his gaming-room tent,

extinguished most of the front lights, and set a bottle of fine scotch on the table.

"I know you're not normally a hard-drinking man, my young friend," Louis said, as he poured two tumblers full of the liquid. "But savor the taste of the Glenlivet. It's the finest made."

Smoke picked up the bottle and read the label. "Was this stuff made in 1824?"

Louis smiled. "Oh, no. That's when the distillery was founded. Old George Smith knew his business, all right."

"Knew?"

"Yes. He died six—no, seven years ago. He was on the Continent at the time."

Smoke sipped the light scotch. It was delicate, yet mellow. It had a lightness that was quite pleasing.

"I had been to a rather obscure place called Monte Carlo." Louis sniffed his tumbler before sipping.

"I never heard of that place."

"I own part of the casino," Louis said softly.

"Make lots of money?"

Louis's reply was a smile.

It silently spoke volumes.

"Prior to that, I was enjoying the theater in Warsaw. It was there I was introduced to Madame Modjeska. It was quite the honor. She is one of the truly fine actresses in the world today."

"You're talking over my head, Louis."

"Madame Mudrzejeweski."

"Did you just swallow a bug, Louis?"

Louis laughed. "No. She shortened her name to Modjeska. She is here in America now. Performing Shakespeare in New York, I believe. She also tours."

Smoke sipped his scotch and kept his mouth shut.

"When I finally retire, I believe I shall move to New York City. It's quite a place, Smoke. Do you have any desires at all to see it?"

"No," Smoke said gently.

"Pity," the gambler said. "It is really a fascinating place. Smoke?"

The young rancher-farmer-gunfighter lifted his eyes to meet Louis's.

"You should travel, Smoke. Educate yourself. Your wife is, I believe, an educated woman. Is she not?"

"Schoolteacher."

"Ah . . . yes. I thought your grammar, most of the time, had improved since last we spoke. Smoke . . . get out while you have the time and opportunity to do so."

"No."

"Pearlie was right, Smoke. There are too many against you."

Smoke took a small sip of his scotch. "I am not alone in this, Louis. There are others."

"Many of whom will not stand beside you when it gets bad. But I think you know that."

"But some of them will, Louis. And bear this in mind: we control the high country."

"Yes, there is that. Tell me, your wife has money, correct?"

"Yes. I think she's wealthy."

"You *think*?"

"I told you, Louis, I'm not that interested in great wealth. My father is lying atop thousands and thousands of dollars of gold."

Louis smiled. "And there are those who would desecrate his grave for a tenth of it," he reminded the young man.

"I'm not one of them."

Louis sighed and drained his tumbler, refilling it from the bottle of scotch. "Smoke, it's 1878. The West is changing. The day of the gunfighter, men like you and me, is coming to a close. There is still a great rowdy element moving westward, but by and large, the people who are now coming here are demanding peace. Soon there will he no place for men like us."

"And? So?"

"What are you going to do then?"

"I'll be right out there on the Sugarloaf, Louis, ranching and farming and raising horses. And," he said with a smile, "probably raising a family of my own."

"Not if you're dead, Smoke." The gambler's words were softly offered.

Smoke drained his tumbler and stood up, tall and straight and heavily muscled. "The Sugarloaf is my home, Louis. Sally's and mine. And here is where we'll stay. Peacefully working the land, or buried in it."

He walked out the door.

10

Smoke made his Spartan camp some five miles outside of Fontana. With Drifter acting as guard, Smoke slept soundly. He had sent Pearlie to his ranch earlier that night, carrying a hand-written note introducing him to Sally. One of the older ranchers in the area, a man who was aligned on neither side, had told Smoke that Pearlie was a good boy who had just fallen in with the wrong crowd, that Pearlie had spoken with him a couple of times about leaving the Circle TF.

Smoke did not worry about Pearlie making any ungentlemanly advances toward Sally, for she would shoot him stone dead if he tried.

Across the yard from the cabin, Smoke and Sally had built a small bunkhouse, thinking of the day when they would need extra hands. Pearlie would sleep there.

Smoke bathed—very quickly—in a small, rushing creek and changed clothes: a gray shirt, dark trousers. He drank the last of his pot of coffee, extinguished the small fire, and saddled Drifter.

He turned Drifter's head toward Fontana, but angling

slightly north of the town, planning on coming in from a different direction.

It would give those people he knew would be watching him something to think about.

About half a mile from Fontana, Smoke came up on a small series of just-begun buildings; tents lay behind the construction site. He sat his horse and looked at Preacher Morrow swinging an axe. The preacher had removed his shirt and was clad only in his short-sleeve undershirt. Smoke's eyes took in the man's heavy musculature and the fluid way he handled the axe.

A lot more to him than meets the eyes, Smoke thought. A whole lot more.

Then Smoke's eyes began to inspect the building site. Not bad, he thought. Jackson's big store across the road, and the offices of the others in one long building on the opposite side of the road. The cabins would be behind the offices, while Jackson and his wife and brother would live in quarters behind but connected to the store.

Smoke's eyes caught movement to his left.

"Everything meet with your approval, Mister Jensen?"

Smoke turned Drifter toward the voice. Ed Jackson. "Looks good. The preacher's a pretty good hand with an axe, wouldn't you say?"

"Oh . . . him? 'Bout the only thing he's good at. He's a sissy."

Smoke smiled, thinking: Shopkeeper, I hope you never push that preacher too hard, 'cause he'll damn sure break you like a match stick.

Hunt, Colton, Haywood, and their wives walked out to where Smoke sat Drifter. He greeted the men and took his hat off to the ladies. Bountiful was not with the group and Smoke was grateful for that. The woman was trouble.

Then he wondered where the shopkeeper's brother was. He wondered if Bountiful and Paul might be . . .

He sighed and put his hat back on, pushing those

thoughts from him. He dismounted and ground-reined Drifter.

"Going into town to vote, Mister Jensen?" Hunt asked.

"No point in it. One-sided race from what I hear."

"Oh, no!" Colton told him. "We have several running for mayor, half a dozen running for sheriff, and two running for city judge."

"Tilden Franklin's men will win, believe me."

"Mister Franklin seems like a very nice person to me," Ed said, adding, "not that I've ever met the gentleman, of course. Just from what I've heard about him."

"Yeah, he's a real prince of a fellow," Smoke said, with enough sarcasm in his voice to cover hotcakes thicker than molasses. "Why just a few days ago he was nice enough to send his boys up into the high country to burn out a small rancher-farmer named Wilbur Mason. Shot Wilbur and scattered his wife and kids. He's made his boast that he'll either run me out or kill me, and then he'll have my wife. Yeah, Tilden is a sweet fellow, all right."

"I don't believe that!" Ed said, puffing up.

Smoke's eyes narrowed and his face hardened. Haywood looked at the young man and both saw and felt danger emanating from him. He instinctively put an arm around his wife's shoulders and drew her to him.

Smoke said, his eyes boring into Ed's eyes, "Shopkeeper, I'll let that slide this one time. But let me give you a friendly piece of advice." He cut his eyes, taking in, one at a time, all the newcomers to the West. "You folks came here from the East. You do things differently back East. I didn't say better, just different. Out here, you call a man a liar, you'd better be ready to do one of two things: either stand and slug it out with him or go strap on iron.

"Now you all think about that, and you'll see both the right and wrong in it. I live here. Me and my wife been here for better than three years. We hacked a home out of the wilderness and made it nice. We fought the hard winters, Indians a few times, and we know the folks in this area. You people, on the other hand, just come in here. You don't know nobody, yet you're going to call me a liar. See what I mean, Shopkeeper?

"Now the wrong of it is this: there are bullies who take advantage of the code, so to speak. Those types of trash will prod a fellow into a fight, just because they think that to fight is manly, or some such crap as that. Excuse my language, ladies. But the point is, you got to watch your mouth out here. The graveyards are full of people ignorant of the ways of the West."

Ed Jackson blustered and sweated, but he did not offer to apologize.

He won't make it, Smoke thought. Someone will either run him out or kill him. And mankind will have lost nothing by his passing.

"Why is Franklin doing these things, Mister Jensen?" Haywood asked.

"Smoke. Call me Smoke. Why? Because he wants to be king. Perhaps he's a bit mad. I don't know. I do know he hates farmers and small ranchers. As for me, well, I have the Sugarloaf and he wants it."

"The Sugarloaf?" Hunt asked.

"My valley. Part of it, that is."

"Are you suggesting the election is rigged?" Haywood inquired.

"No. I'm just saying that Tilden's people will win, that's all."

"Has Mister Franklin offered to buy any of the farmers' or ranchers' holdings?" Hunt asked.

Smoke laughed. "Buy? Lawyer, men like Tilden don't offer to buy. They just run people out. Did cruel kings offer to buy lands they desired? No, they just took it, by force."

Preacher Morrow had ceased his work with the axe and had joined the group. His eyes searched for his wife and, not finding her present, glowered at Ed Jackson.

Maybe I was right, Smoke thought.

"Are you a Christian, Mister Jensen?" he asked, finally taking his eyes from the shopkeeper.

Bad blood between those two, Smoke thought. "I been to church a few times over the years. Sally and me was married in a proper church."

"Have you been baptized, sir?"

"In a little crick back in Missouri, yes, sir, I was."

"Ah, wonderful! Perhaps you and your wife will attend services just as soon as I get my church completed?"

"I knew a lay preacher back in Missouri preached on a stump, Preacher Morrow. Look around you, sir. You ever in all your life seen a more beautiful cathedral? Look at them mountains yonder. Got snow on 'em year-round. See them flowers scattered around, those blue and purple ones? Those are columbines. Some folks call them Dove Flowers. See the trees? Pine and fir and aspen and spruce and red cedar. What's wrong with preaching right in the middle of what God created?"

"You're right, of course, sir. I'm humbled. You're a strange man, Mister Jensen. And I don't mean that in any ugly way."

"I didn't take it in such a way. I know what you mean. The West is a melting pot of people, Preacher. Right there in that town of Fontana, there's a man named Louis Longmont. He's got degrees from places over in Europe, I think. He owns ranches, pieces of railroads, and lots of other businesses. But he follows the boom towns as a gambler. He's been decorated by kings and queens. But he's a gambler, and a gunfighter. My wife lives in a cabin up in the mountains. But she's worth as much money as Tilden Franklin, probably more. She's got two or three degrees from fancy colleges back East, and she's traveled in Europe and other places. Yet she married me.

"I know scouts for the Army who used to be college professors. I know cowboys who work for thirty and found who can stand and quote William Shakespeare for hours. And them that listen, most of them, can't even read or write. I know Negroes who fought for the North and white men who wore the Gray who now work side by side and who would die for each other. Believe it."

"And you, Smoke?" Hunt asked. "What about you?"

"What about me? I raise cattle and horses and farm. I mind my own business, if people will let me. And I'll harm no man who isn't set on hurting me or mine. We need people like you folks out here. We need some stability. Me and Sally are gonna have kids one day, and I'd like for them to grow up around folks like you." He cut his eyes to Ed Jackson. "Most of you, that is." The store-owner caught the verbal cut broadside and flushed. "But for a while yet, it's gonna be rough and rowdy out here." Smoke pointed. "Ya'll see that hill yonder? That's Boot Hill. The graveyard. See that fancy black wagon with them people walking along behind it, going up that hill? That wagon is totin' a gunhawk name of Tay. He braced me last night in Louis's place. He was a mite slow."

"You killed yet *another* man?" Ed blurted out.

"I've killed about a hundred men," Smoke said. "Not counting Indians. I killed twenty, I think, one day up on the Uncompahgre. That was back in '74, I think. A year later I put lead into another twenty or so over in Idaho, town name of Bury. Bury don't exist no more. I burned it down.*

"People, listen to me. Don't leave this area. We got to have some people like you to put down roots, to stay when

Return of the Mountain Man

the gold plays out. And it will, a lot sooner than most folks realize. And," Smoke said with a sigh, "we're gonna need a doctor and nurse and preacher around here . . . the preacher for them that the doc can't patch up."

The newcomers were looking at Smoke, a mixture of emotions in their eyes. They all wanted for him to speak again.

"Now I'm heading into town, people," Smoke said. "And I'm not going in looking for trouble. But I assure you all, it will come to me. If you doubt that, come with me for an hour. Put aside your axes and saws and ride in with me. See for yourself."

"I'll go with you," Preacher Morrow said. "Just let me bathe in the creek first."

All the men agreed to go.

Should be interesting, Smoke thought. For he planned to take Preacher Morrow into Louis's place. Not that Smoke thought the man would see anything he hadn't already seen . . . several times before, in his past.

11

Ralph Morrow was the first one back to where Smoke stood beside Drifter. "Where is your wife, Preacher?"

The man cut his eyes at Smoke. Smoke could see the faded scars above the man's eyes.

A boxer, Smoke thought. He's fought many times in the ring.

"Walking along the creek over there," he said, pointing. "I suppose she's safe. From hostiles," he added, a touch of bitterness in his voice.

"I'd think so. This close to town. Preacher? Anytime you want to talk, I'm available."

The man looked away, stubbornness setting his chin.

Smoke said no more. The others soon joined them and they made their way into Fontana. The newspaper man carried a note pad and had a breastpocket full of pencils. Smoke stabled Drifter with Billy and smiled at the boy. Billy was dressed in new britches and a new shirt, boots on his feet. "Give him some corn, Billy."

"Yes, sir. I heard that was some show last night over to Longmont's place."

Smoke nodded. "He was a tad slow."

Billy grinned and led Drifter into his stall, the big out-law stallion allowing the boy to lead him docilely.

"What a magnificent animal," Colton remarked, look-ing at Drifter.

"Killed the last man who owned him," Smoke said.

The doctor muttered something under his breath that Smoke could not quite make out. But he had a pretty good idea what it was. He grinned.

The town was jammed with people, bursting at its newly sewn seams. American flags were hung and draped all over the place. Notices that Tilden Franklin was going to speak were stuck up, it seemed, almost everywhere one looked.

"Your fine man is going to make a speech, Jackson," Smoke said to the shopkeeper, keeping his face bland. "You sure won't want to miss that."

"I shall make every attempt to attend that event," Ed announced, a bit stiffly.

Several of the miners who had been in Louis's place when Tay was shot walked past Smoke, greeting him with a smile. Smoke acknowledged the greetings.

"You seem to have made yourself well known in a short time, Smoke," Hunt said.

"I imagine them that spoke was some that made money betting on the outcome of the shooting," Smoke informed the lawyer.

"Barbaric!"

"Not much else to do out here, Lawyer. Besides, you should see the crowds that gather for a hanging. Folks will come from fifty miles out for that. Bring picnic lunches and make a real pleasurable day out of it."

The lawyer refused to respond to that. He simply shook his head and looked away.

The town was growing by the hour. Where once no more than fifty people lived, there now roamed some five thousand. Tents of all sizes and descriptions were going up every few minutes.

Smoke looked at Ed Jackson. "I'm not trying to pry into your business, Shopkeeper, so don't take it that way. But do you have any spare money for workmen?"

"I might. Why do you ask?"

"You could get your store up and running in a few days if you were to hire some people to help you. A lot of those men out there would do it for a grubstake."

"A what?"

"A grubstake. You give them equipment and food, and they'll help you put up your building and offer you a percentage of what they take out of the ground. I'd think about it—all of you."

"I thought you didn't care for me, Mister Jensen," the shopkeeper said.

"I don't, very much. But maybe it's just because we got off on the wrong foot. I'm willing to start over."

Ed did not reply. He pursed his perch-mouthed lips in silence. "I thank you for your suggestion," he said, a moment later. "I shall . . . give you a discount on your first purchases in my store for it."

"Why, thank you very much," Smoke replied, a smile on his lips. "That's right generous of you, Ed."

"Yes," Ed said smugly. "It is, isn't it?"

The other men turned their heads to hide their smiles.

"How do I go about doing that?" Ed questioned.

"Just ask somebody," Smoke told him. "Find a man who is afoot rather than riding. Find one carrying everything on his back or pushing a cart. You'll probably get some refusals, but eventually you'll find your people."

Ed, Colton, Hunt, and Haywood walked off into the pushing, shoving hubbub of humanity, leaving Smoke and Preacher Morrow standing alone.

"You have no spare money, Preacher?" Smoke asked.

Ralph's smile was genuine. "Find me one who does

have spare money. But that isn't it. I want to build as much of my church as possible myself. It's . . . a personal thing."

"I understand. I'm a pretty good hand with an axe myself. I'll give you a hand later on."

Ralph looked at the gunfighter. "I do not understand you, Mister Jensen."

Before Smoke could reply, the hard sounds of drumming hooves filled the air. "Tilden Franklin," Smoke said. "The king has arrived."

"Pearlie!" Sally called. "Come take a break and have some coffee. And I made doughnuts."

"Bearsign!" the young puncher shouted. "Yes, ma'am. I'm on my way."

Sally smiled at that. She had learned that cowboys would ride a hundred miles for home-cooked doughnuts . . . something they called bearsign. It had taken Sally a time to learn why they were called bearsign. When she finally learned the why of it, she thought it positively disgusting.

"You mean! . . ." she had puffed to Smoke. "These people are equating my doughnuts to . . . that's disgusting!"

"Bear tracks, Sally," Smoke had told her. "Not what you're thinking."

She had refused to believe him.

And Smoke never would fully explain.

More fun letting her make up her own mind.

"My husband must have thought a lot of you, Pearlie," she said, watching the puncher eat, a doughnut in each hand. "He's not normally a trusting person."

"He's a fine man, Miss Sally," Pearlie said around a mouthful of bearsign. "And got more cold nerve than any man I ever seen."

"Can we win this fight, Pearlie?"

The cowboy pushed his battered hat back on his head. He took a slug of coffee and said, "You want a straight-out honest answer, ma'am?"

"That's the only way, Pearlie."

Pearlie hesitated. "It'll be tough. Right off, I'd say the odds are slim to none. But there's always a chance. All depends on how many of them nester friends of yourn will stand and fight when it gets down to the hard rock."

"A few of them will."

"Yes'um. That's what I mean." He stuffed his mouth full of more bearsign.

"Matlock will, and so will Wilbur. I'm pretty sure Colby will stand firm. I don't know about the others."

"You see, ma'am, the problem is this: them folks you just named ain't gunhands. Mister Tilden can mount up to two hundred riders. The sheriff is gonna be on his side, and all them gun-slingin' deputies he'll name. Your husband is pure hell with a gun—pardon my language—but one man just can't do 'er all."

Sally smiled at that. She alone, of all those involved, knew what her husband was capable of doing. But, she thought with a silent sigh, Pearlie was probably right . . . it would be unreasonable to expect one man to do it all.

Even such a man as Smoke.

"What does Mister Franklin want, Pearlie . . . and why?"

"I ain't sure of the why of it all, ma'am. As for me, I'd be satisfied with a little bitty part of what he has. He's got so much holdin's I'd bet he really don't know all that he has. What does he want?" The cowboy paused, thinking. "He wants everything, ma'am. Everything he sees. I've overheard some of his older punchers talk about what they done to get them things for Tilden Franklin. I wouldn't want to say them things in front of you, ma'am. I'll just say I'm glad I didn't have no part in them. And I'm real glad Mister Smoke gimme a job with ya'll 'fore it got too late for me."

"You haven't been with the Circle TF long, then, Pearlie?"

"It would have been a year this fall, ma'am. I drifted down here from the Bitterroot. I . . . kinda had a cloud hangin' over me, I guess you'd say."

"You want to talk about it?"

"Ain't that much to say, ma'am. I always been mighty quick with a short gun. Not nearabouts as quick as your man, now, but tolerable quick. I was fifteen and workin' a full man's job down in Texas. That was six year ago. Or seven. I disremember exact. I rode into town with the rest of the boys for a Saturday night spree. There was some punchers from another spread there. One of 'em braced me, called me names. Next thing I recall, that puncher was layin' on his back with a bullet hole in his chest. From my gun. Like I said, I've always been mighty quick. Well, the sheriff, he told me to light a shuck. I got my back up at that, 'cause that other puncher slapped leather first. I tole the sheriff I wasn't goin' nowheres. I didn't mean to back that sheriff into no corner, but I reckon that's what I done. That sheriff was a bad one, now. He had him a rep that was solid bad. He tole me I had two choices in the matter: ride out or die.

"Well, ma'am, I tole him I didn't backpaddle for no man, not when I was in the right. He drew on me. I kilt him."

Pearlie paused and took a sip of coffee. Sally refilled his cup and gave him another doughnut.

"Whole place was quiet as midnight in a graveyard," Pearlie continued. It seemed to Sally that he was relieved to be talking about it, as if he had never spoken fully of the events. "I holstered my gun and stepped out onto the boardwalk. Then it hit me what I'd done. I was fifteen years old and in one whale of a pickle. I'd just killed two men in less than ten minutes. One of them a lawman. I was on the hoot-owl trail sure as you're born.

"I got my horse and rode out. Never once looked back. Over in New Mexico two bounty hunters braced me outside a cantina one night. I reckon someone buried both of them next day. I don't rightly know, seein' as how I didn't stick around for the services. Then I was up in Utah when this kid braced me. He was lookin' for a rep, I guess. He didn't make it," Pearlie added softly. "Then the kid's brothers come a-foggin' after me. I put lead in both of them. One died, so I heard later on.

"I drifted on over into Nevada. By this time, I had bounty hunters really lookin' for me. I avoided them, much as I could. Changed my name to Pearlie. I headed north, into the Bitterroot Range. Some lawmen came a-knockin' on my cabin door one night. Said they was lawmen, what they was was bounty hunters. That was a pretty good fight, I reckon. Good for me, bad for them. Then I drifted down into Colorado and you know the rest."

"Family?"

Pearlie shook his head. "None that I really remember. Ma and Pa died with the fevers when I was eight or nine. I got a sister somewheres, but I don't rightly know where. What all I got is what you see, ma'am. I got my guns, a good saddle, and good horse. And that just about says it all, I reckon."

"No, Pearlie, you're wrong," Sally told him.

The cowboy looked at her, puzzlement in his eyes.

"You have a home with us, as long as you want to ride for the brand."

"Much obliged, ma'am," he said, his voice thick. He did not trust himself to say much more. He stood up. "I better get back on the Sugarloaf East, ma'am. Things to do."

Sally watched him mount up and ride off. She smiled, knowing she and Smoke had made yet another friend.

12

Surprisingly, Smoke noted, the election went smoothly. There was one central voting place, where names were taken and written down in a ledger. There was no point in anyone voting more than once, and few did, for Tilden Franklin's men were lopsidedly out in front in the election count, according to the blackboard tally.

By noon, it was clear that Tilden's people were so far ahead they would not be caught.

Hunt, Haywood, Colton, and Ed had voted and vanished into the surging crowds. Preacher Morrow stayed with Smoke.

"You're not voting, Preacher?" Smoke asked.

"What's the point?" Ralph summed it up.

"You're a quick learner."

"It's not Christian of me, Smoke. But I took one look at that Tilden Franklin and immediately formed an acute dislike for the man."

"Like I said, a quick learner."

"The man is cruel and vicious."

"Yes, he is. All of that and more. Insane, I believe."

"That is becoming a catch-all phrase for those who have no feelings for other men's rights, Smoke."

Smoke was beginning to like the preacher more and more as time went by. He wondered about the man's past, but would not ask, that question being impolite. There were scars on the preacher's knuckles, and Smoke knew they didn't get there from thumping a Bible.

Then the call went up: the other candidates had withdrawn. Tilden Franklin's men had won. Within minutes, Monte Carson was walking the streets, a big badge pinned to his shirt.

Smoke deliberately stayed away from the man. He knew trouble would be heading his way soon enough; no point in pushing it.

He felt someone standing close to him and turned, looking down. Billy.

"What's up, Billy?"

"Trouble for you, Smoke," the boy said gravely.

Preacher Morrow stepped closer, to hear better. Haywood and Hunt were walking toward the trio. Smoke waved them over.

"Listen to what the boy has to say," Smoke said.

Billy looked up at the adults standing about him. "Some of the Circle TF riders is gonna prod you, Smoke. Push you into a gunfight and then claim you started it. They're gonna kill you, Smoke."

"They're going to try," Smoke said, softly correcting him.

"Where did you hear this, boy?" Hunt asked.

"I was up in the loft getting ready to fork hay down to the horses when the men came inside the barn. I hunkered down in the loft and listened to them talk. They's five of them, Smoke. Valentine, Suggs, Bolton, Harris, and Wright."

"I've heard of Valentine," Smoke said. "He's a gunhawk. Draws fighting wages from Franklin."

"His name was mentioned too," the boy continued. "They said Mister Franklin told them to nip this matter in the bud and end it. If you was to die, they said, the other nests would crumble like a house of cards. They said the new law was on their side and Mister Franklin told them they didn't have nothin' to worry about from that end."

"I suggest we go see the new sheriff immediately," Hunt said. "Let him handle this matter."

Billy shook his head. "I don't know who you are, mister. But you don't understand the way things are. Monte Carson is Franklin's man. Franklin says frog, Carson jumps. Judge Proctor is an old wine-head from over the Dolores way. Franklin brung him in here to stick him in as judge. It's all cut and dried. All made up agin Smoke."

"Incredible!" Haywood said. "Oh, I believe you, son." He looked at Billy. "Activities of this sort are not confined solely to the West."

Billy blinked and looked at Smoke. "What'd he say?"

"Happens in other places too."

"Oh."

"If that is the case, Smoke," Hunt said, "then you must run for your life."

Smoke's eyes turned icy. He looked at the lawyer. "I don't run, Lawyer."

"Then what are you going to do?" Haywood asked. "You've all three heard Billy's statement. A newspaper man, a lawyer, a minister." Smoke smiled with a grim wolf's baring of his teeth. "Take Billy's story down. I see a way to make Tilden Franklin eat crow on this matter and backpaddle."

"What are you going to do, Smoke?" Preacher Morrow inquired.

"Fight," Smoke said.

"But there's *five* of them!" Hunt protested. "Five against one of you."

"I've faced tougher odds, Lawyer." He looked at Billy. "Where is it going down, Billy?"

"They're gonna brace you in the stable."

Smoke nodded his head. "After these gentlemen take your story on paper, Billy, you get the horses out of there. I don't want to see a good horse die on account of trash like Tilden's men."

"Yes, sir!"

Smoke looked at the three men. "I'll be heading down that way in about an hour, boys. I would suggest you all hunt a hole."

Sally looked toward the eastern slopes of the Sugarloaf. Pearlie was not in sight. Bob Colby was working inside the barn, cleaning it out. She called for him.

"Yes'um?" He stuck his head out of the loft.

"Bob, look and see if you can spot Pearlie. He should be over there." She pointed.

Bob searched the eastern slopes of the Sugarloaf. "Nothing, ma'am," he called. "I can't spot him."

"All right, Bob. Thanks. He's behind a hill, I guess." She put Pearlie out of her mind and thought about what to fix for dinner—supper, as they called it out here, although she had never gotten used to that.

"Now what, boys?" Pearlie asked the half-dozen Circle TF riders facing him.

"I guess you know what, Pearlie," a puncher said. He shook out a loop in his rope.

"You boys is wrong," Pearlie said. "A man's gotta right to ride for the brand he chooses."

"You a turncoat, Pearlie. You should have knowed that no one shows his ass-end to Mister Franklin."

"He ain't God, Lefty."

"He is around here," Lefty responded.

"Then let him bring you back to life," Pearlie said. He jerked iron and blew Lefty out of the saddle, the slug taking the TF rider in the right shoulder, knocking him to the ground.

Pearlie spun his cutting horse and tried to make a run for it. He was just a tad slow. He felt the loop settle around him, and then another circled him and jerked him out of the saddle. He hit the ground hard, the breath knocked out of him.

Pearlie struggled to free himself of the stiff ropes, but he knew he was fighting a losing fight. He lifted his six-gun and thumbed the hammer back. He hated to do it, but he had to leave some proof of who had done this to him.

He shot a TF horse. The animal dropped almost immediately as the slug entered behind its left shoulder and shattered the heart. The rider cursed and jumped free, kicking the six-gun out of Pearlie's hand.

"Drag the son of a bitch!" the horseless rider yelled.

Pearlie was jerked along the ground. Mercifully, his head struck a rock and he was dropped into the darkness of unconsciousness.

"Did you hear a shot?" Sally called.

"Yes'um!" Bob called back. "Probably Pearlie shootin' a rattler, is all."

"Maybe," Sally muttered. She went back into the house and strapped on a pistol. She picked up a rifle and levered a round into the chamber of the Henry. Back outside, she called, "Bob! Are you armed?"

"Yes'um. Got a short gun on and my rifle is right down there." He pointed.

"Get your rifle and stay in the loft. Keep a look-out for riders. I think we're in for some trouble."

"Yes'um!"

"While you're getting your rifle, close and bar all the barn doors. I'll bring Seven inside and put him in a stall."

"Yes'um, Miss Sally."

Sally hurriedly fixed containers of water and a basket of food for the boy. She put in several boxes of ammunition and carried it to him in the barn. "We might be in for a long day, Bob," she told him. "And you might have to stay out here by yourself tonight."

"I ain't skirred, Miss Sally. I can knock the eye out of a squirrel at a hundred yards with a rifle. If anybody comes to fight, we'll stand 'em off."

"Good boy. I'll be in the house. Let them come close, we'll catch them in a crossfire."

Bob grinned. "Yes, *ma'am!*"

It was as if some invisible messenger had passed the word. The town of Fontana grew quiet, then hushed almost entirely. Smoke walked across the street and stepped into the tent of Louis Longmont. Louis waved him to the bar.

"A pall has fallen over us, my young friend," Louis said. "I'm sure it concerns you. Am I correct?"

"Uh-huh. Some of Franklin's men are setting me up for a killing."

"And naturally, you're going to leave town in a cloud of dust, right?"

"Sure, Louis. You know that."

"How many?"

"Five." Smoke named them.

"Valentine is a bad one. I know him. He's a top gun from down near the Tex-Mex border. Watch him. He's got a border roll that's fast as lightning."

"Yeah, I've heard he's good. How good?"

"Very good," the gambler said softly. "He beat Johnny North."

A smile passed Smoke's lips. "But Johnny North is still alive."

"Precisely."

So Valentine was cat-quick, but couldn't shoot worth a damn. Many quick-draw gunhands were blindingly fast, but usually missed their first shots.

Smoke almost never missed.

"I'll back you up if you ask, Smoke," Louis offered.

"It'll come to that, Louis. But not yet. Speaking of Johnny North, where is he?"

"A question I've asked myself a few times since coming here. He'll be here. But he's a strange one, Smoke. He hates Monte Carson."

"So I hear. I've never heard of him teaming up with anyone."

"Lone wolf all the way. Johnny must be . . . oh, about my age, I suppose. But age has not slowed him a bit. When do you meet these gentlemen, and where?"

Smoke opened his watch. "In about fifteen minutes. Down at the stables."

"Anything you need?"

"A shotgun and a pocketful of shells."

Louis reached over the bar and pulled out a sawed-off twelve-gauge express gun. He handed Smoke a sack of shells.

"I loaded these myself," the gambler said. "Full of ball bearings."

Smoke loaded the express gun. "Got a taste of that scotch handy?"

Louis walked behind the long, deserted bar and poured two fingers of scotch for each of them. He lifted his glass. "To your unerring marksmanship."

"And hope I shoot straight too," Smoke said needling the man.

13

Pearlie opened his eyes. He could have sworn he opened his eyes. But he couldn't see a thing. Slowly, painfully, he lifted one hand and wiped his eyes. There. He could see . . . a little bit, at least.

He hurt all over. He wriggled his toes. Something was wrong. His boots were gone. He could feel the cool earth against his skin. His jeans were ripped and his shirt was gone. He carefully poked at himself. He was bruised and cut and torn from head to toes, but he didn't feel any broken bones sticking out. Lucky. Damn lucky.

Pearlie turned his head and felt something flop down over one ear. He carefully inspected his fingertips. A flap of skin was torn loose. He pressed it back against his head and took his bandana from around his neck, tying it around his head. Hurt like hell.

Only then did he think of the danger he might still be in. What if the TF riders were still hanging around?

He looked around him.

Nothing and nobody in sight.

He slowly drew himself up to his knees and looked

around. He could clearly see where he had been dragged. He looked down where he had lain. A hole in the hard ground, blood beside it. He stuck a finger into the hole and pulled out the dirt. His fingers touched something hard. Pearlie dug it out and looked at it. A battered and mangled .44 slug. The bastards had shot him. They thought they'd killed him with a gunshot to the head. That would account for the flap of skin hanging down.

"Boy, you was lucky," he croaked, pushing the words out of a dry throat.

He looked back along the torn path he'd been dragged on. It ran for a ways back toward the cabin. He could see one boot standing all alone in the mangled path. He rose unsteadily to his feet and staggered back toward the boot, one solid mass of aches and pains and misery.

And mad.

Goddamn, was he mad!

He picked up the boot and wandered off in search of his other boot. Pearlie fell down more times than he cared to recall. He banged and bruised and battered his knees and hands each time he fell, but each time he hit the ground, his anger increased. He began cursing Tilden Franklin and all the TF riders who had dragged him and then left him for dead.

The verbal barrage seemed to help.

He found his other boot and sat down to rest, slipping on both his boots. Now he felt better. He could see, just barely, the fallen horse of the TF man. He walked and staggered and stumbled toward it. The animal had fallen on its left side; no way Pearlie could get to the rifle in the saddle boot. But he could salvage the canteen full of water. He sat on the rump of the dead horse and drank his fill. His eyes swept the immediate area. He spotted his six-gun and walked to it, picking it up. He brushed off the dirt, checked the action and the loads, and holstered the weapon. Now he felt better than ever. He dug in the saddlebags of the fallen horse and found a box of .44s, distributing them in his pockets.

Now, by God, just let me find some TF punchers! he thought. He managed to pull the other saddlebag from under the dead horse and rummage through it. Some cold biscuits and beef. As tired as he was and as much as he hurt, he knew he had to have something to eat. Them bearsign was good eatin', but they didn't stay with a man.

He ate the beef and biscuits and washed them down with water. He looked toward the direction of the ranch. A good four or five miles off. With an explosive oath, Pearlie stood up and began walking. Miss Sally and the boy was probably in for a rough time of it. And by *God*, Pearlie was gonna be there to help out.

He put one boot in front of the other and walked and staggered on.

Drops of blood marked his back trail.

Smoke didn't know where all the people had gone, but the streets of Fontana were empty and silent as he walked along, keeping to the near side of the long street, advancing toward the stable.

But he could feel many eyes on him as he walked.

He slipped the thongs from his Colts as he walked, shifting the sawed-off express from right hand to left hand. He looked up as the batwing doors of a saloon swung open. Tilden Franklin and his foreman, Clint, stepped out to stare at Smoke. The new sheriff, Monte Carson, stood beside them, his large, new, shiny badge catching the late-morning rays of the sun.

"We don't like troublemakers in this town, Smoke," Monte said.

Smoke stopped and turned to face the men. With his

eyes on Monte, he said, "What trouble have I caused, Sheriff?"

That took Monte aback. He stared at Smoke. Finally, he said, "Man walks around carrying a shotgun like that one there you got must be lookin' for trouble."

Smoke grinned. "Why, Sheriff, I'm just going down to the stables to see about my horse. Any law against that?"

Monte shook his head.

"Thanks. If there is nothing else, I'll just be on my way."

Tilden grinned at Smoke. His mean eyes shone with evil and power.

Smoke met the man's eyes. "How about you, Franklin? You got anything to say?"

"You talk mighty big standing there with that express gun in your hands," Tilden replied.

"Insurance, Franklin," Smoke said. "Since you're afraid to move without your trained dogs with you."

That stung Clint. His eyes narrowed and his hands balled into fists. But he knew better than to prod Smoke; the gunfighter's rep was that his temper was volatile, and that express gun would turn all three of them into chopped meat at this distance.

"That's right, Clint," Smoke said, a nasty tone to his words. "I forgot. You'd rather make war against farmers and women and kids, wouldn't you?"

"Stand easy, Clint," Tilden quietly warned his foreman.

Smoke laughed and turned, continuing his walk down the street.

Billy darted from the corral and pressed against the side of a newly erected building. "They're all over the place, Smoke," he called in a stage whisper. "Two of 'em up in the loft."

Smoke nodded his thanks and said, "Get out of here, Billy. Hunt a hole."

Billy took off as if the devil was howling and smoking at his heels.

Smoke looked toward the corral. Horse was watching him, his ears perked up.

Smoke walked to the huge open doors and paused. He knew he would be blind for a few seconds upon entering the darkened stable. Out of habit, he rechecked the loads in the express gun and took a deep breath.

He slipped the thongs back on the hammers of his Colts and jumped inside the stable, rolling to his right, into an open stall.

Gunfire blasted the semi-darkness where Smoke had first hit the floor.

"Riders comin', Miss Sally!" Bob called from the barn loft.

"How far off, Bob?" she called from the house.

"'Bout a mile, ma'am. I can't make out no brand yet."

"If they're Circle TF, Bob," she called, "we'll blow them out of the saddle."

"Yes, *ma'am*!"

Woman and boy waited, gripping their rifles.

Pearlie found Lefty's horse and gently approached the still-spooked animal. The horse shied away. Pearlie sat down on a large rock and waited, knowing that the horse would eventually come to him, desiring human company. In less than five minutes, while Pearlie hummed a low tune, the animal came to him and shoved at the puncher with its nose. Pearlie petted the animal, got the reins, and swung into the saddle. Lefty's rifle was in the boot and Pearlie checked it. Full. Pearlie pointed the animal's nose toward the ranch.

"Let's go, boy," Pearlie said, just as the sounds of gunfire reached him. "I wanna get in a shot or two myself."

Sally's opening shot knocked a TF rider out of the saddle. Bob squeezed off a round, the slug hitting a TF gunhawk in the center of his chest. The puncher was dead before he hit the ground. With only three gunslicks left out of the original half a dozen, those three spun their horses and lit a shuck out of that area.

They ran right into Pearlie, coming at them at full gallop. With the reins in his teeth, his right hand full of Colt and his left hand full of Henry rifle, Pearlie emptied two saddles. The last TF rider left alive hunched low in the saddle and made it over a rise and out of range. He then headed for the ranch. They'd been told they were going up against Pearlie and one little lady. But it seemed that Pearlie was as hard to kill as a grizzly and that that little lady had turned into a bobcat.

Meanwhile, Pearlie reined up in a cloud of dust and jumped out of the saddle. "You folks all right?" he yelled.

"My God, Pearlie!" Sally rushed out of the house. "What happened to you?"

"They roped and drug me," Pearlie said. "Then shot me. But they made a bad mistake, ma'am."

She looked at him.

"They left me alive," Pearlie said, his words flint hard.

Smoke darted into the darkness of the first stall just as the lead tore smoking holes where he'd first hit. Rolling to one side, Smoke lifted the sawed-off express gun and eared back both hammers and waited.

"Got the punk!" someone hissed.

"Maybe," a calmer voice spoke from just above Smoke.

Smoke lifted the sawed-off and pulled both triggers. The express gun roared and bucked, and ball-bearing loads tore a great hole in the loft floor. The "maybe" man was flung out of the loft, both loads catching him directly in the crotch, almost tearing him in half. He lay on the stable floor, squalling as his blood stained the horse-shit-littered boards.

Smoke rolled to the wall of the stall, reloaded the express gun, and jumped over the stall divider, into the next stall. His ears were still ringing from the tremendous booming of the sawed-off.

Quietly, he removed his spurs and laid them to one side.

He heard someone cursing, then someone else said, "Jensen shot him where he lived. That ain't right."

The mangled man had ceased his howling, dying on the stable floor.

Smoke waited.

As he had expected, Sheriff Monte Carson was making no effort to interfere with the ambush.

So much for the new law and order in Fontana.

Smoke waited, motionless, his callused hands gripping the express gun. His mentor, Preacher, had taught Smoke well, teaching him, among other things, patience.

One of Tilden's gunhands lost his patience and began tossing lead around where he suspected Smoke to be. He was way off target. But Smoke wasn't.

Smoke blew the man out of the loft, the loads taking him in the belly, knocking him backward. He rolled and thrashed and screamed, the pain finally rolling him off the edge and dropping him to the ground floor.

Smoke heard one man jump from the loft and take off running. The others ran out the back and disappeared.

Smoke waited for a long ten-count, then slipped out the front door. He made sure all watching saw him reload the sawed-off shotgun. Then he walked straight up the dusty street to where Tilden and Monte were standing. Still in the street, Smoke wondered where Clint had gotten off to. No matter. Clint might ride for a sorry no-account, but the man was not a backshooter. Smoke knew that much about him.

Looking straight at Tilden, Smoke said, "Two of your men are on the stable floor. One is dead and I imagine the other won't live long the way he's shot. Your other hands lost their nerve and ran. Maybe you told them to ambush me, maybe you didn't. I don't know. So I won't accuse you of it."

Tilden stood still, smoking a thin cigar. But his eyes were filled with silent rage and hate.

Smoke looked at Monte. "You got anything you want to say to me, Sheriff?"

Monte wanted desperately to look at Tilden for some sign. But he was afraid to take his eyes off Smoke. He finally shook his head. "I reckon not."

"Fine." Smoke looked at Tilden. "See you 'round, Franklin." He knew the man despised to be called by his last name.

Smoke turned and walked to Louis Longmont's place. He handed Louis the shotgun and walked across the street to join the Easterners.

"Go get my horse, Billy. And stay out of the barn until someone cleans up the mess."

"Yes, sir!"

"Is that . . . it?" Hunt asked.

"That's it, Lawyer," Smoke told him. "Out here, for the time being, justice is very swift and short."

Smoke looked at Ed Jackson.

"I'd suggest you bear that in mind," Smoke told him.

14

Tilden sat at a table in a saloon. By himself. The king-pin rancher was in a blue funk and everybody knew it. So they wisely left him alone.

Those six gunhands he'd sent to ambush Jensen were among the best he'd had on his payroll. And they'd failed. And to make matters worse, Jensen had made Tilden look like a fool . . . in front of Monte and countless others who were hiding nearby.

Intolerable.

Tilden emptied his shot glass and refilled it from the bottle. Lifting the shot glass filled with the amber liquid to his lips, Tilden glanced down at the bottle. More than half empty. That too was intolerable. Tilden was not a heavy-drinking man, not a man who liked his thoughts muddled.

He set the shot glass on the table and pushed it from him. He looked up as one of his punchers—he couldn't remember the man's name and that irritated him further—entered the saloon and walked quickly up to Clint, whispering in the foreman's ear.

The foreman stiffened and gave the man a dark look, then cut his eyes to Tilden.

Tilden Franklin rose from the table and walked to Clint and the cowboy. "Outside," he said.

In the shade offered by the awning, the men stood on the boardwalk. "Say it," Tilden ordered the cowboy-gunhand.

"Lefty and five others went over to the Sugarloaf to drag Pearlie. Only one come back and he was shot up pretty bad. He said they drug Pearlie a pretty fair distance and then shot him in the head. But he ain't dead, boss. And they was two people at Jensen's spread. Both of them trigger-pullers."

"Son of a *bitch*!" Tilden cursed low.

"And that ain't all, boss. Billy was over to our western range drivin' the beeves back to the lower slopes. He seen a campfire, smelled beans cookin'. Billy took off over there to run whoever it was off the range. When he got there, he changed his mind. It was Charlie Starr."

Tilden thought about that for a few seconds. He didn't believe it. Last word he'd had of Charlie Starr was five, six years back, and that news had been that Starr had been killed in a gunfight up in Montana.

He said as much.

The puncher shook his head. "Billy seen Charlie over in Nevada, at Mormon Station, seven, eight years ago. That's when Charlie kilt them four gunslicks. Billy bought Charlie a drink after that, and they talked for near-abouts an hour. You've heard Billy brag about that, boss. It ain't likely he'd forget Charlie Starr."

Tilden nodded his head in agreement. It was not very likely. Charlie Starr. Mean as a snake and just as notional as a grizzly bear. Wore two guns, tied down low, and was just as good with one as the other. Charlie had been a number of things: stagecoach guard, deputy, marshal, gambler, outlaw, gunfighter, bounty hunter, miner . . . and a lot of other things.

Charlie was . . . had to be close to fifty years old. But Tilden doubted that age would have slowed him down much. If any.

And Charlie Starr hated Tilden Franklin.

As if reading his thoughts, Clint said, "You don't think . . ."

"I don't know, Clint." He dismissed the cowboy and told him to get a drink. When the batwings had swallowed the cowboy, Tilden said, "That was more than fifteen years ago, Clint. Seventeen years to be exact. I was twenty-three years old and full of piss and vinegar. I didn't know that woman belonged to Charlie. Damnit, she didn't tell me she did. Rubbing all over me, tickling my ear. I had just ramrodded a herd up from Texas and was hard-drinkin' back then." He sighed. "I got drunk, Clint. I've told you that much before. What I haven't told you was that I got a little rough with the woman later on. She died. I thought she liked it rough. Lots of women do, you know. Anyway, I got the word that Charlie Starr was gunning for me. I ordered my boys to rope him and drag the meanness out of him. They got a little carried away with the fun and hurt him bad. He was, so I'm told, a long time recovering from it. Better part of a year. Word got back to me over the years that Charlie had made his brag he was going to brace me and kill me."

"I seen him up on the Roaring Fork nine, ten years ago," Clint said. "Luis Chamba and that Medicine Bow gunslick braced him. Chamba took a lot of lead, but he lived. The other one didn't."

"Where is Chamba?"

"Utah, last I heard."

"Send a rider. Get him."

"Yes, sir."

* * *

It was full dark when Smoke saw the lights shining from the windows of the cabin. He had pushed Horse hard, and the big stallion was tired, but game. Smoke rubbed him down, gave him an extra ration of corn, and turned him loose to roll.

When he opened the door to the cabin and saw Pearlie's battered and torn face, his own face tightened.

"He'll tell you over dinner," Sally said. "Wash up and I'll fix you a plate."

Over a heaping plate of beef and potatoes and gravy and beans flavored with honey, with bearsign for dessert, Pearlie told his story while Smoke ate.

"If there was any law worth a damn in this country I could have Tilden arrested," Smoke said, chewing thoughtfully.

"I don't even know where the county lines are," Pearlie said. He would have liked another doughnut, but he'd already eaten twenty that day and was ashamed to ask for another.

With a smile, Sally pushed the plate of bearsign toward him.

"Well," Pearlie said. "Maybe just *one* more."

"What county does our land lie in, Smoke?" Sally asked.

"I don't know. I'm not sure. It might be split in half. And that's something to think about. But . . . I don't know. You can bet that when it comes to little farmers and little ranchers up against kingpins like Tilden, the law is going to side with the big boys. Might be wiser just to keep the law out of this altogether."

"I thought you folks had bought most of your land and filed on the rest?" Pearlie said.

"We have," Smoke told him. "And it's been checked and it's all legal. But they surveyed again a couple of years ago and drew up new lines. I never heard any more about it."

"Mister Smoke?" Bob asked, from a chair away from the adults.

"Yes, Bob?"

"Who is Charlie Starr?"

Smoke sopped up the last of his gravy with a thick hunk of bread and chewed for a moment. "He's a gunfighter, Bob. He's been a lot of things, but mostly he's a good man. But a strange one. I met him while I was riding with an old Mountain Man called Preacher. Why do you ask?"

"I heard them Jones boys talkin' last week. When we was all gathered over to the Matlocks' for Sunday services. That feller who sometimes works for Mister Matlock said Charlie Starr's been camped out around this country for a month or so."

"I can't believe Charlie is here to hire his gun out to Tilden. He never has hired his guns out against a little man. He's done a lot of things, but he kinda backed into his rep as a gunslick. Maybe that fellow was mistaken?"

"Maybe, Mister Smoke."

Charlie Starr shifted his blankets away from his fire and settled in for the night. He smiled in the darkness, the sounds of his horse cropping grass a somehow comforting sound in the night. Since that puncher had come up on him, he'd moved his location—out of, he thought, the TF range. High up in the mountains, where snow was still capping the crests, above some place called the Sugarloaf. Nice-sounding name, Charlie thought.

Louis Longmont sat at a table playing stud, winning, as usual. Winning even though his thoughts were not entirely on the game. He'd just that evening heard the rumors that Charlie Starr was in the area, and heard too that

Tilden Franklin had sent a rider to Utah to get Luis Chamba, the Sonora gunslick. And he'd heard that Tilden was building up his own forces by half a hundred riders.

Louis pulled in his winnings and excused himself from the game. His mind wasn't on it and he needed a breath of air. He walked outside, into the rambunctious, boom-town night air. The town was growing by hundreds each day. Most of the men were miners or would-be miners, but there was a lot of trash mixed in as well.

With this many people working the area, the town might last, Louis thought, six months—maybe less. There was a strong urge within the man to just fold his tent and pull out. Louis felt there would be a bloodbath before everything was said and done.

But Louis couldn't do that. He'd given his word to Preacher he'd look in on Smoke from time to time. Not that Smoke needed any looking after, Louis thought with a grin. But a man's word was his bond. So Louis would see it through. He tossed his cigar into the street and walked back into his gaming tent.

Tilden Franklin sat alone in his huge house, his thoughts as savage as much of the land that lay around him. His thoughts would have made a grizzly flinch. Tilden had never seen a woman that he desired more than Sally Jensen. Educated, aloof, beautiful. Tilden wondered how she'd look with her dress on the floor.

He shook that thought from him.

Then, with a faint smile curving his lips, he thought about the nester Colby. More specifically, Colby's daughter. Velvet.

Tilden laughed. He thought he knew how to get rid of that nester, and let his boys have some fun in the process.

Yeah. He'd give it some extra thought in the morning. But it seemed like a pretty good idea.

* * *

Billy lay on the hay in the loft, in his longjohns, his new clothing carefully folded and stored on a little ledge. His thoughts were of Smoke. Billy wondered how it would be to have a pa like Smoke. Probably real nice. There was a streak of gentleness in the gunfighter that few adults could see. But a kid could see it right off. Smoke for a pa. Well, it was something to dream about. One thing for sure, nobody would mess with you, leastways.

Ed Jackson lay by his wife's side and mentally counted all the money he was going to make. He'd hired some rough-looking men that day, promising them a grubstake if they'd build his store for him. They had accepted. Ed Jackson dreamed of great wealth. Ed Jackson dreamed of becoming a very important person. Maybe even someone like Tilden Franklin.

Now there was a *really* important man.

Paul Jackson lay in his blankets under a wagon. He was restless, sleep was elusive. He kept thinking about the way Bountiful had looked at him. Something was building between them, he just knew it. And Paul also knew that he wasn't going to hang around here with his stupid, greedy brother any longer than necessary. If he could find gold, that would really make Bountiful sit up and take notice of him.

He grinned.

Or lay down and take notice of him.

Dana lay by her husband, listening to him breathe as he slept. She wondered if they'd made a mistake in coming out West. Haywood didn't think so, but she'd wondered often about it, especially during the past few days. These men out here, they took violent death so . . . so calmly. It frightened her.

Colton closed up his tent and put his money, some of it in gold dust, into a lockbox and carefully stowed it away in the hidden compartment under the wagon. He was tired, but he'd made more money in just two days than most physicians back East made in a month—maybe two months. If this kept up, he'd have enough to travel on to California and set up a practice in real style. In a place that had some class, with a theater and opera and all the rest that civilized people craved. At this rate, he'd have far more than enough in a year's time.

He washed his hands and made ready for bed.

Hunt was wide awake, his thoughts many and most of them confused. True, he'd been busy all day handling gold claims, but no one had come to him for any legal advice concerning the many fights and stabbings and occasional shootings that occurred within the town of Fontana. He simply could not understand that. Didn't these people understand due process? All those fistfights and gunfights. It was positively barbaric. And so needless. All people had to do was come see him; then they could handle it in a proper court of law.

If, Hunt thought with a grimace, they could find the judge when he was sober.

15

Leaving Pearlie with Sally, Smoke escorted Bob back to his home. For the first time since arriving in the area, Smoke saw both Wilbur Mason and Colby armed with short guns and rifles. Dismounting, Smoke ground-reined Drifter and faced the farmer-ranchers.

"Seen any of the others?" Smoke asked.

"Nolan rode by yesterday evenin'," Colby said. "He's scared and admitted it."

"Ray and Betty sent word that they're with us all the way," Mason said.

"How about Peyton?"

Both men shrugged.

"I think he'll stand," Smoke said. "Way he talked to me the other day, he'll stick. How's your food supply?"

"Plenty. The old woman canned enough last summer to last us for a good long time. Potato bin's half full. What's your plans, Smoke?"

Smoke brought them both up to date. Then he said, "I'm staying close to home. Shifting my cattle to a different graze. But if I need something in the way of supplies, nothing or nobody will keep me out of Fontana."

"When you decide to go in," Colby said, "I'll take my wagon and go in with you. The two of us can get supplies for everybody."

"Sounds good. We don't want to leave the whole area without menfolk. I'm going to talk with the others today. Get a better idea of where they stand. I'll see you both later on."

Velvet came out of the house and walked to the well. Smoke's eyes followed her. She was a young girl, but built up like a grown woman. And that worried Smoke. Tilden was ruthless, might do anything. And some of the gunslicks riding for the TF brand were nothing more than pure white trash. They'd do anything Tilden ordered. While most Western men would not bother a good woman, there were always exceptions.

Colby had followed Smoke's eyes. "I still think you're wrong, Smoke. She's just a child."

"Tilden Franklin is a sorry son of a bitch," Smoke told the men. "Don't put anything past him." He swung into the saddle. "See you boys later."

Smoke rode hard that day, stopping in to see all the small outfits he thought might throw in with him and the others. And he had been correct in his thinking. Steve and Mike and Nolan and Ray all agreed to toss in, forming an alliance among all the small spreads. If one got hit, the others would respond.

Their lives and money were sunk deep into this land, and with many, some of their blood as well. They were not going to run.

"What's this talk about Charlie Starr, Smoke?" Nolan asked.

"So far as I know, just that—talk." He told the man what he knew about Starr. "I think, if he is in this area, he's here to kill Tilden Franklin. Lots of bad blood between those two. Goes back years, so the story goes. I'm going to try to pin the rumor down. When I do, I'll get back with you. Stay loose, Nolan, and keep an eye on your womenfolk. I have no way of knowing exactly what Tilden has in mind, but whatever it is, it's bad news for us, that's for sure."

"I'm not going to put up with these miners tearing up my land, Smoke," the rancher said. "If I have to shoot two or three of them, I will."

"Check your land title, Nolan. You might not have mineral rights. Ever think about that?"

The farmer-rancher cursed. "I never thought about that. Could someone buy those rights without my permission?"

"I think so. The law is still kind of raw out here, you know that. I checked on my title last night. I own the mineral rights to my land."

"I just didn't think about it. I'll do just that. See you, Smoke."

Smoke spent a week staying close to home. He received no news about what might be happening in Fontana. Then, on a fine, clear, late spring day, Smoke decided to ride his valley. He found several miners' camps high up, and told the men to clear out—right then.

"And if we don't?" one bearded man challenged him.

"I'll kill you," Smoke told him, ice in the words.

"You talk big, mister," another miner said. "But I'm wonderin' if you got the sand to back up your words."

"My name is Smoke Jensen."

The miners cleared out within the hour.

With the sun directly over his head, Smoke decided to stop in a stand of timber and eat the lunch that Sally had prepared for him. He was just stepping down from the saddle when the smell of wood smoke reached him.

He swung back into the saddle and followed the invisible trail. It took him the better part of an hour to find the well-concealed camp, and when he found it, he knew he had come face-to-face with one of the most feared men in all the West.

Charlie Starr.

"Mind some company?" Smoke asked, raising his voice to be heard over the hundred yards or so that separated the men.

"Is this your land?" the man called.

"Sure is."

"Light and sit then. You welcome to share what I got."

"Thanks," Smoke said, riding in and dismounting. "My wife fixed me a bait of food."

Charlie Starr looked hard at Smoke. "Ain't I seen you afores?"

"Yes," Smoke told him, unwrapping the waxed paper Sally had used to secure his lunch. "Long time ago, up in Wyoming. I was with a Mountain Man called Preacher."

"Well, I'll just be damned if that ain't the truth! You've growed a mite, boy"

There was a twinkle in his eyes as he said it. And Smoke knew that Charlie Starr knew all about him.

Charlie's eyes flicked to Smoke's guns. "No notches. That's good. Only a tinhorn cuts his kills, and half of them are lies."

Smoke thought of Colby's boy, Adam. "I told that to a boy just the other day. I don't think he believed me."

"He might not live to be a man, thinking like that." Charlie's eyes lit up as he spotted the bearsign in Smoke's sack. "Say, now!"

Smoke halved his doughnuts and Charlie put them aside for dessert. "Much obliged, Smoke. Have some coffee."

Smoke filled his battered tin cup and settled back to

enjoy his lunch among the mountain's flowers and trees and cool but pleasant breezes.

"You wonderin' why I'm squatted on your range?" Charlie asked.

"Stay as long as you're friendly, Charlie." Smoke spoke around a mouthful of beef and bread.

Charlie laughed. "And you'd brace me too, wouldn't you, young man?"

Younger eyes met older eyes. Both sets were flint hard and knowing.

"I'd try you, Charlie."

Charlie chuckled and said, "I killed my first man 'fore you was even a glint in your daddy's eyes, Smoke. Way before. How old do you think I am, Smoke?"

"You ain't no young rooster."

Again, the gunfighter laughed. "You shore right about that. I'm fifty-eight years old. I killed my first man when I was fourteen, I think it was. That be, uh, back in '36, I reckon."

"I was fourteen when I killed an Indian. I think we were in Kansas."

"You don't say? I'm be damned. Some folks would say that an Injun don't count, but I ain't one of them folks. Injuns is just like us . . . but different."

Smoke stopped chewing and thought about that. He had to smile. "You don't look your age, Charlie."

"Thank you. But on cold mornin's I shore feel it. Seen me a bunch of boomers headin' this way. They made it to No-Name yet?"

"No-Name is now Fontana. Oh, yeah, the boomers made it and are still coming in."

"Fontana," Charlie said softly. "Right pretty name." His voice had changed, becoming low-pitched and deadly. "Fontana. Now what do you think about that?"

Smoke said nothing. Preacher had told him the story

about Charlie's girl, Rosa Fontana, and about Tilden Franklin killing the girl and dragging Charlie.

The men ate in silence for a time, silently enjoying each other's company. While they ate, they eyeballed each other when one thought the other wasn't looking.

Smoke took in Charlie's lean frame. The man's waist was so thin he looked like he'd have to eat a dozen bearsign just to hold his britches up. Like most cowboys, his main strength lay in his shoulders and arms. The man's wrists were thick, the hands big and scarred and callused. His face was tanned and rugged-looking. Charlie Starr looked like a man who would be hard to handle in any kind of fight.

Then Smoke had an idea; an idea that, if Charlie was agreeable, would send Tilden Franklin right through the roof of his mansion in fits of rage.

"You always sit around grinnin', boy?" Charlie asked.

"No." Smoke had not realized he was grinning. "But I just had me an idea."

"Must have been a good'un."

"You lookin' for work, Charlie?"

"Not so's you'd notice, I ain't."

"My wife is one of the best cooks in the state."

"Keep talkin'." He picked up a doughnut and nibbled at it. Then he stuffed the whole thing in his mouth.

"Wouldn't be a whole lot to do. I got one hand. Name's Pearlie."

"Rat good with a gun, is he?"

"He'll do to ride the river with. Some of Tilden's boys hung a rope on him last week and dragged him a piece." Smoke kept his voice bland, not wanting Charlie to know that he knew about the bad blood between Starr and Franklin. Or why. "Then they shot him in the head. Pearlie managed to live and get lead in two of them. He's back working a full day now."

Charlie grunted. "Sounds like he'll do, all rat. What is he, half 'gator?"

"He's tough. I'll pay you thirty and found."

"Don't need no job. But . . ."

Smoke waited.

"Your wife make these here bearsign now and then, does she?"

"Once a week."

"I come and go as I please long as my work's caught up?"

"Sure. But I have to warn you . . . they'll probably be some shooting involved, and . . . well, with you getting along in years and all, I wouldn't blame you if you turned it down."

Charlie fixed him with a look that would have withered a cactus. Needles and all.

"Boy, are you out of your gawddamned mind or just born slow?"

"Well, no, Charlie . . . but they're gonna be broncs to bust, and with your age and all, I was just . . ."

Charlie threw his battered hat on the ground. "Gawddamn, boy, I ain't ready for no old folks' home just yet!"

"Now, don't get worked up, Charlie. You're liable to have a heart attack, and I don't know nothing about treating heart attacks."

Charlie turned blue around the mouth and his eyes bugged out. Then he began to relax and chuckle. He wiped his eyes and said, "Shore tell Preacher had a hand in your up-bringin', Smoke." He stuck a hard, rough hand across the hat-sized fire. "You got you a man that'll ride the river with you, Smoke Jensen."

Smoke took the hand and a new friendship was born.

16

On the slow ride back to the ranch, Smoke discovered that Charlie and Preacher shared one common bond. They both liked to bitch.

And like Preacher's had been, Charlie's complaints were numerous . . . and mostly made up.

"I stayed in a hospital a week one time," Charlie informed him. "Them doctors found more wrong with me than a human body ought to have to suffer. I swear, if I'd stayed in there another week, I'd have probably died. They told me that no human bein' could be shot twenty-two times and still live. I told them I wasn't shot no twenty-two times, it was twenty-five times, but three of them holes was in a place they wasn't about to look at.

"Boy, was I wrong!"

Smoke was laughing so hard he had to wipe his eyes with a bandana.

"Nurse come in that first day. That was the homeliest-lookin' female I ever did see. Looked like a buffalo. Told me to hike up that gown they had me in. I told her that her and no two others like her was big enough to make me do that.

"I was wrong agin.

"I want to warn you now, Smoke. Don't never get around me with no rubber tubin'. Don't do it. I'm liable to go plumb bee-serk. Them hospitals, boy, they got a thing about flushin' out a man's system. Stay away from hospitals, boy, they'll kill you!"

Pearlie was clearly in awe. Not only was he working for Smoke Jensen, but now Smoke had done gone and hired Charlie Starr.

"Shut your mouth, boy," Charlie told him. "Afore you swaller a bug."

Pearlie closed his mouth.

Charlie was clearly taken aback when Sally came out of the cabin to meet him . . . dressed in men's jeans. With a pistol belted around her tiny waist.

Wimmin just didn't have no business a-runnin' around in men's pants. They'd be smokin' cigarettes 'fore long.

But he forgot all about that when she said, "Fresh apple pie for dessert, Mister Starr."

"Charlie, ma'am. Just Charlie."

The sun was just settling over the Sugarloaf when Sally called them in for dinner. Steaks, beans, potatoes, fresh-baked bread, and apple pie.

Smoke and Sally both noted that, for such a spare fellow, Charlie could certainly eat.

After Charlie had sampled his plate and pleased his palate, he said, "Bring me up to date, Smoke."

Smoke told him what he knew, and then what he guessed. Including Tilden's desires for Sally.

"That's his way, all right," Charlie said. Then he leveled with them, speaking slowly, telling them about Rosa. "Way I hear it, Tilden fancied that she was comin' up on him. But that was her job, hostess at a saloon. Rosa had part of the action, owned about twenty-five percent of it.

When I come to in the hospital, after Tilden's boys drug me, Louis told me what really happened."

Smoke glanced at the man. "Louis!"

Charlie grinned grimly. "Louis Longmont. It was one of his places. And you know Louis don't tolerate no pleasure ladies workin' for him. That's more Big Mamma O'Neil's style. Louis was considerable younger then, and so was I. Louis said one of his bouncers saw it all . . . well, most of it. Tilden was so drunk he got it all wrong. And when Rosa tried to break a-loose from him, he started slappin' her around. Bad. The bouncers come runnin', but Tilden's hands held them at bay whilst he took Rosa in the back room and . . ." He paused, looking at Sally. ". . . had his way with her. Then he killed her. Broke her neck with his bare hands. You see, one of them doctors in that damnable hospital told me, once I got to trust the feller, that Tilden ain't quite right in the head. He's got the ability to twist things all around, and make the bad look good and so forth. He shapes things the way he wants them to be in his mind. I disremember the exact word the doc used. That buffer-faced nurse come by 'bout that time with some rubber tubin' in her hands and things kinda went hazy on me."

"What nurse?" Sally asked.

"I'll tell you later," Smoke said.

Charlie said, "Me and Rosa was gonna get married in the spring. I was unconscious for several days; didn't even get to go to her buryin'." He sighed deeply. "Course, by the time I got on my feet, Tilden and his bunch was long gone. I lost track of him for a time, but by then the fires inside me had burned low. I still hated the man, but I had to make a livin' and didn't have no idea where he might be. I been knowin' he was in this area for some years. I've drifted in and out half a dozen times, stayin' low, watching that low-life build his little kingdom. Then I had me an idea. I'd wait until he got real big, real powerful, real sure of himself. And then I'd kill him . . . slow."

Charlie laid down his knife and fork, pushed his empty plate from him, and stood up. "Bes' grub I've had in many a moon, ma'am. I thank you. Reckon I'll turn in now. Tomorrow I wanna start roamin' the range for a couple of days, learn all the twists and turns and ways in and out. I seen me a cookstove in the bunkhouse. I'll fix me a poke before I pull out in the mornin'. Night, folks."

After the door had closed softly and the sounds of Charlie's jingling spurs had faded, Pearlie said, "I think Tilden Franklin's string has just about run out."

"That hombre who just walked out the door," Smoke said, "I believe means every word he said.

"Story goes that Charlie's folks was kilt by Injuns when he was just a little boy. He was raised by the Cheyenne. If Charlie says he's gonna kill Tilden Franklin slow, that is exactly what he means."

For two days, Charlie prowled the Sugarloaf, getting his bearings and inspecting the cattle and horses that Smoke and Sally were raising.

"You want it known that you're working for me?" Smoke asked him upon his return to the ranch house.

"Don't make no difference to me, Smoke," the gunfighter said. "My bein' here ain't gonna make Tilden back-paddle none. Man sets out to be king, only thing that's gonna stop him is dyin'."

Smoke nodded his agreement. "I'll be gone for several days, Charlie. You and Pearlie stay close to the house, all right?"

"Will do."

Smoke pulled out early the next morning, riding Drifter. It was not like Tilden to wait, once his intentions became known; Smoke wanted to find out what the king-pin had up his sleeve.

As he rode, the sounds of drilling and hammers against rocks and occasional blasting came to him. The miners were in full swing. And they were paying no attention to the No Trespassing signs the farmer-ranchers had posted around their property. Bad trouble was building; the smell of it was in the air.

Smoke figured he'd better check in with Lawyer Brook as soon as he hit town.

"Smoke," the lawyer informed him, "there is nothing your friends can do, not legally."

"But it's their land!"

"But they don't hold the mineral rights to it. The holder of those rights has given the miners permission to mine. The miners get fifty percent, the holder of the rights gets fifty percent."

Smoke leaned back in his chair and built one of his rare cigarettes from the cloth pouch he carried in his vest pocket. He licked the tube and smoothed it, lighting and inhaling before speaking.

"Let me guess," Smoke said. "Tilden Franklin bought all the mineral rights."

"Well . . . if you don't hear it from me, you'll hear it from somebody else. Yes, that is correct."

"It's legal stealing, Hunt."

"I wouldn't phrase it quite like that," the lawyer said stiffly.

"I just did," Smoke told him. He walked out of the lawyer's new offices.

The long building containing the offices of the lawyer, the doctor, and the newspaper had been put up in a hurry, but it was well built nonetheless. Across the street, the big store of Ed Jackson was in business and doing quite well, Smoke observed, eyeballing the many heavily loaded wagons lined up behind it, waiting to be unloaded. And, surprisingly enough, Ralph Morrow's church was up—nearly completed. He walked across the small field to the church and located the minister.

"You do all this yourself, Ralph?" Smoke asked.

"Oh, no! Mister Franklin donated the money for the church and paid the workmen to build it. He's really a very fine man, Smoke. I think you're wrong about him."

Slick, Smoke thought. Very slick on Tilden's part. "Well, I'm happy about your church, Ralph. I wish you a great deal of success."

"Thank you, Smoke." The minister beamed.

Smoke rode to the stable and located Billy. "Take care of him, Billy. Lots of corn and rub him down."

"Yes, sir!"

Smoke walked over to Louis's place and stepped inside. The gambler was sitting at a table, having breakfast. He waved Smoke over.

"Saw you ride in just as I was getting up. Care for a late breakfast?"

"Sounds good."

The gambler called for his cook and ordered breakfast for Smoke. Looking at Smoke, he asked, "Have you spoken to the minister yet?"

Smoke's smile gave him his silent reply.

"Nice move on Franklin's part, don't you think?"

"Very Christian of the man."

Louis enjoyed a laugh at the sarcasm in Smoke's voice. "Slick on his part about the mineral rights."

"I'll tell you the same thing I told Lawyer Brook—it's nothing but legal stealing."

"Oh, I agree with you, Smoke. But it is legal. Were I you, I'd advise the others to walk lightly and don't start any shooting."

"It's their land, Louis. They have a right to protect their herds."

Louis chewed for a moment, a thoughtful look on his face. "Yes, they do," he finally spoke. He took a sip of coffee out of one of the fanciest cups Smoke had ever seen. One thing about Louis Longmont. When he traveled, he went first class all the way, carrying a cook, a valet, and a huge bodyguard with him at all times. The bodyguard usually acted as bouncer in Louis's place, and was rarely seen—except when there was trouble. And then he was seen by the troublemaker only very briefly . . . seconds before the troublemaker died in Mike's bare hands. Providing Louis didn't shoot the troublemaker outright.

Louis buttered a piece of toasted bread and then spread preserves on top of that. The preserves, Smoke was sure, were imported. "Smoke, you know, or I hope you do, that I will back you to the hilt . . . in whatever you do. Regardless of whether I think you are right or wrong. Preacher saved my life a number of times, and besides that, you are a very good young man. But whether our newly elected law is worth a tinker's damn or not, in this mineral rights matter Tilden Franklin is legal. And the law is on his side. Smoke, the land can be repaired. Another hole in the ground is not worth a shooting or a hanging. Your herds? Well, that is quite another matter." He glanced at Smoke, a twinkle in his hard eyes. "There is no law out here that says a man can't hang or shoot a rustler or a horse thief— if you get my drift."

Smoke got it. And he would pass the word to the other small farmer-ranchers. Then they would ride out and advise the miners that there would be no trouble, providing the herds of cattle and horses were left alone. But trample over someone's garden, stampede one herd, cut out one beeve, or steal one horse, and someone was going to die.

And then, if any or all those things happened, they would have to have the raw nerve to carry the threat through.

The French chef placed a plate before Smoke. Smoke looked at the food on the plate. Damned if he knew what it was. He said as much.

Then the chef reached down with a lighted match, set fire to the stuff, and Smoke jumped out of his chair.

Louis had a good laugh out of that. "Sit down, Smoke. Enjoy your breakfast."

"Hell, I can't eat *fire*!"

The flames abated and the chef departed, chuckling. Louis smiled. "Those are *crepes suzette*, my young friend. This dish." He tapped another plate with a knife blade. "Is an *au jambon*."

"Do tell?"

"An omelette, with bits of ham," Louis explained. "Now eat and enjoy."

Them crap susies was a tad too sweet for Smoke's taste, but the omelette was tasty. He made a mental note to tell Sally about what he had had for a late breakfast. Maybe she'd heard of them; damned if he ever had.

"Either way," Smoke said, "I think we're all looking at a lot of trouble just up the road."

"I share your feelings, Smoke. But why not postpone it as long as possible? You know this strike is not going to last. In six months it will have seen its heyday."

"I can't figure you, Louis. I never . . ." He bit off the words just at the last possible second.

The gambler-gunfighter did not take umbrage at what he suspected Smoke had been about to say. Instead, he smiled and finished it for him. "Never knew me to back off from trouble, Smoke?"

"I apologize for thinking it, Louis."

Louis smiled and shook his head. "No need for any of that—not between friends." He sighed. "But you're right,

Smoke. I am trying to avoid trouble. Not for my sake," he was quick to add. "But for yours."

Smoke laid down his fork. "My sake?"

"Listen to me, my young friend. How many guns do you have? A dozen? Maybe fifteen at the most? Tilden has seventy-five hardcases right now and can pull in two hundred more anytime he wishes, and will. Talk is that Luis Chamba is on his way here. And where Luis goes, Sanderson and Kane go with him. Think about it."

Smoke thought about it, and the more he thought about it the madder he got. Louis saw his expression change and tried to calm the young man down.

"No, Louis. No. Don't you see what Tilden is trying to pull?"

"Of course I do, boy! But give it time. In six months this area of the country will be right back where it was a month ago. Farm and ranch country. This town will dry up with only a few of the businesses remaining. I'm betting Tilden won't want to be king of nothing."

"He won't be king of nothing, Louis. For if we don't fight, he'll kill us all one by one. He'll make some grand gesture of buying out the widows or the kids—through some goddamned lawyer—and then he'll own this entire section of the state of Colorado. Everything!"

Louis nodded his head. "Maybe you're right, Smoke. Maybe you're right. If that's the case, then you've got to start hiring guns of your own. You and your wife have the means to do so; if you don't, let me advance you the money."

Suddenly, Smoke thought of something. In a way it was a cruel thought, but it was also a way for a lot of broke, aging men to gather in one final blaze of glory. The more he thought about it, the better he liked it, and his mood began to lighten. But he'd have to bounce it off Charlie first.

"Why are you smiling, Smoke?" Louis asked.

"Louis, you're one of the best gamblers around, aren't you?"

"Some say I am one of the best in the world, Smoke. I should think my numerous bank accounts would back up that claim. Why do you ask?"

"Suppose you suddenly learned you were dying, or suppose some . . . well, call it fate . . . started dealing you bad hands and you ended up broke and old—anything along that line—and then someone offered you the chance to once more live in glory. Your kind of glory. Would you take it, Louis, or would you think the offer to be cruel?"

"What an interesting thought! Say now . . . cruel? Oh, no. Not at all. I would jump at the opportunity. But . . . what are you thinking of, Smoke? I'm not following this line of questioning at all."

"You will, Louis." Smoke stood up and smiled. His smile seemed to Louis to be rather mysterious "You will. And I think you'll find it to your liking. I really believe you will."

Long after Smoke had plopped his hat on his head, left the gaming room, and ridden out of town, Louis Longmont had sat at the table and thought about what his young friend had said.

Then he began smiling. Soon the smile had turned to chuckling and the chuckling to hard laughter.

"Oh . . ." he managed to say over the pealing laughter. "I love it!"

17

Smoke sat with Sally, Pearlie, and Charlie. Charlie listened to what Smoke had on his mind and then leaned back in his chair, a broad smile on his face. He laughed and slapped his knee.

"Smoke, that's the bes' idee I've heard of in a long, long time. Cruel? No, sir. It ain't cruel. What you're talkin' about is what they do bes'. You give me the wherewithal and I'll have an even dozen here in a week, soon as I can get to a telegraph and get hold of them and get some money to them."

"Name them, Charlie."

"Oh . . . well, there's Luke Nations, Pistol Le Roux, Bill Foley, Dan Greentree, Leo Wood, Cary Webb, Sunset Hatfield, Crooked John Simmons, Bull Flagler, Toot Tooner, Sutter Cordova, Red Shingletown . . . give me time and I'll name some more."

Pearlie said, "But all them old boys is *dead*!"

"No, they ain't neither," Charlie corrected. "They just retared is all."

"Well . . ." Pearlie thought a moment. "Then they mus' be a hundred years old!"

"Naw!" Charlie scoffed at that. "You jus' a kid, is all. They all in their sixties."

"I've met some of them. Charlie, I don't want to be responsible for any of them going to their deaths."

"Smoke . . . it's the way they'd want it. If they all died, they'd go out thankin' you for the opportunity to show the world they still had it in them. Let them go out in a blaze of glory, Smoke."

Smoke thought about it. That was the way Preacher would have wanted to go. And those old Mountain Men three years back, that's how they had wanted it. "All right, Charlie. We'll give you the money and you can pull out at first light. Me and Pearlie will start adding on to the bunkhouse. How many do you think will be here?"

"When the word gets out, I'd look for about twenty-five or so." Charlie said it with a smile. "You gonna have to hire you a cook to help Miss Sally. Or you'll work her to a frazzle, Smoke."

"All right. Do you know an old camp cook?"

"Shore do. Dad Weaver. He can cook and he can still pull a trigger too. One about as good as the other."

"Hire him. Oh, 'fore I forget." He looked at Sally. "I had a late breakfast with Louis Longmont. His chef fed me crap susies."

"Fed you *what*?" Sally said.

"The chef set it on fire before he served me. I thought he'd lost his mind."

"You didn't eat it, did you?" Pearlie asked.

"Oh, yeah! It was pretty good. Real sweet."

"*Crepes suzette*," Sally said.

"That's it," Smoke said. "Say it again."

"You pronounce it . . . *krehp sue-zeht*. You all try to say it."

They all tried. It sounded like three monkeys trying to master French.

"I feel like a plumb idiot!" Charlie said.

* * *

"What're those damned nesters up to?" Tilden Franklin asked his foreman.

"I can't figure it," Clint said. "They've all rode out and told the miners there wouldn't be no trouble as long as the miners don't spook their herds or trample their crops. They was firm, but in a nice way."

"Damn!" Tilden said. "I thought Jensen would go in shooting."

"So did I. You want us to maybe do a little night-ridin'?"

"No. I want this to be all the nesters' doing. Wait a minute. Yeah, I do want some night-riding. Send some of the boys out to Peyton's place. Rustle a couple head and leave the butchered carcasses close to some miners' camps. Peyton is hot-headed; he'll go busting up in there and shoot or hang some of them. While we stand clear."

Clint smiled. "Tonight?"

"Tonight."

Sheriff Monte Carson and his so-called deputies kept only a loose hand on the rowdy doings in Fontana. They broke up fistfights whenever they could get to them in time, but rarely interfered in a stand-up, face-to-face shoot-out. Mostly they saw to it that all the businesses— with the exception of Louis Longmont, Ed Jackson, and Lawyer Hunt Brook—paid into the Tilden kitty . . . ten percent of the gross. And didn't hold none back. The deputies didn't bother Doctor Colton Spalding either. They'd wisely decided that some of them just might need the Doc's services sooner or later . . . probably sooner.

And, to make matters just a little worse, the town was attracting a small group of would-be gunslicks; young men who fancied themselves gunfighters and looked to make a reputation in Fontana. They strutted about with their pearl-handled Colts tied down low and their huge California spurs jangling. The young men usually dressed all in black, or in loudly colored silk shirts with pin-striped trousers tucked inside their polished boots. They bragged a lot about who they had faced down or shot, and did a lot of practicing outside the town limits. They were solid looking for trouble, and that trouble was waiting just around the corner for a lot of them.

The town of Fontana was still growing, both in businesses and population. It now could boast four hotels and half a dozen rooming houses. Cafes had sprung up almost as fast as the saloons and the hurdy-gurdy girls who made their dubious living in those saloons . . . and in the dirty cribs in the back rooms.

The mother lode of the vein had been located, and stages were rolling into town twice a day, to carry the gold from the assay offices and to drop off their load of passengers. Tilden Franklin had built a bank, The Bank of Fontana, and was doing a swift business. Supply wagons rolled and rattled and rumbled twenty-four hours a day, bringing in much-needed items to the various businesses.

To give the man a small amount of credit, Tilden Franklin had taken a hard look at his town and quietly but firmly begun rearranging the business district. There were now boundaries beyond which certain types could not venture during specific hours. The red-light district lay at one end of Fontana, and just behind a long row of saloons and greasy-spoon cafes. Those ladies who worked in the red-light houses—In God We Trust, All Others Pay Cash—were not allowed past the invisible line separating the good people from the less desirable people during the time between seven in the morning and four in the afternoon. Heaven forbid that a "decent woman" should have to rub shoulders with . . . that other kind of lady.

* * *

Peyton had found the butchered carcass of two of his beeves close to a miners' camp.

"Take it easy," Smoke said trying to calm the older man. "Those miners have hit a solid strike over there. No reason for them to have rustled any of your cows. Think about it, Peyton. Look here," Smoke said, pointing. "These are horse tracks around these carcasses."

"So?" Peyton angrily demanded. "What the hell has that got to do with it?"

"Those miners are riding mules, Peyton."

That news brought the farmer-rancher up short and silent. He walked over and sat down on a fallen log. He thought about that news for a moment.

"We're not actin' like Tilden would like," Peyton said softly. "So he's tryin' to prod us into doin' something to blow the lid off. I was about to play right into his game, and he would have sent those so-called deputies up to arrest me, wouldn't he, Smoke?"

"Probably." Smoke had told none of the others about the old gunfighters on their way in. Charlie had returned from his travels, all smiles and good news.

The aging gunfighters would begin arriving at any time, trickling in alone or in pairs as they linked up on the trails and roads.

"Go on home," Smoke told the older man, "I'll go see the miners."

Smoke watched the man mount up and leave. He swung into the saddle and rode up toward the miners' camp. He hailed the camp and was told to come on in.

Briefly Smoke explained, but he made no mention of Tilden Franklin.

"Who would try to cause trouble, Smoke?" a burly miner asked.

"I don't know. But I just put the lid back on what might

have been real trouble. You boys be careful from here on in. Tempers are frayed enough around here. The slightest thing could light the fuse."

"We will. Smoke, you reckon Peyton and some of the others would mind if me and the boys pitched in and kind of helped around their places? You know . . . we're all pretty handy with tools . . . maybe some repair work, such as that?"

"I think it would be a hell of a nice move on your part." Smoke grinned and the miners grinned back. "And it's gonna irritate whoever is trying to stir up trouble. I'll tell the others to look for you. I bet y'all would like some home-cooked grub too, wouldn't you?"

That brought a round of cheers from the miners, many of whom had families far away.

Smoke wheeled his horse and rode back down the mountain. Smoke the gunfighter had suddenly become Smoke the peacemaker.

"Nothing," Clint told Tilden. "Smoke made peace with the miners. He figured it all out somehow."

"What's it going to take to prod those goddamned nesters into action?" Tilden asked. "I'm about out of ideas."

Clint didn't like what he was about to suggest, but Clint rode for the brand. Right or wrong. "The Colby girl."

Although it had originally been Tilden's idea, the more he thought about it, the less he liked it. Bother a good woman out West and a man was in serious trouble . . . and it didn't make a damn who you were or how much or how little you had.

"Risky, Clint." He met the man's eyes. "You have a plan?"

"Yes," the foreman said, and stepped across that narrow chasm that separated good from evil, man from rabid beast.

"How long will it take you to set it up?"

"A few days. Them nesters got to be going into town for supplies pretty soon."

Tilden nodded his head. "Do it."

"You better get some sort of platform, Boss," Pearlie told Smoke.

"Platform? What are you talking about?"

"Some of them old gunhands is pullin' in. I swear to God there oughta be a hearse followin' along behind 'em."

Smoke stepped out of the barn just as Charlie was riding up from the Sugarloaf range.

Smoke had never seen a more disreputable, down-at-the-heels-looking bunch in all his life. Some of them looked like they'd be lucky to see another morning break clear.

"See what I mean about that platform, Boss? I swear that them ol' boys is gonna hurt themselves gettin' off their horse."

Smoke had to smile. He was fondly recalling a bunch of Mountain Men who, at eighty, were as spry as many men half their age. "Don't sell them short, Pearlie. I got a hunch they're gonna fool us all."

"Hi, thar, Buttermilk!" Charlie called.

"Aaa-yeeee!" the old man hollered. "You get uglier ever' time I see you, Charlie."

"Talks funny too," Pearlie said.

"I seen now why he's called Buttermilk."

"Why?"

"That's probably all he can eat. He don't have any teeth!"

18

"*That* is The Apache Kid?" Sally said, speaking to Smoke. "I have heard stories about The Apache Kid ever since I arrived in the West. Smoke, he looks like he might topple over at any moment."

"That's him," Smoke said. "Preacher told me about him. And I'll make you a bet right now that that old man can walk all day and all night, stop for a handful of berries and take a sip of water, and go another twenty-four hours."

"I ain't dis-pootin' your word, Boss," Pearlie said. "But I'm gonna have to see it to believe it."

Smiling, Smoke bent down and picked up a small chunk of wood. "Apache!" he called.

The old, buckskin-clad man turned and looked at Smoke.

"A silver dollar says you can't knock it out of the air."

"Toss 'er, boy!"

Smoke tossed the chunk high into the air. With fifty-odd years of gunhandling in his past, Apache's draw was as smooth and practiced as water over a fall. He fired six times. Six times the hardwood chunk was hit, before falling in slivers to the ground.

"Jesus!" Pearlie breathed.

"That's six silver dollars you owe me," Apache said.

Smoke laughed and nodded his head. The Apache Kid turned to talk with Charlie.

"That Jensen?" Apache asked, as the other old gunfighters listened.

"That's him."

"He as good as they say?" Bowie asked.

"I wouldn't want to brace him," Charlie said, paying Smoke the highest compliment one gunhand could pay to another.

"That good, hey?" Luke Nations asked.

"He's the best."

"I heared he was that," Dan Greentree said. "Rat nice of him to in-vite us on this little hoo-raw."

Smoke and Sally had gone into the cabin, leaving the others to talk.

Pearlie shyly wandered over to the growing knot of men. He was expecting to get the needle put to him, and he got just that.

"Your ma know you slipped away from the house, boy?" a huge, grizzled old man asked.

Pearlie smiled and braced himself. "You be Pistol Le Roux?"

"I was when I left camp this mornin'."

"I run acrost a pal of yourn 'bout three years ago— up on the Utah-Wyoming line. South of Fort Supply. Called hisself Pawnee."

"Do tell? How was ol' Pawnee?"

"Not too good. He died. I buried him at the base of Kings Mountain, north side. Thought you'd wanna know."

"I do and I 'preciate your plantin' him. Say a word over him, did you?"

"Some."

"This is Pearlie, Pistol."

"Pleased. Join us, Pearlie."

Pearlie stood silent and listened to the men talk. Charlie said, "This ain't gonna be no Sunday social, boys. And I'll come right up front and tell you that some of you is likely to be planted in these here mountains."

The sounds of horses coming hard paused Charlie. He waited until the last of the old gunslicks had dismounted and shook and howdied.

Charlie counted heads. Twenty of the hardest, most talked-about, and most legendary men of the West stood in the front yard of the sturdy little cabin. Only God and God alone knew how many men these randy old boys had put down into that eternal rest.

The Apache Kid was every bit of seventy. But could still draw and shoot with the best.

Buttermilk didn't have a tooth in his head, but those Colts belted around his lean waist could bite and snarl and roar.

Jay Church was a youngster, 'bout Charlie's age. But a feared gunhawk.

Dad Weaver was in his mid-sixties. He'd opened him a little cafe when he'd hung up his guns, but the rowdies and the punks hadn't left him alone. They'd come lookin' and he'd given the undertaker more business. He'd finally said to hell with it and taken off for the mountains.

Silver Jim still looked the dandy. Wearin' one of them long white coats that road agents had taken to wearing. His boots was old and patched, but they shined. And his dark short coat was kinda frayed at the cuffs, but it was clean. His Colts was oiled and deadly.

Ol' Hardrock. Charlie smiled. What could he say about Hardrock? The man had cleaned up more wild towns than any two others combined. Now he was aging and broke. But still ready to ride the high trails of the Mountain Men.

Charlie lifted his eyes and spotted Moody. Ol' Moody. Standin' away from the others, livin' up to his name. Never had much to say, but by the Lord he was as rough and randy as they could come.

Linch. Big and hoary and bearded. Never packed but one short gun. Said he never needed but one.

Luke Nations. A legend. Sheriff, marshal, outlaw, gunfighter. Had books wrote about him. And as far as Charlie knew, never got a dime out of any of them.

Pistol Le Roux. A Creole from down in Louisiana. As fast with a knife as with a gun . . . and that was plenty fast.

Quiet Bill Foley. Wore his guns cross-draw and had a border roll that was some kind of quick.

Dan Greentree. Charlie had ridden many a trail with Dan. Charlie wondered if these mountain trails around Fontana would be their last to ride.

Leo Wood. Leo just might be the man who had brought the fast draw to the West. A lot of people said he was. And a lot of so-called fast guns had died trying to best him.

Cary Webb. Some said he owned a fine education and had once taught school back East. Chucked it all and came West, looking for excitement. Earned him a rep as a fast gun.

Sunset Hatfield. Supposed to be from either Kentucky or Tennessee. A crack shot with rifle or pistol.

Crooked John Simmons. Got that name hung on him 'cause he was as cross-eyed as anybody had ever seen. Had a hair-trigger temper and a set of hair-trigger Colts.

Bull Flagler. Strong as a bull and just as dangerous. Carried him a sawed-off shotgun with a pistol grip on his left side, a Colt on the other.

Toot Tooner. Loved trains. Loved 'em so much he just couldn't resist holding them up back some years. Turned lawman and made a damn good one. Fast draw and a dead shot.

Sutter Cordova. His mother was French and his dad was Spanish. Killed a man when he was 'bout ten or eleven years old; man was with a bunch that killed his ma and pa. Sutter got his pa's guns, mounted up, and tracked them from Chihuahua to Montana Territory. Took him six years, but he killed every one of them. Sutter was not a man you wanted to get crossways of.

Red Shingletown. Still had him a mighty fine mess of flamin' red hair. He'd been a soldier, a sailor, an adventurer, a rancher . . . and a gunfighter.

And there they stood, Smoke thought, gazing at the men from the cabin. I'm looking at yet another last of a breed.

But did I do right in asking them to come?

Sally touched his arm. Smoke looked down at her.

"You did the right thing," she told him. "The trail that lies before those men out there is the one they chose, and if it is their last trail to ride, that's the way they would want it. And even though they are doing this for you and for Charlie, you know the main reason they're doing it, don't you?"

Smoke grinned, wiping years from his face. He looked about ten years old. All except for his eyes. "Ol' Preacher."

"That's right, honey. They all knew him, and knew that he helped raise you."

"What do you plan on having for supper?"

"I hadn't thought. Why?"

"How about making some bearsign?"

"It's going to run me out of flour."

"Well, I think me and Charlie and some of those ol' boys out there just might ride into Fontana tomorrow. We'll stop by Colby's and get him to take his wagon. Stock up enough for everybody. 'Sides, I want to see Louis's face when we all come ridin' in."

"Uh-huh," she said, poking him in the ribs and tickling him, bending him over, gently slapping at her hands. "But mostly you want to see Tilden Franklin's face."

"Well . . . He suddenly swept her up in his arms and began carrying her toward the bedroom.

"Smoke. Not with all those . . ."

He kissed her mouth, hushing her.

". . . men out . . ."

He kissed her again and placed her gently on the bed.

"Who cares about those men out there?" she finally said.

It came as no surprise to Smoke to find the men up before he crawled out from under the covers. This high up, even the summer nights were cool . . . and this was still late spring. The nights were downright cold.

The men had gotten their bearsign the previous night, but Sally had been just a bit late with them.

Smoke dressed, belted on his Colts, and, with a mug of coffee in one hand, stepped out to meet the breaking dawn, all silver and gold as the sun slowly inched over the high peaks of Sugarloaf.

"Charlie, I thought a few of us would ride into town this morning and pick up supplies. We'll stop at Colby's place and he'll go with us in his wagon."

"Who you want to go in with you?"

"You pick 'em."

Adam Colby had been reading a dime novel about the life and times of Luke Nations, with a drawing of him on the cover, when he looked up at the sounds of horses' hooves drumming on the road. The boy thought he'd been flung directly into the pages of the dime novel.

He looked at the man on the horse, looked at the cover of the book, and then took off running for the house, hollering for his pa.

"Boy!" Colby said, stepping out of the house. "What in tarnation is wrong with . . ."

The man looked at the group of riders still sitting their horses in his front yard. Colby's eyes flitted from man to man, taking in the lined and tanned faces, the hard, callused hands, and the guns belted around the lean waists. Colby knew of most of the men . . . he just never imagined he'd see them in his front yard.

Adam approached Luke, the dime novel in his hand. He stood looking up at the famed gunfighter, awe in his eyes. He held out the book.

"Would you sign my book, Mister Nations?"

"I'd be right honored, boy," the gunfighter said. He grinned. "That's about all I can write is my name." He took the book and a stub of a pencil Adam held out to him and slowly printed his name, giving book and pencil back to the boy.

"Thank you, sir."

"You're welcome."

"We're riding into Fontana, Colby. Sally needs some supplies. Wanna get your wagon and come in with us?"

"Good idea. Wilbur and the boys will stay here. Give me a minute to get my shirt on. Adam, hook up the team, son."

Colby's wife Belle, daughter Velvet, and boys Adam and Bob stood with Wilbur and his wife Edna and watched the men pull out. They would stop at several other small spreads to take any orders for supplies. The men and women and kids left at Colby's place resumed their morning chores.

A mile away, hidden in the timber, a TF rider watched it all through field glasses. When the men had ridden and rumbled out of sight, the TF rider took a mirror from his saddlebags and caught the morning sun, signaling to another TF rider that everything was ready. He didn't know who them hard-lookin' old boys was with Jensen, but they didn't look like they'd be much trouble to handle. Most of 'em looked to be older than God.

Tilden Franklin wanted to make damn sure he was highly visible to as many people as possible until after Clint's plan was over. Tilden had taken to riding into Fontana every morning, early, with Clint and several of his hardcases for bodyguards. He and his foreman usually had breakfast at the best hotel in town and then took their after-meal cigars while sitting on the porch of the hotel, perhaps reading or talking or just watching the passing parade.

This morning, Tilden looked up from the new edition of the *Fontana Sunburst*, Haywood and Dana Arden's endeavor, just as a TF rider rode by. Without looking at either Tilden or Clint, the rider very minutely nodded his head as he passed.

With a slight smile, Tilden lifted the newspaper and once more resumed his reading.

In a way, Tilden thought, he was kind of sorry he was gonna miss out on the action with that built-up little gal of Colby's. Tilden would bet that, once she settled into the rhythm, Velvet would get to liking it. All women were the same when it came to that, Tilden felt. They liked to holler and raise sand, but they wanted it. They just liked to pretend they didn't for the look of things.

Women, to Tilden's mind, were very notional critters . . . and just like critters, not very bright. Pretty to have around, nice to pet, but that was about it.

One of Monte Carson's deputies rode up and looped the reins over the hitch rail in front of the hotel. Dismounting, he stood on the boardwalk facing Tilden.

"Charlie Starr's ridin' in with that Smoke Jensen and the nester Colby, Mister Tilden."

Tilden felt his face stiffen and grow hot as the blood raced to flush his cheeks. He lowered the newspaper and stared at the deputy.

"Charlie *Starr*?"

"Yes, sir. And that ain't all. Smoke's got some mean ol' gunslicks with him, too. The Apache Kid, Sunset Hatfield, Bill Foley, Silver Jim, Moody, and Luke Nations. They ridin' like they got a purpose, if you know what I mean."

A young, two-bit, half-assed punk, who thought himself to be a bad man, was hanging around near the open doors of the hotel. He smiled and felt his heart race at the news. The deputy had just mentioned half a dozen of the most famous gunslingers in all the West. And they were coming into town—here!

Right here, the punk who called himself The Silver Dollar Kid thought, is where I make my rep. Right here, right out there in that street, that's where it all starts. He smiled and walked through the lobby, slipping out the back way. He wanted to change clothes, put on his best outfit before he faced one of those old gunhawks. There was a picture-taker in town; might be a good idea to stop by his studio and tell him about the old gunslicks so's he could have all his equipment set up and ready to pop.

The punk ran back to his tent and began changing into his very finest.

The news of the approaching gunfighters, still several miles out of Fontana, swept through the town like wildfire through a dry forest. Haywood heard it and walked rapidly toward the main business district. He found himself a spot on the boardwalk across the street from where Tilden Franklin sat, surrounded by his hardcases.

Shopkeepers had shooed customers outside, where they stood, lining the boardwalks and packed-dirt sidewalks, waiting for the event of the day.

Louis Longmont came out of his gaming tent to stand on the boardwalk, watching as he smoked his first cigar of the morning. So Smoke had done it, he thought. A smile curved his lips. He'd actually pulled in some of the randiest old boys still living in the West.

"Going to be interesting," Louis murmured. "Very, very interesting."

19

Smoke halted his small group on the edge of town. He looked at Charlie. "A whole passel of two-bit young punks who'll be looking for a reputation in town. They'll be on the prod for a fight."

Charlie spat on the dirt beneath his horse's belly. "They'll damn sure get more than they bargained for with this bunch," he replied.

"We'll ride straight through," Smoke said. "Stopping at Jackson's Mercantile. Colby, pull your wagon up to the loading dock by the side. If there's going to be trouble, let the other side start it. Let's go, boys."

Smoke and Charlie took the point, with Apache and Sunset riding to the left of the wagon, Bill Foley and Silver Jim to the right, and Moody and Luke Nations taking the drag. Smoke rode slowly, so the wheels of the wagon would not kick up much dust. The town had virtually come to a halt, the streets lined with citizens. They stood silently, watching the riders make their way along the street. Trouble hung in the air, as thick as dust.

The riders could practically feel the hate from Tilden Franklin's eyes boring into them as they rode past where he sat like a king on the hotel boardwalk. Smoke met the man's eyes and touched his hat brim in a gesture of greeting.

Tilden did not return the greeting.

They passed Louis Longmont's gaming tent. Most of the old gunfighters knew the gambler and they greeted him. Louis returned the greeting and very minutely nodded his head in the direction Smoke was riding.

There was something or someone down there that Louis wanted Smoke to know about. Smoke's eyes searched both sides of the street. Then he saw them, the three of them, lounging in front of a newly erected tent saloon.

Luis Chamba, Kane, and Sanderson.

The Mexican gunfighter stood with his arms folded across his chest, his sombrero off his head, hanging down his back by the chin cord.

"See them?" Smoke whispered the words, just audible over the clop of hooves.

"I see them," Charlie returned the whisper. "That Chamba, he's a bad one. Kills for pleasure. Gets his kicks that way, you know?"

Smoke knew the type.

Then they were past the killers.

"Kane and Sanderson?" Smoke asked. He knew of them, but did not know them personally.

"Just as bad. They're all three twisted. And they'll kill anything or anybody for money."

"Look at them punks over to your left."

"Seen them too," Charlie said sourly. "Lookin' to make themselves a reputation. I hope they don't try none of this bunch. These guys are all on the shady side of their years, but Lord God, don't sell 'em short."

A young man with a smart-ass look to him and dressed like a San Francisco pimp stood glaring at the men. At least Smoke figured that's how a San Francisco pimp might dress, having never been there.

"Reckon it's time for us to start us a Boot Hill here in Fontana, boys!" the loud-mouthed, loudly dressed young man said, raising his voice so the riders could all hear him.

The Apache Kid favored the young man with a glance and dismissed him just as quickly.

Sunset openly laughed at the dandy.

"Yeah," another duded-up, two-gun-totin' young man agreed, his voice loud. "And them old boys yonder ain't got long to go no ways. Might as well start with them. How 'bout it?"

None of the aging gunfighters even acknowledged the punk had spoken. They rode on.

"Hell!" another would-be gunslinger yelled, fanning the air with his fancy hat. "They so goddamned old they done lost their balls, boys!"

"That one is mine," Luke said, just so his friends could hear.

"He means it, Smoke," Charlie said. "Don't interfere none."

"Far be it from me to interfere," Smoke answered.

Back in the high country, Velvet Colby, her chores done for the morning, thought it would be nice to take a walk through the woods.

"Stay close, Velvet!" her mother called.

"Yes, ma'am, I will."

Adam watched her go. He stuck his dime novel in his back pocket and picked up his .22 rifle, following Velvet but staying back, knowing how his sister enjoyed being alone.

While Ed Jackson and his brother loaded the wagon with supplies, Colby walked with Smoke over to Louis

Longmont's place. He introduced them and Louis invited them inside. Smoke had no intention of trying to shepherd and play check-rein on Charlie and the others. They'd been without his advice for a combination of about three hundred and fifty years. They didn't need it now.

"A taste of the Glenlivet, gentlemen?" Louis asked.

"Huh?" Colby asked.

"Fine scotch whiskey," Smoke told him.

Three tumblers poured three fingers deep, Louis lifted his glass. "Here's to a very interesting summer, gentlemen."

They clinked glasses and sipped.

Louis smiled. "Shall we adjourn to what laughingly passes for a veranda and watch the show, boys?"

"Sure going to be one," Smoke agreed, moving toward the door.

Luke Nations had broken off from the others and was walking toward the knot of would-be gunslicks, walking directly toward the duded-up punk with the fat mouth. Luke stopped about twenty-five feet from him. He stood with the leather thongs off the hammers of his Colts. He stood with his feet slightly spread. He was big and bent and old and mean-looking. And the look in his eyes would have warned off a puma.

"You made a comment a minute or so ago, kid," Luke said, his voice flat and hard. "Well, now is your chance to back up your mouth. Either that . . . or tuck your fancy tail between your legs and carry your ass!"

His name was Lester. But he called himself Sundance. At this moment, he felt more like Lester than Sundance.

The Silver Dollar Kid had backed up against a wall. Unlike Lester, he wasn't afraid; he just wanted to see if the old men still had it in them. When he had studied them, then he would make his move.

"Goddamn you, boy!" Luke's voice was so sharp, it hurt. "Do you hear me?"

"Yeah, I hear you." Sundance surfaced, pushing Lester out of the way.

Monte Carson had come on the run when he heard the news of the impending shoot-out. He came to an abrupt halt, almost falling as his high-heeled boots dug into the dirt of the street. One of his deputies ran into him, and they both almost fell.

"What the hell?" the deputy said.

"Shut up and look around you!" Monte whispered hoarsely.

The Apache Kid was just across the street, standing alone, both hands to his sides, the palms very close to the butts of his Colts.

The deputy cut his eyes. Old Sunset was standing behind them, about thirty feet away.

Bill Foley stood just to their right, poised and ready for anything that might come his way.

"Ssshhittt!" Monte hissed, the breath whistling between his slightly gapped front teeth. He was looking eyeball to eyeball with Silver Jim, his long white duster brushed back, exposing the butts of the Colts, the leather hammer thongs off.

Back of them, facing Tilden Franklin and Clint, stood Moody. Moody said, "You boys come to watch or get dealt in?"

Tilden chewed his cigar soggy in a matter of a heartbeat. He felt no fear, for there was no fear in him. But he had grown up hearing stories about these old gunfighters. And at this distance, everybody was going to get lead in them. And there was something else too. Tilden knew, from hard experience, that when dealing with ballsy old men you'd best walk lightly. With their best years behind them, they had nothing to lose. Old men did not fight fair. Tilden had learned that the hard way too.

Clint cut his eyes. Louis Longmont, his tailored jacket brushed back over the butts of his guns, stood to Clint's right. Smoke was facing Tilden's other hands, and the other hands were looking a little green around the mouth.

And the gunslinger Johnny North had finally made his appearance. The blond-haired Nevada gunhand stood in the street, facing Luis Chamba and his two sidekicks. Johnny was smiling. And those that knew Johnny knew Johnny was not the smiling type.

All in all, as the *Fontana Sunburst* would later say in a column by its editor, it was a most exhilarating and tense moment. These legends of the Wild West, captivating an entire town with their bigger-than-life presence. A moment from the fading past that would be forever etched in the minds of all who had the opportunity to witness this fortuitous encounter of the last of the Bad Men.

Haywood did, on occasion, get a tad bit carried away with his writing.

But since the written word was scarce in the West, folks would read and enjoy nearabout anything. They might not understand what the hell they were reading, but read it they would.

"Do it, punk!" Luke shouted. He began walking toward the dandy. Luke had felt all along the dandy didn't have the cold nerve to pull iron. When he reached the young man, who was beginning to sweat, he balled his left hand into a hard fist and knocked the loud-mouth to the dirt. Lester-Sundance fell hard. He lay on the dirt, looking up at Luke through wide, scared eyes.

Luke reached down and plucked the pearl-handled Colts from the young man's holsters. He stepped to one side and wedged one barrel between a support block and the boardwalk. With a swift jerk, he broke off first one barrel, and then the other. He tossed the ruined pistols to Lester-Sundance.

"I'll tell you something, boy," Luke said. "I wish somebody had done something like that to me when I was your age. I might have amounted to something."

Luke Nations turned his back to the sobbing, humiliated young man and walked away.

"I'll kill him for that," Lester-Sundance sobbed, but not loud enough for Luke to hear. "You just wait and see. I'll get him for that."

The Silver Dollar Kid walked across the street, in the direction Luke had taken.

"Well, boys!" Louis said. "How about the drinks on me? What say you all?"

Smoke looked at Tilden Franklin. "That includes you too, Franklin. Join us?"

His face flushed with rage and hate, Tilden turned his back on the invitation and stomped back up the street, Clint following like a dog behind him.

The TF puppies followed Clint.

Louis watched Tilden wheel around and stalk off. "The man is obviously of low degree," the gambler said.

Smoke, Colby, and the gunfighters had a laugh at that. Tilden had heard the remark, and his back stiffened with new anger. His rage was such that he could hardly see.

"Get the horses, Clint!" he snapped.

"Boss," Clint warned. "Hadn't we best stay in town?"

Tilden's big hands gripped a hitchrail and he trembled in his hot fury. "Yes. Yes," he repeated, then cleared his throat. "You're right. Order your boys to take off their gunbelts, Clint."

"What?"

"You heard me, Clint. We're going to take that invitation for a drink. And then I'm going to stomp Smoke Jensen's goddamned guts out. With my fists and boots!"

20

"What the hell?" Billy said, eyeballing Tilden and Clint and the other TF rowdies removing their gunbelts and looping them on their saddle horns.

The livery stable-swamper darted across the street and into Louis Longmont's gaming place.

"Smoke!" he called. All heads turned toward the small boy in the doorway. "Tilden Franklin and them gunhands of his'n done dropped their gunbelts, and they're all headin' this way. I don't know what they're about, but I betcha it's bad trouble."

"I know what it is," Smoke said. He set his untouched tumbler on the bar. "Thanks, Billy."

"Come here, son," Louis said. "You get over there," he pointed, "and stay put. Andre!" He called for his chef. "Get this young man a sarsaparilla, *s'il vous plait*?"

"But *monsieur . . . ou*?"

"Reasonable question," Louis muttered. "Where indeed? Lemonade?"

Andre's face brightened. *"Oui!"*

A big glass of cool lemonade in front of him, Billy slipped from the table to the eggs-and-cheese-and-beef end of the bar and filled a napkin with goodies. Eating and sipping, Billy sat back to watch the show.

Louis watched the boy's antics and smiled. His big bouncer, Mike, stood close by Billy, his massive arms folded across his barrel chest,

The chef, Andre, had beat it back to his kitchen. Let the barbarians fight, he thought.

Boot heels drummed on the boardwalk and Tilden Franklin's bulk filled the doorway. "I thought I'd take you up on your offer, Gambler," he said.

"Certainly," Louis said. "Be my guest."

Tilden walked to the bar and poured a tumbler of whiskey. He toyed with the shot glass for a moment, then lifted the glass. "To the day when we rid the country of all two-bit nesters."

Tilden and his men drank. None of the others acknowledged the toast.

Tilden smiled. "What's the matter, boys? None of you like my toast?"

Smoke lifted his glass. "To the day when farmers and ranchers all get along."

Smoke's friends toasted that. Tilden, Clint, and the other TF men did not.

"What's the matter, Tilden?" Smoke asked. "You don't like my toast?"

Tilden's smile was thin. Toying with his empty shot glass, his eyes on the polished bar, he said, "I've always had this theory, Jensen . . . or whatever your name is. My theory is that most gunslicks live on their reputations, that without a gun in their hand, they're mighty thin in the guts department. What do you think about that?"

"I think you're mighty thin between the ears, Tilden. That's what I think. I think you sit on your brains. Now what do you think about that?"

"I'm not armed, Jensen," Tilden said, still looking down at the bar.

Smoke unbuckled and untied. He handed his guns to Colby. "Neither am I, Tilden. So the next move is up to you."

Tilden looked at his riders. "Clear us a space, boys."

Gaming tables and chairs were pushed back, stacked against one wall. The barroom floor was empty.

Tilden's smile was ugly and savage. "I'm gonna break you in half, Jensen. Then your wife can see for herself what a real man can do . . . when she comes to my bed."

Smoke laughed at that. "You're a bigger fool than I first thought, Tilden. Now make your move or shut your goddamned flapping mouth."

Tilden spun away from the bar railing and charged Smoke. All two-hundred-forty-odd pounds of him, like an enraged bull, charging at the smaller man.

Smoke stepped to one side, stuck out a boot, and tripped the big man, sending him crashing and sprawling to the barroom floor. Smoke stepped in and kicked Tilden in the side, bringing a grunt of pain from the man. Before Smoke could put the boots to him again, Tilden rolled away and jumped to his feet.

Smoke, weighing some fifty-odd pounds less than Tilden, faced the bigger man. Both men lifted their hands and balled their fists.

"I'm taking bets on Smoke!" Louis announced. "Any takers?"

Clint and the TF men bet on their boss.

Haywood, Colton, Hunt, Ralph, and Ed had quietly slipped into the gaming room, standing close to the front door.

Big Mamma O'Neil bulled her way past those at the door. "A hundred bucks on Tilden!" she yelled.

"Done!" Louis said.

"Barbaric!" Hunt muttered.

Big Mamma laughed and slapped the lawyer on the

back, almost knocking him down. She stepped on past the men at the door and walked to a far wall.

Tilden flicked a right hand toward Smoke, a feeling-out punch. Smoke moved his head slightly, dodging the punch. He jabbed a hard left, catching Tilden in the mouth, snapping the man's head back.

With a roar, Tilden swung a roundhouse left that caught Smoke on the shoulder. A powerfully thrown punch, it brought a grunt of pain from the smaller man. Smoke countered with a right, hitting Tilden in the belly. It was like hitting a piece of hardwood. Tilden grinned at Smoke and the men went after each other, toe to toe, slugging it out.

Smoke realized that if he was to win this fight, and that was something he had to do, for morale's sake if nothing else, there was no way he could stand up and match Tilden punch for punch. The man was bigger and stronger, and in excellent physical shape.

Smoke jumped to one side and lashed out with one boot, the toe of the boot catching Tilden on the kneecap. Tilden howled in pain and, for a second, dropped his guard. A second was all that Smoke needed.

Smoke hit the man twice, a left-and-right combination to the jaw. His punches were savage, and they rocked the bigger man, bringing blood from one side of his mouth. Tilden staggered under the combination. Just for a second, his legs buckled.

Smoke hit the man flush on his mouth. Tilden's lips splattered under the hard-thrown punch, the blood spurting. Tilden grabbed Smoke in a bear hug, holding on until he could recover. Smoke experienced the man's massive strength as the air was crushed out of him. Tucking his head under Tilden's jaw, Smoke brought his head up savagely. Tilden's mouth snapped shut and he squalled in pain as the teeth caught his tongue and more blood was added to the flow from his battered mouth. The big man's grip eased and Smoke slipped out of the bear hug.

Pivoting, Smoke poured on the steam and hit Tilden in the gut with every ounce of strength he could muster. The right fist caught Tilden just above the belt buckle, and the wind whooshed out of the man as he involuntarily doubled over. Smoke stepped in close and grabbed Tilden's head and hair with both hands and brought the head down at the same time he was bringing a knee up. The knee caught Tilden smack on the nose and the nose crunched under the impact. Tilden was flung back against the bar.

The big man hung there, his eyes still wild but glazed over. Smoke stepped in close and went to work on the kingpin.

Smoke hammered at the man's belly and face with work-hardened fists. In seconds, Tilden's face was swollen and battered and bloody.

Clint stepped in to break up the fight and found himself suddenly lying on the barroom floor, hit on the back of the head by The Apache Kid's rifle stock. Clint moaned once and then lay still, out cold.

Smoke went to work on Tilden's belly, concentrating all his punches there, and they were thrown with all his strength. It was a savage, brutal attack on Smoke's part, but Smoke knew, from having the old Mountain Man Preacher as his teacher, that there was no such thing as a fair fight. There was only a winner, and a loser.

He hammered at Tilden's mid-section, working like a steam-driven pile-driver.

Twice, Tilden almost slumped to the floor. Twice, Smoke propped him back up and went to work on him. He shifted his attention to Tilden's face, his punches ruining the man's once-handsome features. Smoke's flat-knuckled fists knocked out teeth and loosened others. His fists completely flattened Tilden's nose. One punch to the side of Tilden's head ripped loose an ear, almost tearing it off the man's head. Still Smoke did not let up. His fists smashed into Tilden's sides and kidneys and belly and face.

Smoke was fighting with a cold, controlled, dark fury. His fists battered the man; this man who had boasted he would take Smoke's wife; this man who had sworn to run Smoke and the others out of this part of Colorado; this man who dared impose his will on all others.

Then Smoke realized he was battering and smashing an unconscious man. He stopped his assault and stepped back, his chest heaving and his hands hurting. Tilden Franklin, the bully of the valley, the man who would be king, the man who would control the destiny of all those around him, slipped to the floor to lie among the cigarette and cigar butts. His blood stained the trash on the floor.

He was so deep in his unconsciousness he did not even twitch.

"I'd have never believed it," Big Mamma O'Neil was heard to whisper. "But I seen it. Lord have mercy, did I ever see it."

"That's a hundred dollars you owe me, Big Mamma," Louis said. "You can give it to Billy over there."

Louis looked at the Tilden riders. "You TF riders can pay Big Mike."

"I have some medication at the office that will ease those swelling hands, Smoke," Colton said. "I'll be waiting for you."

Smoke leaned against the bar and nodded his head.

"Ain't you gonna see to Mister Franklin?" a TF rider asked.

"At the office," Colton said shortly. "I'll prepare a bed for him."

Smoke belted his guns around him and began working his fingers, to prevent them from stiffening any worse than he knew they would.

"Drag that cretin from my premises," Louis said, pointing at the prostrate Tilden Franklin.

Big Mamma O'Neil laid five twenty-dollar gold pieces on the table in front of Billy.

Billy looked up at her with a bit of egg sticking to his upper lip . . .

. . . and grinned!

BOOK TWO

Now this is the law of the jungle—as old and as true as the sky. And the Wolf that shall keep it may prosper, but the Wolf that shall break it must die.

—Kipling

21

Twice, Adam thought he heard something back in the timber behind the Colby house. He lifted his head and concentrated. Nothing. He returned to his reading of the dime novel about the adventures of Luke Nations.

He was just getting to the part about where Luke rides into the Indian camp, both six-guns blazing, to rescue the lovely maiden when he heard kind of a muffled, cut-off scream from in the timber.

"Velvet!" he called.

Only the silence greeted his call. And then it came to him. The silence. The birds and the small animals around the place were used to Velvet's walking through the woods. They seldom stopped their singing and chattering and calling simply because she came gently walking through.

The boy picked up his single-shot .22-caliber rifle and put his dime novel in the hip pocket of his patched and faded work pants. "Velvet!" he shouted.

Nothing.

Not the singing of a bird, not the calling or barking of a squirrel.

Something was wrong.

Adam hesitated, started to go back to the house for Mister Wilbur. Then he shook his head. It would take too long, for Velvet had strayed a pretty good piece from the house.

There was movement from his left. Adam turned just as something hard slammed into the back of his head and sent him spinning into darkness. The darkness blotted out the sunlight filtering through the trees.

When he awakened, the first thing he noticed was that the sunlight through the limbs had changed somewhat, shifting positions. Adam figured he'd been out a good thirty to forty-five minutes. Painfully, he got to a sitting-up position. His head was hurting something fierce and things were moving around like they shouldn't oughta.

He sat very still for a few moments, until his head began to clear and settle down. He thought he heard some sort of grunting sounds. Adam couldn't figure out what they might be.

He got to his feet, swaying for a moment. When things settled down, he looked around for his .22 rifle. He checked it, brushing the dirt from it, and checked the load. He kept hearing that grunting sound. Slowly, cautiously, the boy made his way through the timber toward that odd sound.

He came to a little clearing—must be two miles from the house—and paused, peering through the branches.

What he saw brought him up short and mad.

It was Velvet, and she didn't have no clothes on; her dress was torn off and tossed to one side. And a bunch of them TF riders was standing around, some of them bare-assed naked, some in their long-handles.

And there was money all over the ground. Adam couldn't figure out what all them greenbacks and silver dollars was doing on the ground.

But he knew what them men was doing. He'd never done it with no girl hisself, but he wasn't no fool.

It looked like to him that Velvet wasn't having no

good time of it. It looked like to him she was out cold. He could see bruises on her face and her . . . on her chest. And there was dark marks on her legs where them riders had gripped at her with hard hands. Like that one was doing now. Pokin' at her. From behind. Like an animal.

Adam lifted his rifle and sighted in. It was not going to be a hard shot, but he had the rifle loaded with little shorts for squirrels. He sighted in and pulled the trigger.

It was a good shot, the little chunk of lead striking the rapist in his right eye. The rapist just fell backward, off Velvet, and lay on his back, his privates exposed.

Velvet sort of rolled off the log they'd had her bent over and lay real still.

Adam quickly reloaded and sighted in again. But before he could pull the trigger, a short gun barked and something hard struck him in the chest. The slug knocked him backward. He lost his grip on his rifle. Adam knew he was bad hit, maybe going to die, but he lay still as the men ran up to him.

"Let's get outta here!" he heard one say.

"What about Steve?"

"Take him with us. We'll bury him proper."

"Little son of a bitch kilt him with a lousy .22," another spoke.

"Let's ride."

When the sounds of their horses had faded, Adam tried to reach his sister. He could not. The pain in his chest was getting worse and he was having a hard time seeing. He pulled his dime novel out of his pocket and took his worn stub of a pencil. Slowly, with bloody fingers, he began to print out a message.

A few minutes later, the boy laid his head down on the cool earth and closed his eyes. A moment later he was dead.

* * *

Smoke and the others arrived back a few hours before dark. They had pushed their horses hard. Colby and Charlie were about two hours behind.

Belle Colby met the men in the front yard.

"I can't find Velvet or Adam," she told Smoke. She had been crying, her eyes red-rimmed.

"Bob met us, Belle," Smoke said. "Charlie stayed with Colby just in case. They're a couple of hours behind us. Any idea where they might have gone?"

"No. The girl has her—what she calls her secret places in the timber where she goes to be alone."

The men dismounted. Smoke turned to The Apache Kid. "Apache, Preacher once told me you could track a snake over a flat rock."

"I'll find her trail," the old gunfighter said.

He moved out with a swiftness that belied his age. "Stay behind me," he called to the others. "Jist stay back till I locate some sign. And don't come up to me when I do find it. I don't want none of it all mucked up."

He began moving in a criss-cross manner, looking to anyone who did not understand tracking like a man who had lost his mind. In less than five minutes, he called out, "I got it. Stay behind me."

Apache was following the girl's sign, not Adam's, so they found the girl first.

"Good Jesus Christ!" Silver Jim said. He peeled off his duster and wrapped it around the girl. She was conscious, but in some sort of shock. She seemed unable to speak.

"What's all this money doing piled up here?" Moody asked. "I don't understand none of this."

"Twenty-one dollars," Smoke said, counting the coin and greenbacks. "This isn't making any sense to me."

Then Apache found the body of Adam and called out. The men gathered around.

"They's words writ on this page here," Apache said.

"My readin' ain't good enough to make 'em out." He handed the dime novel to Smoke.

Smoke looked at the bloody, printed words. "IT WAS TF RIDERS WHO DONE IT TO SIS. TF RIDERS WHO SHOT ME. GET THEM FOR ME, LUKE. LUKE, GET THEM."

Smoke read the message and then folded the book.

Luke Nations stood stony-faced. But there were tears running down his tanned, lined, leathery face.

"We play it legal-like, Luke, boys," Smoke said. "When that fails, then we go in shootin'."

"You play it legal-like, Jensen," Luke said, his words like chipped stone. "Me, I'll play it my way."

He turned to go.

Smoke's hard voice stopped the old gunfighter. *"Luke!"*

The gunfighter turned slowly.

"Charlie told me when you signed on, you rode for the brand."

"I do."

"It's my brand."

That stung Luke. He stood for a moment, then slowly nodded his head. "Right, Boss. We play it legal-like. But you know damned well how it's gonna come out in the long haul."

"Yes, I do. Or at least suspect. But when all the shooting is over and the dust settled, we're going to have United States marshals in here, plus all sorts of lawyers and other big-worded people. I don't want anyone to point the finger at us and be able to prove that we started a damn thing. That make sense to you?"

"Put that way, I reckon it do."

"Fine. I hate to ask any of you boys to ride back to town. But we need the sheriff out here first thing in the morning."

Wilbur Mason had walked up. "I'll go," he said quietly.

Smoke nixed that. "You'd be fair game, Wilbur. And you're no hand with a gun. No, I'll go. I'll take the book and give it to Lawyer Brook and tell him the story in the presence of Sheriff Carson. Damn!" he said.

"What's wrong?" Silver Jim said.

"I'll have to take the girl into town to Doctor Spalding. She's in bad shape. Wilbur, hitch up a wagon and fill the back with hay for her comfort. Luke, ride like hell for my place and tell some other men to come hard. They can catch up with me on the way in."

Luke nodded and ran, in his odd, bowlegged, cowboy way, back to his horse.

"I'll borrow a horse from Colby's stable and pick up mine on the way back. You boys tell Sally I'll be back when she sees me."

"You take 'er easy, Smoke," Silver Jim warned. "Them hands of yourn won't be fit for no quick draw for several days yet."

Smoke nodded and left.

Tilden Franklin had tried to sit a saddle. He fell off twice before he would allow himself to be taken back to his ranch in the back of a buckboard. If he was not blind crazy before, he was now. He knew it would be a week, maybe longer, before he was fit to do anything. He was hurt bad, and he had enough sense to know it.

He also had enough sense to know, through waves of humiliation, that since he had started the fight, in front of witnesses, there was not a damn thing, legally, he could do about it.

Except lay in the back of the buckboard and curse Smoke Jensen.

Which he did, wincing with every bounce and jar along the rutted road.

Smoke had met Colby and Charlic on the trail and broken the news to the father. Colby and Wilbur had exchanged wagons and rolled on. Charlie had insisted on returning with Smoke. He didn't say it, but Smoke was glad the gunfighter was with him, for his own hands were in no shape for any standup gunfight.

It was long after dark when they rolled into Fontana and up to the doctor's office. Velvet still had not spoken a word. Nor uttered any sound.

Colton looked at Velvet, looked at Smoke, and silently cursed. He ordered the girl taken into his examining room and called for his wife to be present.

"Tell me what happened," he told Smoke. "As succinctly as possible."

"As what?"

Colton sighed. "Make it short."

Lawyer Hunt made his appearance, with his wife Willow. Mona asked her to assist her with Velvet. The women disappeared into the examining room.

Smoke had sent Billy for the sheriff as they passed the livery stable. For once, Sheriff Carson seemed genuinely concerned. He knew for an ironclad fact that nobody, but *nobody*, messed with a good woman and came off easy. Monte Carson was a hired gun, true, but he respected good womenfolk.

With everyone present, Smoke told his story, handing the bloody, damning dime novel, autographed by Luke Nations, to Lawyer Hunt.

Nobody heard Louis Longmont enter the office. He stood off to one side, listening.

Lawyer Hunt read the message and looked at Monte. "Can you read, Sheriff?"

"Hell, yes!"

"Then read it and pick a side!" There was hard and

genuine anger in the lawyer's voice. God*damn* people who would do this to a girl.

"Hey!" Monte said. "I don't pick sides. I'm the law around here."

"That remains to be seen, doesn't it?" Louis spoke from the darkness near the open door to the office.

Monte flushed and read the bloody words. Now, he thought, I *am* in a pickle.

Doctor Spalding stepped out of the examining room. "The girl's visible wounds will be easily treated. They're mostly superficial. But her mental state is quite another matter. She is catatonic."

Smoke lost his temper. He was tired, sore, hungry, disgusted, and could not remember when he wanted to kill anybody more than at this moment. "Now, what in the goddamn hell does all that jibber-jabber mean?"

"Settle down, Smoke," Louis said. Then the gambler explained the doctor's words.

Smoke calmed down and looked at Sheriff Carson. "You want a war on your hands, Monte?"

"Hell, no!"

"Somebody better hang for this, Monte," Smoke warned, his voice low and menacing. "Or that is exactly what you're going to have on your hands—a war."

Smoke stepped out into the night and walked toward the best of the hotels.

"You ever heard the expression 'caught between a rock and a hard place,' Sheriff?" Louis asked.

"Sure. Why?"

"Because that's where you are. Enjoy it." The gambler smiled thinly.

22

The news swept through the town of Fontana fast. Sheriff Monte Carson found Judge Proctor and jerked him away from the bottle on the bar, leading the whiskered man out of the batwings to the boardwalk.

Monte pointed a finger at the judge. He told him what had gone down, shaking his finger in the judge's face. "Not another drink until this is over," he warned the highly educated rummy. "If you don't think you can handle that, I can damn well put you in a cell and be shore of it."

Judge Proctor stuck out his chest and blustered. "You wouldn't dare!"

"Try me," Monte warned, acid in his voice.

Judge Proctor got the message, and he believed it. He rubbed a hand over his face. "You're right, of course, Sheriff. Goddamn Tilden Franklin! What was he thinking about, authorizing something of this odious nature?"

Sheriff Carson shrugged. "Be ready to go at first light, Judge. No matter how the chips fall, we got to play this legal-like, all the way."

Judge Proctor watched the sheriff walk away into the

night. "Should be interesting," he muttered. "A fair hearing. How quaint!"

Louis Longmont sat in his quarters behind his gaming room and sipped hot tea. At first, the news of the money near where the girl was found puzzled him. Then his mind began working, studying all angles. Louis felt he knew the reason for the money. But it was a thin rope Tilden had managed to grab onto. The man really must be quite insane to authorize such a plan. Colby and Belle and their kids were all deeply religious folk—most farmers were. And the sheriff and judge were going to be forced to handle this right by the law books.

But, the gambler thought with a sigh, there was always the jury to consider. And money, in this case, not only talked, but cursed.

Big Mamma sat at the back of her bar and pondered the situation. In a case like this, wimmin oughta be allowed to sit on the jury . . . but that was years in the future. Even though Big Mamma was as cold-hearted and ruthless as a warlord, something like this brought out the maternal instinct from deep within her. She would have scoffed and cursed at the mere suggestion of that . . . but it was true.

She looked around her. It wouldn't take near as long to tear all this down and get gone as it had to put it all up. Damned if she wanted to get caught up in an all-out shootin' war. But sure as hell, that was what was gonna happen.

That Smoke Jensen . . . well, she had revised her original opinion of that feller. He was pure straight out of Hell, that one. That one was no punk, like she first thought. But one-hundred-and-ten-percent man. And even though Big

Mamma didn't like men, she could respect the all-man types . . . like Smoke Jensen.

Ralph Morrow lay beside his wife, unable to sleep. He was thinking of that poor child, and also thinking that he just may have been a fool where Tilden Franklin was concerned. After witnessing that fight in the gaming room this very day, and seeing the brutal, calculating madness in Tilden's eyes, the preacher realized that Tilden would stop at nothing to attain his goals.

Even the rape of a child.

Hunt sat in his office, looking at the bloody dime novel. Like the gambler, Louis Longmont, Hunt felt he knew why the money had been left by the raped child. And, if his hunch was correct, it was a horrible, barbaric thing for the men to do.

But, his lawyer's mind pondered, did Tilden Franklin have anything to do with it?

"Shit!" he said, quite unlike him.

Of course he did.

Colton dozed on his office couch. Even in his fitful sleep he was keeping one ear out for any noise Velvet might make. But he didn't expect her to make any. He felt the child's mind was destroyed.

He suddenly came wide awake, his mind busy. Supplies! He was going to have to order many more supplies. He would post the letter tomorrow—today—and get it out on the morning stage.

There was going to be a war in this area of the state— a very bad war. And as the only doctor within seventy-five miles, Colton felt he was going to be very busy.

* * *

Ed Jackson slept deeply and well. He had heard the news of the raped girl and promptly dismissed it. Tilden Franklin was a fine man; he would have nothing to do with anything of that nature. Those hard-scrabble farmers and small ranchers were all trash. That's what Mister Franklin had told him, and he believed him.

There had been no rape, Ed had thought, before falling asleep. None at all. The money scattered around the wretched girl proved that, and if he was chosen to sit on the jury, that's the way he would see it.

Sleep was elusive for Smoke. And not just for Smoke. In the room next to his, he could hear Charlie Starr's restless pacing. The legendary gunfighter was having a hard time of it too. Mistreatment of a grown woman was bad enough, but to do what had been done to a child . . . that was hard to take.

War. That word kept bouncing around in Smoke's head. Dirty, ugly range war.

Smoke finally drifted off to sleep . . . but his dreams were bloody and savage.

Not one miner worked the next day . . . or so it seemed at least. The bars and cafes and hotels and streets and boardwalks of Fontana were filled to overflowing with men and women, all awaiting the return of Judge Proctor and Sheriff Monte Carson from the sprawling TF spread.

Luke Nations had stayed at the Sugarloaf with Sally and most of the other gunslicks. Early that morning, however. Pistol Le Roux, Dan Greentree, Bull Flagler, Hardrock, Red Shingletown, and Leo Wood had ridden in.

And the town had taken notice of them very quickly. The aging gunhawks made Monte's deputies very nervous. And, to the deputies' way of thinking, what made it all even worse was that Louis Longmont was solidly on the side of Smoke Jensen. And now it appeared that Johnny North had thrown in with Smoke too. And nobody knew how many more of them damned old gunfighters Smoke had brought in. Just thinkin' 'bout them damned old warhosses made a feller nervous.

Just outside of town, Monte sat his saddle and looked down at Judge Proctor, sitting in a buckboard. "I ain't real happy about bringin' this news back to Fontana, Judge."

"Nor I, Sheriff. But I really, honestly feel we did our best in this matter."

Monte shuddered. "You know what this news is gonna do, don't you, Judge?"

"Unfortunately. But what would you have done differently, Monte?"

Monte shook his head. He could not think of a thing that could have been done differently. But, for the first time in his life, Monte was beginning to see matters from the *other* side of the badge. He'd never worn a badge before, never realized the responsibilities that went with it. And, while he was a long way from becoming a good lawman, if given a chance Monte might someday make it.

"Nothin', Judge. Not a thing."

Judge Proctor clucked to his team and rolled on.

Standing beside Smoke on the boardwalk, Lawyer Hunt Brook said, "Here they come, Smoke. Two went out, two are returning."

"That's about the way I figured it would be."

Judge Proctor halted his team in front of Hunt and Smoke. "Since you are handling this case for Miss Colby, Mister Brook," the judge said, "I'll see you in your offices in thirty minutes. I should like to wash up first."

"Certainly, your honor," Hunt said.

Smoke walked with the lawyer down the long, tightly

packed street to his law office. Hunt went on into his personal office and Smoke sat out in the pine-fresh outer office, reading a month-old edition of a New York City newspaper. He looked up as Colby entered.

"It ain't good, is it, Smoke?" the father asked.

"It doesn't look good from where I sit. You sure you want to be here, listen to all this crap?"

"Yeah," the man said softly. "I shore do want to hear it. I left Belle with Velvet. This is hard on my woman, Smoke. She's talkin' hard about pullin' out."

"And you?"

"I told her if she went, she'd have to go by herself. I was stayin'."

"She won't leave you, Colby."

"Naw. I don't think she will neither. It's just . . . whatever the outcome today, Smoke, we gotta get back, get Adam into the ground. You reckon that new minister, that Ralph Morrow, would come up to the high country and say a few words over my boy?"

The man was very close to crying.

"I'm sure he would, Colby. Soon as this is over, I'll go talk to him."

"I'd be beholden, Smoke."

Judge Proctor and Sheriff Carson entered the office. The judge extended his hand to Colby. "You have my deepest and most sincere condolences, sir."

"Thank you, Judge."

Monte stood with his hat in his hand, looking awfully uncomfortable.

Hunt motioned them all into his office. When they were seated, Judge Proctor looked at them all and said, "Well, this is a bit irregular, and should this case ever come to court, I shall, of course, have to bring in another judge to hear it. But that event appears highly unlikely."

Smoke's smile was ugly.

Monte caught the mocking smile. "Don't, Smoke," he

said quietly. "We done our best. And I mean that. If you can ever prove we slacked up even a little, you can have my badge, and I'm sayin' that in front of witnesses."

For some reason, Smoke believed the man. Queer feeling.

"Here it is," Judge Proctor said. He looked at Colby. "This is highly embarrassing for me, sir. And please bear in mind, these are the words of the TF men who were . . . well, at the scene."

"Just say it," the rancher-farmer said.

"Very well. They say, sir, that your daughter had been, well, shall we say . . . *entertaining* the men at that location for quite some time. They say this has been going on since last summer."

"What's been goin' on?" Colby blurted. "I ain't understandin' none of this."

Smoke had a sudden headache. He rubbed his temples with his fingertips and wished all this crap would be over. Just get all the goddamned lies over and done with.

"Sir," Judge Proctor said. "The TF men claim that your daughter, Velvet, has been entertaining them with sexual favors for some time. For money."

Colby sat rock still for a moment, and then jumped to his feet. "That there's a damned lie, sir! My Velvet is a good girl!"

Smoke pulled the man back into the chair. "We know, Colby. We know that's the truth. It's all a pack of lies. Just like we figured it would be."

"Please, Mister Colby!" Judge Proctor said. "Try to control yourself, sir."

Colby put his face in his hands and began weeping.

Lawyer Brook wet a cloth from a pitcher on his desk and handed the cloth to Smoke, who handed it to Colby. Colby bathed his face and, sighing, looked up. "Go on," he said, his voice strained.

The judge looked at the sheriff. "Would you *please*

take a part in these proceedings, Sheriff? You explain. That's your job, not mine."

"Mister Colby," Monte said. "Them Harris brothers who ride for the TF brand, Ed and Pete? It was them and Billy and Donnie and Singer and . . . two or three more. I got their names writ down. Anyways, they claim that Miss Velvet was . . ." He sighed, thinking, Oh, shit! "Chargin' the men three dollars a turn. There would have been more than twenty-one dollars there this time except that not all the men got their turn."

"Dear God in Heaven!" Hunt Brook exclaimed. "Must you be so graphic, sir?"

"I don't know no other way to say it, Lawyer!" Monte said. "I'm doin' the bes' I can."

Hunt waved his hand. "I know, Sheriff. I know. Sorry. Please continue."

"They say Miss Velvet kep' her . . . earnin's in a secret place back in the timber. They told us where it was. We ain't been there, and you all know we ain't had the time to go to the ranch, into the high country, and back here by now. I'll tell y'all where they said it was. Y'all can see for yourselves.

"Anyways, Miss Velvet's brother come up there and started yellin' and hollerin' and wavin' that rifle of his'n around. Then he just up and shot Steve Babbin. That's for a fact. They buryin' Steve this afternoon. Shot him in the eye with a .22. Killed him. Little bitty hole. Had to have been a .22. Them ol' boys just reacted like any other men. They grabbed iron and started shootin'. Killed the boy. They kinda got shook about it and took off. That's about it, boys."

Monte leaned back in his chair and looked at the newly carpeted floor.

"And you believe their story, Sheriff?" Lawyer Brook asked.

"It ain't a question of believin' or not believin', Lawyer. It's a matter of what can be proved. I don't like it, fellers. I just don't like it. But look at it like this: even if Miss Velvet could talk, which she cain't, it'd still be her word agin theirs. And that's the way it is, fellers."

Smoke stood up and put his hat on his head. "And that's it, huh, boys?"

"I'm afraid so, Mister Jensen," Judge Proctor said. "I don't like it. But we played this straight by the book. If you could bring me evidence to the contrary, I'd certainly listen to it and act accordingly."

"So will I, Smoke," Monte said softly. "Believe it."

"Oddly enough, I do believe you. Come on, Colby. Let's go."

Lawyer Hunt Brook was so angry he was trembling. "This is terrible!" He practically shouted the words. "This is not justice!"

"The lady is blind, Mister Brook," Judge Proctor said. "I shouldn't have to remind you of that." He stood up. "Come, Sheriff."

Stepping outside, the judge almost ran into Pistol Le Roux. "Good Lord!" Proctor said. "It's been years, Pistol. You're looking quite well."

"Thanks. How'd it go in yonder, Judge?"

"Not to anyone's liking, I'm afraid. Are you going to be in town long?"

"I work for Smoke Jensen."

"Oh, my!" the judge said. "How many of you, ah, men did Mister Jensen hire, Pistol?"

Pistol smiled. "Twenty or so."

Judge Proctor suddenly felt weak-kneed. "I see. Well, it's been nice seeing you, Pistol."

"Same here, Judge."

As they walked off, Monte asked, "How come it is you know that old gunslick, Judge?"

"I was up in the Wyoming country hearing a case of his when he was marshal of a town up there. Four pretty good gunhands braced him one afternoon."

"How'd it come out?"

"Pistol killed them all."

"And they's *twenty* of them old gunhawks workin' for Jensen?"

"Yes. Rather makes one feel inadequate, doesn't it, Sheriff?"

"Whatever that means, Judge."

The judge didn't feel like explaining. "You know, Monte, you could be a good lawman if you'd just try."

"Is that what I been feelin' lately, Judge?"

"Probably. But since you—we—are in Tilden Franklin's pocket, what are we going to do about it?"

"We wasn't in his pocket in this one, Judge."

"That is correct. And it's a rather nice feeling, isn't it, Sheriff Carson?"

"Damn shore is, Judge Proctor. Would you like to join me in a drink, Judge?"

"No, Sheriff. I think not. I just decided to quit."

23

When Smoke and Sally and Pearlie and most of the other aging gunhawks rode up to Colby's place the following morning, they were all amazed to see the hills covered with people

"What the hell?" Pearlie said.

"They're showin' Tilden Franklin how they feel," Luke said. "And rubbin' his nose in it."

"Would you look yonder?" Jay said. "That there is Big Mamma. In a *dress*!"

"Musta been a tent-maker moved into town," Apache said.

"Who is that pretty lady beside the . . . large lady I presume you men are talking about?" Sally asked.

Smoke and Sally were in a buckboard, the others on horseback.

"That's Big Mamma's wife, Miss Sally," Silver Jim explained.

Sally looked up at him. "I beg your pardon, Silver Jim?"

"They was married 'bout three year ago, I reckon it

was. Big Mamma had to slap that minister around a good bit 'fore he'd agree to do it, but he done 'er."

Sally turned her crimson face forward. "I do not wish to pursue this line of conversation any further, thank you."

"No, ma'am," Silver Jim said. "Me neither."

The service was a short one, but sincerely given by Ralph. Adam's forever-young body was buried on a hillside overlooking the Colby ranch.

And while most knew the TF riders were watching from the hills, no TF rider showed his face at the funeral. The mood of the crowd was such that if any TF riders had made an appearance, there most likely would have been a hanging.

Belle Colby and Velvet sat in the front yard during the service. Velvet had yet to speak a word or utter any type of sound.

Tilden sat on the front porch of his fine ranch house. He hurt all over. Never, *never*, in his entire life, had he been so badly torn up. And by a goddamned two-bit gunslinger.

Clint walked up to the porch. "Twelve hands pulled out last night, Boss."

"You pay 'em off?" The words were hard to understand and even harder for Tilden to speak. His lips were grotesquely swollen and half a dozen teeth were missing. His nose had yet to be set because it was so badly broken and swollen hideously.

"No. They just packed it all up and rode off. Told Pete Harris they hired their guns to fight men, not to make war on little kids."

"How noble of them. Hell with them!"

"Some of the others say they'll ride for brand—when it comes to punchin' cows. But they ain't gettin' involved in no war."

"Hell with them too. Fire 'em!"

"Boss?"

"Goddamn you! I said fire them!"

Clint stood his ground. He put one boot up on the porch and stared square at Tilden. "Now you listen to me, Boss. We got a hell of a big herd out yonder. And we need punchers to see to that herd. Now I feel sick at my stomach over what I ordered them men to do to that Colby girl, but it's done. And I can't change it. I reckon I'll answer to the Lord for that. If so, that's 'tween me and Him. But for now, I got a herd to look after. Are you so crazy mad you can't understand that?"

Tilden took several deep breaths—as deeply as he dared, that is. For Smoke had broken several of his ribs. He calmed himself. "All right, all right, Clint! You've made your point. I want a tally of how many men are going to fight for me. Those that want to punch cows, do so. But for every one that won't fight, hire two that will. Is that understood?"

"Yes, sir."

"Let's face it. You made a mistake by suggesting what was done to the Colby bitch; I made a mistake by going along with it. All right. Like you say, it's done. I understand that Colby brat wrote in that stupid book about Luke avenging him, right?"

"Yes, sir."

"I figured by now that old bastard would have come storming in here, fire in his eyes and his guns smoking. Maybe he's lost his balls."

Clint shook his head. "You never knew Luke Nations, did you, Boss?"

"Can't say as I ever had the pleasure."

"I do," Clint said softly. "He's . . ." The foreman

searched for a word. "Awesome. There ain't a nerve in his body, Boss. He'll be comin' in smokin', all right. Bet on that. But he'll pick the time and place."

"Hire the gunnies!" Tilden ordered, his voice harsh. "And then tell our gunhawks it's open season on nesters."

Clint hesitated. "Can I say something, Boss?"

"What is it, Clint?"

"Why don't we just drop the whole damned thing, Boss? Call it off? If word of this war gets to the governor's ears, he's liable to send in the Army."

"Hell with the governor. We got the sheriff and the judge in our pockets; how's anything goin' to get out?"

"I don't know about Monte and the judge no more, Boss. They was both pushin' real hard yesterday about that Velvet thing."

"I got them elected, I can get them un-elected."

Clint's smile was rueful. "You're forgettin' something, Boss."

"What?"

"The *people* elected 'em, For four years."

Clint turned around and walked off, leaving Tilden alone on the porch . . . with his hurting body.

And his hate.

Two weeks passed with no trouble . . . none at all. Between Tilden and the smaller spreads, that is. There was still minor trouble in town. But Monte and his men put that down quickly and hard. And the now-sober Judge Proctor hit the offenders with such stiff fines and terms in the new jailhouse that it seemed to deter other potential lawbreakers.

And Monte stopped collecting graft from the saloons and other businesses. He was being paid a good salary as sheriff, and decided that was enough. Any deputy that didn't like the new rules could leave. A few did, most stayed. All in all, it was a good job.

Monte looked up as the front door to his office opened. Johnny North stood there, gazing at him.

"You decide to make your move now, Johnny?" Monte asked.

"I don't know," the gunfighter said. "Mind if I sit down?"

Monte pointed to a chair. "Help yourself."

Johnny first poured himself a cup of coffee. He sat and looked at the sheriff. "What the hell's the matter with you, Monte? You got religion or something?"

Monte smiled. "I ain't got religion, that's for sure. Maybe it's the something. Why do you ask?"

"I been waitin' for you to come brace me for two damn weeks. You forgot we're supposed to hate each other?"

"No, I ain't. But I'll tell you this: I can't remember what we're supposed to hate each other for!"

Johnny scratched his chin. "Come to think of it, neither can I. Wasn't it something about a gal?"

Monte started laughing. "I don't know! Hell, Johnny. Whatever it was it happened so many years ago, what difference does it make now?"

Johnny North joined in the laughter. "You et yet?"

"Nope. You buyin'?"

"Hell, why not? it's gettin' too damn hot outside for a gunfight anyways."

Laughing, the old enemies walked to a cafe.

A few of Tilden Franklin's hands were lounging in a tight knot outside a saloon. These were not the gunhawks employed by the TF brand, but cowboys. And to show they were taking no sides in this matter, they had checked their guns with the bartender inside the saloon.

Monte Carson had made it clear, by posting notices around the town, that TF gunhawks had better not start any trouble in his town, or in any area of his jurisdiction. He'd had to get the judge to spell all the words.

The judge had done so, gleefully.

"Looks like Johnny North and the Sheriff done kissed and made up," one cowboy remarked.

"That's more trouble for Tilden," another observed. There was just a small note of satisfaction in the statement.

Another TF puncher sat down on the lip of a watering trough. "It's May, boys. Past time to move the herds up into the high country for the summer."

"I been thinkin' the same thing."

"I think I'll talk to Clint when we get back to the ranch. Kinda suggest, nice-like, that we get the herds ready to move. If he goes along with it, and I think he will, that'll put us some thirty-five miles from the ranch, up in the high lonesome. Take a hell of a pistol to shoot thirty-five miles."

"Yeah. That'd put us clean out of any war, just doin' what we're paid to do: look after cows."

Another cowboy sat down on the steps. He looked at the puncher who had suggested the high country. "You know, Dan, sometimes you can show some signs of havin' a little sense."

"Thank you," Dan said modestly. "For a fact, my momma didn't raise no fool for a son."

"Is that right?"

"Yeah," Dan said with a smile. "I had a sister."

The aging gunfighters were having the time of their lives. They were doing what most loved to do: work cattle. Smoke's bulls had been busy during the winter, and his herd had increased appreciably now that the calving was over. It was branding time, and the gunfighters were pitching in and working just as hard as Smoke or Pearlie. Some had gone to other small spreads in the area, helping out there, their appearance a welcome sight to the overworked and understaffed ranchers.

It appeared that the area was at peace. Smoke knew, from riding the high country, that Tilden Franklin's punchers were busy moving the TF herds into the high pastures, and doing so, he suspected, for many reasons, not all of them associated with the welfare of the cattle. That was another sign that Tilden had not given up in his fight to rid the area of all who would not bend to his will. Those TF hands who were not gunslicks but cowboys were clearing out of the line of fire.

He said as much to Charlie Starr.

The gunhand agreed. "It ain't even got started good yet, Smoke. I got word that Tilden is hirin' all the guns he can, and they're beginning to trickle in. It's shapin' up to be a bad one."

"They any good?"

"Some of them are bad hombres. Some of them are just startin' to build a rep. But they're alive, so they must be fair hands with a gun."

Smoke looked around him, at the vast, majestic panorama that nature had bestowed on this part of Colorado. "It's all so foolish," he said. "There is more than enough room for us all."

"Not to a man like Tilden," Luke Nations said, walking up, a tin cup of coffee in his hand. He was taking a break from the branding. "Tilden, least for as long as I've known of him, has always craved to be the bull of the woods. He's crazy."

All present certainly agreed with that.

"What'd Colby say or do when you give him that money we found in that holler tree?" Charlie asked Smoke.

"Sent it to Tilden by way of the Sheriff. Wrote him a note too. Told him where to put the money. Told him to put it there sideways."

Charlie and Luke both grinned at that, Luke saying, "I sure would have liked to seen the look on Tilden's face when he got that."

"How's his health?" Charlie asked.

"Coming along," Smoke said with a grin. "Doc Colton goes out there several times a week. 'Bout the only thing wrong with Tilden now—other than the fact he's crazy— is that he don't have any front teeth and his ribs is still sore."

"I figure we got two, maybe three more weeks before Tilden pulls all the stops out," Luke said. "He's not goin' to do nothin' until he's able to sit a saddle and handle a short gun. Then look out."

And they all agreed with that.

"I figure he'll save us for last," Smoke said. "I figure he'll hit Peyton first. That's the ranch closest to his range, and the furtherest from us. I've warned Peyton to be care- ful, but the man seemed to think it's all over now."

"Is he a fool?" Luke asked.

"No," Smoke said softly. "Just a man who tries to see the best in all people. He thinks Tilden has 'seen the light,' to use Peyton's own words."

"He's a fool then," Charlie opined. "There isn't one ounce of good in Tilden Franklin. That little trick with Velvet should have convinced Peyton."

"Speakin' of Velvet . . ." Luke let it trail off into si- lence.

"No change," Smoke said. "She eats, and sits. She has not uttered a sound in weeks."

"Her pa?"

"Colby has turned real quiet-like," Smoke told the men. "Never speaks of her. But I don't like the look in his eyes. Belle told me he takes his pistol out every day and practices drawing and firing."

"He any good?"

"No," Smoke said flatly. "He just doesn't have the eye and hand coordination needed to be any good. He's slow as molasses and can't hit jack-crap with a short gun."

"Then he's headin' for trouble," Luke said. "You want I should go talk to him?"

"Can if you want. But it won't do any good. I tried talking to him. He just turned his back and walked away."

Charlie spat on the ground. "The fool is diggin' his own grave, Smoke."

"Yeah. I know it. But he's all tore up with grief. I'm thinkin' he's gonna brace the Harris Brothers if he ever gets the chance."

"They'll kill him," Luke said. "Them boys is real good."

Smoke nodded his head. He summed up his feelings by saying, "I think Colby wants to die."

24

Paul Jackson walked into his brother's office at the general store and told Ed he was quitting.

Ed looked at his brother as if he was looking at a fool. "To do what?"

"I staked me out a claim. Looks promisin' too. You're makin' all the money here. Hell with you!"

"Fine. But remember this: you'll not get a penny's worth of credit from me."

"I got money of my own." He walked out of the office.

"You're a fool!" Ed shouted after his brother.

His brother turned around and made a very obscene gesture. It was intended for Ed, but Ed's wife caught it as well.

Peg stamped her foot.

Paul laughed and walked on out, feeling as though he had just had a great weight lifted from his shoulders. He swung into the saddle and trotted out, toward the high lonesome, where he had staked his claim.

Paul would show them all. He'd come back a rich man and take Bountiful from that namby-pamby preacher and then, just like in one of them dime novels, the both of them would ride off into the sunset, to be forever together.

Or something like that.

"What side of this fracus is Utah Slim on?" Johnny North asked Monte over coffee one bright early summer morning.

"I can't figure it, myself. He don't appear to be on neither side. And he ain't hurtin' for money. He's always got a wad of greenbacks."

"Gamble?"

Monte shook his head. "No. I ain't never seen nor heard of him gamblin'."

"He's on somebody's payroll," the gunslinger opined. "You can bet on that. Utah don't do nothin' for nothin'. He's here for a reason."

"You find out, you let me know?"

"Why not? I sure ain't got no axes to grind in this here fight."

"Tilden's hirin', you know."

"Screw Tilden Franklin. I got me a little claim staked out and got guys workin' it for shares. 'Bout five years back, I started puttin' back a little bit of money ever' time I had some to spare. Got it in a bank up in Boulder. With the gold I get out of this claim, I aim to start me a little ranch; maybe do a little farmin' too. Hang up my guns."

Monte started grinning.

"What are you grinnin' about, you ape?" Johnny asked.

"Gonna do a little bit of ranchin' and a little bit of farmin', hey?"

"Yeah! What's wrong with that?"

"Nothin'. Nothin' at all. But what happens if you run into some big rancher like Tilden when you decide to settle down?"

"Well . . . I reckon I'll fight."

Monte suddenly felt better. He started chuckling. "Oh, yeah, Johnny, you got an axe to grind in this war—you just ain't realized it yet."

Johnny thought about that, then he too started chuckling. "By God, Monte, you right. I think I'll go see if that feller Colby needs a hand. Might do me some good to do some hard work for a change."

"He can't pay you nothin'."

"I ain't askin' for nothin'."

Boot heels drummed on the boardwalk and someone was hollering for the sheriff.

Monte jumped up and headed for the door, Johnny right behind him. A wild-eyed miner almost collided with them both.

"Come quick, Sheriff! That nester Colby is about to draw down on a TF gunnie named Donnie. Hurry, Sheriff, hurry!"

"Crazy farmer!" Monte yelled, running toward a saloon. He could see a crowd gathered on both sides of a man standing out in the street. He recognized the man as Colby, and with a sick feeling realized he was not going to be able to stop it. He just knew that Colby had started it, and if that was the case, he would not interfere. It was an unwritten rule in the West—and would be for about a decade to come—that a man broke his own horses and killed his own snakes. If one challenged another to a gunfight, and it was a fair fight, few lawmen would interfere.

The gunslick, Donnie, was standing on the boardwalk, laughing at the farmer. Colby was standing in the street, cursing the TF rider.

Monte stopped some distance away, halting both Johnny and the miner. "Who started it?"

"That farmer. He called Donnie out and started cussin' him. Ain't you gonna stop it, Sheriff?"

"There is nothin' I can do, mister," Monte told the

man. "If Colby wants to back off, I'll see that he gets that chance. But I can't stop it. There ain't no city or county law agin a one-on-one fight."

"Colby's gonna get killed," the miner said.

"I reckon," Monte agreed.

"What's the matter, Pig-farmer?" Donnie taunted the older man. "You done lost your nerve?"

"No," Colby said, his voice firm. "Anytime you're ready, draw!"

Donnie and his friends laughed. "Hell, Nester," Donnie said. "I ain't gonna draw on you. You called me out, remember?"

"You raped my Velvet and killed my boy."

"I didn't rape nobody, Nester. Your daughter was sellin' and we'uns bought. Cash money for merchandise. Your boy busted up in there and started throwin' lead around. We fired back. And that's the way it happened."

"You're a goddamned liar!" Colby shouted.

"Now that tears it, Nester," Donnie said, his hands over the butts of his guns. "You make your play." He grinned nastily. "Sorry 'bout Velvet, though. She shore liked it, the more the merrier."

Colby went for his old Navy Colt .36. Grinning, Donnie let the man fumble and then with a smooth, practiced motion drew, cocked, and fired, the slug taking Colby in the right shoulder. The farmer spun around, dropping his Navy Colt onto the dirt of the street.

Colby reached for the gun with his left hand and Donnie fired again, the slug striking Colby in the stomach. The farmer was tossed to one side and Donnie's Colt roared again, the slug raking Colby flush in the face, just above the nose and below the eye sockets. Colby's face was shattered. He trembled once and was still.

"That's it!" Monte shouted. "Holster your gun and ride out of town, Donnie. Right now. Git gone, boy, or face me. Make your choice."

"Hey, I'm leavin', Sheriff." Donnie grinned, returning his Colt to leather. "I mean, you saw it—I didn't start it."

Louis Longmont had watched the whole sickening show from across the street. But, like the sheriff, he had made no attempt to stop it. Such was the code demanded of those who braved the frontier.

Longmont tossed his cigar into the street and walked back to his gaming tent. Then a truth made its way into the light of his mind: he was sick of the whole damned mess. Tired of late hours and tired of taking other people's money—even if his games were honest—tired of sweat-stinking miners and cowboys, tired of the violence and dust and heat and intense cold. Tired of it all. Just plain tired of it.

The gambler realized then that this was to be his last boom town.

That thought made him immensely happy.

From his table in his gaming room, Louis watched the undertaker's black hack rumble past.

He heard a voice saying, "This poor wretch have any family?"

He could not hear the reply.

Louis poured a tumbler of scotch and lifted the glass, silently toasting the dead Colby.

"Not much money in his pockets." The undertaker's voice came to Louis.

"Mike!" Louis called.

The bouncer stuck his big head around the corner "Yeah, Boss?"

"Go tell the undertaker to prepare Colby's body and do it up nice—the best he can offer. I'm paying."

"Yes, sir."

"And tell Johnny North to come see me."

"Yes, sir."

A few minutes later, Johnny North stepped into the gaming tent. "You wanna see me, Louis?"

The two were not friends, but then neither were they enemies. Just two men who were very, very good with a gun and held a mutual respect for each other.

"You know where Colby's spread is located, Johnny?"

"I can probably find it."

"Someone needs to ride up there and tell his wife that she's a widow."

"You tellin' me to do it, Louis?"

"No." The gambler's left hand worked at a deck of playing cards on the table. His right hand was not visible. "But I am asking."

"If that's the case . . . fine. I'll go."

"Ask her . . . no, ride on to Smoke's place and tell him what happened, if you will, please. Ask him to arrange for a wagon to come for Colby's body."

"I'll do that too, Louis. Louis?"

The gambler looked at the gunfighter.

"It wasn't right . . . that shootin'. But we couldn't interfere."

"I know. But the West is changing, Johnny. Going to ranch and farm a bit with the savings you have up in Boulder, Johnny?"

That shook the blond-haired Nevada gunslick. "How in the hell . . ."

"I own part of the bank, Johnny," Louis said with a very slight smile.

Johnny returned the smile. "I think I might just ask the Widder Colby if she needs some help up there, Louis. Not today, now, that wouldn't be fitten. But later on."

"That would be a very decent act on your part, Johnny. I think Belle would appreciate that very much."

"I'll get goin' now. See you, Louis."

"See you. Thanks, Johnny."

As the sounds of Johnny's big California spurs faded on the boardwalk, Andre stuck his head out of the kitchen. "A snack, sir?" the chef asked.

"I think not, Andre. Just coffee, please."

The chef hesitated. "It is a dismal and barbaric place, is it not, *monsieur*?"

"For a while longer, Andre. But it will change as time passes, and time will pass."

"Oui, monsieur."

Johnny North caught up with Donnie about five miles out of town. The young gunslick had several of his friends with him, but numbers had never bothered Johnny North before, and didn't this time.

Johnny North made all the gunslicks and so-called gunslicks of this group nervous. They all kept their hands in plain sight, and as far away from their guns as could be humanly arranged.

"I ain't lookin' for no truck with you, Johnny," Donnie said, his voice sounding a bit shrill.

"Peel off from your friends, Donnie," Johnny told him.

"Why?"

"We're gonna take a ride, just you and me."

"Where we goin'?"

"To deliver a death message"

"I'll be damned if I'm goin'!"

Johnny smiled grimly. "Do you prefer dead to damned, Donnie?"

"Huh?"

"You can either ride to the Colby place with me, and tell the widder how you gunned down her man, or you can be taken back to the TF spread . . . acrost your saddle. It's up to you, Donnie."

"They's five of us, Johnny," a TF gunhawk said.

"There won't be when the smoke clears."

Donnie and the others thought about that for a moment. "I reckon I'll ride with you, Johnny," Donnie said.

"Fine. You others hightail it back to the TF. You tell Tilden Franklin that from now on I'll be workin' out at Colby's place. Tell him to keep his ass and your asses off that range. You got all that?"

"Yes, sir, Johnny," a young TF gunnie said.

"Yes, sir, *Mister North*!"

"Yes, sir, Mister North!"

"Ride!"

The TF gunnies laid the spurs to their horses and left in a cloud of dust and drumming hooves. None of them was lookin' forward to delivering this news to Tilden Franklin. But none of them wanted to tangle with Johnny North neither. Lesser of two evils, they figured.

"You ride in front of me, Donnie," Johnny said. "Move out."

There were a lot of things Donnie wanted to say. Wisely, he said none of them. Just silently cussed.

25

"There was five of you!" Tilden shouted at the men. "Five of you! I'm paying you men good money, fighting wages. But so far, I've seen damn little fighting. But a hell of a lot of running. What does it take to put some backbone in you men?"

The gunslicks stood and took it in silence. Luis Chamba and his sidekicks, Kane and Sanderson, stood by the corner of the big house and smiled at the dressing-down Tilden was giving his gunhands.

When the chastised men had departed, Luis said, "Perhaps, *señor*, it is time for some night-riding, *sí*?"

Tilden shifted his cold eyes to the Mexican gunfighter. "I'll pass the word, Luis. You're in charge. The others take orders from you. *Cooriente*?"

Luis smiled his reply.

"Make your plans, Luis."

"This game, *señor* . . . what are the limits?"

"No limits, Luis. Let the chips fall."

"I likc this game, *señor*," Luis said with a smile.

"I rather thought you would," Tilden said tightly.

* * *

Belle Colby stood in her front yard, Bob by her side, and listened to Donnie haltingly tell what had happened. The TF gunslick's face was flushed with anger, but he told it all, leaving nothing out.

When he had finished, Johnny said, "If I ever see you on this range, Donnie, I'll kill you. Now ride, punk— ride!"

Donnie wheeled his horse and galloped out.

Bob said, "Are you really Johnny North?"

"Yes. Ma'am?" He looked at Belle. "I'll be ridin' over to the Sugarloaf. I should be back by sundown. I'll bunk in the barn if that's all right with you."

"That will be fine, Mister North."

She had taken the news of her husband's death calmly. Too calmly for Johnny. He sat his horse and looked at her.

"You're wondering why I'm behaving in such a calm manner, Mister North?"

"The thought did pass my mind, ma'am."

"My husband told me before dawn this morning, as he was belting on a gun, that he was going into town. I felt then that I would never see him again. I did my grieving this morning."

Johnny nodded his head. He sat looking at the woman for a moment longer. Nice-looking woman; kind of trail worn, but that was to be expected, for this was a hard life for a woman. Then he thought of all the dance-hall floozies and hurdy-gurdy girls he had known down through the long and bloody years. Belle Colby, with her worn gingham dress, sunburned face, and work-hardened hands, seemed beautiful compared to them.

Johnny cleared his throat and plopped his hat back on his head. "You gonna need help around here, ma'am," he said. "If'n it's all right, I'll stick around and pull my weight and then some."

"That would be nice, Mister North," Belle said with a tired smile. "Yes. I'd like that."

Johnny returned the smile and wheeled his horse, heading to the Sugarloaf.

The crowd was respectable at Colby's burying, but not near so many people showed up as had at Adam's planting. Most men, whether they would say it aloud or not—and it was the latter if they were married—felt that Colby had done a damn fool thing. And while most of them didn't condone what Donnie had done, they probably would not have interfered. They might have done something similar had they been in Colby's boots, but it would have been done with a sawed-off express gun in their hands, not with a pistol in a fast-draw type of situation.

Out here, a man had damned well best know his limitations and capabilities.

And behave accordingly.

Once again the Reverend Ralph Morrow conducted the funeral services, and once again he and Bountiful and lots of others stayed for lunch. That was no problem, for everyone who attended the services had brought some sort of covered dish.

Like hangings, funerals also served as quite a social event.

Louis Longmont was there, all fancied up in a tailored black suit . . . carefully tailored to hide the shoulder-holster rig he wore under the jacket.

The aging gunfighters were all in attendance, gussied up in their best. They made no attempts to conceal their Colts, wearing them openly, low and tied down.

Pearlie had stayed behind at the Sugarloaf, just in case some TF riders decided to use the occasion to come calling. With a funeral of their own in mind.

Monte Carson and Judge Proctor were there, and so

were Hunt and Willow Brook, Colton and Mona Spalding, Haywood and Dana Arden.

Ed Jackson did not show. He figured he might lose a dollar or so by closing down his store.

Besides, Ed felt that Colby had gotten exactly what he deserved. And the next time he saw that Smoke Jensen, Ed just might give him a good piece of his mind about the totally uncalled-for beating of a fine man like Tilden Franklin. Well . . . he'd think about doing that, anyways.

"Going to stay on up here for a time?" Monte asked Johnny.

"Thought I might. Belle has her hands full all day just tryin' to look after Velvet, and I think me and Bob can pretty well handle it. And some of them old gunslingers come over from time to time, Belle says. Them old boys know a lot about farming and such."

Monte and Judge Proctor said their goodbyes to Belle and returned to Fontana.

By late afternoon, most of those attending had left for home, since many had traveled miles to get there. About half of the old gunslicks had left, returning to the Sugarloaf to give Pearlie a break.

Louis had returned with Monte and Judge Proctor, riding a magnificent black stallion.

"Like to ride over and spend the night at our place?" Smoke asked Reverend Morrow. "It's a lot closer than town, and we have the room. 'Sides, I'd like Sally and Bountiful to get to know each other."

After he consulted with his wife, the young couple agreed. Those returning to the Sugarloaf made their way slowly homeward, Smoke and Sally and Ralph and Bountiful in buckboards, the rest on horseback.

"It's so beautiful up here," Bountiful said, squeezing her husband's arm. "So peaceful and lovely and quiet. I think I would like to live up here."

"Might have a hard time supporting a church up here, Bountiful."

"Yes, that's true. But you could do what you've always wanted to do, Ralph."

He looked at her, beautiful in the sunlight that filtered through the trees alongside the narrow road.

"You would be content with that, Bountiful? A part-time preacher and a full-time farmer?"

"Yes."

"You're sure?"

"I'm sure of several things, Ralph. One is that I'm not cut out to be a preacher's wife. I love you, but that isn't enough. Secondly, I'm not so sure you're cut out to be a preacher."

"It's that obvious, Bountiful?"

"Ralph, nothing happened back East. It was a harmless flirtation and nothing more. I think you've always known that. Haven't you?"

"I suspected. I should have whipped that scoundrel's ass while I was feeling like it."

He spoke the words without realizing what he had really said.

Bountiful started laughing.

"What is so . . ." Then Ralph grinned, flushed, and joined his wife in laughter.

"Ralph, you're a good, decent man. I think you're probably the finest man I have ever known. But you went into the ministry out of guilt. And I think that is the wrong reason for choosing this vocation. Look at us, Ralph. Listen to what we're saying. We've never talked like this before. Isn't it funny, odd, that we should be doing so now?"

"Perhaps it's the surroundings." And for a moment, Ralph's thought went winging back in time, back almost eight years, when he was a bare-knuckle fighter enjoying no small amount of fame in the ring, open-air and smokers.

The young man he'd been fighting that hot afternoon was good and game, but no match for Ralph. But back then, winning was all that Ralph had on his mind, that and money. And he was making lots of money, both fighting and gambling. The fight had gone on for more than thirty rounds, which was no big deal to Ralph, who had fought more than ninety rounds more than once.

And then Ralph had seen his opportunity and had taken it, slamming a vicious left-right combination to the young man's head.

The young man had dropped to the canvas. And had never again opened his eyes. The fighter had died several days later.

Ralph Morrow had never stepped into another ring after that.

He and Bountiful had known each other since childhood, and it was taken for granted by all concerned that they would some day marry. Bountiful's parents were relieved when Ralph quit the ring. Bountiful was a bit miffed, but managed to conceal it.

Both had known but had never, until now, discussed the obvious fact that Ralph simply was not cut out to be a minister.

"What are you thinking, Ralph?"

"About the death I caused."

"It could just as easily have been you, Ralph," she reminded him. "You've told me a thousand times that the fight was fair and you both were evenly matched. It's over, Ralph. It's been over. Stop dwelling on it and get on with the matter of living."

Quite unlike the strait-laced minister, he leaned over and gave Bountiful a smooch on the cheek. She blushed while the old gunfighters, riding alongside the buckboards, grinned and pretended not to notice.

* * *

After supper, the young couples sat outside the cabin, enjoying the cool air and talking.

"How many acres do you have, Smoke?" Ralph asked.

"I don't really know. That valley yonder," he said, pointing to the Sugarloaf, "is five miles long and five miles wide. I do know we've filed on and bought another two thousand acres that we plan to farm. Right now we're only farming a very small portion of it. Hay and corn mostly. Right over there"— again he pointed—"is seven hundred and fifty acres of prime farmland just sittin' idle. I think we overbought some."

"That acreage is just over that little hill?" Bountiful asked.

"Yes," Sally said, hiding a smile, for it was obvious that the minister and his wife were interested in buying land.

"We'll ride over in the morning and take a look at it, if you'd like," Smoke suggested.

"Do you have a proper saddle for Bountiful?" Ralph asked.

"We're about the same size," Sally told him. "She can wear some of my jeans and ride astride."

Bountiful fanned her suddenly hot face. She had never had on a pair of men's britches in her life. But . . . this was the West. Besides, who would see her?

"I don't know whether that would be proper for a minister's wife," Ralph objected.

"Don't be silly!" Sally said, sticking out her chin. "If it's all right for a man, why should it be objectionable for a woman to wear britches?"

"Well . . ." Ralph said weakly. Forceful women tended to somewhat frighten him.

"Have you ever read anything by Susan B. Anthony, Bountiful?" Sally asked.

"Oh, yes! I think she's wonderful, don't you?"

"Yes. As well as Elizabeth Cady Stanton. You just wait, Bountiful. Someday women will be on an equal footing with men."

"Lord save us all!" Smoke said with a laugh. He shut up when Sally gave him a dark look.

"Do you think the time will come when women will be elected to Congress?" Bountiful asked.

Ralph sat stunned at the very thought.

Smoke sat grinning.

"Oh my, yes! But first we have to work very hard to get the vote. That will come only if we women band together and work very hard for it."

"Let's do that here!" Bountiful said, clapping her hands.

"Fine!" Sally agreed.

"But how?" Bountiful sobered.

"Well . . . my mother knows Susan B. very well. They went to school together in Massachusetts. I'll post a letter to Mother and she can write Miss Anthony. Then we'll see."

"Wonderful!" Bountiful cried. "I'm sure Willow and Mona and Dana would be delighted to help us."

Smoke rolled a cigarette and smiled at the expression on Ralph's face. The man looked as though he might faint at any moment.

The ladies rose and went chattering off into the cabin.

"My word!" Ralph managed to blurt out.

Smoke laughed at him.

"Boss!" Pearlie stilled the laughter and sobered the moment. "Look yonder." He pointed.

In the dusk of fast-approaching evening, the western sky held a small, faint glow.

"What is that?" Ralph asked. "A forest fire?"

"No," Smoke said, rising. "That's Peyton's place. Tilden's hands have fired it."

26

There was nothing Smoke could do. Peyton's spread was a good twenty-five miles away from Sugarloaf, his range bordering Tilden's holdings.

It was not long before the fire's glow had softened, and then faded completely out.

"Peyton refused our offer of help," Buttermilk said. "Some of us offered to stay over thar with him. But he turned us down flat."

"We'll ride over in the morning," Smoke said. "At first light. There is nothing we can do this evening."

"Except wonder what is happening over there," Ralph stated.

"And so many funerals you gonna have to hold," Luke added.

Peyton, his wife June, and their kids had been forced to retreat into the timber when it became obvious they were hopelessly outnumbered and outgunned. The family had made it out of the burning, smoking area with the clothes on their backs and nothing else.

They had lain quietly in the deep timber and watched their life's work go up, or down, in fire. They had watched as the hooded men shot all the horses, the pigs, and then set the barn blazing. The corral had been pulled down by ropes, the garden trampled under the hooves of horses. The Peyton family was left with nothing. Nothing at all.

They could not even tell what spread the men had come from, for the horses had all worn different or altered brands.

The family lay in the timber long after the night-riders had gone. They were not hurt, not physically, but something just as important had been damaged: their spirit.

"I tried to be friends with Tilden," Peyton said. "I went over to his place and spoke with him. He seemed to be reasonable enough, thanked me for coming over. Now this."

"They turned the wagon over," June said, her eyes peering into the darkness. "Broke off one wheel. But that can be fixed. There's lots of land to be had just north of here. I won't live like this," she warned. "I will not. And I mean that."

"I got a little money. I can buy some horses. We'll see what we can salvage in the morning."

"Nothing," June said bitterly. "Nothing at all."

"And you don't have any idea who they were?" Smoke asked Peyton.

Dawn had broken free of the mountains only an hour before. Smoke and some of his old gunhawks had left the Sugarloaf hours before first light, stopping along the way at the other small spreads.

"No," Peyton said, a note of surrender in his voice.

The Apache Kid returned from his tracking. "Headin' for the TF spread," he said. "Just as straight as an arrow, that's where they're headin'."

"So?" June demanded, her hands on her hips. "So what? Prove that them riders come from the TF. And then even if you do that, see what the law will do about it."

"Now, June," Peyton said.

The woman turned around and walked off, her dress dirty and soot-covered.

"What are you gonna do?" Smoke asked Peyton.

"Pull out. What else is there to do?"

"We'll help you rebuild, just like we're doing with Wilbur Mason."

"And then what?" Peyton demanded. "What happens after that? I'll tell you," he blurted out. "The same thing all over again. No. I'll find me some horses, fix that busted wheel, and take off. This land ain't worth dyin' over, Smoke. It just ain't."

"That's not what you told me a few weeks back."

"I changed my mind," the man replied sullenly. "I don't feel like jawin' about it no more. My mind is made up. We're taking what we can salvage and pullin' out. Headin' up north of here. See you men." He turned and walked off, catching up with his wife.

"Let him go," Charlie said to Smoke. "He's not goin' to last anywhere out here. First time a drought hits him, he'll pack up and pull out. The locust come, he'll head out agin, always lookin' for an easy life. But he'll never find it. You know yourself it takes a hard man to make it out here. Peyton's weak, so's his woman. And them kids are whiners. He'll leave the land pretty soon, I'm figurin'. He'll get him a job in some little store, sellin' shoes and ribbons, and pretty soon he'll find something wrong with *that* job. But it ain't never gonna be his fault. It'll always be the fault of someone else. Forget him, Smoke. He ain't got no good sand bottom to him."

Smoke hated to say it, but he felt Charlie was right in his assessment of Peyton. Tilden had burned Wilbur

Mason out; that had just made Wilbur and his family all the more determined to stay and fight.

"Good luck, Peyton!" Smoke called.

The man did not even turn around. Just waved his hand and kept on walking.

Somehow that gesture, or lack of it, made Smoke mad as hell. He wondered if he'd ever see Peyton or his family again. He thought, if he didn't, he wouldn't lose any sleep over the loss.

The few other small rancher-farmers in the high country met that afternoon on a plateau just about halfway between Smoke's Sugarloaf and the beginning of the TF range. And it was, for the most part, a quiet, subdued gathering of men.

Mike Garrett and his two hands; Wilbur Mason and Bob Colby; Ray Johnson and his hired hand; Nolan Edwards and his two oldest boys; Steve Matlock; Smoke and his gunhands.

And Reverend Ralph Morrow, wearing a pair of jeans and checkered shirt.

"Ralph is gonna buy some land from me," Smoke explained. "Farm some and ranch a little. Preach part time. The minister come up with a pretty good idea, I'm thinking. But we'll get to his idea in a minute. Anybody got any objections to Ralph joinin' our group?"

"I ain't got no objections," Ray said. "I'm just wonderin' if, him bein a preacher and all, will he fight?"

Ralph stepped forward. "Some of you might know me. For five years, I went by another name. I fought under the name of the Cincinnati Kid."

Matlock snapped his fingers. "I read about you in the *Gazette*. You kilt a man . . . ah . . ."

He trailed off into an uncomfortable silence.

"Yes," Ralph said. "I killed a man with my fists. I didn't mean to, but I did. As to whether I'll fight. Yes. For my family, my land, my friends. I'll fight."

And everyone there believed him. Still, one had to say, "But, Reverend Morrow, you're a minister; you can't go around shootin' folks!"

Ralph smiled . . . rather grimly. "Smoke and Charlie and some of the boys are going to help me build my cabin, first thing in the morning. You let some sucker come around and start trouble, you'll see how fast I'll shoot him."

The laughter helped to relieve the tension.

And Reverend Ralph Morrow suddenly became just "one of the boys."

"How about that other idea, Smoke?" Wilbur asked.

Smoke walked to the edge of the flats. He pointed down at the road. "That road, right there, connects Danner and Signal Hill. Seven, eight miles further down, you got to cut south to get to Fontana. Right?"

All agreed that was true. So?

"Pearlie is ridin' hard to the county seat right now. The reverend and his wife, Bountiful, come up with this idea at noonin'. Right here, boys, right here on this plateau, but back yonder a ways, there's gonna be a town. We don't need Fontana. The land the town will be built on is gonna be filed on by Pearlie; he's carrying the money to buy some of it outright. When that surveyor was through here last year, he left a bunch of his markings and such at the house. Never did come back for them. Sally remembered 'em this morning. Everything is gonna be legal and right. My wife is puttin' up the money to build a large general store. I figure that once I explain it all to Louis Longmont, he'll see the humor in it and drop some of his money in. I'm hopin' he will. Pretty sure. Pearlie is carryin' a letter to the bank at the county seat; me and my wife have some money there." He grinned. "She has a heap more than I do. Wilbur Mason and his wife is gonna run the store for us. Wilbur owned a store back east of here at one time. So they both know what to do.

"Day after tomorrow, there's gonna be wagons rolling in here. Lumber, and a lot of it. We're gonna have several buildings here, including a sheriff's office and a jail."

Everybody was grinning now. Some of the men were laughing outright.

"We're gonna have a saloon, 'cause you all know that a saloon is just as much a meetin' place as it is a place to drink. We're gonna have us a cafe, with home-cookin'. The women will see to that. It'll bring in some money— and I know you all could use that. A church too, where we can all go to services come Sunday morning. And . . . a school. Both Sally and Bountiful are schoolmarms. And I'm gonna tell y'all something: once the wives of Beaconfield and Jackson hear about this town, with a church and proper schoolhouse, don't you think they won't be putting the pressure on their husbands to lean toward us."

"Who's gonna be the sheriff?" Matlock asked.

"Charlie Starr," Smoke said with a grin. "He's still got an old badge he wore some years back down close to Durango. I think he'd make a damned good one. Any objections?"

None.

"Now we want this to be kept secret as long as possible. Soon as the wagons start rolling in, though, the cat's gonna be out of the bag. But by that time, there won't be a damned thing Tilden Franklin can do about it except cuss. Now here is something else. There ain't no post office in Fontana. Never has been. We've always had to ride over to either Danner or Signal Hill to the post office. We can post a letter on the stage that comes through Fontana, but that don't always mean it'll get where it's goin'. Sally wrote a letter this morning to the proper people up in Denver and also to her folks who have a lot of high-up connections back East. So I think we'll get us a post office.

"Now the name. That come pretty easy too. Last evenin', as Ralph and Bountiful was ridin' along, talkin', they come to this point, right down there." He pointed. "And she said, 'Oh, look at that beautiful big rock.'"

Smoke grinned. "Big Rock. Big Rock, Colorado!"

27

"The son of a bitch is doing *what*?" Tilden Franklin screamed the question at Clint.

"Buildin' a town," Clint said woefully. "Big Rock, Colorado."

Tilden sat down. "Well, he can't do that," he said with something very close to a pout. *"I* done built a town. A proper one."

"Maybe he can't, Boss. But somebody forgot to tell him that. Him and that goddamned preacher and their wives. And lemme tell you something about that preacher man. He's done up and bought some land from Smoke Jensen and his cabin is damn near complete. And maybe you oughta know this too: that preacher is more than just a preacher. He fought for some years under the name of the Cincinnati Kid."

Tilden stared at his foreman as if the man had lost his mind. Then he slowly nodded his head. "I read about him. He killed a man with his fists right before he was scheduled to fight . . . somebody big-named. Iron Mike or something like that. What's the point of all this, Clint? What does Jensen hope to prove by it?"

Clint sat down, rather wearily, and plopped his hat down on the floor beside the chair. "Damned if I know, Boss. I figured with his reputation, when we burned Mason out, he'd come shootin'. He didn't. I figured when we . . . they done it to Velvet and killed Adam, Smoke would come a-shootin'. He didn't. Luis and his bunch burned out Peyton. And Smoke builds him a town. I can't figure it."

"I won't even ask if the town is legal."

"It's legal, and that Lawyer Hunt Brook and his wife done moved his practice out of Fontana and up to Big Rock. I spied on them some this morning. Then I nosed around Big Rock myself. That's a mighty fine store that's goin' up. And the smells from that cafe got my mouth waterin'. Some of the nesters' wives and older girls is doin' the cookin'. And them miners is swarmin' all over the place. They got 'em a saloon too. Big Rock Saloon. No games, no girls. A nice church and school combination goin' up too. And a jail."

"And I guess they elected themselves a sheriff, did they?"

"Shore did. Charlie Starr is the sheriff, and Luke Nations is his deputy."

Tilden pounded his fists on the desk and cursed. He looked and behaved like a very large, spoiled, and petulant child.

Clint waited patiently. He had seen his boss act like this before.

When Tilden had calmed down, Clint said, "Herds look good."

Tilden fixed him with a baleful look. "That's wonderful, Clint. I can't tell you how impressed I am. I'm making thousands of dollars a week on gold shares. I should be making several more thousands in kickbacks, except that goddamned sheriff I put into office has turned holy-roller on me. I am paying several thousands of dollars a month for some of the finest gunhands in the West, and they can't seem to rid the country of one Smoke Jensen. The son of a bitch rides all over the country, usually by himself, and my so-called gunslicks can't or won't, tackle him."

Clint sat quietly, knowing his boss was not yet through.

"Now Johnny North has taken up with a damned nester woman. Judge Proctor hasn't had a drink in weeks; he's turned just as righteous as Monte Carson. My men are afraid, *afraid,* to go into *my goddamn town*!"

Tilden rose from behind his desk to pace the study. He turned to face Clint's back.

"Turn around and look at me!" he ordered. "Tell Luis to take his men into town and rid it of Monte and Proctor. Right now, Clint. Right now!"

Clint retrieved his hat and stood up. "Boss," he said patiently. "Are you talkin' about treein' a town?"

"Exactly."

Clint sighed and shook his head. He wished Tilden would get Smoke Jensen out of his mind and just get on with the business of ranching. The big foreman wished a lot of things, but he knew that Smoke Jensen had become an obsession with Tilden. He wasn't even talkin' much about Sally no more. His hatred of Smoke had nearly consumed the man.

And Clint felt—no, *knew*—somehow that Tilden wasn't goin' to win this fight. Oh, he would succeed in runnin' out the nesters who were weak to begin with. Like Peyton. But Peyton was long gone. And them that remained was the tough ones. Not cold-eyed tough like Luis Chamba and Kane and Sanderson and Valentine and Suggs and them other gunslicks Tilden had on the payroll, but tough like with stayin' power.

And now Tilden wanted to tree a Western town. He lifted his eyes, meeting the just-slightly-mad eyes of Tilden Franklin.

"Are you not capable of giving those orders, Clint?"

"Don't push on me, Boss," Clint warned. "Don't do it."

Tilden's face softened a bit. "Clint . . . we've been together for years. We've spent more than a third of our lifetimes together. We've had rough times before. You own ten percent of this ranch. You could have taken your profits and left years ago, started your own spread, but you stayed with me. Just stay with me a while longer, you'll see. Things will be like they were years ago."

"Boss, things ain't *never* gonna be like they was. Not ever agin."

Tilden picked up a vase and hurled it against a far wall, breaking the vase, showering the carpet with bits of broken ceramic. "It will!" he screamed. "You'll see, Clint. Just get rid of Smoke Jensen and those nesters will fold up and slink away. Now get out, Clint. Carry out my orders. *Get out,* damn you!"

Crazy! Clint thought. He ain't just obsessed . . . he's plumb crazy. *He's* the one who's livin' in a house of cards. Not them nesters, but Tilden Franklin.

"All right, Boss," Clint said. There was a different note in his voice, a note that Tilden should have picked up on. But he didn't. "Fine. I'll get out."

Clint left the big house and stood for a moment on the front porch. His eyes swept the immediate holdings of Tilden Franklin. Thousands and thousands of acres. Too goddamn much for one man, and that silly bastard isn't content with it. He wants more.

But not with my help.

Clint walked to his own quarters and began packing. He would take only what he had to have to travel light. One packhorse. Clint had money. Being a very frugal man, he had banked most of his salary and the profits from selling the cows over the years.

He smiled, not a pleasant smile. Tilden didn't know

that he owned land up on the Gunnison, up near Blue Mesa. Owned it under the name of Matthew Harrison. Everybody around here knew him as Clint Harris. He'd changed his name as a snot-nosed boy, when he'd run off from his home down in Texas, after he'd shot his abusive stepfather. Clint never knew whether he'd killed the man, or not. He'd just taken off.

And that was what he was going to do now. Just take off.

The foreman—no! he corrected that—ex-foreman . . . had not had a good night's sleep since that . . . awfulness with Velvet Colby. He sat down at his rough-hewn desk and slowly wrote out instructions on a piece of paper. Finished with the letter, he walked to the door and opened it, calling for a puncher to get over there.

"Billy, can you read and write?"

"Yes, sir, Mister Clint," the cowboy said. "I finished sixth grade."

"Fine. Come on in." With the cowboy inside Clint's quarters, Clint pointed to the letter. "Sign your name where it says Witness."

"Yes, sir, Mister Clint." The cowboy did not read the letter; that wasn't none of his business. He signed his name. "You want me to date this, Mister Clint?"

"Yes. Good thought, Billy."

After Billy had gone, Clint looked around his spartan living quarters. Looked around for one last time. He could see nothing left that he wished to take. Outside, he rigged the packhorse and swung onto his own horse. Looking around, he spotted several punchers just down from the high country. They walked over to him.

"Where you goin', Mister Clint?" a puncher called Rosie asked.

"Haulin' my ashes, Rosie. And if you got any sense about you, you will too." He looked at the others. "All of you."

"You got a new job, Mister Clint?" a cowboy named Austin asked.

"Yeah, I do, Austin. And I'm hirin' punchers. I'm payin' forty a month and found. You interested?"

They all were.

Clint figured he could run his place with four hands, including himself. At least for a time.

"Pack your warbags, boys. And do it quiet-like. Meet me just north of Big Rock, south of Slumgullion Pass."

He swung his horse's head and moved out.

The punchers moved quietly to the bunkhouse and packed their meager possessions. One by one, they moved out, about thirty minutes behind Clint. None of them knew why the foreman was pullin' out. But with Clint gone, damned if they was gonna stay around with all these lazy-assed, overpaid gunhands.

As they rode over and out of TF range, they met other TF punchers—not hired guns, cowboys. The punchers looked at those leaving, put it all together, and one by one, silently at first, made their plans to pull out.

"I ain't seen my momma in nigh on three years," one said. "I reckon it's time to head south."

"I got me a pard works over on the Saguache," another said. "Ain't seen him in two, three years. It's time to move on anyway."

"I know me a widder woman who owns a right-nice little farm up near Georgetown," yet another cowboy said. "I'm tared of lookin' at the ass end of cows. I think I'll just head up thataway."

"I ain't never seed the ocean," another cowboy lamented. "I think I'll head west."

Clint rode into Big Rock and tied his horses at the post outside the Big Rock Saloon. As he was stepping up onto the still-raw-smelling boardwalk, he saw Johnny North and that Belle Colby woman coming out of the general store. They stopped to chat with Lawyer Hunt Brook.

Clint removed his gunbelt and walked slowly over to them. Johnny saw the man coming at him and instinctively slipped the thongs off the hammers of his Colts. Then he noticed that Clint was not armed. His eyes found the packhorse.

"What the hell . . ." he muttered.

Clint had some papers in his right hand.

Clint stopped about twenty-five feet from the trio. "I'm friendly," he said.

"Come on," Johnny said.

Clint held the papers out to Belle. Slowly, she took them. Clint said, "It won't make up for what was done to your daughter and your husband, but it's something I'd like to do." He turned and walked back to his horses.

Belle, Johnny, and Hunt watched him swing into the saddle and ride out of their lives.

"Let me see those papers, Belle," Hunt said. The lawyer quickly scanned first one paper, then the others— older, slightly yellowing around the edges. He began to smile.

"What is it, Mister Brook?" Belle asked.

"Why, Belle . . . you own ten percent of the TF Ranch. I think you have just become a very wealthy woman."

Tilden called for his houseboy.

"Yes, sir?"

"Get Clint for me, boy."

"Yes, sir."

The houseboy returned a few minutes later. "Sir? Mister Clint is gone."

"Gone . . . where, damnit?"

"He packed up and rode out. His quarters is empty, and so is the bunkhouse. Old Ramon at the stable says all the punchers packed up and left. Following Mister Clint."

"Get out!" Tilden said, real menace in his voice.

"Yes, sir," the houseboy said. "I most certainly will do that, Mister Tilden."

Thirty minutes later, the servant had packed his kit and was walking toward Fontana.

In his study, Tilden called for his houseboy. "Bring me a cup of coffee, boy!"

The big house creaked in empty silence.

"Boy!" Tilden roared. "You bring me a cup of coffee or I'll take a whip to your lazy greaser ass!"

Silence. And Tilden Franklin, the man who would be king, knew he was alone in his large, fine home.

He walked to a large window and looked out. His thoughts were savage. "I'm gonna kill you, Jensen. I'm gonna bring Fontana to its knees first. Then I'm gonna burn your goddamn Big Rock to the ground. Then I'm gonna kill you and have your woman."

He walked to a rack and took down his gunbelt, buckling it around his hips. He put his hat on his head and walked outside.

"Ramon?" he yelled.

"Sí, señor?" the old man called.

"Bring me my horse. Then you find your mule and get Luis for me."

"Sí, señor." Son of a bitch! he silently added.

28

The houseboy heard the thundering of hooves long before he saw them. He did not know what they meant, other than a lot of riders were in a big hurry. He shifted his heavy satchel to his other hand and trudged on, walking along the side of the rutted dirt road. As the thunder grew louder, he turned around, fear and panic on his face.

"Ride the insubordinate bastard down!" he heard Tilden Franklin scream, his voice just carrying over the steel-shod thunder.

The houseboy tried to run. He dropped his belongings and leaped to one side. He was too slow.

The rushing shoulder of a horse hit him in the back, tossing him to the road. Pain filled him as he heard his bones break. He looked up in time to see Tilden's crazed face and his stallion rear up, the hooves flashing in the hard sunlight.

The houseboy screamed.

His screaming was cut off as the steel hooves came down on his face, crushing his skull. The riders galloped on, leaving the houseboy lying in the road, his blood staining and dampening the dust.

They were fifty-odd strong, drunk not with alcohol, but with the power given them by Tilden Franklin. Raw, unbridled, killing power. He was paying them good money, and offering them immunity and total impunity.

From the law. None of them was taking Smoke Jensen into consideration as any form of punishment. They should have.

One deputy saw them coming hard and ran for his horse. He hauled his ashes, leaving everything he owned behind him in Fontana. If it ever calmed down, he might be back. If not, to hell with it!

Yet another deputy, nicknamed Stonewall, saw the riders coming and ran across the street to the sheriff's office. "Monte!" he hollered, jumping into the office and running to the shotgun rack. "Tilden and his gunhawks comin' fast. Get ready."

A third deputy ran inside the office-jail just as gunfire ripped the street. Like Monte and Stonewall, he grabbed a Greener from off the rack and stuffed his pockets full of shells.

"Take the back, Dave," Monte said, his voice calm. "Where are the others?"

"I seen Slim haulin' his ashes outta here," Dave told him. "I think Joel is out in the county somewheres servin' a notice from Judge Proctor."

"Stay calm," Monte told his men. "We got some food, and we got a pump for water. Tilden wanted this place built of stone for strength, so that's gonna work agin him. It'd take a cannon to bring these walls down."

"Hey!" a miner back in lockup hollered. "What about me?"

"Turn him loose and give him a shotgun," Monte ordered. "If he tried to get of here, those gunnies would cut him to rags."

The miner looked out at the angry group of heavily armed riders. "Who the hell is all them people?"

"That's your buddy, Tilden Franklin, and his gun-hands," Stonewall told him. "Would you like to go out and kiss him hello?"

"Would you like to kiss another part of me?" the miner challenged.

Stonewall laughed and handed the man a sawed-off shotgun and a sack of shells.

Monte called out through an open but barred window "As sheriff I am ordering you to break this up and leave this town or you'll all be under arrest."

"That's gonna be a good trick," Dave muttered.

A TF gunhand made the mistake of firing into the jail. Monte lifted his express gun and blew the rider clear out of the saddle.

The street erupted in gunfire, the hard exchange returned from those in the fortlike jail.

Blood dropped onto the dusty street as the shotguns cleared half a dozen saddles of living flesh, depositing dead, dying, and badly wounded men into the dirt.

Monte reloaded his express gun and lined up a gunhand he knew only as Blackie. He gave Blackie both barrels full of buckshot. The double charge lifted the gunhand out of the saddle, a hole in his chest so large it would take a hat to cover it.

The screaming of frightened and bucking horses filled the gunsmoke air. The riders were hard pressed to control their mounts, much less do any fighting.

Louis Longmont stepped out of his gaming tent, a Colt in each hand. As calmly as in a seconded duel, Louis lifted first one Colt and then the other, firing coolly and with much deliberation. He emptied two saddles and then paused, not wanting to shoot a horse.

The man who owned and cooked at the Good Eats Cafe stepped out of his place with a Sharps .50. The man, a Civil War veteran with four hard years of fighting as a

Union cavalryman, lifted the Sharps and emptied yet another saddle.

Big Mamma ran out of her place and literally jerked one gunhand off his horse. She began smashing his face with big, hard fists, beating the man into bloody unconsciousness.

Billy, up in the loft of the stable with his newly bought .22 caliber rifle, grinned as he took careful aim at the big man on the big horse. Gently he squeezed the trigger.

And shot Tilden Franklin smack in one cheek of his ass.

With a roar of rage, Tilden wheeled his horse around and took off at a gallop, out of town, the gunhands following closely.

Nobody treed a Western town in the 1870s. Nobody. Nearly every man in every town was a combat veteran of some war, whether it be against Indians, outlaws, the Union Blue, or the Rebel Gray. But nobody treed a Western town.

Two years prior to the formation of Fontana, back in September of 1876, Jesse James and his outlaw gang had tried to collar Northfield, Minnesota. They were shot to rags by the townspeople.

The dust settled slowly, and a quiet settled over Fontana. Only the moaning of the badly wounded TF gunslicks could be heard. Doctor Spalding came wheeling up in his buggy, sliding to a halt in the street. His unbelieving eyes took in the carnage before him. He began counting. He stopped at ten, knowing there were several more scattered about in the dirt and dust.

Monte and his deputies stepped out of the jail building. "Get 'em patched up, Doc," he said. "Them that is able, bunk 'em in yonder." He jerked his thumb toward the jail. "You!" His eyes found a man lounging about. "Git the undertaker on down here."

The photographer was coming at an awkward run, his tripod-and-hood, camera-and-flash container a cumbersome burden. He set up and began taking pictures.

"Sheriff!" Doc Spalding called. "Most of these men are dead. Several more are not going to make it much longer."

"Good," Monte said. "Saves the town the expense of a trial."

Tilden Franklin lay on his belly, in bed, while the old camp cook probed and poked at his buttock, finally cutting out the small .22 slug. He dropped the bloody pellet into a pan.

"Somebody was a-funnin' you with that thing," the cook observed.

Tilden swore, loud and long.

News of the attempted collaring of Fontana was quick to reach Big Rock and the small spreads scattered out from it. When Smoke took the news to Ralph, the minister sat down on a log he was hewing and laughed.

"Billy shot Tilden Franklin in the ass!" he hollered, then started laughing again.

Bountiful came on the run, sure something was wrong with her husband. Sally was with her. The ladies had been working, making a list of prospective members for the Big Rock Women for Equal Rights Club.

"What's wrong?" Bountiful asked.

"Billy shot Tilden Franklin in his big ass!" Ralph again hollered, then bent over with laughter.

The laughter was infectious; soon they were all howling and wiping their eyes.

Judge Proctor was furious. Since he had begun his program of alcohol abstention, he had realized he was supposed to help maintain law and order, not make a mockery of it by drunken antics.

The judge signed arrest warrants for Tilden Franklin and as many of the TF gunslicks that people on the street could recall being present during the shooting spree.

Louis Longmont put up a five-thousand-dollar reward for the arrest and conviction of Tilden Franklin, and the judge had Haywood's printing press cranking out wanted posters for Tilden Franklin. He then had them posted throughout the county.

Louis thought it all hysterically amusing.

Now everybody, or most everybody, knew that no one was really going to try to arrest Tilden Franklin. Or, for that matter, any of the TF gunhawks. But it did keep them out of Fontana and Big Rock and, for the most part, confined to the TF ranges. Punching cattle. Which pissed off the gunslicks mightily.

"You got no choice," Tilden said to his new foreman, Luis Chamba. Tilden was unshaven, and sitting on a pillow. "Not if you want to stay alive. All them damned old gunslingers have ringed my range. They're just waiting for you or me or some of the others to step off of this range. Anyway, what are you boys bitching about? You're all drawing top wages for sitting around really doing nothing." Tilden did manage a rueful smile. "Except herdin' beeves, that is."

Luis did not see the humor in it. He stalked out of the

great house. But Luis was no fool. He knew that, for the time being, he was stuck. Herding cattle.

And then two things happened that would forever alter the histories of Fontana and Big Rock and the lives of most of those who called them home.

Belle Colby, accompanied by Johnny North and Lawyer Hunt Brook, claimed her ten percent of the TF.

And Utah Slim finally made his move, setting out to do what he had been paid to do.

Kill Smoke Jensen.

29

"Riders coming, Boss!" Luis Chamba hollered through an open window of the large home.

"Who are they?" Tilden shouted, returning the holler. He was sitting in his study, drinking whiskey. The interior of the home was as nasty as Tilden Franklin's unwashed body and unshaven face.

"Can't tell yet," the gunslinger called. "But there's a woman in a buckboard, I can tell that much."

Tilden heaved himself up and out of his chair. For a moment, the big man swayed unsteadily on his booted feet. He stumbled to a water basin and washed his face. Lifting his dripping face, he stared into a mirror. He was shocked at his appearance. A very prideful man, Tilden had always been a neat dresser and almost fastidious when it came to washing his body.

He could smell his own body odors wafting up to assail his nostrils. With a grimace, he called to Luis.

"Tell them I'll be out in fifteen minutes, Luis."

"*Sí*, Boss."

Hurriedly, Tilden washed himself best he could out back of the great house and toweled himself dry. He had water on the stove heating for shaving. He shaved, very carefully, noting his shaking hands. Somehow, he managed not to nick his face.

For some reason, his crazed mind felt that the woman in the buckboard was Sally Jensen, coming to see him.

Tilden splashed Bay Rum on his face and sprinkled some on his body, then dressed in clean clothes. He was shocked when he stepped out onto the porch and saw it was not Sally Jensen.

The woman was Belle Colby. With her were Johnny North, the lawyer Hunt Brook, Sheriff Monte Carson, and someone Tilden had never seen before. A man dressed in a dark suit, white shirt, and string tie. His face was tanned and his eyes were hard. He had a drooping mustache.

He cleared up who he was in a hurry. "My name is Mitchell," he said. "United States Marshal. I don't know who started the war in this part of the country, Franklin, and I don't much care. But I'm delivering two messages today. One to you, another to Smoke Jensen. The war is over. If I have to come back in here, I'll bring the Army with me and declare a state of martial law. You understand all that?"

"Yes . . . sir," Tilden said, the words bitter on his tongue. He glared at Carson.

"Fine," Mitchell said. "Now then, Lawyer Brook is here representing Mrs. Colby. Me and Sheriff Carson will just sit here and see that the lady gets her due."

"Her . . . *due*?" Tilden questioned.

Briefly, Hunt Brook explained. He further explained that the papers given Belle Colby were now part of court records.

"I want to see your books, Mister Franklin," Hunt told Tilden. "When that is done, I shall determine how much is owed Mrs. Colby. She has confided in me that she is willing to sell her ten percent back to you. Once a fair price is determined. By me. Shall we get to it, Mister Franklin?"

Speaking through an almost blind rage, Tilden started to choke out his reply. Then some small bit of reason crept into his mind. He did not want these people inside his smelly house. That would not look good, and the word would get around.

"I'll get my books. We'll go over them on the porch. All right?"

"Fine, Mister Franklin," the lawyer said.

Luis Chamba had discreetly disappeared into the bunk house. He had known who Mitchell was at first sighting. And while the Mexican gunfighter felt he could best him, no one in their right mind killed a federal marshal. He told his men to stay low and out of sight.

Chamba felt, along with many of the other gunhands, that Tilden Franklin had just about come to the end of his string. But as long as he could pay the money, they would stay. Anyways, Luis wanted his chance at Smoke Jensen. Now that the elusive gunfighter had finally surfaced, a lot of gunslicks wanted to try their skills against his.

Tilden was seething as the lawyer went over his books. As far as the money went, the money to buy out Belle Colby, Tilden had that much in his safe inside the house. It wasn't the money. It was the fact that Clint had given his percentage to this trashy nester woman. Husband not even cold in the grave and she was probably hunchin' and bumpin' the gunslinger Johnny North. Trash, that's all she was.

Tilden listened as the lawyer quoted an absurdly high figure. But Tilden wasn't going to quibble about it. He just wanted his holdings intact, and this hard-eyed U.S. marshal out of the area. Mitchell was damn sure wrong on one count, though: the war was not over. Not by a long shot.

"All right," Tilden said, agreeing to the figure.

The lawyer reached into his case and handed Tilden what the man knew was a binding note. He signed it, Belle signed it, and then Mitchell and North both witnessed it. Belle Colby was now a woman of some means.

Tilden Franklin sat in a chair and watched them leave. Slowly, the gunfighters began to once more gather around the porch.

"Play it close to the vest for a time," Tilden said. "Let that damned marshal get clear of this area. Then you'll all start earning your wages. I don't care who you have to kill in order to get to him, but I want Smoke Jensen dead. Dead, goddamnit . . . *dead*!"

U.S. Marshal Mitchell looked at the legendary gunfighter Smoke Jensen. He was even younger than Mitchell had been led to believe. The man was still a ways from thirty.

"If I tried real hard, Jensen, I probably could come up with half a dozen arrest warrants for you. You know that, don't you?"

Smoke grinned boyishly. "But findin' people to stand up in court, look me in the eyes, and testify against me might give you some problems."

Smart too, Mitchell thought. The marshal returned Smoke's smile. "There is always that to consider, yes."

"The war is not over, Marshal. You must know that."

"I mean what I say, Jensen. If I have to, I'll bring the Army in here. The Governor of the State of Colorado is tired of hearing about this place. In terms of blood."

"Tilden Franklin is a crazy man, Marshal. I don't know why he hates me, but he does. He will never rest until one of us is dead."

"I know that," Mitchell said. "But don't sell him short, Jensen. Not even Luis Chamba is as fast as Tilden Franklin. He's poison with a short gun."

"He thought he was poison with his fists too," Smoke replied, again with that boyish grin.

"So I heard." The marshal's reply was very dry. "That beating you gave him didn't help matters very much."

"It gave me a great deal of satisfaction."

"I really hope I never see you again, Jensen. But somehow I feel I will."

"I didn't start this, Marshal. But if it comes down to it, I'll damn sure finish it."

The marshal looked at Smoke for a moment. "Other than Tilden Franklin, you know anyone else who might pay a lot of money to have you killed?"

Smoke thought about that for a moment. Then he shook his head. "No, not right off hand."

Time took him winging back more than three years, back to the ghost town of Slate, where Smoke had met the men who had killed his brother and his father, then raped and killed his wife Nicole, and then killed Nicole and Smoke's son Arthur.

Mitchell, as if sensing what was taking place in Smoke's mind, stood motionless, waiting.

"Them old mountain men is pushin' us toward Slate," a gunhand said.

The one of the Big Three who had ordered all the killing, Richards, smiled at Smoke's choice of a show-down spot. A lot of us are going to be ghosts in a very short time, he thought.

As the old ghost town loomed up stark and foreboding on the horizon, located on the flats between the Lemhi River and the Beaverhead Range, a gunslick reined up and pointed. "The goddamn place is full of people."

"Miners," another of the nineteen men who rode to kill Smoke said. "Just like it was over at the camp on the Uncompahgre."

The men checked their weapons and stuffed their pockets full of extra shells and cartridges.

They moved out in a line toward the ghost town and toward the young gunfighter named Smoke.

"There he is," Britt said, looking up the hill toward a falling-down store.

Smoke stood alone on the old curled-up and rotted boardwalk. The men could just see the twin .44s belted around his waist. He held a Henry repeating rifle in his right hand, a double-barreled express gun in his left hand. Suddenly, Smoke ducked into the building, leaving only a slight bit of dust to signal where he once stood.

"Two groups of six," Richards said. "One group of three, one group of four. Move out."

Smoke had removed his spurs, hanging them on the saddlehorn of Drifter. As soon as he'd ducked out of sight, he had run from the store down the hill, staying in the alley. He stashed the express gun on one side of the street in an old store, his rifle across the weed-grown street.

He met the gunslick called Skinny Davis in the gloom of what had once been a saloon.

"Draw!" Skinny hissed.

Smoke put two holes in his chest before Davis could cock his .44s.

"In the saloon!" someone yelled.

Williams jumped through an open, glassless window of the saloon. Just as his boots hit the old warped boards, Smoke shot him, the .44 slug stopping him and twisting the gunhawk back out the window to the boardwalk. Williams was hurt, but not out of it. He crawled along the side of the building, one arm broken and dangling, useless.

"Smoke Jensen!" the gunnie called Cross called. "You ain't got the sand to face me."

"That's one way of putting it," Smoke muttered. He

took careful aim and shot the man in the stomach, doubling him over and dropping him to the dirty street.

The miners had hightailed it to the ridges surrounding the old town. There they sat, drinking and betting and cheering. The old Mountain Men, Preacher among them, watched expressionless.

The young man called Smoke, far too young to have been one of that rare and select breed of adventuring pioneers called Mountain Men, had, nonetheless, been raised, at least in part, by Preacher, so that made Smoke one of them. Indeed, the last of the Mountain Men.

A bullet dug a trench along the old, rotting wood, sending splinters flying, a few of them striking Smoke in the face, stinging and bringing a few drops of blood.

Smoke ran out the back, coming face-to-face with Simpson, the outlaw gunfighter having both his dirty hands filled with .44s.

Smoke pulled the trigger on his own .44s, the double hammer-blows of lead taking Simpson in the lower chest, knocking him dying to the ground.

Smoke reloaded, then grabbed up Simpson's guns and tucked them behind his belt. He ran down the alley. A gunslick stepped out of a gaping doorway just as Smoke cut to his right, jumping through a windowless opening. A bullet burned his shoulder. Spinning, he fired both Colts, one slug taking Martin in the throat, the second striking the outlaw just above the nose, almost removing the upper part of the man's face.

Smoke caught a glimpse of someone running. He dropped to one knee and fired. His slug shattered the hip of Rogers, sending the big man sprawling in the dirt, howling and cussing. Another gunslick spurred his horse and charged the building where Smoke was crouched. He smashed his horse's shoulder against the old door and came thundering inside. The animal, wild-eyed and scared, lost its footing and fell, pinning the outlaw to the floor, crushing the man's stomach and chest. The outlaw, Reese, cried in agony as blood filled his mouth and darkness clouded his eyes.

Smoke slipped out the side door.

"Get him, Turkel!" a hired gun yelled.

Smoke glanced up roof-level high; he ducked as a rifle bullet flattened against the building. Smoke snapped off a shot and got lucky, the slug hitting Turkel in the chest. He crashed through an awning, bringing down the rotting awning. The hired gun did not move.

A bullet removed a small part of Smoke's right ear; blood poured down the side of his face. He ran to where he had stashed the shotgun, grabbing it up and cocking it, leveling the barrels just as the doorway filled with gun-slicks.

Smoke pulled both triggers, fighting the recoil of the 12-gauge. The blast cleared the doorway of all living things.

"Goddamn you, Jensen," a hired gun yelled, his voice filled with rage and frustration. He stepped out into the street.

Smoke dropped the shotgun and picked up a rifle, shooting the gunhand in the gut.

It was white-hot heat and gunsmoke for the next few minutes. Smoke was hit in the side, twisting him into the open doorway of a rotting building where a dead man lay. Smoke picked up the man's bloody shotgun and stumbled into the darkness of the building just as spurs jingled in the alley. Smoke jacked back both hammers and waited.

The spurs came closer. Smoke could hear the man's heavy breathing. He lifted the shotgun and pulled both triggers, blowing a bullet-sized hole in the rotting pine wall.

The gunslick stumbled backward, and slammed into an outhouse. The outhouse collapsed, dumping the dying gunhand into the shit-pit.

Smoke checked his wounds. He would live. He reloaded his own Colts and the guns taken from the dead gunnie. He listened as Fenerty called for his buddies.

There was no response.

Fenerty was the last gunslick left.

He called again and Smoke pinpointed his voice. Picking up a Henry, Smoke emptied the rifle into the storefront. Fenerty came staggering out, stumbled on the rotting steps, and pitched face-forward into the street. There, he died.

Smoke laid down the challenge to Richards, Potter, and Stratton. "All right, you bastards!" he yelled. "Face me in the street if you've got the balls!"

The sharp odor of sweat mingled with blood and gunsmoke filled the summer air as four men stepped out into the death-street.

Richards, Potter, and Stratton stood at one end of the block. A tall, bloody figure stood at the other. All guns were in leather.

"You son of a bitch!" Stratton lost his cool and screamed, his voice as high-pitched as an hysterical girl's. "You ruined it all!" He clawed for his .44.

Smoke drew, cocked, and fired before Stratton's pistol could clear leather.

Screaming his outrage, Potter jerked out his pistol. Smoke shot him dead with his left-hand Colt. Holstering both Colts, Smoke faced Richards and waited.

Richards had not moved. He stood with a faint smile on his lips, staring at Smoke.

"You ready to die?" Smoke asked him.

"As ready as I'll ever be." There was no fear in his voice that Smoke could detect. Richards was good with a short gun, and Smoke kept that in mind. Richards's hands were steady. "Janey gone?"

"Took your money and pulled out."

Richards laughed. "Well, it's been a long run, hasn't it, Smoke?"

"It's just about over."

"What happens to all our—" He looked down at his dead partners. "—*my* holdings?"

"I don't care what happens to the mines. The miners can have them. I'm giving all your stock to decent, honest punchers and homesteaders."

A puzzled look crawled over Richards's face. "I don't understand. You mean, you did all . . . *this*!" He waved his left hand. "For nothing?"

Someone moaned, the sound painfully inching up the bloody, dusty, gunsmoke-filled street.

"I did it for my pa, my brother, my wife, and my baby son. You, or your hired guns, killed them all."

"But it won't bring them back!"

"Yeah, I know."

"I wish I had never heard the name of Jensen."

"After this day, Richards, you'll never hear it again."

"One way to find out," he replied with a smile, and went for his Colt. He cleared leather fast and fired. He was snake-quick, but he hurried his shot, the lead digging up dirt at Smoke's feet.

Smoke shot him in the right shoulder, spinning the man around. Richards drew his left-hand gun and Smoke fired again, the slug striking the man in the left side of his chest. He struggled to bring up his Colt. He managed to cock it before Smoke's third shot struck him in the belly. Richards sat down in the street, the pistol slipping from suddenly numbed fingers.

He opened his mouth to speak, and tasted blood on his tongue. The light began to fade around him. "You'll . . . meet . . ."

Smoke never found out, that day, who he was supposed to meet. Richards toppled over on his side and died.

Smoke looked up at the ridge where the Mountain Men had gathered.

They were gone, leaving as silently as the wind.

And to this day, he had never seen or heard from any of them again.

"You been gone a time, boy," Marshal Mitchell said.

Smoke sighed. "Just a few years. Bloody ones, though."

He told the marshal about that day in the ghost town.

"I never knew the straight of it, Smoke. But you did play hell back then. That person Richards told you you'd meet?"

"Yeah?"

"He was talkin' about the man who will be faster than you. We who live by the gun all have them in our future."

Smoke nodded his head. "Yeah, I know. And yeah, I know who would pay to see me dead."

"Oh?"

"My sister. Janey."

30

"Your own sister would pay to have you killed!" Bountiful said, appalled at just the thought. "How dreadful. What kind of person is she?"

Ralph and Bountiful were having supper with Smoke and Sally. "She must have a lot of hate in her heart," Ralph said.

"I reckon," Smoke said. "Well, I'll just have to be more careful and keep looking over my shoulder from now on." He smiled. "That's something I'm used to doing."

Then he remembered Utah Slim. The man had aligned with no side in the mountain country war. No, Smoke thought, he didn't have to. He already had a job.

U.S. Marshal Mitchell had told Smoke that his office had received word that a gunslick had been paid to kill Jensen. But none of their usual sources could, or would, shed any light on who that gunslick might be.

Or why.

Smoke felt he knew the answer to both questions.

Utah Slim.

"You've got a funny look in your eyes, Smoke," Sally said, looking at her husband.

"I'm not going to sit around and wait for a bullet, Sally. I just made up my mind on that."

"I felt that was coming too."

"What are you two talking about?" Bountiful asked.

"A showdown," Smoke told her, buttering a biscuit. He chewed slowly, then said, "Might as well brace him in the morning and get it over with."

Ralph and Bountiful stopped eating and sat staring at the young gunfighter. Ralph said, "You're discussing this with no more emotion than if you were talking about planting beets!"

"No point in gettin' all worked up about it, Ralph. If I try to avoid it, it just prolongs the matter, and maybe some innocent person gets caught up in it and gets hurt. I told you and your friends a time back that we do things differently out here. And I'm not so sure that it isn't the best way."

"In the morning?"

"In the morning."

"I'll go in with you," the minister turned farmer said. His tone indicated the matter was not up for debate.

"All right, Ralph."

Ralph was a surprisingly good horseman, and Smoke said as much.

"I was raised on a farm," he said. "And I'm also a very good rifle shot."

"I noticed you putting the Henry in the boot this morning."

The morning was very clear and very bright as the two men rode toward Fontana. As they worked their way out of the mountains and toward the long valley where Fontana was located, the temperature grew warmer.

"Ever shot a man, Ralph?"

"No."

"Could you?"

"Don't ever doubt it."

Smoke smiled faintly. He didn't doubt it for a minute.

The town of Fontana seemed to both men to be a bit smaller. Ralph commented on that.

"The easy pickings have been found and taken out, Ralph. For however long this vein will last, it's going to be hard work, dirty work, and dangerous work. Look yonder. One whole section of Fontana is gone. Half a dozen bars have pulled out."

"Why . . ." Ralph's eyes swept the visibly shrinking town that lay below them. "At this rate, there will be nothing left of Fontana by the end of summer."

"If that long," Smoke said, a note of satisfaction in his statement. "If we all can just settle the matter of Tilden Franklin, then we can all get on with the business of living."

"And it will have to be settled by guns." Ralph's remark was not put in question form. The man was rapidly learning about the unwritten code of the West.

"Yes."

Smoke reined up in front of Sheriff Monte Carson's office. The men dismounted and walked toward the bullet-scarred stone building. As they entered, Monte smiled and greeted them.

His smile faded as he noted the hard look in Smoke's eyes.

"I've had that same look a few times myself, Smoke," Monte said. "Gonna be a shootin'?"

"Looks that way, Monte. I'd rather not have it in town if I can help it."

"I'd appreciate that, Smoke. But sometimes it can't be helped. I got to thinkin' after talkin' with that marshal. It's Utah Slim, ain't it?"

"Yeah." Smoke poured a tin cup of coffee and sat down. "I got a strong hunch my sister hired him to gun me."

"Your . . . *sister*?"

Smoke told him the story of Janey. Or at least as much as he knew about her life since she'd taken off from that hard-scrabble, rocky, worthless farm in the hills of Missouri. Back when Smoke was just a boy, after their ma had died, when their pa was off fighting in the War Between the States. And Smoke had had to shoulder the responsibilities of a boy forced into early manhood.

It was a story all too common among those who drifted West.

It sounded all too painfully familiar to Monte Carson, almost paralleling his own life.

"I seen Utah early this mornin', sittin' on the hotel porch." He smiled. "The only hotel we got left here in Fontana, that is."

"Won't be long now," Smoke told him. "How many businesses are you losing a day?"

"Half a dozen. As you know, up there in Big Rock, the stage is runnin' twice a day now, carryin' people out of here."

"Seen some TF riders in town as we rode in," Smoke said. "And didn't see any of those flyers the judge had printed up. What happened?"

"Some state man was on the stage three, four days ago, from the governor's office. He looked at the charges I had agin Tilden and his men and told me to take them dodgers down. They wasn't legal." He shrugged. "I took 'em down."

Smoke grinned. "It was fun while it lasted, though, wasn't it?"

"Damn shore was."

Conversation became a bit forced, as both Monte and Smoke, both gunfighters, knew the clock was ticking toward a showdown in the streets of Fontana. Stonewall and Joel came into the office.

"Git the people off the boardwalks," Monte told his deputies. "And have either of you seen Utah Slim?"

"He's standin' down by the corral, leanin' up agin a post," Joel said. "He's got a half dozen of them punk gunslingers with him. They lookin' at Utah like he's some sort of god."

"Run 'em off," Monte ordered. "I'll not have no mismatched gunfight in this town."

The deputies left, both carrying sawed-off express guns.

Monte looked at Smoke after the office door had closed. "Utah is fast, Smoke. He's damn good. I'd rate him with the best."

"Better than Valentine?"

"He don't blow his first shot like Valentine, but he's just as fast."

Ralph looked out a barred window. "Streets are clear," he announced. "Nobody moving on the boardwalks."

Smoke stood up. "It's time." He slipped the leather thongs from the hammers of his Colts and put his hat on his head. "I'd like to talk to Utah first, find out something about my sister. Hell, I don't even know if she's the one behind this. I'll give it a try."

Smoke walked out onto the shaded boardwalks outside the sheriff's office. He pulled his hat lower over his eyes and eased his Colts half out of leather a few times, letting them fall back naturally into the oiled leather. He stepped out into the street and turned toward the corral.

As he walked down the center of the street, his spurs jingling and his boots kicking up little pockets of dust, he was conscious of many unseen eyes on him, and even a few he could associate with a body.

Stonewall and Joel were on the opposite sides of the broad street, both still carrying shotguns. The duded-up dandies who fancied themselves gunslingers had gathered as close to the corral as the deputies would allow them. Smoke saw the young punk Luke had made eat crow that day. Lester Morgan, Sundance. He had himself some new Colts. And that kid who called himself The Silver Dollar Kid was there, along with a few other no-names who wanted to be gunfighters.

Smoke wondered how they got along; where did they get eating money? Petty thievery, probably.

Louis Longmont had stepped out of his gaming tent. "How many you facing, Smoke?" he asked, as Smoke walked by.

"Just one that I know of. Utah Slim. I think my sis, Janey, sent him after me."

Louis paced Smoke, but stayed on the boardwalk. "Yes, it would be like her."

"Where is she, Louis?"

"Tombstone, last I heard. Runnin' a red-light place. She's worth a lot of money. Richards's money, I presume."

"Yeah. Richards ain't got no use for it. I never heard of no Wells Fargo armored stage followin' no hearse."

Louis laughed quietly. "I'll watch your back, Smoke."

"Thanks."

Smoke kept on walking. He knew Louis had fallen back slightly, to keep an eye on Smoke's back trail.

Then the corral loomed up, Utah Slim standing by the corral. Smoke's eyes flicked upward to the loft of the barn. Billy was staring wide-eyed out of the loft door.

"Billy!" Smoke raised his voice. "You get your butt outta that loft and across the street. Right now, boy— move!"

"Yes, sir!" Billy hollered, and slipped down the hay rope to the street. He darted across the expanse and got behind a water trough.

"That there's a good kid," Utah said. "Funny the other week when he shot Tilden in the ass."

"Yeah, I'd like to have seen that myself."

"I ain't got nothin' personal agin you, Jensen. I want you to know that."

"Just another job, right, Utah?"

"That's the way it is," the killer said brightly.

"My sister hire you?"

"Damned if'n I know. Some woman named Janey, down in Tombstone paid me a lot of money, up front." He squinted at Smoke. "Come to think of it, y'all do favor some."

"That's my darlin' sister."

"Makes me proud I ain't got no sister."

"Why don't you just get on your horse and ride on out, Utah? I don't want to have to kill you."

The killer looked startled. "Why, boy! You ain't gonna kill me."

"You want to wager on that?" Louis called.

"Yeah." Utah smiled. "I'll bet a hundred."

"Taken," Louis told him.

"How much did she pay you, Utah?" Smoke asked the man.

"Several big ones, boy." He grinned nastily. "She's a whoor, you know."

"So I heard." Smoke knew the killer was trying to anger him, throw him off, make him lose his composure.

"Yeah, she is," Utah said, still grinning. "I tole her, as part of the payment, I'd have to have me a taste of it."

"Is that right?"

"Shore is. Right good, too."

"I hope you enjoyed it."

"I did for a fact." This wasn't working out the way Utah had planned it. "Why do you ask?"

Smoke drew, cocked, and fired twice. Once with his right-hand Colt, that slug taking Utah in the chest and staggering him backward, and the second slug coming from his left-hand gun and striking the gunslick in the stomach, dropping the killer to his knees, his left arm looped around the center railing of the corral.

Smoke holstered his left-hand Colt and waited for Utah. The killer managed to drag his Colt out of leather and cock it. That seemed to take all his strength. He pulled the trigger. The slug tore up the dirt at his knees.

Utah dropped the Colt. He lifted his eyes to Smoke. Just as the darkness began to fade his world, he managed to gasp, "How come you axed me if I enjoyed it?"

" 'Cause you damn sure ain't gonna get no more, Utah."

Utah died hanging onto the corral railing. He died with his eyes open, staring at emptiness.

Smoke holstered his pistol and walked away.

31

The undertaker's hack rumbled past Louis Longmont's tent just as the gambler and the gunfighter were pouring tumblers of scotch.

Louis lifted his glass. "May I pay you a compliment, Smoke Jensen?"

"I reckon so, Louis."

"I have seen them all, Smoke. All the so-called great gunfighters. Clay Allison, John Wesley Hardin, Bill Longley, Jim Miller. I've drank with Wild Bill Hickok and Jim, Ed, and Bat Masterson. I've gambled with Doc Holliday and Wyatt Earp. I've seen them all in action. But you are the fastest gun I have ever seen in my life."

The men clinked glasses and drank of the Glenlivet.

"Thank you, Louis. But I'll tell you a secret."

Louis smiled. "I'll bet you a double eagle I already know what it is."

"No bets, Louis, for I imagine you do."

"You wish you were not the faster gun."

"You got that right."

The men finished their drinks and stepped out onto the

boardwalk. The photographer had set up his equipment at the corral and was taking his shots of Utah Slim. The duded-up dandies had gathered around, managing to get themselves in almost every shot the man took.

"Fools!" Smoke muttered.

"Look at them with their hands on the butts of their guns," Louis pointed out. "They'll be bragging about that picture for the rest of their lives."

"However short they may be," Smoke added.

"Yes."

Ralph walked up, joining the gambler and the gunfighter. Louis smiled at him.

"I would offer you a drink, Mister Morrow, but I'm afraid I might offend you."

"I'm not averse to a cool beer, Mister Longmont."

Louis was more than slightly taken aback. "Well, I'll just be damned!" he blurted.

"Oh, I think not, sir," Ralph replied. He met the man's cool eyes. "How is your orphanage up in Boulder doing? Or that free hospital out in San Francisco?"

Louis smiled. "For a man of the cloth, you do get around, don't you, Ralph?"

"But I wasn't always a preacher, Mister Longmont," he reminded the gambler.

"Tell me more," Smoke said with a grin, looking at Louis.

"Don't let the news of my . . . philanthropic urges get out," the gambler said. "It might destroy my reputation."

Smoke looked at him and blinked. "Hell, Louis! I don't even know what that means!"

Laughing, the men entered the gaming tent for a cool one.

And the photographer's flash pan popped again.

And Utah Slim still clung to the corral railing.

* * *

The town of Fontana had begun to die, slowly at first, and then more rapidly as the gold vein began to peter out. More businesses shut down, packed up, and pulled out. The rip-roaring boom town was not yet busted, but a hole had been pierced in the balloon.

Those who elected to stay until the very end of the vein had been found were slowly shifting their trading to the new town of Big Rock. But since the Mayor of Big Rock, Wilbur Mason, refused to allow gaming and hurdy-gurdy girls in, the town of Fontana soon became known as the pleasure palace of the high country.

But that was both a blessing and a curse for Sheriff Monte Carson and his three remaining deputies. A curse because it kept them on the run at all hours; a blessing because it kept them all in steady work, and doubly so for Monte, because it gave him a new direction in life to pursue. One that he found, much to his surprise, he enjoyed very much.

Louis had, of course, noticed the change in Monte, and in his quiet way tried to help the man, as did Judge Proctor, Louis helping the man with his reading and Proctor loaning him books on the law.

And Tilden Franklin maintained a very low profile, as did most of his gunslicks. Tilden wanted the area to settle down, stop attracting the governor's attention. More importantly, he wanted that damned hard-eyed U.S. marshal to stay out of the high country.

But both Tilden and Smoke knew that the undeclared war in the high country was not over, that the uneasy truce was apt to break apart at any time. And when it did, the high lonesome was going to run red with blood.

Someone was going to come out on top, and Tilden was making plans for that someone to be named Tilden Franklin. And he had not given up on his plans to possess Sally Jensen. Not at all. They had just been shelved for a time. But not forgotten.

* * *

The festering blot on the face of the high country began to leak its corruption when Paul Jackson rode into Fontana after a lonely six weeks in the mountains. Paul had heard talk of the new town of Big Rock, but had never seen it. He had heard talk of Fontana slowly dying, but had given it little thought. Paul had been busy digging gold. Lots of gold. More gold than even he had ever imagined he would ever find. His saddlebags were stuffed with the precious dust. His packhorses were loaded down.

He rode slowly into Fontana and could not believe his eyes. He had remembered a town, just six weeks past, full of people.

Place looked dead.

No, he corrected that. Just dying.

And where had the good people gone? Place looked to be full of whores and gamblers and pimps and ne'er-do-wells.

Made Paul feel kind of uncomfortable.

He reined up in front of the bank. But the damn bank was closed. He saw a deputy and hailed him.

Stonewall ambled over. "Something wrong, Paul?"

"Where's the bank?"

"Ain't got no bank no more, Paul," the deputy informed him. "It shut down when the gold began to peter out."

Paul, not a bright person to begin with, had to think about that for a minute or so.

"The gold is petering out?"

Now Stonewall never figured himself to be no genius, but even he was a shining light compared to this yo-yo sitting his horse in front of the empty bank building.

"Yeah, Paul. The vein is about gone. If you got gold, we can store it at the jail until you can figure out what to do with it."

"I plan on taking my woman and my gold out of here,"

Paul said. "We are going to San Francisco and becoming man and wife."

"Your . . . woman?"

"Yes. I should like to see Bountiful now. So if you'll excuse me . . ."

"The minister's wife . . . Bountiful?" Stonewall asked.

"Yes."

"Paul . . . they don't live here in Fontana no more. The preacher quit his church and took to farmin'. He bought hisself some land up near the Sugarloaf. He preaches ever' Sunday morning at the new church up in Big Rock."

"Bountiful?"

Stonewall was rapidly losing patience with this big dumbbell. "Why, hell, man! She's with her husband."

"Not when she sees me," Paul said, then swung his horses and rode slowly out of town, toward the high lonesome and the town of Big Rock.

And Bountiful.

"What the hell was all that about?" Monte asked, walking up to his deputy.

Stonewall took off his hat and scratched his head. "Sheriff, I don't rightly know. That Paul Jackson never was too bright, but I think the time up in the mountains has flipped him over the edge."

He told Monte the gist of the conversation.

"Strange," Monte agreed. "But Paul is gonna be in for a surprise if he tries to mess with Ralph's wife. That preacher'll whip his butt up one mountain and down the other."

"Surely Paul ain't *that* dumb!"

"Don't bet on it. Did he really have them horses loaded with gold?"

"Said he did."

"Outlaws workin' the high country; he'll be lucky if he makes it to Big Rock."

* * *

"Bountiful," Paul said, sitting his horse in front of the Morrow cabin. "I've come for you."

Bountiful blinked her baby blues. "You've . . . *come* for me?"

"Yes. Now get your things. I'm a rich man, Bountiful. We can have a beautiful life together. I'll buy you everything you ever dreamed of."

"Paul, everything I have ever dreamed of is right here." She waved her hand. "What you see is what I want. I have it all."

"But . . . I don't understand, Bountiful. The way you looked at me . . . I mean . . . I was sure about your feelings."

It had been that way all her life; men were constantly misreading her. Mistaking friendliness for passion. It was very difficult for a beautiful woman to have men friends.

"Paul, I like you. You're a good man. And I'm happy that you found gold. I hope it brings you a lot of happiness. And you'll find a nice lady. I just know it. Now you'd better leave."

Smoke and Ralph rode into the yard. Sally stepped out of the cabin where she had been helping Bountiful make curtains.

"Hello, Paul," Ralph said. "How have you been?"

"Very well, thank you, Ralph. I've come for your wife."

Ralph blinked. "I beg your pardon?"

Bountiful looked at Sally and shook her head. Sally knew the story; Bountiful had told her that Paul was infatuated with her.

"Leave, Paul," Sally told the man. "You've got everything all mixed up in your mind. It isn't the way you think it is."

"Is too!"

"Now Paul," Ralph said soothingly. "You don't want to make trouble for us. Why don't you just leave?"

Paul shook his head and dismounted. With a knife, he cut open one saddlebag, the yellow dust pouring out onto the ground.

"See, Bountiful?" Paul cried. "See? It's all for you. I did it for you. You can have it all."

"I don't want it, Paul," Bountiful said softly. "It's yours. You keep it."

Paul stood like a big, dumb ox, slowly shaking his head. It was all so confusing. He had thought he had it all worked out in his mind, but something was wrong.

Then he thought he knew what would bring Bountiful to him. "I know," he said. "You're afraid to leave because of Tilden Franklin. I can fix that for you, Bountiful. I really can."

"What do you mean, Paul?" Smoke asked.

Paul turned mean eyes toward Smoke. "You stay out of this. You're one of the reasons Bountiful won't go with me."

Smoke blinked. "Huh?"

"I can use a gun too," Paul said, once more looking at Bountiful. "I'll show you. I'll show you all."

Smoke looked at Paul's pistol. It was in a flap-type holster, the flap secured. Smoke figured he could punch Paul out before any real damage was done—if he went for his gun.

"I'll come back a hero, Bountiful," Paul said. "I'll be the hero of the valley, Bountiful." He cut the saddlebags loose and let them fall to the ground. He tossed the reins of the packhorses to the ground. "You keep this for me, Bountiful. Play with it. It's not as pretty as you. But it's pretty. I'll be back, Bountiful. You go on and pack your things. Wait for me."

Paul swung awkwardly into the saddle and rode off.

"Paul is not very bright," Ralph said. "What in the world do you suppose he's going to do?"

No one would even venture a guess.

Smoke squatted down and fingered the dust and the nuggets. He looked at them closely. Then he stood up with a sad smile on his face.

"It's all fool's gold."

"If it wasn't so pitiful, it would be funny," Ralph said. "But Paul really believes, after he does whatever in the world he plans to do, that Bountiful is going with him. I wonder what he has in mind."

"What was that about Tilden Franklin?" Sally asked.

"He said I was afraid to leave because of Tilden Franklin," Bountiful said. "But that's silly. Why should I be afraid of that man?"

No one could answer that.

And in a few hours, it wouldn't matter to Paul either.

32

"Rider comin', Boss," Valentine called to Tilden.

Tilden stepped out onto the porch and squinted his eyes against the sun. It was that fool shopkeeper's brother, Paul Jackson. "What in the hell does he want?"

"That one ain't playin' with a full deck," Slim said. "That's the one used to foller the preacher's wife around with his tongue a-hangin' out like a big ugly hound dog."

"He looks like a hound dog," Donnie observed. "A goofy one."

The gunfighters had a good laugh at that remark; even Tilden laughed. But for some reason he could not explain, the big man slipped the thongs off his six-guns.

Luis Chamba noticed the movement. "What's wrong, Boss?"

"I don't know. Just something about the way he's riding that bothers me."

"You want me to kill him?" Donnie asked.

Tilden waved that off. "No. Let's see what he's got on his mind."

Paul rode up to the house and sat his weary horse. "May I dismount?"

"Ain't he polite?" a gunfighter said, laughing.

"Sure, Jackson," Tilden said. "Climb down. What can I do for you?" Tilden noticed that the flap on the military-type holster was missing. Looked like it'd been freshly cut off. Paul's gun was riding loose.

"I've come to meet you man to man, Mister Franklin," Paul said.

"Well, Jackson, here I am. Speak your piece and then carry your ass off my range."

"I've come to kill you," Paul stated flatly.

"Is that so? Why?"

"Personal reasons."

"Don't I deserve better than that?" Tilden asked. This stupid sod was beginning to irritate him.

Several of the gunhands were beginning to giggle and titter and circle in the area of their temples with their forefingers.

Paul looked at the giggling gunslicks. "You men seem to find this amusing. Why?"

That brought them all down laughing. Tilden joined in the laughter. "Get off my range, you silly bastard!"

"Draw, goddamn you!" Paul shouted, and began fumbling for his gun.

Tilden drew, cocked, and fired with one blindingly fast motion. His slug hit Paul in the right shoulder, knocking the man to the dirt.

"You stupid son of a bitch!" Tilden snarled at the man, cocking the .44.

As Paul struggled to get to his feet, Tilden shot him again, this time the slug hitting the man in the right leg. Paul's feet flew out from under him and he landed hard in the dirt.

Screaming his rage at the rancher, Paul tried to claw his pistol out of leather. Tilden shot him in the other shoulder, rendering the man helpless.

Laughing, Tilden cocked and fired, the bullet striking Paul in the stomach.

"Tie him on his goddamned old nag and send him on his way," Tilden ordered, punching out the empties and reloading.

The gunslicks tied Paul upright in his saddle and slapped the already spooked horse on the rump. Paul went bouncing and swaying down the road, unconscious.

It was almost breaking dawn when Charlie Starr knocked on Smoke's cabin door. "Charlie Starr, Smoke. Got news for you."

In his longhandles, a Colt in his right hand, Smoke lifted the latch and peered out. "Mornin', Charlie. Come on in. I'll make us some coffee."

"Put your pants on first," Charlie said drily. "You ain't no sight to see first thing in the mornin'."

Smoke put on coffee to boil, visited the outhouse, then sat down at the kitchen table. "What's wrong, Charlie?"

"Paul Jackson was found late yesterday afternoon by some miners. He was tied to his horse. Somebody had a good time putting a lot of unnecessary lead in the fool. He's alive, but just barely. He told Doc Spalding he braced Tilden Franklin out at the TF ranch house. Then he went into a coma. Doc says he probably won't come out of it. My question is, why'd he do it?"

Sipping coffee, Smoke told Charlie about Paul's visit the day before.

"But there ain't nothin' between Bountiful and Paul Jackson. Is there?"

"No. It was all in Paul's mind."

"Fool's gold," Charlie muttered. "Finding that and thinkin' it was real might have been what pushed him over the edge."

"Probably was. How many times was he shot, Charlie?"

"Both shoulders, leg, and stomach. Me and Monte been up all night talkin' about it. He admitted goin' out there and bracin' Tilden. Tilden had a right to protect hisself. But tyin' the man on that horse was cruel. Still, the judge says there ain't no laws to cover that."

"How's Ed taking it?"

"Harder than he'll let on. Monte said the man was cryin' last night after leavin' the Doc's office. He's tore up pretty bad. And . . . he's talkin' about goin' out there and seein' Tilden."

"That wouldn't be smart on his part."

"He's a growed-up man, Smoke. I sure can't stop him if that's what he wants to do."

"And he thought Tilden hung the stars and the moon."

"Lots of folks seein' the light about that crazy bastard. Monte told me to tell you something else too."

Smoke lifted his eyes.

"Tilden's replaced all them gunhawks that was shot in town. But he's scrapin' the bottom of the slime pit doin' it. He's hirin' the real hardcases. Cold-blooded killers. Range-war types. He's hiring some of them that was vigilantes down on the Oklahoma-Texas border. He's hirin' thugs, punks, cattle thieves, horse thieves . . . anybody who can pack a gun and even just brag about usin' one. Them dandies in town, The Silver Dollar Kid and Sundance and them other punks? Tilden hired them too."

"I guess we'd all better get ready for the balloon to bust, Charlie. I don't see any other way out of it."

Sally entered the kitchen and poured coffee. She set a plate of doughnuts on the table between the two men. Charlie grinned and helped himself.

"You heard?" Smoke asked his wife.

"I heard. I feel sorry for Paul. He wasn't quite right in the head."

Speaking around a mouthful of bearsign, Charlie said,

"Out here, ma'am, man straps on a six-shooter, that gun makes him ten feet tall. Out here, they's a sayin'. God didn't make man equal. Colonel Colt did."

Paul Jackson died mid-morning, the day after he was shot. And once more, the undertaker's hack rumbled through the streets of Fontana. The streets were far less busy than they had been just a week before. The one remaining hotel had already announced plans to close.

Several TF riders had come to town, and the story of what had happened at the TF ranch was beginning to spread throughout the rapidly shrinking town. The TF gunhawks were drinking and laughing in the Blue Dog Saloon, telling the story of how Paul Jackson braced Tilden Franklin and how Paul had flopped around on the ground like a headless chicken after Tilden started putting lead into the man.

Stonewall stepped into the saloon just in time to hear the story being told for the umpteenth time. Each time it had been told with a bit more embellishment. Stonewall had not really cared much for Paul Jackson, but Jackson had been a decent sort of fellow . . . if a bit off in the head. But he had been no thief or footpad, just a hardworking guy who deserved a better death than the one he'd received.

The deputy said as much to the gunhands.

The saloon suddenly became very quiet as the TF gunslicks set their shot glasses and beer mugs on the bar and turned to face Stonewall.

"You makin' light of Mister Franklin, Deputy?" a gunslinger asked.

Stonewall thought about that for a few seconds. "Yeah," he said. "I reckon I am. A fair shootin' is one thing. Torturin' a man for sport is another thing."

"Well, Mister Franklin ain't here to defend hisself."

"You here," Stonewall said softly.

Monte took that time to step onto the boardwalk.

The TF gunhawks jerked iron and Stonewall matched their draw. The Blue Dog started yelping and barking with gunfire. Monte stepped through the batwing doors, his hands full of Colts. Stonewall was leaning against the bar, hard hit, but he had managed to drop two of the TF gunslingers. The front of Stonewall's shirt was stained with blood.

Monte's Colts started belching smoke and fire and lead. Two more TF riders went down, but not before Monte was hit twice, in the side and upper chest.

Stonewall died on his feet, his gun still clutched in his fingers. Monte was knocked back against a wall, losing one Colt on the way. He lifted his second Colt and got lead into the last remaining TF gunslick before he slid into darkness.

The wounded TF rider stumbled outside and made it to his horse, galloping out of town, holding on to the saddle horn with bloody fingers. Joel ran out of the sheriff's office and lifted his rifle. The TF rider twisted in the saddle and shot the deputy through the head before he could get off a shot.

Dave jumped into the saddle and took off after the TF gunslick. He ran slap into a dozen TF riders, on their way into town, the wounded TF rider in the middle of the pack. Dave was literally shot out of the saddle, a dozen holes in him.

Slim turned in his saddle and said, "Singer, take him back to the ranch with you." He indicated the wounded gunhawk. "And tell Mister Franklin that Fontana is ours!"

Dave was left where he had fallen, the deputy's horse standing over its master, nudging at Dave with its nose.

* * *

Bob Colby reined up in Smoke's yard in a cloud of dust. "Mister Smoke!" he hollered.

Smoke and Sally both ran from the cabin. "What's the matter, Bob?"

"Mister Luke tole me to tell you to come quick. Tilden Franklin's men done took over Fontana and this time they done 'er good. Sheriff Carson is hard hit, and all his deputies is dead!"

"Where's Johnny?"

"He took Ma over to a neighbor's house, then said he would meet you at Big Rock."

"I'm on my way, Bob."

Smoke instructed some of the old gunfighters to stay at the ranch in case any TF riders might choose to attack either the ranch or Ralph's new cabin, and told Ralph to keep his butt close by, and to carry his rifle wherever he went.

Smoke and the old gunslingers lit out for Big Rock.

" 'Bout time," Pistol Le Roux muttered. "I was beginnin' to think we wasn't never gonna see no action."

In the town of Fontana, the bully-boys who made up Tilden Franklin's army were having a fine ol' time exercising their muscle on the citizens.

The Silver Dollar Kid and the punk who called himself Sundance were strutting up and down the boardwalk, shooting at signs and anything else they took a mind to fire at.

Big Mamma lay on the floor of her pleasure palace, her head split open from a rifle butt. A few of the TF riders were busying themselves with her stable of red-light girls. Free of charge.

At Beeker's store, the shopkeeper and his wife had barricaded themselves in a sturdy storeroom. They huddled together, listening to the rampaging TF gunslicks loot their store.

Billy lay in the loft of the stable, watching it all, his .22 rifle at the ready, in case any of the TF riders tried to hurt him.

Louis Longmont sat in his gaming room, riffling a deck of cards. His Colts were belted around his lean waist. A rifle and double-barreled shotgun lay on a table. Mike sat across the room, armed with two pistols and a rifle. Louis was not worried about any TF riders attempting to storm his place. They knew better.

Colton and Mona Spalding and Haywood and Dana Arden sat in the newspaper office, listening to the occasional bursts of gunfire from the town.

All had made up their minds they were leaving Fontana at the first chance. Perhaps to Big Rock, perhaps clear out of the state.

And at his general store, Ed Jackson and his wife were being terrorized.

33

"How in the hell did they manage to tree the town?" Smoke asked.

"I reckon the townspeople—them that's left—was in shock over the sheriff and his deputies bein' gunned down the way they was," Luke said. "And Tilden's bunch just overpowered them that stood to fight."

"How many men are we looking at?" Silver Jim asked.

"I'd say over a hundred," Charlie replied. "But Beaconfield sent word in about two hours ago that Tilden left a good-sized bunch at the ranch. I'd say he's got a good hundred and twenty-five to a hundred and fifty men under his command."

"You got any ideas, Smoke?"

"Where is Monte?"

"At the Doc's clinic. He's hanging on, so I was told."

"Judge Proctor?"

"Out of town. Denver, I think," Luke said.

Smoke paced the street in front of the large general store of Big Rock. "It would be foolish for us to try to retake the town. If we leave here, Tilden would probably send his men from the ranch to take this place, burn it probably. And any ranch or farm up here he could find."

"You're right," Hunt Brook said.

"Damn!" Charlie said. "I hate to just sit here and do nothing, but I don't know what else we can do."

"I just wish I knew what was going on down at Fontana," Wilbur said.

Smoke grimaced. "I got a pretty good idea."

Smoke was silent for a moment. "I hope Billy is all right. I should have got that kid out of there before this."

The men fell silent, all looking in the direction of Fontana.

A group of TF riders had stripped Peg Jackson naked and were raping her, enjoying her screaming. Ed Jackson had been trussed up like a hog and tossed to the floor, forced to watch his wife being violated.

"You don't understand," Ed kept saying. "I like and respect Mister Franklin. We're friends."

One TF rider named Belton got tired of listening to Ed and kicked him in the mouth, then in the stomach. Ed lay on the floor, vomiting up blood and bits of teeth and the ham and eggs he'd had for breakfast.

Peg continued screaming as yet another TF gunhand took her.

In Louis's gaming tent, the gambler looked at his bouncer. "Mike, go get our horses and bring them around to the back. And if you find that boy, Billy, bring him along. I'm thinking that at full dark, when those rowdies get enough booze in them, they'll rush us. I'd like to get that boy out of this place."

"Yes, sir, Mister Longmont," Mike said, and was gone into the night.

Louis looked at the roulette wheels, the faro cue boxes, the card presses, the keno gooses . . . all the other paraphernalia of gambling.

"I shall not be needing any of it," Louis muttered. "When I again gamble, it will be in the company of ladies and gentlemen . . . with champagne and manners and breeding."

He rose from his chair, picked up his weapons, and walked into the back of the tent.

Mike returned in less than fifteen minutes, with saddled horses and Billy in tow.

"Any trouble?" Louis asked.

"One TF rowdy braced me," the huge bouncer replied. "I broke his neck."

The men and the boy mounted up. Andre said, "I will not miss this miserable place."

"Nor will I, Andre," Louis said. He pointed his horse's nose toward the high lonesome. "Quiet now," he cautioned. "Ride light until we're clear of the town."

"Boss?" Mike said. "Them thugs is rapin' the shopkeeper's woman. I could hear her screamin'."

Louis's face was tight as he said, "If she's lucky, that's all they'll do."

They cleared the town and then rode hard for the town of Big Rock.

"Grim," was Louis's one-word reply to Smoke's asking about Fontana.

"Can't we ride for the Army?" Hunt asked.

"Nearest Army post is four days away," Smoke explained. "And the next stage isn't due for twenty-four hours. If then." He looked at the old gunfighter called Buttermilk. "Think you boys could handle those gunhawks left at the TF ranch?"

Buttermilk smiled his reply.

"All right. Leave Dad Weaver and three others at the Sugarloaf. One in the barn with a rifle and lots of shells. Let me have Crooked John and Bull, and the rest of you take off to the TF. Pin 'em down and wear 'em down with rifle fire, then cut 'em down when they get enough and try to pull out."

Buttermilk nodded and turned to his compadres. "Let's ride, boys!"

Louis smiled. "Those old boys will lay up on the ridges around the TF spread and put so much lead in that house those gunhawks will be crying to get out."

"Those old men will allow their adversaries to surrender, won't they?" Hunt asked.

Louis cut his eyes to the lawyer. "You just have to be joking!"

Crooked John and Bull rode with Louis, Smoke, and Johnny North. Pearlie stayed behind with Luke and Charlie. The men rode slowly, sparing their horses, and making plans as they rode.

"I think we should let them get good and drunk," Louis remarked. "A full twenty-five percent of them will be passed out by night. That will make our work easier."

"Good idea," Johnny said. "And we need to get Monte outta there. Come night, I'll slip in from the blind side, through all them shacks that was left behind, and get to the Doc's place. We can hitch up the horses, put some hay in the back to keep Monte comfortable, and point the pilgrims on the way to Big Rock."

Smoke nodded his approval. "All right. While you're doing that, I'll ease in and see about Ed and his wife. Johnny, let's make it a mite easier for us. Bull, you and Crooked John create a diversion on this end of town. At full dark. You can leave your horses in that dry run behind the stable. Louis, how about you?"

Louis smiled. "I'll be doing some head-hunting on my own."

What they were going to do firmly implanted in their minds, the men urged their horses into a trot and began putting the miles behind them.

It was full dark when they pulled up, the lights of Fontana below them. They could hear an occasional gunshot and a faint, drunken whoop.

"I wonder where Tilden is," Smoke said, expressing his thought aloud. "If I could get lead in him, this would be over."

"Well protected, wherever he is," Louis said. "But what puzzles me is this: why is he letting his men do this?"

"He's gone over the edge," Smoke said. "He's a crazy man, drunk with power. He's made no telling how many thousands of dollars on gold shares with the miners and doesn't care how much of it he spends. And he hates me," Smoke added.

None of the men needed to add that Tilden Franklin also wanted Sally Jensen.

"Let's go, boys," Smoke said. "And good luck."

The men separated, Smoke turning his horse's head toward the right, Johnny moving out to the left. Bull and Crooked John headed straight in toward the lights of Fontana, and Louis Longmont moved out alone into the night.

Each man stashed his horse in the safest place he could find and slipped into the town to perform his assigned job.

The diversion that Crooked John and Bull made was a simple one. They set several buildings blazing, lighting up one end of the town.

Smoke slipped to the rear of Jackson's general store and eased up onto the loading dock. His spurs were left hanging on his saddle horn and he made no noise as he pushed open the back door and entered the storeroom area of the building. Listening, he could hear the faint sobbing of Peg Jackson and the drunken grunting of men.

He wondered what had happened to Ed.

Smoke heard the excited shouting out in the street and wondered what kind of diversion the gunslingers had set. He glanced behind him, out the open back door of the store, and saw the reflection of the dancing, leaping flames reddening the night sky.

Grinning, he slipped closer to the cracked-open door that would lead into the store. He peeked through the crack and silently cursed under his breath.

He could see Ed, trussed up like a hog, on the floor of the store. The man's face appeared to be badly swollen. There was blood and puke on his shirt front.

Lifting his eyes, searching, he saw Peg. The woman had been badly used and appeared to be just conscious enough to sob. A TF gunhawk, his pants down around his boots, his back to Smoke, was having his way with the woman. Several TF riders were sprawled on the floor and on the counters. They seemed to be dead drunk and out of it.

Two TF gunslicks were leaning against a counter, drinking whiskey straight out of the bottle, an amused look on their faces as they watched the rape of Peg Jackson.

Those men seemed to be the only ones still conscious enough to give Smoke any cause for worry.

The sounds of gunfire came hard through the night air. It was followed by a choking scream. The two TF men looked at each other.

"Let's check that out," one said.

The other man nodded and they both walked out onto the boardwalk in front of the general store.

Smoke slipped into the large area of the store. Looking down, he saw that Ed was awake and staring at him through wide and very frightened eyes. Smoke nodded his head at the man and put a finger to his lips, urging Ed to keep silent. Ed nodded his head.

Picking up an axe handle, Smoke slipped up behind the rapist, busy at his ugly work. Smoke hit him on the side of the head with the axe handle. The man's skull popped under the impact and he fell to one side, dying as he was falling. Smoke glanced at him for a second. The man's head was split open, his brains exposed.

Smoke jerked Peg to her unsteady feet and handed her a blanket. She looked at the blanket through dull and uncomprehending eyes. Glancing toward the open front door, Smoke could not see the two TF gunnies who had stepped outside. Walking swiftly to the counter, he picked up one half-empty bottle of whiskey and returned to Peg. He tilted her head back and poured the raw booze down her throat. She coughed and gagged and gasped as her eyes cleared a bit.

She pulled the blanket over her nakedness and slowly nodded her head in understanding.

"Get to the back of the store," Smoke whispered. "And wait there for us."

She walked slowly, painfully, toward the rear of the store.

Smoke didn't bother cutting Ed's bonds. He just picked the man up and slung him over his shoulder. He walked swiftly out of the show and business area of the store, joining Peg on the loading dock. There, he dumped Ed on the dock and cut his bonds.

"Hitch up your team, Ed," he spoke softly. "And do it very quietly and very quickly. Take the old road that circles the town and head for Big Rock. A couple of miles out of town, pull up and wait for Spalding and Arden."

"My store!" the man protested.

Smoke almost hit the man. He controlled his temper at the last second and said, "Get your goddamned ass moving, Ed. Or I'll turn you back over to those TF riders. How do you want it?"

Shocked at the cold threat in Smoke's voice, Ed moved quickly to his barn, Peg walking slowly behind him, the blanket clutched tightly around her.

Smoke walked back into the store just as more gunfire erupted throughout the town. Smoke entered the store just as the two TF gunslicks walked back in through the front door.

They all saw each other and jerked iron at the same time. Smoke's Colts roared and bucked in his hands. The TF men were thrown to the floor as the .44 slugs from Smoke's guns hit big bones and vital organs. Smoke's draw was so fast, his aim so true, the men were unable to get off a single shot before death took them into its cold arms.

Smoke quickly reloaded and holstered his .44s. He walked to the gun rack and took down a sawed-off shotgun, breaking it down and loading it with buckshot, then stuffing his pockets full of shells. He took two new .44 pistols from the arms showcase, checked the action, and loaded them full, tucking them behind his gunbelt. Shotgun in hand, Smoke stepped out onto the boardwalk and prepared to lessen the odds just a tad.

The passed-out gunslicks in the store snored on, probably saving their lives . . . for the time being.

A TF gunslick made the mistake of riding up just at that moment. Lifting the Greener, Smoke literally blew the man out of the saddle, dumping him, now a bloody mass, onto the dusty ground.

He looked around him, his eyes picking up the black-dressed figure of Louis Longmont, standing on the boardwalk across the street. Louis had a Colt in each hand, the hammers back.

"Where's Johnny?" Smoke called.

"Right up there," Louis said, returning the call, pointing with a Colt.

Smoke looked through the smoky night air and spotted Johnny North, about half a block away.

"I got the pilgrims on the way!" Johnny called. "Looks like Monte's gonna make it if he can stand the trip."

Reloading the Greener, Smoke called, "Let's do some damage and then get the hell out of here!"

One of the duded-up dandies who had been strutting about picked that time to brace Johnny North. "Draw, North!" he called, standing in the dusty street.

Johnny put two holes in the punk before the would-be gunhand could blink. The dandy died on his back in the dirt, his guns still in leather.

Two gunhawks came running up the street, on Louis's side. The gambler dropped them both, his guns roaring and belching gray smoke and fire.

Smoke heard a noise to his left and spun around, dropped to one knee and lifted the shotgun. As he dropped, lead whistled over his head. He pulled both triggers on the Greener, the buckshot spreading a TF rider all over a storefront and the boardwalk.

At the far end of town, Bull Flagler was holding his own and then some, the old gunfighter Crooked John Simmons by his side, both gnarled hands full of Colts. Bull's shotgun roared and Crooked John's pistols belched death with each cocking and firing.

"Let's go!" Smoke shouted, and began falling back. He stepped into Ed's store just as one of the drunken TF riders reared up, a pistol in his hand.

Smoke shot him in the chest with the sawed-off and the gunnie died amid the corsets and the bloomers.

Running out the back, Smoke got his horse and swung into the saddle. He cut into an alley and came out just on the far edge of Fontana. With the reins in his teeth, both hands full of guns, Smoke galloped straight up the last few blocks of the boom town now going bust. Johnny North was right behind him and Louis Longmont just behind Johnny. Bull and Crooked John were waiting at the end of town, rifles in their hands, and their aim was deadly.

The five gunfighters took a fearful toll on Tilden Franklin's gunhands those last few blocks.

Most of the gunnies were busy with a bucket-line, trying to keep the raging fires contained at one end of town. Smoke, Johnny, and Louis rode right through the bucket-brigade, guns sparking the fiery night, adding death and confusion to the already chaotic scene.

Louis, Johnny, and Smoke sent the gunhands turned firemen running and diving and sprawling for their lives. Most made it; a few did not.

Louis knocked a leg from under a TF gunnie and the man fell backward, into the raging inferno. His screams were hideous in the fiery, smoky, gunshot-filled night.

Tilden Franklin stood in the best suite of the hotel and watched it all, his hate-filled eyes as hot as the flames that threatened to consume the town. He turned to the small woman who had been the sole property of Big Mamma and, in his rage, broke the woman's neck with his powerful hands.

He screamed his hate and rage and picked up the naked, ravaged woman and threw her body out the second-floor window.

The young woman lay dead on the street.

Then, with slobber wetting his lips and chin, Tilden Franklin emptied his guns into the battered body.

"I'll kill you, Jensen!" the man howled. "I'm gonna burn your goddamned town to the ground and have your woman . . . right in front of your eyes!"

34

The old gunfighters who had ridden to the TF ranch house lay on the ridges that surrounded the huge home and made life miserable for those TF gunhawks who had survived the initial attack.

The moon was full and golden in the starry night skies, the illumination highlighting the bodies of those gunnies who now lay sprawled in death on the grounds surrounding the bunkhouse and the main ranch house.

Those trapped in the bunkhouse and in the main house were not at all happy about their situation. Several had thought the night would cover them as they tried to escape. Those with that thought now lay dead.

"What are we gonna do?" a TF gunslick, who felt more sick than slick, asked.

"Hold out 'til the boss gets back," was the reply. "There ain't that many of 'em up there on the ridges."

"Yeah, but I got me a peek at who they is," another paid gunhand said. "That's them old gunfighters. And I think I seen The Apache Kid 'mong 'em."

Nobody said anything for a long time. Nobody had to. They were all thinking the same thing. Toot Tooner and

Red Shingletown had already been spotted, briefly. Now The Apache Kid. They all knew what that meant: these hard ol' boys didn't take prisoners. Never had. They expected no quarter, and they gave none.

"I ain't goin' out there, boys," a gunman said. "No way."

"I wish to hell someone had told me this Jensen feller was raised up by Preacher. I'd have kept my butt up in Montana."

"He ain't so good," another said.

Nobody paid any attention to him. The man was speaking without any knowledge of the subject. He was too young to have any real awareness of the legendary Mountain Man known as Preacher. If he had, he'd have kept his mouth shut.

"So we wait, is that it?" The question was thrown out of the darkened room.

"You got any better ideas?"

Silence, and more silence.

Even with only the sounds of their breathing to be heard, none of the TF gunhands could hear the moccasined feet of The Apache Kid as he slipped through the kitchen and into the large dining area. Sutter Cordova was right behind him. There had been a guard at the back door. He now lay on the porch, his throat cut, his blood staining the ground.

Both men had their hands full of pistols, the hammers jacked back.

"Something is wrong!" a TF gunslick suddenly said, his voice sharp in the darkened house.

"What?"

"I don't know. But there ain't a shot fired in more 'un fifteen, twenty minutes."

"Maybe they pulled out?"

"Sure they did, and a hog is gonna fly any day now."

Apache and Sutter stepped into the room and started

letting the lead fly. They were grateful to Smoke Jensen for giving them this opportunity to go out as gunfighters should. They had all outlived their time, and they all knew it. They had no one to live for, and no one to grieve for them when they died.

They were a part of the West's rapidly vanishing past. So they would go out as they lived.

The room filled with gray smoke, the booming of Colts and Remingtons deafening.

The Apache Kid died with his back to a wall, his hands full of guns. But the old man had taken a dreadful toll while he had lived this night.

Sutter Cordova went into that long sleep with a faint smile on his lips. His guns empty, the gunfighter buried his knife into the chest of a TF gunhawk and rode him down to the floor.

When the booming of the gunfire had faded away into the night, the other aging gunfighters walked slowly down to the big house. They checked out the bunkhouse and found no life there.

Carefully, they went into the house and lighted a lamp. They found one TF rider alive, but not for long.

"You old . . . bastards played . . . hell!" he managed to gasp.

"You got a name, boy?" Dan Greentree asked, squatting down beside the young man.

"It . . . don't matter." He closed his eyes and died.

"Funny goddamn name," Red Shingletown said.

"We'll bury them in the morning," Smoke said. "I'll come back into town and bring the minister with me."

"What'd y'all do with the dead TF gunnies?" Luke asked.

"Left 'em where they lay," Red replied. "Let somebody else worry with them."

" 'Pache and Sutter both tole me they was a-goin' out this run," Luke Nations said. " 'Pache had a bad ticker and Sutter was havin' a hard time passin' his water. It's good they went out this way. I'm right happy for 'em."

"You're happy your friends died?" Hunt asked, his robe pulled tightly around him against the night chill.

"Shore. That's the way they wanted it."

The lawyer walked away, back to his cabin. He was thinking that he would never understand the Western way of doing things.

"Peg Jackson?" Louis asked.

"Physically, not hurt too badly," Belle Colby said. "But like my Velvet, she's not good in the head. She said they did terrible things to her."

Belle walked back into the store where they had set up a hospital.

"Monte?" Bull asked.

"He's in rough shape, but the Doc says he thinks he's gonna pull through."

"How about Ed?" somebody finally asked, although few if any among them really gave a damn how Ed was.

"He's all right," Haywood said, joining the group. "He's bitching about losing his store. It's just his way, gentlemen. And he'll never change. He's already talking of pulling out."

"He don't belong here," Charlie Starr said, lighting a tightly rolled cigarette. "This country's still got some rough and woolly years ahead of it. And it's gonna take some tough-minded men and women to see it through."

"What's the plan, Smoke?" Louis asked. "I know you've got one. You've been thinking hard for about an hour now."

"I'm gonna get a few hours' sleep and then get the preacher. After the services, I'm riding into Fontana and get this matter settled, one way or the other. Anybody who wants to come along is welcome to ride."

* * *

They left the graveyard at nine o'clock the next morning. They had said their goodbyes to The Apache Kid and Sutter Cordova, and then those that had family to worry about them said their goodbyes to womenfolk and kids and swung into the saddle.

They left behind them some heavily armed hands who worked for Beaconfield and Mike Garrett, but who were hands, not gunhands, and half a dozen teenagers who were excellent shots with a rifle. In addition, Hunt, Colton, and Haywood were armed with rifles and shotguns. All the Western women could shoot rifles and shotguns as well as, and sometimes better than, the men. Mike, the big bouncer, was there, as well as Wilbur Mason, Dad Weaver, and Billy. The general store had been turned into a fort in case of attack.

Twenty-eight men rode toward the town of Fontana. They had guns in leather, guns tucked behind gunbelts, guns stashed in their saddlebags, and rifles and shotguns in saddleboots.

Smoke had warned them all that even though the previous night's raid into Fontana had taken some TF riders out, they were probably facing four- or five-to-one odds, and anyone who wanted out had damn well better speak up now.

His words had been met with a stony silence.

Smoke had nodded his head and pulled his hat brim down low, securing the chin strap, "Let's ride."

There had been no stopping Ralph Morrow. He had stuck out his chin, picked up his Henry rifle, and stuffed his pockets full of cartridges. "I'm going," he had said. "And that's final."

The men trotted their horses for a time, and then walked them, alternating back and forth, eating up the miles.

Then they looked down on the town of Fontana . . .

and stared at the long line of wagons that were pulling out.

Smoke looked at Silver Jim. "Find out about that, will you, Jim?"

Silver Jim rode down to the lead wagon, talked for a moment, then rode back to where Smoke sat his horse with the others.

"Big Mamma's dead," Silver Jim said. "She stormed into a saloon last night, after she learned that Tilden Franklin had raped and killed her . . . wife. Tilden ordered her hanged. They hung her slow. That feller I talked to said it took a long time for her to die. One of Big Mamma's girls tried to run away last night. Tilden's gun-slicks caught her and . . . well, done some perverted things to her, then they dragged her and set her on far. Tilden personal kilt Beeker at the store. Then his boys had they way with his wife. She set up such a squall, they shot her."

"Dear Jesus Christ!" Ralph muttered.

"Them people down there," Silver Jim said, pointing to the line of wagons, "is near 'bouts all that's left of any decent folks, and some of them would steal the pennies off a dead man's eyes. That's how bad it's got down in town."

"So Tilden and his men are waiting for us?" Smoke asked.

"Dug in tight."

"Proctor didn't come back, did he?"

"They didn't say and I didn't think to ask."

Smoke stepped down from the saddle and said, "Let's talk about this some."

Dismounted, the men sipped water from canteens and ate a few biscuits and some beef packed for them before they pulled out.

"If we go in there," Smoke said, "we're going to have to take the place building by building, and like Silver Jim said, they're dug in and waiting. The cost, for us, will be too high."

"What choice do we have?" Luke said.

"Well, let's talk about that," Mike Garrett said. "We could wait them out while someone rides for the Army."

"No!" Ralph said, considerable heat in his voice.

"You want to explain that, Ralph?" Johnny said.

"Maybe I wasn't cut out to be a minister," the man said. "There is violence and hate in my heart. Anyway, it is my belief that people like Tilden Franklin should not be allowed to live. Back East—and I know, that's where I'm from—lawyers are already using the insanity pleas to get killers off scot free. And it's going to get worse. Let's not start a precedent out here."

"A what?" Johnny asked.

"Let's not let Tilden Franklin go free," Ralph said.

All present loudly and profanely agreed with that.

"There is another way," Smoke said.

"And that is?" Louis asked, knowing full well what was coming.

"I challenge Tilden Franklin. Best man with a gun wins."

"No," Louis said. "No. Tilden Franklin is a man totally without honor. Basically, he is a coward, a backshooter. He'd set you up, Smoke. No to your plan."

And all agreed with Louis on that.

"Well," Moody said. "We could burn the bastards out."

"How many days since we've had rain?" Smoke asked. "Too long. That's why Tilden ordered his men to put out the fire last night instead of concentrating on us. We can't risk a grass fire. Feel this hot wind? It would spread faster than anyone could contain it."

Charlie Starr grinned. "Besides, ol' tight-fisted Ed Jackson would probably sue us all for destroying his goods."

All the men enjoyed a tension-relieving laugh at that.

"Well, boys," Pistol Le Roux said, "that don't leave us with too gawddamned many options, do it?"

The men turned to tightening saddle cinches. They knew the discussion was over.

Hardrock swung into the saddle and looked at his friends. "You know what my momma wanted me to be?" he asked.

They stared at him.

"An apothecary, that's what."

Toot Tooner climbed into the saddle. "Shit, I wouldn't let you fix up nuttin' for me. You'd probably mix up something so's I couldn't get a boner up."

Sunset laughed. "Hell, you ain't had one in so long it'd probably scare you to death!"

The men swung their horses toward Fontana, lying hot under the sun and wind.

35

Hardrock, Moody, and Sunset were sent around to the far end of town, stationed there with rifles to pick off any TF gunhand who might try to slip out, either to run off or try and angle around behind Smoke and his party for a box-in.

The others split up into groups of twos and threes and rode hunched over, low in the saddle, to present a smaller target for the riflemen they had spotted lying in wait on the rooftops in Fontana. And they rode in a zig-zagging fashion, making themselves or their horses even harder to hit. But even with that precaution, two men were hit before they reached the town limits. Beaconfield was knocked from the saddle by rifle fire. The one-time Tilden Franklin supporter wrapped a bandana around a bloody arm, climbed back in the saddle, and, cursing, continued onward. Hurt, but a hell of a long way from being out.

The old gunfighter Linch was hit just as he reached the town. A rifle bullet hit him in the stomach and slapped him out of the saddle. The aging gunhand, pistols in his hands, crawled to the edge of a building and began laying down a withering line of fire, directed at the rooftops. He managed to knock out three snipers before a second bullet ended his life.

Leo Wood, seeing his long-time buddy die, screamed his outrage and stepped into what had once been a dress shop, pulled out both Remington Frontier .44s, and let 'em bang.

Leo cleared the dress shop of all TF riders before a single shot from a Peacemaker .45 ended his long and violent life.

Pearlie settled down by the corner of a building and with his Winchester .44-40 began picking his shots. At ranges up to two hundred yards, the .44-40 could punch right through the walls of the deserted buildings of Fontana. Pearlie killed half a dozen TF gunhawks without even seeing his targets.

A few of Tilden's hired guns, less hardy than they thought, tried to slip out the rear of the town. They went down under the rifle fire of Moody, Hardrock, and Sunset.

Bill Foley, throwing caution to the wind, like most of his friends, having absolutely no desire to spend his twilight years in any old folks' home, stepped into an alley where he knew half a dozen TF gunnies were waiting, and opened fire. Laughing, the old gunfighter took his time and picked his shots while his body was soaking up lead from the badly shaken TF men. Foley's old body had soaked up a lot of lead in its time, and he knew he could take three or four shots and still stay upright in his boots. Bill Foley, who had helped tame more towns than most people had ever been in, died with his boots on, his back to a wall, and his guns spitting out death. He killed all six of the TF gunslicks.

Toot Tooner, his hands full of Colts, calmly walked

into what was left of the Blue Dog Saloon, through the back door, and said, "I declare this here game of poker open. Call or fold, boys."

Then he opened fire.

His first shots ended the brief but bloody careers of two cattle rustlers from New Mexico who had signed on with the TF spread in search of what Tilden had promised would be easy money. They died without having the opportunity to fire a shot.

Toot took a .45 slug in the side and it spun him around. Lifting his pistol, he shot the man who had shot him between the eyes just as he felt a hammer-blow in his back, left side. The gunshot knocked him to his knees and he tasted blood in his mouth.

Toot dropped his empty Colts and pulled out two Remington .44s from behind his gunbelt. Hard hit, dying, Toot laughed at death and began cocking and firing as the light before his eyes began to fade.

"Somebody kill the old son of a bitch!" a TF gunhand shouted.

Toot laughed at the dim figure and swung his guns. A slug took him in the gut and set him back on his butt. But Toot's last shots cleared the Blue Dog of hired guns. He died with a very faint smile on his face.

Louis Longmont met several TF gunhands in an alley. The gambler never stopped walking as his Colts spat and sang a death song. Reloading, he stepped over the sprawled bloody bodies and walked on up the alley. A bullet tugged at the sleeve of his coat and the gambler dropped to one knee, raised both guns, and shot the rifleman off the roof of the bank building. A bullet knocked Louis to one side and his left arm grew numb. Hooking the thumb of his left hand behind his gunbelt, the gambler rose and triggered off a round, sending another one of Tilden Franklin's gunslicks to hell.

Louis then removed a white linen handkerchief from an inside breast pocket of his tailored jacket. He plugged the hole in his shoulder and continued on his hunt.

The Reverend Ralph Morrow stepped into what had been the saloon of Big Mamma and the bidding place of her soiled doves and began working the lever on his Henry .44. The boxer-turned-preacher-turned-farmer-turned-gunfighter muttered a short prayer for God to forgive him and began blasting the hell out of any TF gunhand he could find.

His Henry empty, Ralph jerked out a pair of .45s and began smoking. A lousy pistol shot, and that is being kind, Ralph succeeded in filling the beery air with a lot of hot lead. He didn't hit a damn thing with the pistols, but he did manage to scare the hell out of those gunhands left standing after his good shooting with the rifle. They ran out the front of the saloon and directly into the guns of Pistol Le Roux and Dan Greentree.

Ralph reloaded his rifle and stepped to the front of the building. "Exhilarating!" he exclaimed. Then he hit the floor as a hard burst of gunfire from a rooftop across the street tore through the canvas and wood of the deserted whorehouse.

"Shithead!" Ralph muttered, lifting his rifle and sighting the gunman in. Ralph pulled the trigger and knocked the TF gunman off the roof.

Steve Matlock, Ray Johnson, Nolan, Mike Garrett, and Beaconfield were keeping a dozen or more TF gunslicks pinned down in Beeker's general store.

Charlie Starr had cleared a small saloon of half a dozen hired guns and now sat at a table, having a bottle of sweetened soda water. He would have much preferred a glass of beer, but the sweet water beat nothing. Seeing a flash of movement across the street, Charlie put down the bottle and picked up a cocked .45 from the table. He sighted the TF gunhand in and pulled the trigger. The slug struck the man in the shoulder and spun him around. Charlie shot him again in the belly and that ended it.

"Now leave me alone and let me finish my sodie water," Charlie muttered.

The Silver Dollar Kid came face-to-face with Silver Jim. The old gunfighter grinned at the punk. Both men had their guns in leather.

"All right, kid," Silver Jim said. "You been lookin' for a rep. Here's your chance."

The Silver Dollar Kid grabbed for his guns.

He never cleared leather. Silver Jim's guns roared and bucked in his callused hands. The Kid felt twin hammer blows in his stomach. He sat down in the alley and began hollering for his mother.

Silver Jim stepped around the punk and continued his prowling. The Kid's hollering faded as life ebbed from him.

Smoke met Luis Chamba behind the stable. The Mexican gunfighter grinned at him. "Now, Smoke, we see just how good you really are."

Smoke lifted his sawed-off shotgun and almost blew the gunfighter in two. "I already know how good I am," Smoke said. "I don't give a damn how good you . . . were."

Smoke reloaded the 10-gauge sawed-off and stepped into the stable. He heard a rustling above him and lifted the twin muzzles. Pulling the triggers, blowing a hole the size of a bucket in the boards, Smoke watched as a man, or what was left of a man, hurled out the loft door to come splatting onto the shit-littered ground.

Smoke let the shotgun fall to the straw as the gunfighter Valentine faced him.

"I'm better," Valentine said, his hands over the butts of his guns.

"I doubt it," Smoke said, then shot the famed gunfighter twice in the belly and chest.

With blood streaking his mouth, Valentine looked up from the floor at Smoke. "I . . . didn't even clear leather."

"You sure didn't," the young man said. "We all got to meet him, Valentine, and you just did."

"I reckon." Then he died.

Listening, Smoke cocked his head. Something was very wrong. Then it came to him. No gunfire.

Cautiously, Smoke stepped to the stable door and looked out. Gunsmoke lay over the town like a shroud. The dusty streets were littered with bodies, not all of them TF gunhands.

Smoke was conscious of his friends looking at him, standing silently.

Louis pointed with the muzzle of his pistol.

Smoke looked far up the street. He could make out the shape of Tilden Franklin. Smoke stepped out into the street and faced the man.

Tilden began walking toward him. As the man came closer, Smoke said, "It's over, Tilden."

"Not yet," the big man said. "I gotta kill you, then it's over."

"Make your play," Smoke said.

Tilden grabbed for his guns. Both men fired at almost the same time. Smoke felt a shock in his left side. He kept earing back the hammers and pulling the triggers. Dust flew from Tilden's chest as the slugs slammed into his body. The big man took another step, staggered, and then slumped to his knees in the center of the street.

Blood leaking from his wounded side, Smoke walked up to the man who would be king.

"You had everything a man could ask for, Tilden. Why weren't you satisfied?"

Tilden tried to reply. But blood filled his mouth. He looked at Smoke, and still the hate was in his eyes. He fell forward on his face, in the dust, his guns slipping from his dead fingers.

It was over.

Almost.

36

They all heard the single shot and whirled around. Luke Nations lay crumpled on the boardwalk, a large hole in the center of his back.

Lester Morgan, a.k.a. Sundance, stepped out of a building, a pistol in his hand. He looked up and grinned.

"I did it!" he hollered. "Me. Sundance. I kilt Luke Nations!"

"You goddamned backshootin' punk!" Charlie Starr said, lifting his pistol.

"No!" Smoke's voice stopped him. "Don't, Charlie." Smoke walked over to Lester, one hand holding his bleeding side. He backhanded the dandy, knocking him sprawling. Lester-Sundance landed on his butt in the street. His mouth was busted, blood leaking from one corner. He looked up at Smoke, raw fear in his wide eyes.

"You gonna kill me, ain't you?" he hissed.

The smile on Smoke's lips was not pleasant. "What's your name, punk?"

"Les . . . Sundance. That's me, Sundance!"

"Well, *Sundance*." Smoke put enough dirt on the name to make it very ugly. "You wanna live, do you?"

"Yeah!"

"And you wanna be known as a top gunhand, right, Sundance?"

"Yeah!"

Smoke kicked Lester in the mouth. The punk rolled on the ground, moaning.

"What's your last name, craphead?"

"M . . . Morgan!"

"All right, Les Sundance Morgan. I'll let you live. And Les, I'm going to have your name spread all over the West. Les Sundance Morgan. The man with one ear. He's the man who killed the famed gunfighter Luke Nations."

"I got both ears!"

Before his words could fade from sound, Smoke had drawn and fired, the bullet clipping off Lester's left ear. The action forever branded the dandy.

Lester rolled on the dirt, screaming and hollering.

"Top gun, huh, punk?" Smoke said. "Right, that's you, Sundance." He looked toward Johnny North. "Get some whiskey and fix his ear, will you, Johnny?"

Lester really started hollering when the raw booze hit where his ear had been. He passed out from the pain. Ralph took that time to bandage the ugly wound.

Then Smoke kicked him awake. Lester lay on the blood- and whiskey-soaked ground, looking up at Smoke.

"What for you do this to me?" he croaked.

"So everybody, no matter where you go, can know who you are, punk. The man who killed Luke Nations. Now, you listen to me, you son of a bitch! You want to know how it feels to be top gun? Well, just look around you, ask anybody."

Lester's eyes found Charlie Starr. "You're Charlie Starr. You're more famouser than Luke Nations. But I'm gonna be famous too, ain't I?"

Charlie rolled a cigarette and stuck it between Lester's

lips. He held the match while Lester puffed. Charlie straightened up and smiled sadly at Lester.

"How is it, punk? Oh, well, it's a real grand time, punk. You can't sit with your back to no empty space, always to a wall. Lots of backshooters out there. You don't never make your fire, cook, and then sleep in the same spot. You always move before you bed down, 'cause somebody is always lookin' to gun you down . . . for a reputation.

"You ain't never gonna marry, punk. 'Cause if you do, it won't last. You got to stay on the move, all the time. 'Cause you're the man who kilt Luke Nations, punk. And there's gonna be a thousand punks just like you, lookin' for you.

"You drift, boy. You drift all the time, and you might near always ride alone, lessen you can find a pard that you know you can trust not to shoot you when you're in your blankets.

"And a lot of towns won't want you, punk. The marshal and the townspeople will meet you with rifles and shotguns and point you the way out. 'Cause they don't want no gunfighter in their town.

"And after a time, if you live, you'll do damn near anything so's people won't know who you are. But they always seem to find out. Then you'll change your name agin. And agin. Just lookin' for a little peace and quiet.

"But you ain't never gonna find it.

"You might git good enough to live for a long time, punk. I hope you do. I hope you ride ten thousand lonely miles, you backshootin' bastard. Ten thousand miles of lookin' over your back. Ten thousand towns that you'll ride in and out of in the dead of night. Eatin' your meals just at closin' time . . . you can find a eatin' place that'll serve you.

"A million hours that you'll wish you could somehow

change your life . . . but you cain't, punk. You cain't change, 'cause *they* won't let you.

"Only job you'll be able to find is one with the gun, punk. 'Cause you're the man who kilt Luke Nations. You got your rep, punk. You wanted it so damned bad, you got 'er." He glanced at Johnny North.

Johnny said, "I had me a good woman one time. We married and I hung up my guns, sonny-boy. Some god-damned bounty-hunters shot into my cabin one night. Killed my wife. I'd never broke no law until then. But I tracked them so-called lawmen down and hung 'em, one by one. I was on the hoot-owl trail for years after that. I had both the law and the reputation-hunters after me. Sounds like a real fine life, don't it, punk? I hope you enjoy it."

Smoke kicked Lester Sundance Morgan to his boots. "Get your horse and ride, punk! 'Fore one of us here takes a notion to brace the man who killed Luke Nations."

Crying, Lester stumbled from the street and found his horse, back of the building that once housed a gun shop.

"It ain't like that!" the gunfighters, the gambler, the ranchers, and the minister heard Lester holler as he rode off. "It ain't none at all like what you say it was. I'll have wimmin a-throwin' themselves at me. I'll have money and I'll have . . ."

His horse's hooves drummed out the rest of what Lester Sundance Morgan thought his reputation would bring him.

"Poor, sad, silly son of a bitch," Ralph Morrow said.

Charlie Starr looked at the minister. "I couldn't have said 'er no better myself, preacher."

The bodies of the gunfighters and Tilden Franklin were dragged to a lone building just at the edge of what was left of the boom town named Fontana. The building was doused with kerosene and torched just as a very gentle rain began falling.

"Lots of folks comin', Smoke," Charlie said, pointing toward the road leading to the high lonesome.

It was Sally and Belle and Bountiful and nearly all of those the men had left behind.

Sally embraced and kissed her man, getting blood all over her blouse as she did so. "How'd you folks know it was done with?" Smoke asked her.

"Hook Nose's people set up relay points with runners," she said. "They were watching from the hills over there." She pointed.

"What a story this will make," Haywood Arden said, his eyes wide as he looked at the bullet-pocked buildings and empty shell-casings on the ground.

"Yeah," Smoke said wearily. "You be sure and write it, Haywood. And be sure you spell one name right."

"Who is that?" the newspaperman asked.

"Lester Morgan, known as Sundance."

"What'd he do?" Haywood was writing on a tablet as fast as he could write.

Smoke described Lester, ending with, "And he ain't got but one ear. That'll make him easy to spot."

"But what did this Lester Sundance Morgan *do?*"

"Why . . . he's the gunfighter who killed Luke Nations."

37

Ed Jackson and his wife went back East . . . anywhere east of the Mississippi River. They did not say good-bye to anybody, just loaded their wagon and pulled out early one morning.

Louis Longmont, Mike, and Andre left the town of Big Rock. Louis thought he'd retire for a time. But Smoke knew he would not . . . not for long. The raw and woolly West had not seen the last of Louis Longmont.

Word drifted back that Lester Sundance Morgan had been braced by a couple of young duded-up dandies look-ing for a reputation down in New Mexico Territory. Sun-dance had managed to drop them both and was now riding low, keeping out of sight. The report that Smoke received said that Lester was not a very happy young man.

Monte Carson recovered from his wounds and became the sheriff of Big Rock, Colorado. He married himself a grass widow and settled down.

The aging gunfighters pulled out of the area, riding out in small groups of twos and threes . . . or alone. Alone. As they had lived.

Charlie Starr shook hands with Smoke and swung into

the saddle. With a smile and a small salute, he rode out of Big Rock and into the annals of Western history. Smoke would see the famed gunslinger again . . . but that's another story.

The *Fontana Sunburst* became the *Big Rock Guardian.* And it would remain so until the town changed its name just before the turn of the century.

Colton Spalding remained the town's doctor until his death in the 1920s.

Sally and Mona and Bountiful and Dana and Willow would live to "see the vote." But, there again, that's another story.

Judge Proctor returned and was named district judge. He lived in the area until his death in 1896.

The gold vein ran dry and all the miners left as peace finally settled over the High Lonesome.

The gold still lies in the ground on Smoke and Sally's Sugarloaf. They never touched it.

The last store in Fontana closed its doors in 1880. The lonely winds hummed and sang their quiet Western songs throughout the empty buildings and ragged bits of tent canvas for many years; the songs sang of love and hate and violence and bloody gunfights until the last building collapsed in the 1940s. Now, nothing is left.

Danner and Signal Hill died out near the turn of the century, but the town that was once called Big Rock remains, and the descendants of Smoke and Sally Jensen, Johnny and Belle North, Pearlie, and all the others still live there . . . finally in peace.

But peace was a long time coming to that part of Colorado, for not all the gunslicks were killed that bloody day in Fontana. Those few that managed to escape swore they'd come back and have their revenge.

They would try.

It would be many more years before Smoke Jensen could hang up his guns for good. Many years before Smoke and Sally Jensen's sons and daughters could live in peace. For Smoke Jensen was the West's most famous gunfighter. And for years to come, there would be those who sought a reputation.

But before that, on a bright, sunny, warm, late-summer morning, Velvet Colby called out for her mother and for Johnny.

The newly wed man and woman ran to Velvet's bedroom. Johnny North, one of the West's most feared gunfighters, knelt and took the girl's hands in his hard and callused hands.

"Yes, baby?" he said, his voice gentle.

Velvet smiled. Her voice, husky from lack of use, was a lovely thing to hear. She had not spoken in months. "Can I go outside?" she asked. "It looks like such a beautiful day."

And a gentle, peaceful breeze stirred the branches and the flowers and the tall lush grass of the High Lonesome . . .

. . . along the trail of the last Mountain Man.

RETURN OF THE MOUNTAIN MAN

To my friend who answers my endless questions concerning weapons of the old west: Hollis Erwin

Back of the bar, in a solo game, sat Dangerous Dan McGrew. And watching his luck was his light-o'-love, the lady that's known as Lou.

—Robert W. Service

1

The man called Smoke looked at the new wanted poster tacked to a tree. This one had his likeness on it. He smiled as he looked at the shoulder-length hair and the clean-shaven face on the poster. The artist had done a dandy job.

But it in no way resembled the man who now called himself Buck West.

Kirby Jensen had been sixteen years old when the old mountain man called Preacher hung the nickname Smoke on him. Preacher had predicted that Smoke would turn out to be a very famous man. And he had. As one of the most feared gunfighters in all the west.

It was not a reputation Smoke had wanted or sought.

Smoke now wore his hair short-cropped. A neat, well-trimmed beard covered his face. He no longer wore one pistol in cross-draw fashion, butt-forward. He now wore his twin .44s butt back and the holsters tied down low. He was just as fast as before. And that was akin to lightning.

He had turned his Appaloosa, Seven, loose in a valley several hundred miles to the east. A valley so lovely it was nearly impossible to describe.

Nicole would have loved it.

Seven had gone dancing and prancing off, once more running wild and free.

Nicole.

He shook his head and pushed the face of his dead wife from his mind. He turned his unreadable, cold, emotionless brown eyes to the west. The midnight-black stallion he now rode stood steady under his weight. The man now called Buck stood six feet, two inches, barefooted. He weighed one eighty: all hard-packed muscle and bone. His waist was lean and his short hair ash-blond.

The stallion shook his head. Buck patted him on the neck. The stallion quieted immediately. The animal's eyes were a curious yellow/green, a vicious combination that vaguely resembled a wolf's eyes. The stallion had killed its previous owner when the man had tried to beat him with a board. Smoke had bought the horse from the man's widow, gentled him, and learned to respect the animal's feelings and moods.

The stallion's name was Drifter.

Smoke had carefully hidden his buckskins, caching them with his saddle and other meager possessions in the valley where the Appaloosa, Seven, now grazed and ran free with his brood of mares.

Smoke had very carefully pushed all thoughts of the past behind him. He had spent months mentally conditioning himself not to think of himself as the gunfighter Smoke. His name was now Buck. Last names were not terribly important in the newly opened western frontier, and it had been with a smile that Buck chose West as his last name.

Buck West. Smoke was gone—for a time.

Buck laughed. But it was more a dark bark, totally devoid of humor.

Drifter swung his head around, looking at the man

through cold killer eyes. Buck's packhorses continued to graze.

High above, an eagle soared, pushing and gliding toward the west. Buck could have sworn that it was the same eagle he had seen months back, after the terrible shootout at the silver camp not far from the Uncompahgre. At least fourteen men had died under his guns that smoky, bloody day. And he had taken more than his share of lead, as well. It had taken him months to fully recover.

Many months back, in the southwestern corner of Wyoming, he had seen the first wanted poster.

WANTED
DEAD OR ALIVE
THE OUTLAW AND MURDERER
SMOKE JENSEN
10,000.00 REWARD
CONTACT THE SHERIFF AT BURY, IDAHO
TERRITORY

He had removed the wanted poster and tucked it in his shirt pocket. He knew he would see many, many more of the dodgers as he made his way west. He had looked up to watch an eagle soar high above him, gliding majestically northwestward.

He had said, with the big skies and grandeur of the open country as witnesses, "Take a message with you, eagle. Tell Potter and Richards and Stratton and all their gunhands that I'm coming to kill them. For my Pa, for Preacher, for my son, and for making me an outlaw. And they'll die just as hard as Nicole did. You tell them, eagle. Tell them I'm coming after them."

The eagle had circled, dipped its wings, and flown on.

Buck shook away the memories, clearing his head of things dead and buried and gone. He let the smoldering coals of revenge burn on, deep within his soul. He would fan the coals into white-hot flames when branding time arrived. And he would do the branding—with hot lead.

The man who had earned the reputation as one of the most feared gunfighters in the newly opened west spoke gently to Drifter and the big cat-footed stallion moved out through the timber.

Buck was just west of the Rockies, skirting south of the Gros Ventre Range. He would—unless he hit some sort of snag—make Moose Flat in two days. Once at the Flat, he would camp for a few days and rest Drifter. Then he would ride for Bury, Idaho Territory.

Bury was a good name, Buck thought. For that is exactly what I intend to do to Stratton and Richards and Potter: bury them!

It was cool during the day and flat-out cold at night; early spring when Buck crossed the still ill-defined line into Idaho Territory. He had seen several bands of Indians, but they had left him alone. He knew they'd seen him, for this was their country, and they knew it as intimately as the roots of a tree knows the earth that nurtures it. But Indians, as Preacher had once put it, were notional critters.

Buck moved out, slowly. He would take his time, get accustomed to the country, and eyeball everything in sight. For if he made it out of Bury alive, he was going to need more than one back door and one hell of a good hiding place.

Buck wore gray pin-striped trousers tucked into soft calfskin boots. Black shirt. His hat was black, low-crowned, and wide-brimmed. His leather vest was black. His belt was silver-studded with a heavy buckle. A jacket and slicker were tied behind the saddle, over the saddlebags. A Henry repeating rifle rested in a boot, butt forward instead of the usual fashion of the butt facing back. He did not ride in the usual slump-shouldered manner of the old mountain men, but instead sat his saddle ramrod straight, cavalry fashion. Because of this, many who saw the handsome, cold-eyed young man believed him to be ex-cavalry. He let them think it, knowing that helped to further disguise his past.

He carried a two-shot derringer in his left boot, in his right boot a long-bladed, double-edged dagger—that knife in addition to the Bowie he wore on his gunbelt, behind his left-hand gun.

Buck was an expert with all the weapons he carried. The legend growing around the man stated there was no faster gunhand in all the west. He was faster than the Texas gun Hardin; even more steel-nerved than Wild Bill; meaner than Curly Bill; when he was in the right, crueler than any Apache; as relentless in a hunt as any man who ever lived.

The old mountain man, Preacher, who helped raise him from a lad, had taught him fistfighting and boxing and Indian wrestling. But even more importantly, Preacher had taught him how to win, teaching him that it don't make a good gawddamn how you win—just win.

The old mountain man had said, and the boy had remembered, "Long as you right, Smoke, it don't make no difference how you win. Just be sure you in the right."

And Lord God, how fast the young man was with those deadly .44s.

Buck gave Drifter his head, letting the horse pick his own way at his own pace, staying close to the timber, away from open places, always edging slightly south and west. He wanted to enter the mostly uncharted center of the Territory from the south. Just north of the Craters of the Moon, Buck would turn Drifter's nose north until he hit the Big Lost River. He would follow that through some of the most beautiful and wild country in the Territory. He would then track the Big Lost for a time, then head more north than west until reaching the new town of Challis. There, he would resupply and head north, following the Salmon River for about thirty-five miles. Bury was located about midway between the Salmon and the town of Tendoy.

But if Buck had his way, the town of Bury would soon cease to exist.

It would be several more years before the toll road would be started from Challis, reaching to Bonanza, with a spur to Salmon. Only then would the big-scale silver mining at Bay Horse get underway.

But that was future. This was now. And Buck was not heading for Bury to pan for gold, search for silver, or start a ranch. And he really didn't care all that much if he died doing what he'd set out to do—just so long as he got it done. The men now living and prospering in and around Bury had directly killed his brother. They had ordered out the men who had killed his father; raped, tortured, and murdered Buck's wife, Nicole; killed his baby son; and killed his best friend and mentor, the old mountain man, Preacher.

And then they had done their cruel best to kill the man who now called himself Buck West.

Stratton, Potter, and Richards had thrown their best gunhands at the young man. He had killed them all.

Thus far, Stratton, Potter, and Richards had failed to stop Buck.

Buck had no intention of failing.

2

Buck was being followed. He had yet to catch a glimpse of his pursuers, but he knew someone was tracking him; knew it by that itchy feeling between his shoulder blades. Twice in as many days he had stopped and spent several hours checking his backtrail. But to no avail. Whoever or whatever it was coming along behind him was laying way back, several miles at least. And they were very good at tracking. They would have to be, for Buck not to have spotted them, and Preacher had taught the young man well.

Puzzled, Buck rode on, pushing himself and his horses, skirting the fast-growing towns in the eastern part of the state, staying to the north of them. Because of the man, or men, tracking him, Buck changed his plans and direction. He rode seemingly aimlessly, first heading straight north, then cutting south into the Bridger Wilderness. He crossed into Idaho Territory and made camp on the north end of Grays Lake. He was running very low on supplies, but living off the land was second nature to Buck, and doing without was merely a part of staying alive in a yet wild and untamed land.

The person or persons following him stayed back, seemingly content to have the young man in sight, electing not to make an appearance—yet.

Midafternoon of his second day at Grays Lake, Buck watched Drifter's ears prick up, the eyes growing cautious as the stallion lifted his head.

Buck knew company was coming.

A voice helloed the camp.

"If you're friendly, come on in," Buck called. "If you want trouble, I'll give you all you can handle."

Buck knew the grizzled old man slowly riding toward his small fire, but could not immediately put a name to him. The man—anywhere between sixty-five and a hundred and five—dismounted and helped himself to coffee and pan bread and venison. He ate slowly, his eyes appraising Buck without expression. Finally, he belched politely and wiped his hands on greasy buckskins. He poured another cup of coffee and settled back on the ground.

"Don't talk none yet," the old man said. "Jist listen. You be the pup Preacher taken under his wing some years back. Knowed it was you. Ante's been upped some on your head, boy. Nearabouts thirty thousand dollars on you, now. You must have a hundred men after you. Hard men, boy. Most of 'em. You good, boy, but you ain't that good. Sooner 'er later, you'll slip up, git tared, have to rest, then they'll git you." He paused to gnaw on another piece of pan bread.

"The point of all this is . . . ?" Buck said.

"Tole you to hush up and listen. Jawin' makes me hungry. 'Mong other things. Makes my mouth hurt too. You got anything to ease the pain?"

"Pint in that pack right over there." Buck jerked his head.

The old mountain man took two huge swallows of the rye, coughed, and returned to the fire. "Gawddamn farmers and such run us old boys toward the west. Trappin's fair, but they ain't no market to speak of. Ten of us got us a camp just south of Castle Peak, in the Sawtooth. Gittin' plumb borin'. We figured on headin' north in about a week." He lifted his old eyes. "Up toward Bury. We gonna take our time. Ain't no point in gettin' in no lather." He got to his feet and walked toward his horses. "Might see you up there, boy. Thanks for the grub."

"What are you called?" Buck asked.

"Tenneysee," the old man said without looking back. He mounted up and slowly rode back in the direction he'd come.

"You're not any better lookin' than the last time I saw you!" Buck called to the old man's back, grinning as he spoke.

"Ain't supposed to be," Tenneysee called. "Now git et and git gone. You got trouble on your backtrail."

"Yeah, I know!" Buck shouted.

"Worser'n Preacher!" Tenneysee called. "Cain't tell neither of you nuttin'!"

Then he was gone into the timber.

Fifteen minutes later, Buck had saddled Drifter, cinched down the packs on his pack animal, and was gone, riding northwest.

He wondered how many men were trailing him. And how good they were.

He figured he would soon find out.

Staying below the crest of a hill, Buck ground-reined Drifter and scanned his backtrail. It was then he caught the first glimpse of those following him. Four riders, riding easy and seemingly confident. He removed a brass spyglass from his saddlebags and pulled it fully extended, sighting the riders in. He did not recognize any of them, but could see they were all heavily armed. Hardcases, every one of them.

Buck looked back over his shoulder, toward the west. He smiled at the sight. Blackfeet. And the way they were traveling, the gunhands and the warlike Blackfeet would soon come face-to-face.

The Blackfeet had not always hated the white man. Long before the Lewis and Clark expedition, the Blackfeet had been in contact with the French-Canadian trappers of the Hudson's Bay Company. For the most part, they had gotten along. But in 1806, when the Lewis and Clark expedition split up, Clark turning southward to explore the Yellowstone River, Lewis taking the Blackfoot Branch as the best route to the Missouri, Lewis had encountered a band of Blackfeet. No one knows who started the fight, or why, and the journals of Lewis don't say, but the battle had a long-lasting effect. Since the Blackfeet were the most powerful and warlike tribe in the Northwest, their hatred following the battle closed both rivers to American travel.

Buck was puzzled why so many Blackfeet were in this part of the Territory, somewhat off their beaten path. He concluded, after looking them over through his spyglass, that they were a war party, and had been quite successful, judging from the scalps on their rifles and coup sticks and wound into their horses' manes.

Buck smiled as the Blackfeet spotted the white men first. Within seconds, the Blackfeet had vanished, the war party splitting up, lying in silent wait to spring the deadly ambush.

Buck didn't wait around for the fun. He quickly mounted up and took off in the other direction. Blackfeet had a reputation for being downright testy at times.

And from the north, a pair of old eyes watched as Buck rode out. The eyes followed the young man until he was out of sight.

Buck heard the shots from the short battle as he continued to put more distance between himself and the Blackfeet. The old man waited almost an hour before leaving his hiding place. Leading a pack animal, he slowly rode after Buck. He was in no hurry, for he knew where Buck was going and what he was going to do. He just wanted to be there to help the young man out.

1874 in most of Idaho Territory was no place for the faint-hearted, the lazy, the coward, or the shirker. 1874 Idaho Territory was pure frontier, as wild and woolly as the individual wanted to make it. It would be three more long, bloody, and heartbreaking years for the Nez Percé Indians before Chief Joseph would lead his demoralized tribe on the thirteen-hundred-mile retreat to Canada. There, the chief would utter, "I am tired; my heart is sick and sad. From where the sun now stands I will fight no more forever."

But in 1874, the Indians were still fighting all over Idaho Territory, including the Bannocks and Shoshones. It was a time for wary watchfulness.

It had been fourteen years since an expedition led by Captain Elias D. Pierce of California had discovered gold on Orofino Creek, a tributary of the Clearwater River. It wasn't much gold, but it was gold. Thousands had heard the cry and the tug of easy riches, and thousands had come. They had poured into the state, expecting to find nuggets lying everywhere. Many had never been heard from again. As Buck rode through the southern part of the state, heading for the black and barren lava fields called the Craters of the Moon, even here he was able to see the mute heartbreak of the gold-seekers: the mining equipment lying abandoned and rusting, the dredges in dry creek beds. Now, in early summer, a time when the creeks and rivers were starting to recede, Buck spotted along the banks a miner's boot, a pan. He wondered what stories they could tell.

He rode on, always checking his backtrail. He had a vague uneasy feeling that he was still being followed. But he could never spot his follower. And that was cause for alarm, for Buck, even though still a young man, was an expert in surviving in the wilderness.

He skirted south of the still-unnamed village of Idaho Falls, a place one man claimed "openly wore the worst side out."

Buck rode slowly but steadily, coming up on the south side of the Big Lost, north of the Craters of the Moon. He stopped at a trading post at what would someday become a resort town called Arco. Inside the dark, dirty place, filled with skins and the smell of rotgut whiskey, Buck bought bacon and beans and coffee from a scar-faced clerk. The clerk smelled as bad as his store.

Buck's eyes flicked over several wanted posters tacked to the wall. There he was.

"Last one of them I seen had ten thousand dollars reward on it," he said, to no one in particular. He noticed several men at a corner table ceased their card playing.

"Ante's been upped," the clerk/bartender said with a grunt.

"Man could do a lot with thirty thousand dollars," Buck said. He walked to the bar and ordered whiskey. He didn't really care for the stuff but he wanted information, and bartenders seldom talked to a non-drinking loafer. "The good stuff," he told the bartender. The man replaced one bottle and reached under the counter for another bottle.

He grinned, exposing blackened stubs of teeth. "This one ain't got no snake heads in it."

Buck lifted the glass. Smelled like bear piss. Keeping his expression noncommittal, he sipped the whiskey. Tasted even worse.

"Have any trouble coming from the east?" the bartender asked.

"How'd you know I come from the east?"

"That's the way you rode in."

"Seen some Blackfeet two-three days ago. But they didn't see me. I didn't hang around long."

"Smart."

"You see four men, riding together?" the voice came from behind Buck, from the card table.

"Yeah. And so did the Blackfeet."

"Crap! You reckon the Injuns got 'em?"

"I reckon so. I didn't hang around to see."

"You mean you jist rode off without lendin' a hand?"

"One more wouldn't have made any difference," Buck said quietly, knowing what was coming.

"Then I reckon that makes you a coward, don't it?" the cardplayer said, standing up.

Buck slowly placed the shot glass of bear piss back on the rough bar. He eyeballed the man. Two guns worn low and tied down. The leather hammer thongs off. "Either that or careful."

"You know what I think, Slick? I think it makes you yellow."

"Well, I'll tell you what I think," Buck said. "I think you don't know your bunghole from your mouth."

The man flushed in the dim light of the trading post. His dirty hands hovered over his guns. "I think I'll jist kill you for that."

"Bet or fold," Buck said.

The man's hands dipped down. Buck's right-hand .44 roared. The gunhand was dead before he hit the floor, the slug taking him in the center of the chest, exploding his heart.

"I never even seen the draw," the bartender said, his voice hushed and awe-filled.

"Any of you other boys want to ante up in this game?" Buck asked.

None did.

The dead man broke wind as escaping gas left his cooling body.

"He were my partner," a man still seated at the table said. "But he were in the wrong this time. I lay claim to his pockets."

"Suits me," Buck said. No one had even seen him holster his .44. "He have a name?"

"Big Jack. From up Montana way. Never spoke no last name. Who you be?"

"Buck West. I been trackin' that damned Smoke Jensen for the better part of six months."

Big Jack's partner visibly relaxed. "Us, too. I would ask if you wanted some company, but you look like you ride alone."

"That's right."

"Name's Jerry. This here's Carl and Paul. Don't reckon you'd give us a hand diggin' the hole for Jack?"

"I don't reckon so."

"Cain't much blame you."

"Bury him out back," the bartender said. "Deep. If he smells any worser dead than alive I'll have to move my place of business."

3

The men watched as Buck rode away, ramrod straight in the saddle. Jerry said, "That young feller is faster than greased lightning."

"Faster than Jesse, I betcha!"

"Ain't no faster than Wild Bill, though," Paul said.

Jerry spat on the ground. "Wild Bill ain't crap!"

"You don't say!" Carl turned on his friend. "I suppose you gonna tell us Wild Bill didn't clean up Abilene?"

"He sure as hell didn't. I know. I were there. Me and Phil Coe. I seen Wild Bill shoot him with a pair of derringers after Phil done put his gun away. Then he turned around and shot the marshal, Mike Williams. Wild Bill better not ever try to brace that there Buck West. Buck's a bad one, boys. Cold-eyed as a snake."

It would be almost exactly two and one half years later, on the afternoon of August 2, 1876, in Deadwood, South Dakota, when a cross-eyed, busted-nose wino named Jack McCall would blow out Hickok's brains as he studied his poker hand of Aces and Eights. Wild Bill would be thirty-nine years old.

"I think Potter ought to know about this here Buck

West," Jerry said. "Think I'll take me a ride later on. Let Buck get good and gone."

"We'll tag along."

Late that afternoon a stranger rode up to the trading post and walked inside. He cradled a Henry repeating rifle in the crook of his left arm. "I seen the fresh grave out back," he said to the barkeep. "Friend of yourn?"

"Hell, no! Don't git me to lyin'."

"Man ought to have a marker on his grave, don't you think?"

"I'll git around to it one of these days. Maybe. Big Jack was all they called him."

"Better than nothin'. I don't reckon he died of natural causes?"

"Not likely. You gonna talk all day or buy a drink of whiskey?"

The buckskin-dressed old man tossed some change on the wide rough board that passed for a counter. "That buy a jug?"

"And then some. No, sir. That Big Jack fancied hisself a gunhand, I guess." He placed a dirty cup and a clay jug of rotgut on the counter. "But he done run up on a ringtailed-tooter this day. Feller by the name of Buck West. You heard of him?"

"Seems I have, somewheres. Bounty hunter, I think. But he's a bad man to mess with."

"Tell me! Why, he drew so fast a feller couldn't even see the blur! Big Jack's hand could just touch the butt of his .36 when the lead hit him in the center of the chest. Dead 'fore he hit the ground."

The old man smiled. "That fast, hey?"

"Lord have mercy, yes!" He eyeballed the old man. "Ain't I seen you afore? You a mountain man, ain't you? Ain't so many of you old boys left."

"Not me, podner. I'm retared from the east. Come out

here to pass my golden years amid the peace and tranquility of the High Lonesome."

The bartender, no spring chicken himself, narrowed his eyes and said, "And you jist as full of shit now as you was forty year ago, you old goat!"

The old man laughed. "Wal, you jist keep that information inside that head of yourn and off your tongue. You do that and I won't tell nobody I know where Rowdy Jake Kelly was retared to. You still got money on your head, Rowdy."

"Man, I heard you got kilt! Shot all to hell and gone over to Needle Mountains."

"Part of it's true. I got all dressed up in my finest buckskins, rode an old nag up into the hills, and laid me down to die. Lordy, but I was hurtin' some. Longer I laid there the madder I got. I finally got up, said to hell with this, and rode off. Found me one of my Injun kids—or grandkids, I ain't real sure which—and she took care of me. You keep hush about this, now, you hear?"

"I never saw you afore this day," Rowdy Jake Kelly said.

The old man nodded, picked up his jug of whiskey, and rode off.

Buck had left the trading post and followed the Big Lost River north. He pushed his horses, rested them, then pushed them hard again, putting as many miles as possible between himself and the trading post. He had a hunch the men back at the trading post would be hell-bent for Bury. They were bounty hunters; he knew from the look. He smiled grimly at what they might think if they knew they had been within touching distance of the man called Smoke.

Buck found himself a hidden vantage point where he could watch the trail, and settled in for the evening. He built a hand-sized fire and fixed bacon and beans and coffee. Using tinder-dry wood, the fire was virtually smokeless. He kept his coffee warm over the coals.

Just at dusk, he heard the sounds of riders. Three riders. He watched as they passed his hiding place at a slow canter, heading north, toward the trading post at Mackay. He watched and listened until the sounds of steel-shod hooves faded into the settling dusk. Using his saddle for a pillow, Buck went to sleep.

Just as the first rays of dawn streaked the horizon, Buck was fording the Big Lost, heading for the eastern banks and the Lost River Range. He did not want to travel those flats that stretched for miles before reaching Challis, preferring to remain in the timber.

He wanted to take his time getting to Bury for two reasons: One, he wanted the story of the shoot-out at the trading post to reach the right ears—namely, Potter, Stratton, and Richards. Men like that could always use another gun, and Buck intended to be that other gun. Two, he still had that nagging sensation of being followed. And it annoyed him. He knew, *felt,* someone was back there. He just didn't know who.

The eighty-mile ride from the trading post to Challis passed slowly, and Buck took his time, enjoying the sights of new country. Buck was a man who loved the wilderness, loved its great beauty, loved the feeling of being alone, although he knew perfectly well he certainly was not alone. There were the eagles and hawks who soared and glided above him. The playful camp-robber birds, the squirrels and bears and puma, the breathless beauty of wild flowers in early summer. No, he was not alone in the wilderness. Alone was just a state of mind. Buck had only to look around him for company, compliments of nature.

Sensing more than hearing movement, Buck cut toward the west and into the deep timber of the Lost River Range. He quieted his horses and waited in the timber.

Then he spotted them. It was a war party, and a big one. From this distance—he couldn't risk using his spyglass, for it was afternoon and he was facing west, and didn't want to risk sunlight bouncing off the lens—he could only guess the tribe. Nez Percé, Bannock—maybe Sheepeater. Preacher had told him about the little known but highly feared Sheepeaters.

Buck counted the braves. Thirty of them, all painted up and looking for trouble. He cursed under his breath as they reined up and dismounted, after sending lookouts in all directions.

Were they going to make camp? Buck didn't know. But he knew it was awfully early for that.

To the south, Borah Peak, almost thirteen thousand feet high, loomed up stark in the high lonesome. The highest peak in the state, Borah dominated matters for miles.

Buck sat it out for several hours, watching and waiting out the long minutes. The horses seemed to sense the urgency of the moment and were very quiet. Occasionally, Buck would slip back to them to pat and water them, whispering gently to the animals, keeping them still and calm.

Returning from his last trip to the animals, Buck looked out over the valley he was high above. He grunted, not in surprise, but rather an "I should have known" grunt.

The Indians were gone, having left as swiftly and silently as they had come. Buck lay still for another ten minutes, mulling the situation over in his mind.

The war party had built no fires, either cook or signal. They had met with no other Indians. Why had they stopped? Buck had no idea. But he knew one thing: he damn sure wasn't going to head out after them. Whichever direction the war party had taken, he planned to head in the other direction. And he did. Before two minutes had passed, Buck had tightened cinches and was heading out. He found where the war party had ridden south, so he swung Drifter's head and pointed his nose north, toward the muddy, brawling town of Challis, located just to the northwest of the Salmon River. Buck would hang around Challis for a few days, listening to the miners talk and attempting to get the feel of what the townspeople thought of Bury, some thirty-five miles north and slightly east.

Challis was one short business street, more saloons than anything else, with tents and shacks and a few permanent-looking homes to the north. Most of the shacks appeared to have been tossed in their location by some giant crap-shooter.

Buck stabled his horses—he wasn't worried about anyone stealing Drifter, for the stallion would kill anyone who entered his stall—and taking his Henry repeating rifle, a change of clothing, and his saddlebags, Buck walked toward the town's hotel.

After checking in, Buck went to a barber shop and took a hot bath, a young Chinese man keeping the water hot with additional buckets of water. After Buck had soaped off the weeks of dirt and fleas, he dressed in dark trousers, white shirt, and vest. He left his boots to be shined and settled in the barber chair.

"Short," he told the barber. "And trim my beard."

"Passin' through?" the barber asked.

"Could be. Mostly just drifting."

The barber had noted Buck's tied-down guns. Being an observant man, and one raised on the frontier, he knew a fast gun when he saw one. And this man sitting in his chair was a gunhand, and no tinhorn. The butts of his .44s were worn smooth from handling, with no marks in the wood to signify kills. Only a tinhorn did that, and tinhorns didn't last long in the west.

But there was something else about this young man. Confidence. That was it. And a cold air about him. Not unfriendly, just cold.

"If it's silver you're huntin'"—he knew it wasn't—"big strike north and east of here. Close to the Lemhi River."

"Not for me," Buck told him. "Too much work involved in that."

"Uh-huh. You be handy with them .44s?"

"Some folks say that."

"You head north from here, follow the Salmon until the river cuts through the Lemhi range, then head east. You'll come up on the town of Bury."

"Hell of a name for a town."

"It's right proper, considerin' the size of their Boot Hill. You'll see."

"Why would I want to go to someplace called Bury?"

"Maybe you don't. Then again, you might find work up there."

"Might do that. How's the law in this town?" Buck set the stage with that question.

"Tough when they have to be. Long as it's a fair fight, they won't bother you."

"I never shot no one in the back," Buck replied, putting it just a bit testily.

"You don't have that look about you, that's for sure." The barber's voice was very bland.

"Where's the best place to eat?"

"Marie's. Just up the street. Beef and beans and apple pie. Good portions, too. Reasonable."

They weren't just good portions; they were huge. The food simple but well-prepared. The apple pie was delicious. Buck pushed the empty plate away and settled back, leaning back in his chair, his back to a wall. He lingered over a third cup of coffee and watched the activity in the street through the window.

He was waiting for the marshal or sheriff to make his appearance. It didn't take long.

The town marshal entered the cafe, a deputy behind

him. The deputy held a sawed-off double-barrel twelve-gauge express gun in his hands. And it appeared he had used it before.

The marshal was not a man to back up or mince words. He sat down at Buck's table, facing him, and ordered a cup of coffee. He stared at Buck.

Buck returned the stare.

"Passin' through?" the marshal asked.

"Might stay two or three days. I'm in no big hurry to get anywhere."

"You got a name?"

Buck smiled. "I'm not wanted."

"That don't answer my question."

"Buck West." Buck then placed the man. Dooley. He'd been a lawman over in Colorado for years. A straight, no-nonsense lawman. But a fair one.

Dooley pointed up the street. "Them houses with paint on them beginning at the end of the street is off-bounds for drifters. Decent folks live there. The dosshouses is on the other end of the street." He pointed. "Thataway." He jerked his thumb. "The road out of town is thataway. Feel free to take it as soon as possible."

"I don't intend to cause you or your men any trouble, Marshal," Buck said softly.

"But you will," the marshal replied just as softly. "You just got that air about you."

"You're a very suspicious man, Marshal."

"Goes with the job, son." The marshal drained his coffee cup, stood up, and started to leave. He looked once more at Buck. "You sure look familiar, mister."

"I just have a friendly face," Buck said solemnly.

"Yeah," the marshal said drily. "I'm sure that's it."

4

As he stood facing the two men in the saloon, it occurred to Buck that perhaps the marshal just might have been right. Buck had entered the saloon, ordered a beer, and had nursed it for about fifteen minutes before the cowboy with a loud and arrogant mouth had begun needling him.

"You gonna drink that beer or stand there and look at it with your face hangin' out?"

Buck ignored him.

"Boy, you better talk to me!" the cowhand said.

"I intend to drink this beer," Buck said, "in my own good time. Not that it's any of your business."

The cowboy took a step backward, a puzzled look on his face. Buck knew the type. He was big and broad and solid with muscle. And he was used to getting his way.

He had been a bully all his life. He belittled anything he was too stupid to comprehend—which was nearly everything.

"That's Harry Carson, stranger," the barkeep whispered.

"Is that supposed to mean something to me?" Buck said, not bothering to keep his voice to a whisper.

"And his buddy is Wade Phillips," the barkeep plunged ahead.

"I wonder if either one of them can spell 'unimpressed,'" Buck said. He felt the old familiar rage fill him. He had never been able to tolerate bullies; not even as a boy back in Missouri.

The deputy who had been with Marshal Dooley earlier that day leaned against the bar, silently watching the show unfold before him. Carson and Phillips were both loud-mouthed troublemakers. But he felt he had pegged this tall young man right. If he was correct in his assumption, Carson and Phillips would never pick another fight after this night.

The deputy slipped out of the line of possible gunfire and sipped his beer.

"What'd you say, buddy?" Carson stuck his chin out belligerently.

Buck fought back his anger. "Go on, Carson. Back off, drink your drink, and leave me be."

"You got a smart mouth, buddy." Phillips stuck his ugly, broad-nosed and boozy face into it.

Upon entering the place, Buck had slipped the hammer thongs off his .44s. He slowly turned to face the twin loudmouths.

"I'm saying now I'm not looking for trouble. But if I'm pushed into it, so be it."

"Talks fancy, don't he?" Phillips's laugh was ugly. But so was he, so it rounded out.

"Yeah," Carson said. "And got them fancy guns on, too. But I betcha he ain't got the sand in him to duke it out."

Buck's smile was faint. He had pegged the men accurately. Both men probably realized that neither one of them could beat Buck in a gunfight, so they would push him into a fight with fists and boots. And if he didn't fight them at their own game, he would be branded a coward.

The bully's way.

Buck took off his gunbelt and laid it on the bar. Spotting the deputy, he slid the hardware down the bar to him. "Look after those, will you, please?"

"Be glad to, West. Watch 'em. They're both dirty at the game."

Buck drained his beer mug and said, "Not nearly as dirty as I am."

Then Buck smashed the mug into Carson's face. The heavy mug broke the man's nose on impact. Buck then jabbed the jagged broken edges into the man's cheek and lips, sending the bully screaming and bleeding to the sawdust-covered floor.

Buck hit Phillips a combination left and right, glazing the man's eyes with the short, brutal punches. Buck did not like to fight with his bare fists, knowing it was a fool's game. But sometimes that was the only immediate option. Until other objects could be brought into play.

Phillips jumped to his boots, in a crouch. Buck stepped close and brought one knee up, at the same time bringing both hands down. As his hands grabbed the man's neck, his knee came in contact with the man's face. The crunch of breaking bones was loud in the saloon.

The fight was over. Carson lay squalling and bleeding on the floor beside the unconscious Phillips. Buck turned around. Marshal Dooley was standing by his deputy.

"Any law against a fair fight, Marshal?" Buck asked. "It was two against one."

"And they were outnumbered at those odds," Dooley said. "No, West, there is no law against it. Yet," he added. "But someday there will be."

Buck retrieved his guns and buckled them around his waist. "Not as long as there are people so stupid as to place and praise physical brawn over the capacity of reason."

Dooley blinked. "Who are you, West? You're no drifting gunhand. You've got intelligence."

"Anybody who wishes to do so can read, Marshal. And most of us can think and reason. That's who I am. Good night, Marshal."

Buck picked up his hat from the bar and walked out into the night.

"More to him than meets the eyes, Marshal," the deputy observed.

"Yeah," said the marshal. "But it's that unknown about him that I'm afraid of."

Buck spent the next three days loafing and listening around Challis. He read a dozen six-month-old newspapers, bought a well-worn book of verse by Shelley and began reading that. He played a little poker, winning some, losing some, and ending up breaking about even. Twice he saw a couple of the most disreputable-looking men he'd seen in years. He knew they were mountain men, and he knew they were checking on him. The men had to be close to seventy years old, but they still looked like they could wrestle a grizzly bear. And probably win.

Some of the so-called "good people" of the community sniffed disdainfully at the sight of the buckskin-clad old men, snubbing them, having highly uncomplimentary things to say about them. Buck wanted to say, "But these men opened the way west. These men faced the dangers, most of the time alone. And many of their compadres were killed opening the way west. Had it not been for them, you folks would still be waiting to make the trek westward. These men are some of the true heroes of our time; living legends. You should welcome them, praise them, not snub and insult them."

But Buck kept his mouth shut, knowing he would be wasting his words. He recalled the words of that fellow called Thoreau: If a man does not keep pace with his companions, perhaps it is because he hears a different drummer. Let him step to the music which he hears, however measured or far away.

But Buck knew there was more to it than that. And he silently cursed his lack of education, vowing to read and retain more wisdom of words. He had left his books, his precious books, back at the cabin in that lovely lonely meadow, where he had buried his wife and son. Nicole and Arthur. He knew someday he'd return to that valley. If he lived through his mission.

He leaned back in his chair on the boardwalk, his back to a storefront, and pondered away a few moments, wondering why so many people built false and unworthy idols. These old mountain men were, in some cases, like military men. Looked down on and cursed until the need for them arises, then, as that moment passes, they are once more shunted aside. Like those signs Buck had been seeing on some stores: NO IRISH WANTED HERE.

Buck's philosophical meanderings were shoved aside as his eyes found the two men walking slowly down the center of the dirt main street.

Phillips and Carson. Both of them wearing two pistols. Their hands were near the pistols, ready to draw. With a sigh, Buck stood up and looked around him. Then he remembered: Marshal Dooley and his deputy had left that morning to ride out to a ranch; something about rustling.

"Get out in the street, West!" pig-face Phillips yelled.

Buck stepped off the boardwalk, slipping the leather thongs from the hammers of his .44s as he walked.

Front doors and windows facing the street banged shut as the residents headed for cover. Gunfights were nothing new to these people. They just wanted to view it from a safe place.

"It doesn't have to be this way, boys!" Buck called. But he knew it did. With people like Carson and Phillips, winning was the only way. So-called "loss of face" was totally unacceptable. Reasoning was beyond their comprehension.

Something is wrong with this method of settling disputes, Buck thought. And something is very wrong with my own personal vendetta. But the young man, self-educated as far as his education went, knew that, at this point in the advancement of civilization, a dusty street and the smell of gunsmoke was judge and jury.

But he also knew that lawyers weren't the final answer, either. They mucked matters up too much, twisting and reshaping the truth.

There had to be a better middle ground. But damned if he knew what it was.

"You ready to die, boy?" Carson yelled.

Buck cut his eyes for just an instant. Standing in front of a saloon was one of the men from back at the trading post. What was his name? Jerry. Yeah. Big Jack's buddy. And standing a few yards from him, an old buckskin-dressed mountain man. The mountain man, old and big and still solid, cradled a Henry repeating rifle in the crook of one massive arm.

"We all have to see the elephant sometime," Buck said. He could tell the men facing him were nervous. Since he had whipped them that night, Buck had heard stories about Carson and Phillips. They were thugs and ne'er-do-wells. Shiftless troublemakers. Buck had heard that the pair had used guns before, but were not gunhands, per se. They were back-shooters, cowards. But of course, as Buck knew well, most bullies were cowards.

Buck stood in the center of the street, standing tall and straight, his big hands, rough and work-hardened, close to his guns.

There was fifty feet between the men when Carson

and pig-face Phillips stopped. Buck could see the sweat on the men's faces. Buck knew he could not afford to draw first. Even though the men were trash, this was their town; Buck was a stranger. They had to draw first in order for it to be called self-defense. Even if it was two on one.

Buck stood quietly, waiting.

"You had no call to scar us up like you did," Carson yelled. "You don't fight fair."

Buck waited.

Then Buck knew what had been wrong with his philosophical thinking of a few moments ago. These men were mentally ill-equipped to face the day-to-day struggles of living peacefully. But was that Buck's fault? Was he, and others like him, responsible for Carson and Phillips and others like them? What would happen if he presented them with an armload of books, saying to them, "Here, gentlemen, within these pages lie the answers. Here is a thousand years of wisdom. Understand this and you'll learn how to cope; how to live decently . . ." Buck shook those thoughts away.

We are all put here on this earth with the capability to learn to reason. These men, and others like them, don't want to learn. Therefore, it lies on their head, not mine. We come into this world naked and helpless and squalling. Yes. But we are equal to the task of learning.

Buck mentally settled it.

To hell with them!

"Ain't you got no tongue?" Phillips hollered. "Cain't you talk?"

"What do you want me to say?" Buck asked.

"Beg and we'll let you turn tail and run on out of here!" Carson yelled.

"I beg to no man," Buck's words were softly offered.

"Then die!" Phillips screamed. He reached for his gun.

Buck let him clear leather before he drew his right-hand .44. He fired twice, one slug taking Phillips in the belly, the second slug hitting the man in the center of his chest. Phillips fell backward, mortally wounded.

Carson had not drawn. The man's face was chalky white. He watched as Buck holstered his .44. Buck waited patiently.

The street was silent as a hundred pairs of eyes watched in awe and disbelief, the incredible speed of the tall young man an astonishing thing to witness. His hand had been like a blur as he drew, cocked, and fired.

"Back off, Carson," Buck said. "Just turn around and walk away and it's over. How about it?"

A hundred pairs of ears heard him offer the man his life.

A hundred pairs of ears heard Carson refuse the offer. "Hell with you!" Carson snarled, and went for his gun.

Born with the gift of ambidextrousness, Buck was as fast with his left hand as with his right. In a heartbeat, Carson lay dead on the dusty street. The man's bootheels and spurs beat a death march on the dirt as his spirit joined that of Phillips, winging their way to their just rewards.

Buck reloaded his .44s and holstered them. He walked across the street to his chair and sat down.

People began streaming out of offices and stores and saloons. They gathered around the fallen pair of would-be gunhands. They looked at Buck, sitting calmly on the boardwalk.

"Mind if we get the man to take your picture?" some called.

Buck didn't mind at all. He wanted Stratton and Potter and Richards to hear of this.

The town's only photographer gathered up his bulky equipment and came on a run.

Buck sat calmly, waiting for the marshal.

5

"When you gonna tell the boy you still alive and kickin'?" Beartooth asked the mountain man who had been following Buck.

He was called Beartooth because he didn't have a tooth in his mouth. And hadn't had in forty years. No one knew what his Christian name was, and it wasn't a polite question to ask.

"I might not never," the mountain man said. "He thinks I'm dead. Might be best to keep it thataway. I'm only goin' in if and when he needs help."

"He'll need help," Dupre said. "Plenty guns up at Bury. And they all going to be aimed at your friend."

Dupre had drifted up from New Orleans in the late '20s. His accent was still as thick as sorghum.

"You ain't seen Smoke—'scuse me, *Buck*—git into action," the mountain man said. "He's hell on wheels, boys. Best I ever seen. And I seen 'em all."

"Don't start lyin', Preacher," Greybull said.

Greybull was a mountain of a man. It took a mule to pack him around.

"What do you think about it, Nighthawk?" Preacher asked.

"Ummm," the old Crow grunted.

"Whutever the hell that means," Tenneysee said. "Damned Injun ain't said fifteen words in the fifty year I been knowin' him."

"Ummm," Nighthawk said.

"Might make the lad feel better if'n he knowed you was still breathin'," Pugh said. Pugh was commonly referred to as "Phew!" He hated water. "Then again," Pugh said. "It might make him irritable. He probably said all sorts of kind words 'bout you. An' thinkin' of enough kind words 'bout you to bury you probably took him the better part of a month."

"Phew," Preacher said. "Would you mind changin' positions just a tad. Right there. Don't move. Now the wind is right. Why don't you take a bath? Damn, you'd make a vulture puke."

"Well, if you ask me—" Audie said.

"Nobody did," Beartooth said. "Hell, nobody can *see* you."

Audie was a midget. About three and a half feet tall. And about three and a half feet wide. He was a large amount of trouble in a very compact package.

"As I was saying," Audie said, "before your rudeness took precedent." Audie had taught school in Pennsylvania before the wanderlust hit him and he had struck out for the west, on a Shetland pony. When the Indians had seen him, they'd laughed so hard they forgot to kill him. "I think it best that Preacher keep his anonymity for the period preceding our arrival in Bury. Should Preacher reveal his living, breathing self to the young man, it might prove so traumatic as to be detrimental to Jensen's well-being."

"Ummm," Nighthawk said, nodding his head in agreement.

"Whut the hale's far you shakin' your head about, you dumb Injun?" Greybull said. "You don't know no more whut he said than us'ins do."

"Ummm," Nighthawk said.

"Whatever Audie said, I agree with him," Matt said. Matt was a Negro. Big and mean and one-eyed.

Matt was probably the youngest man present. And he was at least sixty-five. He had lost his eye during a fight with an angry mountain lion. Matt had finally broken the puma's back.

"Good Gawd, Audie!" Deadlead said. "Cain't you talk American? What the hell did you jist say?"

Deadlead had earned his nickname from being a crack shot with a pistol. Like most of the mountain men, no one knew what his Christian name was.

"Ummm," Nighthawk said.

"I say we break camp and meander on up towards Bury," Powder Pete said. "Old as we is, some of us might not make the trip if we wait much longer."

"I opt fer that myself," Tenneysee said. "What do you say, Nighthawk?"

"Ummm."

"I'll not have this town filled up with would-be gunhands looking to make themselves a reputation," Marshal Dooley said. "Get your truck together and hit the trail, West."

"Friendly place you have here, Marshal," Buck said with a double-edged smile.

"Yes, it is," Dooley said, ignoring the sarcasm in Buck's tone. "Something about you invites trouble, boy." He waved a hand absently. "I know, I know. You didn't start the fight. And I understand from talking with witnesses you even tried—slightly—to back away from it. That's good. But not good enough. Clear out, West."

"In the morning soon enough?"

Dooley wavered. He nodded his head. "Stay out of the saloons tonight and be gone by dawn."

Buck stepped out of the office onto the boardwalk. He didn't object to being asked to leave town. He didn't blame the law. It was time to be moving on. And there was no point in delaying his departure until morning. Buck was getting that closed-in feeling anyway. And so was Drifter. Last time he'd looked in on the animal, Drifter had rolled his eyes and tossed his head. And then proceeded to kick in the back of his stall.

Buck walked to the hotel, gathered up his gear, and headed for the stable. He had bought his supplies earlier and was ready to go.

"Ready to go, Drifter?" Buck asked the stallion.

Drifter reared up and smashed the front of his stall.

"Guess so," Buck mumbled.

The band of mountain men met Lobo at the base of Greyrock Mountain, about halfway between the Saw-tooth Wilderness area and Challis. Lobo briefed the men on what he'd seen in town.

It was rumored that Lobo had once lived with wolves.

"Faster than greased lightnin'," Lobo said. "I never seen nothin' like it afore in my life. An' the lad didn't even blink an eye doin' it."

"Tole you!" Preacher said to the men, grinning.

"Don't start braggin'," Powder Pete told Preacher. "It's bad 'nuff jist havin' to look at you." Powder Pete was so called because of his expertise with explosives.

"Did the law run him out of town?"

"Don't know. Didn't hang around to see. Law might *ask* him to leave. But if that there boy gits his back up, there ain't nobody gonna *run* him nowheres."

"Wal, les' us just sorta amble on toward the northeast," Preacher said. "If I know Smoke—and I do, I raised him—he'll take his time gettin' to Bury. He'll lay back in the timber for a day 'er so and look the situation over. We'll cross the Lost River Range, head acrost the flats, and turn north, make camp in the narrows south of Bury. I know me some Flatheads live just west of Bitterroot. Once we set up camp, I'll take me a ride over to the Divide, palaver some with 'em. They'll be our eyes and ears. That sound all right to you boys?"

"Quite inventive," Audie said.

"Ummm," Nighthawk grunted.

Buck crossed the Salmon to the east bank and began following the river north. He stayed on the fringe of the timber that made up the northern edge of the Lemhi Range. He would follow the river for about thirty-five miles before cutting to the east for about ten miles. That should put him on the outskirts of Bury. Once there, he would make camp south of the town and look it over.

The dozen mountain men, with about six hundred years of survival and fighting experience between them, were riding hard just south of Challis. With their rifles held across the saddlehorns, their fringed buckskins and animal-hide caps and brightly colored shirts and jackets and sashes, the last of the mountain men were returning for one more fight. They were riding hard to help—if he needed it—the youngest mountain man. One of their own. A young man who had chosen the lonely call of the wilderness as home. A young man who preferred the high lonesome over the towns and cities. A young man they had taken under their wing and helped to raise, imparting to him the wisdom of the wilderness, hopefully perpetuating a way of life that so-called civilized people now sneered at and rejected. This gathering, this aging motley crew, knew they were the last—the very last—of a select breed of men. After this ride, never again would so many gather. But hopefully, just maybe, their young protégé would live on, known for the rest of his life as the last mountain man.

6

The town of Bury, with a population of about five hundred, sat on a road first roughed out by Mormon settlers in the mid-1850s. Bury had a bank, probably the best school in that part of the country—a large, two-story building—a large mercantile store, a weekly newspaper, several saloons, several cafes, a large hotel, a sheriff, several deputies, a jail, a leather shop, and several other businesses, including a whorehouse located discreetly outside of town. The town also boasted several churches. A handful of ranches lay around the town, and a lot of producing mines as well.

And nearly all of it was owned by three men: Stratton, Potter, and Richards.

Bury also had a volunteer fire department. They were going to need a fire department before Buck was through.

The business district of Bury was three blocks long, on both sides of the wide street. It was down that street that Buck rode at midmorning. He had camped some miles from the town, watching the one road for two days. A stagecoach rolled in every other day. Wagons bringing supplies rolled by. Peddlers and tinkers and snake-oil salesmen rattled past.

Booming little town, Buck thought. For a while longer, that is.

The first thing Buck noticed in his slow ride up the street was the number of gunhands lounging about on the boardwalk, and not just in front of the saloons. A couple always seemed to be in front of the bank, as well. Buck guessed there had been some attempts to hold up the place. Or perhaps the Big Three were just cautious men.

He located the livery stable and arranged a stall for Drifter, warning the stable boy not to enter Drifter's stall.

"He's got a mean eye for sure," the boy said, eyeballing the stallion.

"He killed one man," Buck said, knowing that tale would soon spread throughout the small town.

The boy solemnly nodded his head.

Buck handed the boy a five-dollar gold piece. "Just between you and me, now. Make certain he gets an extra ration of grain."

"Yes, *sir*!"

"Both Drifter and the packhorse, now."

"Yes, *sir*!"

Taking his personal gear and his rifle, Buck stashed the rest of his gear in Drifter's stall. He walked toward the hotel. As he walked, he passed by a very pretty, dark-haired, hazel-eyed young woman. He smiled at her and she blushed. Buck paused and watched her walk on toward the edge of town. Buck crossed the street to better watch her and saw her push open the gate on a small picket fence and walk up onto the porch of a small house. She disappeared from view.

"Nice," he muttered.

"Sure is," a voice came from behind him.

Buck slowly turned around to face the sheriff and one

of his deputies. Neither one of them would win any prizes for good looks.

"Sheriff Reese. This is Rogers, one of my deputies. I don't know you."

That's good, Buck thought. But you will, Sheriff. You will. "Buck West."

"Ahh," Reese said. "Now I know you. The gunhand."

"Some say I am."

"Going to be in town long?"

"That depends."

"On what?"

"On how fast I get rested up, resupplied, and find out more about this Smoke Jensen and how I go about collecting the reward money."

Reese smiled. "First you have to catch him, hombre."

"I'll catch him," Buck said, without changing expression.

Reese stared at the young man. Something about this tall young man was just slightly unsettling. Even for a man like Dan Reese, who had worked on both sides of the law nearly all his life. Reese had worked the hoot-owl trails many times, in several states, ducking and dodging the law that sought him.

Beside him, Rogers stood and glared at Buck, forming an instant dislike for the young man. Rogers was big and solid, including that space between his ears. He was not just dumb; he was stupid. And very dangerous. He had killed more times than he could remember—with fists, guns, knife, or club.

"You stay away from Sally Reynolds," Rogers said. "I got my eyes on her. 'Sides, she likes me."

Buck cut his eyes to the deputy. He doubted that even Rogers's own mother liked him very much. Sally Reynolds. He wondered what the pretty lady did in Bury? "Sally Reynolds is one of our schoolteachers," Reese said. "She wouldn't want notin' to do with no damned bounty hunter like you, West."

"Uh-huh," Buck said. "You're probably right, Sheriff. Anything else I need to know about Bury and its citizens?"

Reese got the accurate impression that he had just been dismissed by Buck. The feeling irritated him. "Jist stay out of trouble."

Buck turned his back to the men and walked on up the boardwalk, toward the hotel.

"I don't lak him," Rogers said. "I think I'll kill him."

"I don't like him either. But you don't do nothin' 'til you're told to do it. You understand that, Rogers?"

"Yes, sir."

"Let's find out what Stratton thinks about this West."

"What's your impression of him?" Stratton asked.

Reese hesitated, then leveled with one of his three bosses. He didn't much care for Buck West, but he knew better than to play the game any way other than straight. "I think he's who he says he is. And I think the rumors are right. He's one hell of a gunfighter."

"Keep an eye on him."

"Yes, sir."

Buck checked into the hotel, a very nice one for a town so far away from the beaten path, and stowed his gear. He bathed, took a shave, and dressed in a dark suit, white shirt and black string tie, polished boots. He checked and cleaned his .44s, and belted them around his waist, tying down the low-riding holsters.

He stepped out onto the boardwalk, carefully looked all around him, as was his habit, and then headed for the cafe, preferring that over the hotel dining room. He took a seat one table over from Miss Sally Reynolds. They were the only customers in the cafe, the lunch hour over. He felt eyes on him and looked up into her hazel eyes. He smiled at her.

"Pleasant day," Buck said.

"Very," Sally replied. "Now that school is out for the summer, it's especially so."

"I regret that I don't have more formal education," Buck said. "The War Between the States put a halt to that."

"It's never too late to learn, sir."

"You're a schoolteacher?"

"Yes, I am. And you . . . ?"

"Drifter, ma'am."

"I . . . don't think so," the young woman said, meeting his gaze.

Buck smiled. "Oh? And why do you say that?"

"Just a guess."

"What grades do you teach?"

"Sixth, seventh, and eighth. Why do you wear two guns?"

"Habit."

"Most of the men I've seen out here have difficulty mastering one gun," Sally said. "My first day out here I saw a man shoot his big toe off trying to quick-draw. I tried very hard not to laugh, but he looked so foolish."

Buck again smiled. "I would imagine so. But I should imagine the man minus the toe failed to find the humor in it."

"I'm sure."

Conversation waned as the waitress brought their lunches. Buck just couldn't think of a way to get the talk going again.

Deputy Rogers entered the cafe, sat down at the counter, and ordered coffee.

Rogers glared at Sally as she said to Buck, "Will you be in Bury long?"

"All depends, ma'am."

"Lady of your quality shouldn't oughta be talkin' to no bounty hunter, Miz Reynolds," Rogers said. "Ain't fittin'."

Buck slowly chewed a bite of beef.

"Mr. Rogers," Sally said. "The gentleman and I are merely exchanging pleasantries over lunch. I was addressing the gentleman, not you."

Rogers flushed, placed his coffee mug on the counter, and abruptly left the cafe.

"Deputy Rogers doesn't like me very much," Buck said.

"Why?" Sally asked bluntly.

"Because . . . I probably make him feel somewhat insecure."

"A very interesting statement from a man who professes to have little formal education, Mr. . . . ?"

"West, ma'am. Buck West."

"Sally Reynolds. Western names are very quaint. Is Buck your Christian first name?"

"No, ma'am. But it might as well be. Been called that all my life."

"Are you a bounty hunter, Mr. West?"

"Bounty hunter, cowhand, gunhand, trapper. Whatever I can make a living at. You're from the east of the Mississippi River, ma'am?"

"New Hampshire. I came out here last year after replying to an advertisement in a local paper. The pay is much better out here than back home."

"I . . . sort of know where New Hampshire is. I would imagine living is much more civilized back there."

"To say the least, Mr. West. And also much duller."

Hang around a little longer, Sally, Buck thought. You haven't seen lively yet. "Would you walk with me, Miss Reynolds?" Buck blurted. "And please don't think I'm being too forward."

"I would love to walk with you, Mr. West."

The sun was high in the afternoon sky and Sally opened her parasol.

"Do you ride, Miss Reynolds?" Buck asked.

"Oh, yes. But I have yet to see a sidesaddle in Bury."

"They ain't too common a sight out here."

"*Ain't* is completely unacceptable in formal writing and speech, Mr. West. But I think you know that."

"Yes, ma'am. Sorry."

She tilted her head, smiling, looking at him, a twinkle in her eyes. As they walked, Buck's spurs jingled. "Which line of employment are you currently pursuing, Mr. West?"

"Beg pardon, ma'am?"

"Bounty hunter, cowhand, gunhand, or trapper?"

"I'm lookin' for a killer named Smoke Jensen. Thirty-thousand-dollar reward for him."

"Quite a sum of money. I've seen the wanted posters around town. What, exactly, did this Jensen do?"

"Killed a lot of people, ma'am. He's a fast gun for hire, so I'm told."

"Faster than you, Mr. West?"

"I hope not."

She laughed at that.

A group of hard-riding cowboys took that time to burst into town, whooping and hollering and kicking up clouds of dust as they spurred their horses, sliding to a stop in front of one of the saloons.

Buck pulled Sally into a doorway and shielded her from the dust and flying clods.

When the dust had settled, Buck stepped aside and Sally stepped once more onto the boardwalk. "Those are men from the PSR Ranch," she said. "Rowdies and ruffi-ans, for the most part."

"PSR?" Buck asked, knowing full well what the letters stood for.

"Potter, Stratton, Richards. It's the biggest ranch in the state, so I'm told."

"How do they get their cattle to market?" Buck asked. "I know they don't drive them over the Divide."

"They haven't made any big drives yet. I understand that so far they've sold them to people in this area. Leesburg, Salmon, Lemhi. Small communities within a fifty- to seventy-mile radius. The big drive is scheduled for late next spring. They'll be using a hundred or more cowboys."

"Quite an undertaking."

"Oh, yes."

A door opened behind them. A very pretty lady emerged from the dress shop. "Sally," she said. She gave Buck a cool glance and walked on down the boardwalk.

"That is, ah, Mr. Richards's mistress, Buck. Her name is Jane."

Buck had just seen his sister for the first time in almost ten years.

7

"You have an odd look in your eyes, Buck," Sally said.

"I never have gotten used to being snubbed, I suppose. But I suppose I should have, by now. But to be snubbed by a common whore irritates me."

"She may be a whore, but she isn't common," Sally corrected that. "I'm told she speaks three languages very fluently; her home is the showcase of the state; and her carriage was built and brought over from France."

"Oh?" Now where in the devil did Janey learn three languages? he thought. She quit school in the eighth grade.

"Here she comes now," Sally said.

It was a grand carriage, all right. The coachman was a black man, all gussied up in a military-looking outfit. Four tough-looking riders accompanied the carriage. Two to the front, two to the back.

As the carriage passed, Buck removed his hat and bowed gallantly.

Even from the boardwalk, Sally could see the woman

in the carriage flush with anger and jerk her head to the front. Sally suppressed a giggle.

"Oh, you made her mad, Buck."

"She'll get over it, I reckon." Buck remembered the time, back before the war, when he had rocked the family outhouse—with his sister in it. She'd chased him all over the farm, throwing rocks at him.

"That funny look is back in your eyes, Buck. What are you thinking?"

"My own sister," he said.

"Does Jane remind you of her?"

"Not really. I haven't seen the sister I remember in a long time. I'll probably never see that girl again."

Sally touched his arm. "Oh, Buck. Why do you say that?"

"There is nothing to return to, Sally. Everything and everyone is gone."

He took her elbow and they began to walk toward the edge of town. They had not gone half a block before the sounds of hooves drumming on the hard-packed dirt came to them. Two of the bodyguards who had been with Jane reined up in the street, turning their horses to face Buck and Sally.

Buck gently but firmly pushed Sally to one side. "Stand clear," he said in a low voice. "Trouble ahead."

"What—?" she managed to say before one of Richards's gunhands cut her off.

"You run on home now, schoolmarm. This here might git messy."

Sally stuck her chin out. "I will stand right here on this boardwalk until the soles of my shoes grow roots before I'll take orders from you, you misbegotten cretin!"

Buck grinned at her. Now this lady had some *sand* to her.

"What the hell did she call me?" the cowboy said to his friend.

"Durned if I know."

The cowboy swung his eyes back to Buck. "You insulted Miss Janey, boy. She's madder than a tree full of hornets. You got fifteen minutes to git your gear and git gone."

"I think I'll stay," Buck said. He had thumbed the thongs off his .44s after pushing Sally to one side.

"Boy," the older and uglier of the bodyguards said, "do you know who I am?"

"Can't say I've had the pleasure," Buck replied.

"Name's Dickerson, from over Colorado way. That ring a bell in your head?"

It did, but Buck didn't let it show. Dickerson was a top gun. No doubt about that. Not only was he mean, he was cat quick with a pistol. "Nope. Sorry."

"And this here," Dickerson jerked a thumb, "is Russell."

Buck hadn't heard of Russell, but he figured if the guy rode with Dickerson, he'd be good. "Pleased to meet you," Buck said politely.

Dickerson gave Buck an exasperated look. "Boy, are you stupid or tryin' to be smart-mouthed?"

"Neither one. Now if you gentlemen will excuse me, I'd like to continue my stroll with Miss Reynolds."

Both Dickerson and Russell dismounted, ground-reining their ponies. "Only place you goin' is carried to Boot Hill, boy."

Several citizens had gathered around to watch the fun, including one young cowhand with a weather-beaten face and a twinkle in his eyes.

"Stand clear," Buck told the crowd.

The gathering crowd backed up and out of the line of impending fire. They hoped.

"I've bothered no one," Buck said to the crowd, without taking his eyes from the two gunhands facing him.

"And I'm not looking for a fight. But if I'm pushed, I'll fight. I just wanted that made public."

"Git on your hoss and ride, boy!" Russell said. "And do it right now."

"I'm staying."

"You a damn fool, boy!" Dickerson said. "But if you want a lead supper, that's up to you."

"Lead might fly in both directions," Buck said calmly. "Were I you, I'd think about that."

Some odd light flickered quickly through Dickerson's eyes. He wasn't used to being sassed or disobeyed. But damn this boy's eyes, he didn't seem to be worried at all. Who in the devil was they up against?

"That's Buck West, Dickerson," the young cowboy with the beat-up face said.

"That don't spell road apples to me," Russell said. He glared at Buck. "Move, tinhorn, or the undertaker's gonna be divvyin' up your pocket money."

"I like it here," Buck said.

"Then draw, damn you!" Dickerson shouted. He went for his gun. Out of the corner of his eye, he saw Russell grab for his .45.

Buck's hands swept down and up with the speed of an angry striking snake. His matched .44s roared and belched smoke and flame. The ground-reined horses snorted and reared at the noise. Dickerson and Russell lay on the dusty street. Both were badly wounded. The guns of the PSR men lay beside them in the dirt. Neither had had time to cock and fire.

"Jumpin' jackrabbits!" the young cowboy said. "I never seen nothin' like that in my life."

Buck calmly punched out the spent brass and dropped the empties to the dirt. He reloaded and holstered his .44s, leaving the hammer thongs off.

Sheriff Dan Reese and Deputy Rogers came at a run

up the wide street. Many townspeople had gathered on the boardwalks to crane their necks.

"Drop those damn guns, West!" Reese yelled before arriving at the scene. "You're under arrest."

"I'd like to know why." Sally said, stepping up to stand beside Buck. Her face was very pale. She pointed to Dickerson and Russell. "Those hooligans started it. They ordered Mr. West to leave town. When he refused, they threatened to kill him. They drew first. And I'll swear to that in a court of law."

"She's right, Sheriff," the young cowhand said.

Reese gave the cowboy an ugly look. "Which side are you on, Sam?"

"The side of right, Sheriff."

Dickerson cried out in pain. The front of his shirt was covered with blood. The .44 slug had hit him squarely in the chest, ricocheted off the breast bone, and exited out the top of his shoulder, tearing a great jagged hole as it spun away.

Russell was hardest hit. Buck's .44 had struck him in the stomach and torn out his lower back. The gunhand was not long for this world and everybody looking at him knew it.

"Any charges, Sheriff?" Buck asked, his voice steady and low.

There was open dislike in Reese's eyes as he glared at Buck. He stepped closer. "You're trouble, West. And you and me both know it. I hope you crowd me, gunfighter. 'Cause when you do, I'll kill you!"

"You'll try," Buck replied in the same low tone.

Reese flushed. He stepped back. "No charges, West. It was a fair fight."

Russell groaned, blood leaking from his mouth. He jerked once on the dirt and died.

"Have his full name recorded," Buck said, playing the

part of the hard hunter. "There might be a reward on him."

"You're a sorry son of a you-know-what," Reese said. "Ain't you got no feelin's at all?"

"Only for those who deserve it," Buck said. He turned and took Sally's elbow. "Shall we continue?"

As the tall young gunfighter and the pretty lady strolled off, the young cowpuncher named Sam looked at them. He thought he knew who the gunfighter was, and his name wasn't Buck West. But Sam thought he'd keep that information to himself for a time. Might come in handy.

"Your first gunfight?" Buck asked as they walked.

"Yes. And I hope my last."

"It won't be. Not if you continue living out here. It's a big, wild, raw country still. The laws are simple and straight to the point. Justice comes down hard. Out here, a man's word is his bond. That's the way it should be everywhere. Tinhorns and shysters and crooks don't last long in the west."

"And you, Buck?"

"What do you mean?"

"Will you last long out here?"

"No way I can answer that. I hung up my guns once. Thought I would never put them on again. It didn't work out. Maybe I can walk away from it one more time. I don't know. Worth a try, I guess."

They paused at Sally's front gate. "Would you like to have supper with me this evening?" Buck asked. "At the hotel dining room?"

"You're awfully young to have already retired once from gunfighting."

"Some of us had to start young, Sally."

"Yes, I suppose. It's an interesting land, your wild west. I'll be ready at six. Good afternoon, Mr. Buck West." She smiled. "Or whatever your name is."

* * *

Jane looked out the window of her bedroom. Ever since she had seen the arrogant young man she had struggled to recall where she'd seen him before. She knew she had. But where? She just could not remember. And now the startling news that the young man had bested Russell and Dickerson in a stand-up gunfight.

Incredible.

She sighed and turned away from the window that overlooked the northern vastness of the PSR ranchlands. She had time for a bath before Stratton and Richards and wives came out for their monthly business and dinner meeting.

The face of the tall gunslick remained in her mind. His name would come to her in time.

Sheriff Dan Reese had gone through all his dodgers twice, looking for anyone who resembled Buck West. Nothing. But anybody that fast and sure had to have a backtrail. Trick was in finding it. Russell and Dickerson were both hard men. Or had been. And they both had been almighty quick. Yet this Buck West had handled them as easily as children. Just blew in out of nowhere. Probably came from Texas, way down on the border.

Sheriff Reese stood up and stretched. One thing for certain, he thought: Buck West was trouble. Best way to handle him was to get him on the PSR payroll. He'd talk to Richards about it. First thing this evening.

He glanced up at the clock. Had to shave and bathe now, though. Get out to PSR headquarters.

The dozen old mountain men made their camp about ten miles south of the town of Bury, in the timber of the Lemhi Range. As soon as they were set up, Preacher changed ponies and headed east, toward the Continental Divide and the Bitterroot Range. At first light, Dupre was to head into Bury for a look-see. Pick up some bacon and beans and coffee and salt and keep his ear open.

"Better wash them jug-handle things first," Beartooth told him. "Probably git five pounds of dirt out of 'um."

"I'd talk," Dupre retorted. "Last time you took a bath it killed the fish for five miles downstream."

"Ummm," Nighthawk said.

8

Buck had ordered his one suit pressed, had bought a new set of longhandles and a new pearl-gray shirt, and was ready to knock on Miss Sally Reynolds's door promptly at six.

As he walked the short blocks from the hotel to Sally's house, Buck had been conscious of eyes on him. Not unfriendly eyes, but curious ones. He had passed several ladies during his walk. They had batted their eyes and swished their bustles at him. Buck had smiled at the ladies and continued walking, his spurs jingling.

He had spoken to the crowd of little boys that had followed him—at a safe distance. He had noticed that several of them were wearing two wooden guns in makeshift holsters, the leather tied down low.

Buck didn't know whether he liked that or not. He didn't want any young people aping his lifestyle. But he didn't know what he could do about it.

Miss Sally Reynolds was dressed in gingham, in a bright summer color with matching parasol, the light, bright color setting off her dark hair. She wore just a touch of rouge on her cheeks.

Dusk when they closed the gate to her picket fence and began their stroll to the hotel dining room. The crowd of boys had been called in to supper by their mothers, so Buck and Sally could walk in peace.

They had just left Sally's house when two carriages, accompanied by half a dozen outriders, rolled stately past them.

"Wiley and Linda Potter in the first carriage," Sally said. "Keith and Lucille Stratton in the second carriage. They're going out to Josh Richards's. He lives on the PSR Ranch. They have a monthly dinner and business meeting. The sheriff will be there too, I should imagine."

"Same time, every month?" Buck asked.

"Oh, yes. Very punctual and predictable."

Buck smiled at that. But his smile was only to hide his true inner feelings. And those thoughts were dark and dangerous.

For one hot, flashing instant, Buck's thoughts were flung back in time.

La Plaza de los Leones—Square of the Lions, later to be renamed Walsenburg—was a major farming and ranching community in 1869, when Smoke and Preacher rode in from the west.

They were met by the town marshal and told to keep on riding.

They planned to do just that. But first they wanted to know about the Casey ranch.

"Southeast of here. On the flats. Casey's got eight hands. They all look like gunnies."

"You got an undertaker in this town?" Smoke asked.

"Sure. Why?"

"Tell him to dust off his boxes—he's about to get some business."

Ten miles out of town, they met two hands riding easy, heading into town.

"You boys is on the TC range," one of the riders warned.

"Get the hell off. The boss don't like strangers and neither do I."

Smoke smiled. "You boys been ridin' for the brand long?"

"You deef?" the second hand asked. "You been told to git—now git!"

"You answer my question and then maybe we'll leave."

"Since '66. That's when we pushed them longhorns up here from Texas. If that's any of your damned business. Now git!"

"Who owns TC?"

"Ted Casey. Boy, are you plumb crazy or jist stupid?"

"My Pa knew a Ted Casey. Fought in the war with him—for the Gray."

"Oh? What be your name?"

"Some people call me Smoke." He grinned. "Jensen."

Recognition flared in the eyes of the TC riders. They grabbed for their guns. They were far too slow. Smoke's left-hand .36 belched flame and smoke as Preacher fired his Henry one-handed. Horses reared and snorted and bucked at the noise. The TC gunnies dropped from their saddles, dead and dying.

The one TC gunhand alive pulled himself up on one elbow. Blood poured from two chest wounds, the blood pink and frothy, one .36 ball having passed through both lungs, taking the rider as he turned in the saddle.

"Heard you was comin'," he gasped. "You quick, no doubt 'bout that. Your brother was easy." He smiled a bloody smile. "Potter shot him low in the back; took him a long time to die. Died hard. Hollered a lot." The TC rider closed his eyes and died.

Smoke and Preacher burned the house down, driving the men from it after a prolonged gunfight. They took only Casey alive.

"What are you figurin' on doin' with him?" Preacher asked.

"I figure on going back to town and hanging him."

"I don't know how you got that mean streak, boy. Seein' as how you was raised—partly—by a gentle old man like me."

Despite the death he had brought and the destruction wrought, Smoke had to laugh at that. Preacher was known throughout the West as one of the most dangerous men ever to roam the high country and vast Plains. The old mountain man had once gone on the prowl, spending two years of his life tracking down and killing—one by one— a group of men who ambushed and killed a friend of his, stealing the man's furs.

Smoke tied the unconscious Casey across a saddle. "'Course you never went on the hunt for anyone, right?"

"Well . . . mayhaps once or twice. But that was years back. I've mellowed a mite since then."

"Sure." Smoke grinned. Preacher was still as mean as a cornered puma.

By the banks of a creek outside of town, a crowd had gathered for the hanging. Marshal Crowell was furious as he watched Smoke build a noose.

"This man has not been tried!" the marshal protested.

"Yeah, he has," Smoke said. "He admitted to me what he done."

The marshal looked at the smoke to the southeast.

"House fire," Preacher said. "Poor feller lost everything."

Casey spat in the direction of the crowd. He cursed them.

"This is murder!" the marshal said. "I intend to file charges against you both."

"Halp!" Casey hollered.

A local minister began praying for Casey's poor wretched soul.

Casey soiled himself as the noose was slipped around his neck.

The minister prayed harder.

"That ain't much of a prayer," Preacher opined sourly. "I had you beat hands down when them Injuns was fixin' to skin me alive on the Platte. Put some feelin' in it, man!"

The local minister began to shout and sweat. The crowd swelled; some had brought their supper with them. A hanging was always an interesting sight. There just wasn't that much to do in small western towns. Some men were betting how long it would take for Casey to die—providing his neck didn't snap when his butt left the saddle.

A small choir had assembled. The ladies lifted their voices to the sky.

"'Shall We Gather at the River,'" they intoned.

"I personally think 'Swing Low' would be more like it," Preacher opined.

A local merchant looked at Casey. "You owe me sixty-five dollars."

"Hell with you!" Casey tried to kick the man.

"I want my money!" the merchant shouted.

"You got anything to say before you go to Hell?" Smoke asked Casey.

"You won't get away with this!" Casey screamed. "If Potter or Stratton don't git you, Richards will."

"What's he talkin' about?" the marshal asked.

"Casey was with the Gray—same as my Pa and brother," Smoke explained. "Casey and some others waylaid a patrol bringing a load of gold into Georgia. They shot my brother in the back and left him to die. Hard."

"That was war," the marshal said.

"It was murder."

"Hurry up," a citizen shouted. "My supper's gettin' cold."

"I'll see you hang for this," the marshal told Smoke.

"You go to hell!" Smoke told him.

Casey swung in the cool, late afternoon air.

"I'm notifying the territorial governor of this," the marshal said.

Casey's bootheels drummed the air.

"Shout, man!" Preacher told the minister. "Sing, sisters, sing!" he urged the choir.

"What about my sixty-five dollars?" the merchant shouted.

All the memories had flashed through Buck's mind in the space of two heartbeats.

"You've gone away again," Sally said.

Buck looked at her. She was smiling up at him. "Yes, I guess I was, Sally. I apologize for that."

They continued walking toward the hotel. Sally said, "Buck, are you here to slay dragons or to tilt at windmills?"

"Beg pardon?"

"Are you familiar with Cervantes?"

"Is he a gunhand?"

She looked at him to see if he was serious. He was. "No, Buck. A writer."

"No, I guess I missed that one. I know what slaying dragons means. But what's that about tilting windmills?"

"Oh, I suppose you're not. I didn't notice Sancho riding in with you."

Now Buck was thoroughly confused. "I never had a Mex sidekick, Sally."

"I have a copy of *Don Quixote*—somewhere. I'll find it and loan it to you. I think you'll enjoy it."

"All right." Buck was well-read, considering his lack of formal education and allowing for the locale and his lifestyle. But he sure as hell had never heard of any Don Quixote.

Heads turned as they entered the dining room. Some dining there gave the young couple disapproving looks. A few smiled. They took a table next to the wall, affording them maximum privacy, and ordered supper. PSR beef, naturally, with boiled potatoes and beans, and apple pie for dessert.

Neither admitted it, for separate reasons, but both wondered what might be taking place at the grand house of the PSR ranch.

"And it was a fair fight?" Josh Richards asked Sheriff Reese.

"Stand up and square," Reese said. "I didn't see it, but Sam did. He said he ain't never seen nothin' like that Buck West's draw. Lightnin' fast. Neither Dickerson nor Russell got a shot off. And they drew first."

"And he's a bounty hunter?" Stratton asked. He was a big man gone to fat. Diamond rings glittered on his soft fat fingers.

"That's what Jerry told me."

"Jerry saw him fight back at the trading post, that right?" Potter asked.

"Yes, sir."

Wiley Potter, like his two partners, had pushed his past from him. He almost never thought of his outlaw and traitor days. He was a successful man, a man under consideration to be territorial governor. And he played his political power to the hilt. He was always well dressed, well groomed.

Josh Richards listened, but had little to say on the subject of the bounty hunter Buck West. If this West was as good as described, Richards wanted him on the payroll. Of the three men, Richards had changed the least. Physically. He was still a powerful man. Something he had always been proud of. That and his reputation with the ladies. But he knew it was time for him to be thinking of settling down. And while Janey's reputation was a bit scarlet, she was, nevertheless, the woman he planned to marry. She was just as ruthless and cunning as Richards. Would do anything for money. They made a good team.

"I'll see him in the morning," Richards said. "Let's eat. I'm hungry."

Potter was big politically—the front man, all smiles and congeniality, territory-wide. Stratton was the local big shot—the president of the bank and so forth. But Richards ran the show, always staying quietly in the background. That's the way he wanted it.

The men trooped out of the study into the dining room. Richards looked at Jane. "Something the matter?" he asked in a whisper.

"That Buck West. I've seen him before. Somewhere."

"Can you remember where?"

She shook her head. "Not yet. But I will." She looked him directly in the eyes. "He's trouble, Josh."

"Your imagination, my dear. He'd be a good man to have on our side."

"Watch him," she cautioned. "I don't trust him."

"You don't even *know* him, Jane!"

"Yeah, I do. I just can't remember where I met him, that's all."

"It'll come to you."

"Bet on it."

9

Buck knew he wasn't going to tolerate much living in the hotel. He didn't like the closed-in feeling. The sheets were clean, and that was nice, but the bed was soft and made his back hurt. Buck was not accustomed to the finer things in life. So-called finer things. To Buck, the finer things were the clean smell of deep timber; the high thinness of clean air in the mountains; the rush of a surging stream, wild white water whipping and singing; the cough of a puma and the calling of a bird. Now *that* was fine living!

He walked down to the cafe in the coolness of the early morning. The eastern sky was just beginning to streak with silver, but the cafe was busy, the smell of bacon and eggs and frying potatoes filling the air.

Conversation stopped when Buck walked in and took a seat at a far table, his back to the wall. When the waitress came to take his order, Buck said, "If the food's as good as it smells, I'll take one of everything on the menu."

The waitress smiled at him. Buck ordered breakfast

and said, "The owner must make a fortune in this place, the food's so good."

"The owner?" the waitress asked, a curious look in her eyes.

"Yes. Are you the owner?"

She laughed. "Not hardly, sir. Mr. Stratton is the owner. Mr. Stratton owns everything in Bury. Every building and every business."

"Interesting," Buck said. *"Everything?"*

"Everything, sir."

Buck mulled that over in his mind while he ate. The buzz of conversation had returned to normal and the towns-people were ignoring Buck, concentrating on eating. Eating was serious business in the west. Not to be taken lightly. Not at all. Buck thought, The waitress might think Stratton owns everything in sight, but Potter and Richards are right in there as well.

So no one owns their own business. Good. That will make it easier when I burn the damn place to the ground.

Buck was halfway through his breakfast when Deputy Rogers blundered in, closing the door just a bit too hard. Obviously, he wanted everyone to know he had arrived.

Rogers plopped down in a chair facing Buck and said, "Mr. Richards wants to see you."

"When I finish eating. Now go away."

Rogers could not believe his ears. "Hey, gunslick! I said—"

"I heard what you said. So did the entire crowd. I'll see Mr. Richards when I'm finished. Now go away."

Rogers wanted to start something. He wanted it so badly he could taste his personal rage. But he had orders to leave Buck alone. Uttering an oath, he stumbled from the table and slammed the door behind him.

The cafe was totally silent. Even the cook had stepped out and was staring in disbelief at Buck. The one collective thought among them all was, *No one, absolutely* no one *keeps Mr. Richards waiting.*

The front door opened. Josh Richards stepped in. He nodded politely to the crowd and walked to Buck's table, pulling out a chair and calling to the waitress to bring him coffee.

"Ham and eggs are real fine," Buck said. "I recommend them."

Richards smiled. "All right. Ham and eggs, Ruby!"

"Yes, sir."

Buck held out his right hand. "Buck West."

Richards took the offered hand. "Josh Richards. You don't much care for Deputy Rogers, do you Mr. West?"

"I don't think he's got both hands in the stirrups, that's for sure."

"Quaint way of putting it. I'll have to remember that. Oh, you're right, Mr. West. Rogers is a bit weak between the ears. But he does what he is told to do."

"That's important to you, Mr. Richards?"

"Very."

"Money's right, I can be as loyal as any man. More than most, I reckon."

"I imagine you can. Are you looking for a job, Mr. West?"

"I'm lookin' for Smoke Jensen, sir. But that gunhand's backtrail is gone cold."

"Yes. I've had a lot of men looking for Jensen. So far, to no avail. Tell you what I'll do, Mr. West. I can put you on the payroll today. Right now. Fighting wages. That's good money. Five or six times what the average puncher makes. You hang around town, the ranch. Just let your presence be known. Every now and then, I'll have a job for you. Sometimes, Mr. Stratton, Mr. Potter, or myself have to transfer large sums of money from place to place. Highwaymen have taken several of those pouches. I need a good man to see that it doesn't happen again. How about it?"

"All right," Buck said with a smile. "Oh, one more thing?"

"Certainly."

Buck pointed with his fork. "Eat your breakfast. It's getting cold."

Buck met Stratton and Potter. It was all he could do to conceal his raw hatred from the men. He shook hands with them and smiled, nodding in all the right places.

When the meeting was over, he returned to his hotel room and washed his hands with lye soap. They still felt dirty to him.

He saw to his horses and found the livery boy true to his word. Both Drifter and the pack animal were getting extra rations of grain.

He walked the town, getting to know the layout of Bury. As he walked, he noticed a buckskin-clad old mountain man leaning against the wall of the not-yet-opened general store. The mountain man appeared not to be watching Buck, but Buck knew he was watching him. His name came to Buck. Dupre. The Louisiana Frenchman. He remembered him from the rendezvous at the ruins of Bent's Ford, back in . . . was it '66? Buck thought it had been.

Dupre looked as old as time itself, and as solid as a granite mountain. Buck had been raised among mountain men, and he knew these old boys were still dangerous as grizzly bears. Not a one of the mountain men still left alive could tell you how many men they'd killed. White men. Indians didn't count.

When Buck again caught his eyes, Dupre was talking to the store owner. Not owner, Buck corrected himself—manager. The two men went inside. Buck continued walking. Unlike most men who spent their lives on the hurricane deck of a horse, Buck enjoyed a good stroll.

It was a pretty little town, Buck thought. And not just thrown haphazardly together, like so many frontier towns. He took his time, speaking to the men and doffing his hat to the ladies he passed. He noticed suspicion in many of the eyes; open hostility in a like amount. He wondered about that.

"You're up early," a voice called from Buck's left.

He stopped and slowly turned. Sally Reynolds sat on her front porch, drinking what Buck guessed was coffee.

"I enjoy the early morning, Sally."

"So do I. Would you care for a cup of tea?"

"Tea?"

"Tea."

"Sure. I guess so. Never acquired much of a taste for it."

"I can make coffee."

"No, no. Tea will be fine." He pushed open the gate and took a chair on the porch.

It wasn't fine. Buck thought he was going to gag on the stuff. It didn't taste like nothing. But he smiled bravely and swallowed. Hard.

Sally laughed at him. "Please let me make you some coffee, Buck. It will only take a few minutes."

"Maybe you'd better. I sure would appreciate it. This stuff and me just don't get along."

Buck sat alone on the small porch and watched as Dupre rode past, riding slowly, his Henry repeating rifle held in one hand, across the saddle. As he rode past, the old mountain man nodded his head to Buck. "Nice mornin', ain't it, son?"

"Yes, it is. Have yourself a good day."

"My good days are twenty year down my backtrail," Dupre said. "But I still manage to git by." He rode on, soon out of sight.

"Who in the *world* was that?" Sally asked. She placed a cup of coffee on the small table between their chairs.

"You probably read about them in school," Buck said. "Mountain men?"

"Oh, yes! But I thought they were all dead."

"Most of them are. The real mountain men, that is. But there's still some salty ol' boys out there, still riding the high lonesome."

"The high lonesome? That's beautiful, Buck. Do I detect a wistful note in your voice?"

"Wistful?"

"Means a longing, or a yearning for something."

Could he trust her? Buck didn't know. She could very well be a spy for Stratton or Potter or Richards. Then he remembered how she had stood up to Sheriff Reese. He made up his mind. All right, he would tell her just enough to bait her.

"I guess so, Sally. I came out here just a boy. Alone," he lied. "I grew up in the mountains. Met a lot of mountain men. They was, were, old men even then. But tough and hard as nails. They knew their way of life was about gone, even then. But it was a fine way of life—for them; not for everybody."

"And for you, Buck?"

"For me? Do you mean did I enjoy it?"

She nodded.

Buck smiled. "Oh, yes. I'll get a burr under my saddle one of these days and you won't see me for several days. I'll have to shake the staleness of town off me; head for the high country. Me and the horses. But I'll be back. If it matters to you, that is."

She was silent for a very long moment. So long that Buck thought he had offended her with the statement.

"Yes, Buck. I think it does matter to me. In . . . a way that I can't explain. Not just yet. Buck, I am a very perceptive person . . ."

"A what kind of person?"

"Perceptive. That means I have a keen insight, or understanding, of things."

"Terrible to be as ignorant as I am," Buck said.

Sally did not pursue that, for she did not believe Buck to be an ignorant person. Just a person who was hiding something. For whatever reason.

"And your insight tells you what about me, Sally?"

"That you don't fully trust me."

"I don't fully trust anybody, Sally. Out here in the west, trust is something that has to be earned. It has to be that way 'cause your life might depend on it."

"Yes. I've heard that from several people since I've been out here."

"It's very true. You have a lot of outlaws working out here. You have a half-dozen Indian tribes on the warpath. Long as you stay close to Bury, you probably won't have to worry about the Indians attacking. It's too big for them. But get a mile away from town, and your life is in constant danger. You've got to know the man or men you ride with. Will they stand with you or turn tail and run? See what I mean about earning trust?"

"Yes. I suppose so. I won't tell you what else my insight tells me about you, Buck. Not until I've earned your trust. Do you suppose that will happen?"

"I imagine so."

Buck checked in with the Big Three's office manager, the office located in a building in the center of town, and told the dour-faced and sour-dispositioned little man he was riding out; be gone for a day or two. Give his horse some exercise.

MacGregor grunted and told Buck to be back day after tomorrow. He had to ride south to deliver a pouch.

"I'll be back."

He rode north out of Bury, following the Salmon River. He headed for a small town called Salmon. A rough-and-tumble mining camp.

He had no intention of going to Salmon; Buck just wanted to see if he was being followed. He wanted to test how much trust Richards had in him.

"Not much," Buck grunted. He was back in the deep timber, hidden, watching his backtrail. He was watching a half-dozen riders slowly tracking him. Using his spyglass, Buck pulled them into closer view. He knew their faces, having seen them loafing around Bury, but didn't know their names.

Buck rode deeper into the timber, making a slow circle, coming out of the timber behind the riders. Now he was tracking them. He wore an amused look on his face as he watched the gunhands slowly circling, having lost Buck's trail, trying to once more find it. Buck rode up to within five hundred or so yards of the men and sat his horse, watching the men.

One rider finally lifted his head, feeling, sensing eyes on him. "Crap!" the man's voice drifted faintly to Buck. "He's watchin' *us*, boys."

The PSR riders bunched and rode slowly toward Buck, reining up a respectable distance from him. One said, "This ain't nothin' personal, partner. We ride for the brand, just like you."

"No offense taken, boys. Town was closing in on me. I wanted some space. You know what I mean?"

"Know exactly what you mean," a scar-faced rider said. "We got biscuits and coffee and it's 'bout noon. Let's build a fire and jaw some."

Cinches loosened, bits out, the horses ground-reined, they grazed. The riders sat on the ground, munching biscuits and drinking cups of strong black coffee. The scar-faced rider was Joiner. The oldest of the men, a hard-eyed puncher, was Wilson. Buck took an immediate dislike to

Wilson and he sensed the feeling was mutual. McNeil had practically nothing to say. But he kept eyeballing Buck. The man's head was totally bald. Long was short and stocky. He wore one gun tied down low and his second gun in a shoulder-holster rig. Davis was a long lean drink of water; looked like a strong wind would blow him slap out of the saddle. Simpson was big and mean-looking.

"You familiar with Brown's Hole?" Joiner asked Buck.

"Been there. Went there lookin' for Jensen. Grave close to the base of Zenobia Peak. Looks like that's where Jensen planted his pa."

"You dig the grave up?" Wilson asked.

"*Hell*, no!"

Davis said, "That'd be a sin. Sorry no good would do that. Let a man rest in peace."

Wilson looked pained. "Mayhaps that'd be where the gold is buried."

"How would a dead man do that?" Simpson asked.

Wilson nodded his head. "Ain't thought about that. You right."

Then another piece plopped into place in Buck's mind.

10

1867. Emmett Jensen's horses had been picketed close to the base of Zenobia Peak. His gear was by his grave, covered with a ground sheet and secured with rocks. The letter from his pa, given him by the old mountain man, Grizzly, was in Smoke's pocket.

"You read them words on that paper your pa left you?" Preacher asked.

"Not yet."

"I'll go set up camp at the Hole. I reckon you'll be along directly."

"Tomorrow. 'Bout noon."

"See you then." Preacher headed north. He would cross Vermillion Creek, then cut west into the Hole. Smoke would find him when he felt ready for human company. But for now, the young man needed to be alone with his pa.

Smoke unsaddled his horse, Seven, and allowed him to roll. He stripped the gear from the pack animals, setting them grazing. Taking a small hammer and a miner's spike from his gear, Smoke began the job of chiseling his father's name into a large, flat rock. He could not remember exactly when his pa was born, but he thought it about 1815.

Headstone in place, secured by rocks, Smoke built a small fire, put coffee on to boil in the blackened pot, then sat down to read the letter from his pa.

Son,

I found some of the men who killed your brother Luke and stolt the gold that belonged to the Gray. Theys more of them than I first thought. I killed two of the men work for them, but they got led in me and I had to hitail it out. Came here. Not goin to make it. Son, you dont owe nuttin to the Cause of the Gray. So dont get it in your mind you do. Make yourself a good life and look to my final restin place if you need help.

Preacher kin tell you some of what happen, but not all. Remember—look to my grave if you need help.

I allso got word that your sis Janey leff that gambler and has took up with an outlaw down in Airyzona. Place called Tooson. I woodn fret much about her. She is mine, but I think she is trash. Dont know where she got that streek from.

I am gettin tared and seein is hard. Lite fadin. I love you Kirby Smoke.

Pa

Smoke reread the letter. Look to my grave. He could not understand that part. He pulled up his knees and put his head on them, feeling he ought to cry, or something. But no tears came.

Now he was alone. He had no other kin, and he did not count his sister as kin. He had his guns, his horses, a bit of gold, and his friend, Preacher.

He was eighteen years old.

* * *

Now, five years later, it all came back to him. Sure, he thought. His pa had dug his own grave, put the gold in the bottom, and then crawled in on top of it to die. The old mountain man, Grizzly, had buried him.

Well, the gold could just stay there. Damned if he'd dig up his pa's grave for it.

"Where else you been lookin' for this Smoke?" McNeil asked.

"Name someplace. I thought I had him cornered over near Pagosa Springs, but he gave me the slip. I drifted down into New Mexico Territory after him. But he was always one jump ahead of me. He's slick."

"He'll screw up," Long said.

"When he does I'm gonna be there," Buck said. And he noticed out of the corner of his eyes that the men seemed to relax. He had passed their test.

Buck prowled the area about Bury for two days, planting a permanent map in his brain. He would remember the trails and roads and landmarks. They would come in handy when Buck made his move and sought his escape.

And he learned from the PSR gunhands about the townspeople of Bury. They were a pretty scummy lot, according to the riders. There were men who had skipped out on partners back east: men who were wanted for everything from petty crimes to murder. In exchange for loyalty, the Big Three had offered them sanctuary and a chance to bury their past. After twenty years, the businesses they ran for the Big Three would revert to the shopkeepers. Free and clear.

So Buck could expect no help from them.

In a way, that knowledge made it easier.

* * *

The saddlebags handed to Buck by MacGregor were heavy. The canvas and leather saddlebags were flap-secured by padlocks. Buck did not ask what was in the bags; the sour little Scotsman did not volunteer that information.

"It's about a sixty-five-mile ride," Buck was told. "Head out east to the Lemhi River and follow it down. Little mining operation down in the Lemhi Valley. Town ain't got no name. So it's called No Name. Be a man there waitin' for you. Name is Rex. Give the saddlebags to him, wait 'til he checks them out, and he'll give you a receipt. Come back here."

The Scotsman turned away and stumped back to his rolltop desk, leaving Buck with the heavy bags. Buck smiled. "Gimme some expense money, friend."

The Scotsman sighed and reached into a tin box, pulling out a thin sheaf of bills. He made Buck sign for them. "Bring back anything that's left. Not that I think there will be anything left, that is."

Buck rode out at nine that morning. He stopped by Sally's place and found her sitting on the front porch. Drinking that damnable tea. "Be back in about three days." He smiled. "I'll bring you back a couple of pounds of coffee." He wheeled Drifter and was gone.

Staying close to the timber, with the flats to his left, Buck let Drifter pick his own pace. About ten miles out of town he reined up and sat his horse. He rubbed his eyes in disbelief. Was that an elf up ahead, sitting on a spotted pony? Buck walked Drifter slowly toward the sight. Sure looked like an elf.

"Since I care nothing for life in caves or other subterranean dwellings, I can assure you that I am not a troll," the little man said, when Buck was within earshot.

"A what?"

"Never mind, young man. My name is Audie. I, along with others of our vanishing breed, have made our meager camp just to the west of where we are now engaged in this somewhat less than loquacious confabulation."

Buck blinked. "Huh?"

Audie sighed. "Very well." He took a deep breath. "Me and them there other ol' boys who was pards with Preacher is a-camped over yonder." He jerked his thumb.

"Oh. All right. For a little fellow you got a smart mouth, you know that?"

Audie jerked out a .44 with the barrel sawed off short. "But I carry a very large friend, do I not?"

"I'd say so. An' quick with it, too."

"Did you think I might be an elf?" Audie smiled after the question.

"Well, sir. Ah . . . yeah!"

"How quaint," the remark was very drily given. "But . . . given the fact that elves are rumored to engage in somewhat capricious interference in human affairs, and are usually represented in diminutive human form, I suppose your first impression might be forgiven. But I cannot, for the life of me, envision Greybull as an elf."

"Mister Audie, I don't *even* know what it is you just said."

"We're watching you," Audie plunged onward, undaunted. "We'll be there when you need us." He wheeled his pony around and trotted off.

Buck watched him disappear from view. Buck removed his hat and scratched his head. "I've seen the seasons change, the birthing of human life, and been in love. But I ain't *never* seen nothin' like that!"

At No Name, Buck tied up in front of a building with the name PSR on the false front. *Rex Augsman* was painted on the door. Buck pushed open the door and stepped inside, pausing for a moment to allow his eyes to adjust to the dimmer light.

"You Rex Augsman?" Buck asked the man who was rising from behind his desk.

"That's me."

"You got some proof of that?"

He pointed to a diploma hanging on the wall. Mining engineer. Rex M. Augsman.

"I'm from PSR headquarters up in Bury." He held out the saddlebags. "I'm supposed to give this to you."

"You look like you might just have some sense," Rex said. "A definite improvement over the others." He opened the padlocks and looked inside. He smiled and said, "Welcome to the team. You passed the final test."

"What do you mean?" Buck asked.

The engineer dumped the contents of the heavy saddlebags onto the counter. The bags had been filled with cut-up pieces of newspaper and lots of rocks.

"The young man is not exactly a paragon of intelligence," Audie said. "But there is something about him that suggests there might be a glimmer of hope."

"Smart as a whip, you dwarf!" Preacher fired at the former schoolteacher. Halfway to the Divide, Preacher had run into a band of friendly Flatheads. Yes, they had been into Bury many times to trade. Yes, they would keep their eyes and ears open and report back to Preacher. Preacher had returned to the base camp.

"No doubt you speak nonprejudicially," Audie said.

"Don't you cuss me!" Preacher warned. "I'll rap you up-side the head."

Audie reached for the sawed-off .44. Preacher reached for his Colt.

Lobo suddenly growled like a wolf and the two old friends settled down, dropping their hands from the butts of pistols.

"Sorry 'bout that, little friend," Preacher said.

"I, too, offer my sincere apologies, Preacher," Audie said. "It's the tension of waiting for the unknown."

Dupre grinned and walked to his bedroll. He pulled two clay jugs out of the blankets. "I tink perhaps we have a drink or three," he said.

"Right good idee," Greybull said.

"I could stand a taste myself," Matt said. "How 'bout you, Nighthawk?"

"Ummm."

Buck had asked for a receipt for the newspapers and rocks. Back in Bury, he solemnly presented it to Mac-Gregor. The Scotsman looked at Buck, then the receipt, and a sour smile slowly formed on his lips.

"You're a damn fool for staying, boy," MacGregor said. "I told Richards you were an honest man. That impressed him. But honest men won't last long in a town filled with scalawags and hooligans. Tell him I said it, if you wish—but you won't. You've stepped into a snake pit, young man. There isn't a handful of people—men *and* women—in this town and surrounding area that is worth spit. Oh, I know why you're here, Mr. Kirby Jensen, aka Smoke, aka Buck West. You're here to avenge your wife, your son, your father, your friend Preacher. You're so full of hate it's consuming you, eating you alive. If you let it, boy, it will destroy you."

"How many others know who I am?" Buck asked, keeping his voice calm.

"I think the red-haired gunman, Sam, probably knows. Sam is quite like you. An honest man. The schoolteacher you've been sparking about, Sally. She probably suspects. Don't worry about me, Buck. I am a federal marshal."

11

Buck had asked the Scotsman how he had known about him. MacGregor had shown him a wanted dodger on Smoke. He had cut off the hair and added a beard. It was eerie; almost like looking into a mirror.

"Your skill and speed with your guns gave you away, Buck," MacGregor said. Then he smiled. "What are you planning to do here?"

"I'm going to kill Potter and Richards and Stratton and then burn this damn town to the ground."

"Warn me before you start putting your suicidal plan into action. I need to gather up my evidence and get out of here."

Buck had looked at the smaller man, not knowing how to take the man. "But you're a federal marshal, Mac-Gregor. Aren't you going to arrest me?"

"On what charges, Buck? I'm not aware of any federal charges against you. You haven't committed any acts of treason against the government of the United States. You haven't robbed any federal mints. You haven't assaulted any federal agents or destroyed any federal property. Hell,

I personally hope you are successful in destroying this cesspool. Good day, Mr. West."

Buck stabled Drifter and went back to the hotel for a bath and shave. MacGregor hadn't told him very much as to the why of a federal marshal being in Bury; just that if he, MacGregor, was successful, another chapter in that regrettable bloody insurrection referred to as the Civil War would be closed. And perhaps a young man would finally be at peace with himself.

MacGregor had left it at that.

After cleaning up, Buck walked to Sally's house carrying a small package wrapped in brown paper. He found her working in the yard, planting flowers. She turned at the sounds of his bootheels and the jingle of his spurs and smiled at him.

Brushing off her hands, Sally asked, "Did you have a good trip?"

"Oh, yes." Buck held out the package. "Brought you something."

She waved him onto the porch and they both took chairs. She opened the package and laughed out loud. Two pounds of coffee.

"I'll grind these beans and make some coffee right now," she said. "While it's perking I'll clean up. It won't take me five minutes."

They chatted away the remainder of the morning. Sally fixed sandwiches for lunch, then the two went for a stroll around town. While resting on the cool banks of a creek, Buck said, "Sally, I want to tell you something."

She glanced at him. "Sounds serious."

"Might be. Sally, if I ever come to you and tell you to pack up and get out of town, don't question it. Just do as I say. If I ever tell you that, it's because a lot of trouble is about to pop wide open."

"If there is an Indian attack, wouldn't it be safer in town rather than outside of town?"

"It won't be Indians, Sally."

"There are children in this town, Buck," she reminded him.

"I'm aware of that."

"Are you saying the sins of the father are also on the head of the son?"

"No," Buck's reply was given slowly, after much thought. "Why would I think that?"

She touched his face with her small hand. "Who are you, Buck?"

And just before his lips touched hers, Buck said, "Smoke Jensen."

"Well, this cinches it," Richards told MacGregor. "I've got a man I can trust. You agree?"

"Oh, most assuredly," the Scotsman said. "I like the young man."

Richards gave his bookkeeper a sharp glance. Damned little sour man had never seemed to like anybody. But if MacGregor gave his OK to Buck West, then Buck was all right.

"Boss," Jerry stuck his head into the office. "Some range-rider just reported a group of old mountain men's gatherin' south and west of here."

"Mountain men?" Richards said. "That's impossible. All those people are dead."

"No, sir," Jerry respectfully disagreed with his boss. "There's still a handful of 'um around. They old, but they mean and crotchety and not to be fooled with. Dangerous old men. I've run up on 'um time to time. And Benson over to the general store reports that one was in his place 'bout three days back. Bought supplies and sich."

"Mountain men," Richards vocally mused. "Now why would those old characters be hanging around here?"

Neither Richards nor Jerry noticed the faint smile on

MacGregor's face. The Scotsman now knew what Buck/ Smoke was up to. And it amused him. But, he cautioned himself silently, you damn sure don't want to be around when Buck and his friends lift the lid on Pandora's Box. Best start making arrangements to pull out. It isn't going to be long.

"Don't know, boss," Jerry said. "Just thought you'd want to know about it."

"Yeah, right, Jerry. Thanks."

MacGregor watched the men leave the office. The undercover federal marshal sat down at his desk and took up his pen, dipping the point into the inkwell. He returned to his company ledger book. But he had a difficult time entering the small, precise figures. His shoulders kept shaking from suppressed laughter.

"I must keep reminding myself that I'm a lady," Sally told Buck. But the twinkle in her eyes told Buck that while a lady she might be, there were a lot of hot coals banked within.

"Aren't you going to run away, screaming in fear?" Buck asked her. "After all, I'm the murderer, Smoke Jensen."

"You took an awful chance, telling me that."

"Maybe I have some insight, too."

"Yes, I suppose you do. Now tell me about Smoke."

She listened attentively for a full ten minutes, not interrupting, letting him tell his painful story, his way. Several times during the telling he lapsed into silence, then with a sigh, he would continue.

When he had finished, she sat on the cool creek bank, her long skirt a fan of gingham around her, and mentally digested all she had heard.

Finally she said, "And to think I work for those creatures." She hurled a small stone into the water. "Well, I shall tender my resignation immediately, of course."

Buck's smile was hard. "Stick around, Sally. The show's just about to begin."

"What would you do if I told you . . . well, I am quite fond of you, Buck?"

"What would you want me to do?"

"Well," she smiled, "you might kiss me."

Just as their lips touched, a voice came from behind them. "Plumb sickenin'. Great big growed-up man a-moonin' and a-sparkin' lak some fiddle-footed kid. Disgustin'."

Buck spun around, on his feet in a crouch, his hands over the butt of his guns. His mouth dropped open.

"Shut your mouth, boy," Preacher said. "Flies is bad this time of year."

"*Preacher!*" Buck croaked, his voice breaking.

"It damned shore ain't Jedediah Smith," the old man said drily. "We lost him back in '35, I think it was. Either that or he got married. One and the same if'n you's to ask me."

Buck ran toward Preacher and grabbed him in a bear hug, spinning around and around with the old mountain man.

"Great Gawd Amighty!" Preacher hollered. "Put me down, you ox!"

Buck dropped the old man to the ground. His big hands on Preacher's shoulders, Buck said, "I can't believe it. I thought you were dead!"

"I damn near was, boy! Took this old body a long time to recover. Now if'n you're all done a-slobberin' all over me, we got to make some plans."

"How'd you find me, Preacher?"

"Hell's fire, boy! I just followed the bodies! Cain't you keep them guns of yourn in leather?"

"Come on, Preacher! Tell the truth. I know you'd rather lie, but try real hard."

"You see how unrespectful he is, Missy?" Preacher looked at Sally. "Cain't a purty thang lak you do no better than the laks of this gunslick?"

"I'm going to change him," Sally said primly. She was not certain just how to take this disreputable-looking old man, all dressed in buckskins and looking like death warmed over.

"Uh-huh," Preacher said. "That's whut that white wife of mine said, too."

"White wife!" Buck looked at him. "You never had no wife except squaws!"

"That's all you know, you pup. I married up with me a white woman that was purtier than Simone Jules Dumont's mustache."

"Heavens!" Sally muttered.

Simone Jules Dumont, also known as Madame Mustache, was either from France or a Creole from the Mississippi Delta region—it had never been proven one way or the other. She'd showed up in California during the 1849 gold rush and had soon been named head roulette croupier at the Bella Union in San Francisco. Eventually, Simone had moved on to a livelier occupation: running a gambling saloon/whorehouse at Bannack, Montana. It was there she is rumored to have taught the finer points of card dealing to Calamity Jane. And her mustache continued to grow, as did her reputation. She killed what is thought to be her first husband—a man named Carruthers—after he conned her out of a sizable amount of money. She moved on to Bodie, California, mustache in full bloom, and killed another man there when he and another footpadder tried to rob her one night. She lost most of her money in a card game on the night of September 6, 1879, and passed on through the Pearlies that same night after drinking hydrocyanic acid.

"Did you have any children from that union, Mister Preacher?" Sally asked.

"Durned if'n I know, Missy. I lit a shuck out of there one night. Walls was a-closin' in on me. I heard she took up with a minister and went back east. I teamed up with John Liver-Eatin' Johnston for a time. He lost his old woman back in '47 and went plumb crazy for a time. Called him Crow Killer. He kilt about three hundred Crows and et the livers out of 'em."

Sally turned a little green around the mouth. Buck had heard the story; he yawned.

"I didn't think crows were good to eat, Mister Preacher," Sally said.

"Not the bird, Missy," Preacher corrected. "The Indian tribe. You see, it was a bunch of Crows on the warpath that kilt Johnston's old woman. John never did lak Crows after that. Et a bunch of 'em."

"You mean he was a . . . *cannibal?"*

"Only as fer as the liver went," Preacher said blandly. "He got to lookin' at me one night while we's a-camped in the Bitterroot. Right hongry look in his eyes. I took off. Ain't seen him since. Last I heard, old Crow Killer was a scout for the U.S. Army, over on the North Plains."

Sally sat back on the bank, averting her eyes, mumbling to herself.

"I wish you had gotten word to me that you were still alive, you old coot," Buck said.

"Couldn't. I were plumb out of it for a couple of months. By the time I could ride out of that Injun camp, Nicole and the baby was dead and buried and you was gone. I'm right sorry about Nicole and the boy, Smoke."

Buck nodded. "Better get used to calling me Buck, Preacher. You might slip up in town and that would be the end of it."

"I ain't goin' into town. Not until you git ready to make your move, that is. You wanna git a message to me,

Smoke, they'll be a miserable-looking old Injun in town named Hunts-Long. Flathead. Wears a derby hat. He'll git word to me. Me and the boys was spotted last yesterday, so we'll be changin' locations." He told Buck where. "I's tole you met up with Audie." That was said with a grin.

"I thought I was seeing things. I thought he was an elf."

"He's the furrtherest thang from an elf. That little man will kill you faster than you can spit. Yessir, Smoke, you got some backup that'll be wrote up strong when they writes about the buryin' of Bury. Got Tenneysee, Audie, Phew, Nighthawk, Dupre, Deadlead, Powder Pete, Greybull, Beartooth, and Lobo. And me. 'Course I'm a better man than all them combined," Preacher said, in his usual modest manner. "And Matt."

"Phew?" Sally said. "Why in Heaven's name would you call a man that?"

" 'Cause he stinks, Missy."

"I know Matt. The negro."

"That's him. Ol' one-eye." Preacher stuck out his hand. "Be lookin' at you, Smoke. You take care, now." He whistled for his pony and the spotted horse trotted over. Preacher jumped onto the mustang's back and was gone.

Sally looked at Buck. A load seemed to have been removed from his shoulders. His eyes were shining with love as he watched the old man ride out. He seemed to stand a little taller.

He met her eyes. "It's sad. When those men are gone, a . . . time will have passed. And it will never be again."

"That is not entirely true, Smoke Jensen," Sally said.

"Oh? What do you mean?"

"You'll be here to carry on."

12

The day after seeing Preacher, Buck was witness to a scene that lent credence to what MacGregor had said about the men and women who made up the population of Bury. Buck was sitting on the boardwalk in front of one of Bury's hurdy-gurdy houses, leaned back in his chair, when a man and woman and three children walked up the main street. The man and woman wore rags and the kids looked as though they had not eaten in days. The ragged little band of walkers stopped in front of the large general store. Buck drifted over that way just as the red-headed cowboy, Sam, walked over from another direction. Buck and Sam looked at each other and nodded greetings.

"Watch this," Sam said out of the corner of his mouth. "This might change your mind about the men you're working for. And the sorry people in this town."

"You get your money out of the same hand that pays me," Buck reminded him.

"But I don't have to like it . . . Smoke."

"Do I know you from somewheres else?" Buck asked.

"I was in Cañon City when you and that old mountain

man drew down on Ackerman and his boys. Took me awhile to put it all together. But I knowed I'd seen you before."*

"Why haven't you tried to collect the bounty on my head, then?"

Sam hesitated. "I don't know," he finally admitted. "Mayhaps I'm havin' some second thoughts 'bout the way my life's been goin' up to date. And then mayhaps I just want to hang around and see the show. 'Cause I know when the time gets right, you're goin' to put on one hell of a show."

"You gonna watch my back?"

"I don't know. Talk to you later. Listen to this."

The ragged emaciated-looking man was talking to the store manager. "I'm begging you, mister. Please. My kids are starving and my wife is worn out. I ain't asking nothing for myself. Just a bite of food for my wife and kids. I'll work it out for you."

The storekeeper waved his broom at the ragged man. "Get on with you. Get out of here. Go beg somewhere else."

"I'll get down on my knees and beg you, mister," the man said. He was so tired, so worn out, he was trembling.

The man who ran the leather shop next to the general store stepped out onto the boardwalk to watch the show. "What happened to you, skinny?" he called to the ragged man.

"Indians. They ambushed the wagon train we was on. We didn't have time to circle. They split us up. Most of the others died. We lost everything and have been walking for days. Brother, can you find it in your heart to give my kids and woman something to eat?"

"Only if you got the money to pay for it. If you don't, then haul your ashes on, beggar."

*The Last Mountain Man.

The man's shoulders sagged and tears began rolling down his dusty face.

Buck could not believe what he was hearing and seeing. But he knew he could not afford to step out of character—not yet. He watched and waited.

Other shopkeepers had gathered on the boardwalk. The man who ran the apothecary shop laughed and said, "There's a joyhouse down the end of this street. Why don't you put your woman in there? Clean 'er up some and she'll make enough to get you goin' again." The gathering crowd roared with laughter.

Sam explained. "Man poisoned his partner back in Illinoise," he said. "Then stole his woman and come out here. Real nice feller. Name's Burton."

"Yeah," Buck returned the low tone.

The hotel manager stepped out. He waved his arms at the ragged little band. "You ne'er-do-wells get out of here. That little girl looks like she's got galloping consumption. No one here wants to catch that. Stir up the dust and get gone from here."

"Morgan," Sam said. "Ran a hotel in Ohio until he burned it down. Killed several sleepers. Another nice feller."

"I just don't believe the heartlessness of these people," Buck said.

"You ain't seen nothin' yet, partner," Sam said. "Stick around."

"The Lord helps those who help themselves," Reverend Necker said, appearing on the scene. "But He frowns on shirkers. Now be gone with you."

"A minister?" Buck whispered.

"About as holy as you and me," Sam said. "Come from Iowa, so he says. He's a drunk and a skirt-chaser."

The woman had gathered her children close to her and was fighting back tears. The man's shoulders were slumped in defeat.

Sheriff Reese and Deputy Rogers walked up. "You vagabonds keep on moving," the sheriff ordered. "Get on with you now before I put a loop on you all and drag you out of town."

"I don't believe I'm seeing this!" Sally shouted from the fringe of the crowd. Her hot eyes found Buck and bored invisible holes into his heart. She swung her eyes back to the merchants gathered on the boardwalk. "What is the matter with you people?"

"Warn her off," Sam whispered. "You and me will get some grub and clothes for them people; give it to them on the outskirts of town. But warn her off, Buck. She's treadin' on dangerous ground."

"How?" Buck whispered.

Sam grunted. "Good question, I reckon. That lady would stand up to an Injun attack armed with a broom, I'm thinkin'."

"You people should be ashamed of yourselves!" Sally shouted. "Look at those children. *Look at them!* They're starving."

"This ain't none of your business, Miz Sally," Sheriff Reese said. "You just go on back home and tend to your knittin'."

"Well, I'll make it my business!" Sally flared, sticking her chin out and standing her ground. She looked at the ragged, starving family. "You people come with me. To my house. I'll give you all a hot meal."

"No, you won't, Miss Reynolds," the voice came from the edge of the crowd.

All heads turned to stare at Keith Stratton, mounted on a showy white horse.

"What do you mean, Mr. Stratton?" Sally asked.

"Those people are losers, Miss Reynolds," Stratton said. "No matter what or how much one does for them, they will be begging again tomorrow. Trash. That's all they are. All they ever will be. And you don't own that house you're living in. I do. You are staying there rent-free. And you are paid to teach school, not meddle in town affairs. Now please leave."

"And if I choose to stay?" Sally asked.

"You will neither have a job, nor a place to stay," Stratton warned.

"Stratton just stepped into a pit full of rattlers," Sam projected accurately. "All dressed up in gingham."

"Yep," Buck said.

"I see," Sally said. "Will you allow me the time to gather up my personal belongings, or do you intend to seize those along with the house?"

"You're about to make a very bad mistake, Sally," Stratton informed her.

"There is quite a popular phrase out here, Mr. Stratton," Sally said. "It is said that out in the west, a person saddles their own horses and kills their own snakes."

"I'm familiar with the saying," Stratton said, his triple chins quavering as he spoke. The sunlight glinted off his diamond rings.

"Then I stand by that maxim, sir."

"A what?" Sam whispered.

"Don't ask me," Buck said.

"You're a very foolish and headstrong young woman, Miss Reynolds. But if that is your decision, then you have one hour to gather up your possessions and vacate that house."

Sally nodded and looked at the ragged family. "You people come with me."

Buck started toward Sally. She waved him back. "You have made your choice, Buck. So long as you work for the other side, I do not wish to see you."

She winked at him.

Buck hid his smile, knowing then what Sally was

doing. She was jeopardizing her own position in order to strengthen his own. *Gal has guts*, Buck thought. *But where in the hell is she going to stay the night?* he wondered.

"She's going to stay *where*?" Buck shouted at Sam.

Sam backed up. "Easy now, partner." He kept his hands away from his guns. "She's gonna stay down at Miss Flora's place."

"A whorehouse!"

"It wasn't my idea, Buck. It was Miss Flora's. She likes Sally 'cause Sally was always nice and polite to them, ah, ladies that work the Pink House."

"Sally Reynolds in a whorehouse!"

The red-headed cowpuncher-turned-gunslick took another step backward. The last thing in this world he wanted was for Buck to reach for those guns. Sam was fast, but Lord knows not nearabouts that fast. "Miss Flora done closed the doors to the Pink House, Buck. Shut 'er down tight. She's been wanting to pull up stakes for a year. Take her girls and head out. Stratton and them blocked that move. Made her mad. Now she's locked the doors to the Pink House. This is liable to bring things to a head 'round here, Buck."

Buck began to relax as the humor of the situation struck him. He had been told that the Big Three built the joyhouse to keep their randy gunhands happy. If Miss Flora had indeed shut the Pink House down, a lot of gunhands were going to be walking around with a short fuse.

Leave it to Sally to light the fuse.

Buck asked, "What happened to that poor family?"

"Sally give 'um a big poke of food and money enough to buy clothes and a wagon and horses. You knew she was rich, didn't you?"

"Sally? Rich?"

"Folks is. Her daddy owns a lot of factories and such back east. Her momma has money too. Stratton and Potter and Richards just might have grabbed ahold of a puma's tail this time. I hear Wiley Potter was all upset about what Stratton done today. He sent word to Sally to go on back to her little house and forget what happened. Sally told him, through Miss Flora, that she would forget only when pigs fly."

Deputy Rogers walked up, a grim look on his face. "Buck West! You go see Mr. Richards over to the office. And you, Sam, is fired. Them words come from Mr. Stratton. He's done found out about you helpin' them dirt farmers over in the flats. Git your gear and be out of town by sundown." He looked at Buck. "Move, West!"

Buck silently stared the big deputy down. With a curse, Rogers wheeled around and stalked away.

"What dirt farmers, Sam?"

"It's a big country, Buck. They's room for lots of folks. The Big Three don't object to farmers comin' in, but only if they agree to the terms set up by Potter and Stratton and Richards. If they don't, they git burnt out and run off the land. I don't hold none with the likes of that. A young couple with two little kids moved in last year. Just after I joined up. Started homesteadin'. Richards sent some of his hardcases in. When the man got his back up, Long shot him dead. Becky—that's the widder woman's name—stayed on the place, workin' it herself. I kinda helped along from time to time. I was raised on a farm in Minnesota. Guess they heard about my helpin' out."

Buck looked hard at the man. Could he trust him, or was this a set-up? He decided to play along, test Sam. "You stick around. I'm going to see Richards. When I'm through, we'll take a ride out to the Widow Becky's place. OK?"

"All right, Buck. I'll be at the livery."

Buck walked to the PSR offices. Richards was waiting for him. He pointed to saddlebags on the counter. "No test this time, Buck. The corporation is buying more land. Those bags contain gold dust and the contracts. Man named Gilmore is waiting for you in Challis. Get the papers signed, give him the dust, and get back here."

"Yes, sir."

Buck picked up the saddlebags and walked to the stable. Sam was waiting for him, talking with the little boy Buck had given the gold piece to. Sam grinned at Buck.

"This here is Ben. This stable is his home. His pa was kilt in a cave-in a couple of years ago. He ain't got no ma. He's a good boy. Keeps his mouth shut. And he don't like none of the Big Three. Stratton took a whip to him last year. Marked him up pretty good. Richards kicked him off the boardwalk later on. Bust a rib. He's all right, Buck."

"You go to school, Ben? Buck asked.

"No, sir. Mister Rosten won't let me. Says I gotta work here all the time."

Ben looked to be about nine years old.

Buck nodded. He mentally added Rosten's name to his list of sorry people. "You seen an old Indian around? Wears a derby hat?"

"Hunts-Long. Yes, sir. When he's in town he camps down by the creek yonder." Ben pointed.

"You go tell Hunts-Long I said it's time. Get the word out. He'll know what you mean." Buck gave the boy some coins. Ben took off.

"We can't be seen leaving town together, Sam. Where do you want to meet?"

"Crick just south of town, 'bout four mile. I'll meet you there in a couple of hours."

Buck nodded. "If you playin' a game, Sam, workin' for the other side, you'll never live to see the game finished."

"I believe you, Buck. Or Smoke. No games. I'm done with that. See you at the crick."

Buck watched the cowboy ride out. He wondered if he was going to have to kill him.

13

Buck took his time saddling Drifter. He watched the old Flathead, Hunts-Long, ride out. He was conscious of Little Ben looking at him.

"You know Miss Flora, boy?"

"Yes, sir. Down to the Pink House."

"After I'm gone, you walk down there and tell Miss Sally Reynolds I said to keep her head down. She'll know what I mean. You got that?"

"Yes, sir. Mister Buck? Sam's a nice feller. He ain't no real gunhand. He got backed into it."

"How's that, Ben?"

"Story is—I heard some men talkin'—a deputy over in Montana Territory pushed Sam hard one day. Sam tried to get out of it, but the deputy drew on him. Sam was faster. Kilt the man and had to take the hoot-owl trail." The boy grinned. "Sam's sweet on Miz Becky."

"Sam told me he was from Minnesota."

"Yes, sir. That's what I heard, too. Sam wants to go back to farmin', way I heared it."

"A lot of us would like to be doin' something other than what we're doin', Ben. But a man gets his trail stretched out in front of him, sometimes you just got to ride it to trail's end, whether you like it or not."

"You be careful, Mister Buck."

"See you, boy."

Buck rode out easy. He could feel . . . *something* in the air. A feeling of tension, he thought. And he wondered about it. The pot was about to boil over in Bury, and Buck didn't know what had caused the fire to get too hot. But he knew that sometimes just the slightest little push could turn over a cart—if the contents weren't stacked right.

A mile out of town, Buck cut off the road and reined up, hidden in the timber. He waited for half an hour. No riders passed him. He rode out of the timber, heading for the creek.

"Buck, this here is Becky," Sam said. He was trying very hard not to grin, and not being very successful.

Becky's hair was as red as Sam's, her tanned face pretty and freckled across the nose. She was a slender lady, but Buck could sense a solid, no-nonsense quiet sort of strength about her. Two red-headed kids stood close by her. A boy and a girl. About four and six, Buck guessed. They grinned shyly up at Buck. He winked at them and they both giggled.

Buck took the lady's hand and was not surprised to find it hard and callused from years of hard work.

After talking with Becky and the kids for a few moments, Buck took Sam aside. "You stay here with her, Sam. Until I get back from Challis. Don't be surprised if you spot some old mountain men while I'm gone. I'm going to swing by their camp and tell them I'm just about ready to strike. I'll tell them about your lady friend here, too. They'll probably ride by to see if they can get her anything. And they'll be by. They don't hold with men who hurt womenfolks."

"Who are your friends, Buck? These mountain men, I mean?"

Sam stood open-mouthed as Buck reeled off the names of some of the most famous mountain men of all time. Sam finally blinked and said, "Those are some of the meanest old codgers that ever forked a bronc."

"Yeah," Buck said with a grin as he swung into the saddle. "Ain't they?"

He waved good-bye to Becky and the kids and pointed Drifter's nose south. A mile from Becky's cabin, Buck turned straight east, toward the new camp of Preacher and his friends. Even Buck, knowing what to expect, drew up short at the sight that soon confronted him.

Greybull and Beartooth were wrestling. Dupre was fiddling a French song while Nighthawk and Tenneysee were dancing. Together. Audie was standing on a stump, reciting pretty poetry to the others.

"I hate to break this up," Buck said.

"Then don't!" Preacher said. "Jist sit your cayuse and listen and learn. Go ahead, Audie. Tell us some more about that there Newton."

"*Isaac* Newton, you ignorant reprobate! I was merely stating Sir Newton's theory that to every action there is always opposed an equal reaction: or, the mutual actions of two bodies upon each other are always equal, and directed to contrary parts."

"Then direct it to him," Buck said, pointing at Preacher. "'Cause he sure is contrary."

Audie looked pained while the others laughed. He glowered at Buck. "If I had you in a classroom I'd take a hickory stick to the seat of your pants, young man."

"I don't know nothing about Newton," Buck said, still sitting on Drifter. "But I did like that poetry. Can you say some more of that?"

"But of course, young outlaw called Smoke," Audie said with a wave of his hand. "Dismount and gather around."

Dupre had stopped his fiddling, Nighthawk and Tenneysee their dancing, Greybull and Beartooth their wrestling.

"'I came to the place of my youth'," Audie said, "'and cried, The friends of my youth, where are they? And echo answered, Where are they?'"

"That don't make no damn sense," Phew said.

"And it don't even rhyme," Deadlead growled.

"It doesn't have to rhyme to be poetry!" Audie said. "I have told you heathens that time and again."

"Say something that's purty," Preacher said.

"Yeah, that fits us'ns," Powder Pete said.

"What a monumental task you have verbally laid before me," Audie said. "Very well. Let me think for a moment."

"And I don't reckon it has to rhyme," Matt said.

Audie smiled. He said, "'And in that town a dog was found. As many dogs there be, both mongrel, puppy, whelp, and hound, And curs of low degree. The dog, to gain some private ends, Went mad, and bit the man. The man recovered of the bite, The dog it was that died.'" Still smiling, Audie stepped off the stump and walked off, leaving the old mountain men to scratch their heads and ponder what he'd just said.

"Is he callin' us a bunch of *dogs*?" Lobo asked.

"I don't think so," Preacher said.

Deadlead looked at Nighthawk. "What do you think about it, Nighthawk?"

"Ummm."

Buck's ride to Challis was uneventful. He found the man named Gilmore, completed his business, and headed back. When he rode into Bury, past Miss Flora's Pink

House, he noticed the front door was closed, a hand-lettered sign hanging from a string. CLOSED, the sign read. Smiling, Buck rode to the PSR office and handed the receipt to MacGregor. The Scotsman had a worried look on his now-more-than-ever dour face.

"What's wrong?" Buck asked.

"New territorial governor was just named. It wasn't Potter. He's fit to be tied."

"You knew it wouldn't be all along, didn't you?"

"I had a rather strong suspicion."

"Now what?"

"I don't know. I haven't got enough evidence to bring any of the Big Three to court and make it stick. The Big Three violate a number of *moral* laws. But they run their own businesses on the up and up —so far as I've been able to find out. They have committed murder—either themselves or by hiring it out—but since this town, and all the people in it, belong to the Big Three, no one will talk. But there is a sour, rancid feeling hanging in the air, Buck, Smoke—what *is* your real name?"

"Kirby."

MacGregor nodded absently. "I gather those mountain men in the timber are friends of yours?"

"Preacher helped raise me. I know most of the others." He named them.

MacGregor chuckled. "Old bastards!" he said, with no malice in the profanity. "Did you know Audie is the holder of several degrees?"

"Yes. How did you know about that?"

"Oh, ever since I came out here, fifteen years ago, I have maintained a journal of sorts. I should like to take all those pages and turn them into a book someday. A book about mountain men. I've talked with many of them. But my God, they *lie* so much. I can't tell what is truth and what is fiction."

"I've discovered that most of what they say is true."

"Really now, Smoke! A human being cannot successfully fight a grizzly bear and win!"

"Negro Matt fought a mountain lion with his bare hands and killed it. Preacher fought a bear up on the North Milk in Canada and killed it. Jedediah Smith fought a grizzly and killed it—by himself. Bear chewed off one of his ears, though. Shoo Fly Miller had a grizzly bear for a pet. Those old boys are still about half hoss, half alligator."

"My word!" MacGregor said.

"Stick around, Mac," Buck said cheerfully. "If you live through what's coming up shortly, you can write the final chapter to the lives of the mountain men."

It was going sour, Buck thought, walking from the PSR offices back to his hotel. He could sense it; an almost tangible sensation. The gunhands that were constantly in view were behaving in a surly manner. Cursing more and drinking more openly. Buck noticed a distinct lack of kids playing on the boardwalks and streets. He noticed a couple of loaded-down wagons parked in front of the general store.

Buck stopped in front of a saloon and asked the scar-faced Joiner, "What's going on?"

"Two schoolteachers and their families pullin' out. Didn't like the way Miz Sally was treated. The boss is some sore, let me tell you."

Buck smiled.

Joiner looked sourly at him. "You find something funny about that, West?"

"Just that a man can't push some women, is all."

Joiner grunted. It was obvious to Buck that he was looking for a fight. And Buck wasn't.

When Joiner saw that Buck wasn't going to fight, he said, "There can't be much sand to your bottom, boy."

Buck met him eye to eye. "If you want to get a shovel

and start digging for that sand, Joiner, feel free to do so. But I'd suggest you make one stopover first for a little digging."

"Oh? And where's that?"

"Boot Hill." Buck turned and walked on up the street. As he turned, his right side blocked to Joiner's view, Buck slipped the hammer thong off his .44.

He could feel Joiner's eyes boring into his back as he walked.

"Buck West!" Joiner shouted. "Turn and fight, you tinhorn!"

Buck heard Joiner's hand as his palm struck the wooden grips of his pistol.

Turning, Buck drew, cocked, and fired, all in one fluid motion. Joiner's pistol clattered to the wooden boardwalk as the .44 slug from Buck's gun hit him squarely in the center of the chest. Joiner staggered backward, grabbed at a wooden chair for support, missed the arm of the chair, and sat down heavily on the boardwalk, one hand supporting himself, holding himself up, the other hand covering the hole in his chest.

"You bassard!" Joiner hissed at Buck.

"You pushed me, Joiner," Buck reminded the man.

Joiner groaned and let himself slump to the boards.

Burton ran out of the apothecary shop, crossed the street, and knelt by the dying Joiner. When he looked up at Buck, his face was flushed with hate. "If you're so damned good with a gun, why didn't you just shoot the gun out of his hand? You didn't have to kill him."

"I ain't dead!" Joiner protested weakly.

"You ain't far from it," Burton told him.

"Get me a preacher!" Joiner said.

"He'd probably do you more good than a doctor," Burton agreed.

Buck punched out the spent brass and slid a live round into the chamber. He dropped the empty brass to the dirt of the street just as the sounds of a carriage approaching rattled through the air. The carriage whoaed up beside the blood-slicked boardwalk and the tall gunhand standing impassively over the dying Joiner.

"Oh, my word!" the woman seated in the carriage said.

"Help me, Miz Janey!" Joiner cried.

A group of Cornish miners, in town from their work at a nearby silver mine, gathered around, beer mugs in callused hands.

"The bloke's nearly done," one immigrant from Cornwall observed. "Shall we sing him a fare-thee-well, mates?"

"Aye. Let's."

A half-dozen voices were raised in song, drunkenly offering up a hymn.

A jig dancer from the hurly-gurdy in front of which Joiner lay dying stepped out. "Can I have your pockets, love?" she asked Joiner.

"Get away with you!" Reverend Necker said, running up. "You filthy whore!"

"Careful, Bible-thumper," the jig dancer said. "Or I'll tell everybody where you was the other evenin'."

Necker flushed and bent down over the dying Joiner.

"He kilt me!" Joiner said, pointing a trembling finger at Buck.

"Damn sure did," Necker said.

Buck raised his eyes to look squarely at the woman seated in the fancy carriage.

Janey met the tall young man's direct stare.

The elegantly dressed woman flushed as Buck's eyes stared directly at her.

"Save me, Preacher!" Joiner groaned. "I don't wanna go to Hell. I got a family to take care of."

"Where are they, son?" Necker asked. He looked at the blood on his hands. Joiner's blood. "Yukk!" Necker said.

"Damned if I know," Joiner said. Then he closed his

eyes and did the world the greatest favor men of his ilk could do. He died.

Janey stared at Buck. Her eyes widened as Buck smiled. She watched as Buck turned and walked away.

It couldn't be! she thought. That was impossible. Kirby was back in Missouri, probably working that damned hardscrabble farm.

But she knew the man who had killed Joiner. She knew him. It was her brother.

14

Janey stood in her bedroom, absently gazing out the window. So Buck West was really Kirby Jensen, aka Smoke. She laughed, but the laugh was totally devoid of mirth. She suddenly remembered all the good times they'd shared as children, back in Missouri. It had been a hard life, but despite that, there had been plenty of love to go around. Never enough money for nice things, but none of them had gone hungry.

"Crap!" Janey said, turning away from the window. She didn't know what to do. The gunfighter was blood kin, but Janey felt no warmth toward him. She looked around her. Damned if she was going to give all this up for a man she hadn't seen since he was a snot-nosed kid tryin' to farm forty rocky acres with a damned ol' mule.

She walked downstairs, searching for Josh.

"Gone, ma'am," the Negro houseman informed her.

"Gone, where?"

"Up to the north range to inspect the herds, ma'am. Won't be back for several days."

"Bull-droppings!" Janey blurted.

The houseman's eyes widened.

"Thank you, Thomas," Janey said. "That will be all."

Now she sure didn't know what to do.

MacGregor ceased his pacing, his mind made up. He would not leave Bury, as had been his original plan. He would stick it out here. If Buck West, aka Smoke Jensen, was successful in his plan, what a book that would make! And, the Scotsman smiled grimly, he could close the federal pages on Potter, Stratton, and Richards.

"He's really the outlaw Smoke?" Flora asked Sally.

"He's Smoke Jensen, but he's no outlaw," Sally told the gathering of joy-girls.

"We can't get out of town, Miss Sally," Rosa said. "The little boy, Ben, says Potter and Stratton gave orders to that nasty Rosten not to rent us wagons or horses. We're stuck."

Sally nodded. As Josh Richards had once explained to her, the Pink House was one of the best constructed buildings in town. The two-story structure was built of logs, with excellent craftsmanship in the construction, with carefully fitted corners. Instead of a mixture of clay and moss filling the chinks, solid mortar had been used. With a little rearranging of furniture, the house could easily withstand any stray bullets.

"All right, ladies," Sally said. "Here's what we'll do . . ."

"What's happening!" Deputy Rogers said. "I don't understand none of it. It's like . . . it's like ever'thang was just fine one day, and the next day it's all haywire!"

Sheriff Dan Reese knew what was happening, but he didn't feel like explaining it to this big dummy standing before him. He'd seen boom towns go sour before. And he knew that sometimes a feller could skin the clabber off the top and salvage the milk. Not often, but sometimes.

But he had a sinking feeling it was too damn late for Bury.

"Shut up, Rogers," he said. He looked at his other deputies, Weathers and Payton. "You men check them shotguns and rifles. Git over to the store and stock up on shells. I don't know why, but something tells me everything that's happenin' is the fault of that Buck West. Damn his eyes!"

"So we is gonna do what?" Payton asked. Like Rogers, Payton was no mental giant.

"I think the bosses is gonna tell us to kill him."

Potter turned from the second-floor window of the PSR offices to look at Stratton. "You feel it?" he asked.

"Yes," Stratton said with a sigh. "Whatever *it* is."

"I had the territorial governorship in the palm of my hand," Potter said. "And suddenly, for no reason, I lose it. Why? A seemingly intelligent, reasonable young woman, a very capable schoolteacher, suddenly falls for a gunslick. Why? And now I discover that Buck West—or whatever his name is—is buddy-buddy with Sam, and Sam is sharing the blankets with a squatter. What's happening around here?"

"Don't forget the mountain men gathering up in the deep timber."

"That's right."

The two men looked at each other and suddenly their brains began to click and hum in unison.

"Mountain men helped raise Kirby Jensen," Stratton said.

"We've all heard the rumors that Preacher wasn't killed," Potter said.

"All our troubles started when Buck West arrived in town."

The men sent a flunky for Sheriff Dan Reese.

"Anybody have any idee whatever happened to old Maurice Leduc?" Deadlead asked.

The mountain men were camped openly and brazenly about two miles outside of Bury. They knew their reputation had preceded them, and they likewise knew that none of the Big Three's gunhands were about to attack the camp. For one thing, they held the vantage point—the crest of a low hill. For another, no twenty-five cowboys-turned-gunhands were about to attack a dozen old hardbitten mountain men; especially not the most notorious bunch of mountain men to ever prowl the high lonesome. No matter that none of the mountain men would ever see seventy years of age again. That had nothing to do with it. Even at seventy, most of them could still outshoot and outfight men half their age.

Lobo said, "Last I heard, ol' Leduc come back up to near Bent's fort and built hisself a cabin; him and a teenage Mex gal. Took up gardenin'." That was said very contemptuously.

"Hale's far!" Powder Pete said. "That was back in '58."

"Wal, what year is this here we're in?" Dupre asked.

"Oh . . . about '75, I reckon," Tenneysee said.

"You don't say," Greybull said. "My, time does git away from a man, don't it?"

"If that is the case," Audie said. "And I will admit that I don't even know what year it is, not really, I was born seventy-one years ago."

"And got uglier every year," Preacher said.

"You should talk. You're so ugly you could pose for totem poles."

"I 'member thc furst time I seen one of the things," Phew said. "Up in Washington Territory. Like to have plumb scared me out of my 'skins."

"That'd probably been a good thing for all concerned," Matt said. "Least you'da took a bath then. You ain't been out of them skins in fifty year."

"I wish Smoke would git things a-smokin' down yonder," Beartooth said. "I'm a-cravin' a mite of action."

"He'll start stirrin' it up in a day or three," Preacher opined. "And then we'll all have all the action we can handle. Bet on it."

"Reckon whut he's a-doin' down there?" Lobo asked.

"Probably tryin' to spark that schoolmarm," Preacher said. "He's shore stuck on her."

"What do you mean, I can't come in?" Buck said, standing on the front porch of the Pink House.

"Buck," Sally's voice came through the closed door. "You'd better get out of town. Little Ben just slipped up to the back door and told us Sheriff Reese and his deputies are looking for you. Word just drifted into town that you're Smoke Jensen."

So the cat was out of the bag. Fine. He was getting tired of being Buck West. "You . . . ladies have plenty of food and water?"

"Enough for a month-long siege. Go on, Buck."

"Call me Smoke."

15

Smoke slipped around the side of the Pink House and into the weed-grown alley in the rear. He carefully picked his way toward the rear of the stable. He felt sure the front of the stable would be watched.

For the first time since he had arrived in Bury, the town was silent. No wagons rattled up and down the streets. No riders moving in and out of town. No foot traffic to be seen in Bury. A tiny dust devil spun madly up the main street, picking up bits of paper as it whirled away.

Smoke slipped from outhouse to outhouse, both hammer thongs off his .44s.

Reese and his deputies apparently believed Smoke would not take to the alleys, but instead stroll right down the center of the main street, spurs jingling, like some tinhorn kid who fancied himself a gunhand. But Smoke had been properly schooled by Preacher, whose philosophy was thus: if you're outnumbered, circle around 'hind 'em and ambush the hell out of 'em. Ain't no such thang as a fair fight, boy. Just a winner and a loser.

Smoke didn't want to open the dance just yet. He was

in a very bad position, being on foot and armed with only his short guns.

And he was still about a block and a half from the stable. His eyes picked up the shape of a small boy, frantically and silently waving his arms. Little Ben. Smoke returned the wave. Ben disappeared into the stable and returned seconds later, leading a saddled and ride-ready Drifter. Smoke grinned. Drifter must have taken a liking to Little Ben, for had he not, the stallion would have stomped the boy to death.

"Jensen!" The harshly spoken word came from his right, from the shadows of an alley.

Out of the corner of his eye, Smoke could see the young man had not drawn his pistol. The cowboy was a PSR rider, but Smoke did not know his name.

Smoke slowly turned, facing the young rider. "Back away, cowboy," Smoke stated softly. "Just walk back up the alley and no one will ever have to know. If you draw on me, I'll kill you. Turn around and you'll live. How about it?"

"That thirty thousand dollars looks almighty good to me, Jensen," the puncher replied, his hands hovering over his low-tied guns. "Start me up a spread with that."

"You'll never live to work it," Smoke warned him.

Ben was slowly leading Drifter up the alley.

"Says you!" the cowboy sneered.

"What's your name, puncher?"

"Jeff Siddons. Why?"

"So I'll know what to put on your grave marker."

Jeff flushed. "You gonna draw or talk?"

"I'd rather not draw at all," Smoke again tried to ease out of the fight.

"You yellow scum!" Jeff said. "Draw!" His hands dipped downward.

Jeff's hands had just touched the wooden handles of

his guns when he felt a terrible crushing double blow to his chest. The young cowboy staggered backward, falling heavily against the side of the building. Smoke was already turning away from the dying cowboy as light faded in Jeff's eyes. "Ain't no human man that fast!" Jeff spoke his last words, sitting in his own dusty blood.

Smoke looked back at the dying cowboy. "Just remember to tell Saint Peter this wasn't my idea."

But he was talking to a dead man.

He heard the drum of bootheels on the boardwalk, all running in his direction. He turned just as a voice called out, "Hold it, Jensen!"

Smoke ducked in back of the building just as a shot rang out, the bullet knocking a fist-sized chunk of wood out of the building. Smoke dropped to one knee and fired two fast shots around the side of the building, then he was up and running toward Ben and Drifter, ignoring the howl of pain behind him and in the alley. At least one of his snap shots had struck home.

"That damned little stableboy's helpin' Jensen!" a man's voice yelled. "I'll take a horsewhip to that little son of a bitch!"

Smoke reached Ben and Drifter. "Run to Miss Flora's, Ben. Them women won't let anything happen to you. Run, boy, run!"

Ben took off as if pursued by the devil. Smoke mounted up. His saddlebags were bulging, so Ben must have transferred a lot of his gear from the packs normally borne by the pack animal. He looked back over his shoulder. Sheriff Reese was leading a running gang of men. And they weren't far behind Smoke.

"Hold up there, Jensen!" Reese yelled, just as Smoke urged Drifter forward and cut into the alley where the dead cowboy lay. Reese lifted a double-barreled coach gun and pulled the trigger. The buckshot tore a huge hole in the corner of the building.

Drifter leaped ahead and charged through the alley, coming out on the main street. Smoke turned his nose north for a block and then whipped into another alley, coming out behind Reese and his men. Smoke had reloaded his Colts and now, with the reins in his teeth, a Colt in each hand, he charged the knot of gunslicks headed by Sheriff Reese.

"I want that thirty thousand!" a man yelled. Smoke recognized the man as Jerry, from back at the trading post.

"Hell with you!" Reese said. "I want that—" He turned at the sound of drumming hooves. "Jesus Christ!" he hollered, looking at the mean-eyed stallion bearing down on him.

The charging stallion struck one gunhand, knocking the man down, the man falling under Drifter's steel-shod hooves. The gunnie screamed, the cry cut off as Drifter's hooves pounded the man's face into pulp.

Reese had jumped out of the way of the huge midnight black horse with the killer-cold yellowish eyes, losing his shotgun as he leaped. One of Drifter's hooves struck the sheriff's thigh, bringing a howl of pain and a hat-sized bruise on the man's leg. Reese rolled on the ground, yelling in pain.

"You squatter-lovin' son!" Jerry screamed at Smoke, bringing up a .45.

Smoke leveled his left-hand .44 and shot the man between the eyes.

As blood splattered, the foot-posse broke up, fear taking over. Men ran in all directions.

Smoke urged Drifter on, galloping up the alley and once more entering the main street. He looped the reins loosely around the saddlehorn and screamed like an angry cougar, the throaty scream, almost identical to a real cougar's war cry, chilling the shopowners who were huddling behind closed doors. Stratton, Potter, and Richards had promised them a safe town and lots of easy money; they hadn't said anything about a wild man riding a horse that looked like it came straight out of the pits of Hell.

Preacher sat straight up on his blankets. He slapped one knee and cackled as the gunshots drifted out of Bury. The shots were followed by the very faint sounds of a big mountain lion screaming.

"Hot damn, boys!" Preacher hollered. "Somebody finally grabbed holt of Smoke's tail and gave 'er a jerk. Bet by Gawd they'll wish they hadn't a done it."

"He a-havin' all the fun!" Beartooth gummed the words.

"They's plenty to go around," Lobo growled. "When he needs us, he'll holler."

"Ummm," said Nighthawk.

"How eloquently informative," said Audie.

Leaning close to Drifter's neck, presenting a low profile, Smoke charged up the main street. He was not going to shoot up the town, for he did not want to harm any woman or child. He had made up his mind that he was going to give the shopkeepers and the storeowners and their families a chance to pull out. But he was doing that for the sake of the kids only. To hell with the adults; man or woman, they knew who they worked for. One was as bad as the other.

Ten minutes later, Smoke had reined up and dismounted in the camp of the mountain men.

"Howdy, son!" Preacher said. "You been havin' yourself a high old time down there, huh?"

"That's one way of putting it," Smoke said, putting one heavily muscled arm around the old man's wangleather-tough shoulders.

"You grinnin' like a chicken-eatin' dog, boy," Preacher said. "What you got a-rattlin' 'round in 'at head of yourn?"

Smoke looked at Powder Pete. "You got any dynamite with you?"

"Only time I been without any was when them durned Lakotas caught me up near the Canadian border and wanted to skin me. Since I was somewhat fond of my hide, I were naturally disinclined to part with it."

Smoke laughed aloud, and the laughter felt good. He felt as though he was back home, which, in a sense, he was. "What happened?"

"The chief had a daughter nobody wanted to bed down with," Powder Pete said, disgust in his voice. "Homeliest woman I ever seen. 'At squaw could cause a whirlwind to change directions. The chief agreed to let me live if'n I'd share Coyote Run's blankets. How come she got that name was when she was born the chief had a pet coyote. Coyote took one look at her and run off. Never did come back. 'At's homely, boy. I spent one winter with Coyote Run, up in the MacDonald Range, on the Flathead. Come spring, I told 'at chief he might as well git his skinnin' knife out, 'cause I couldn't stand no more of Coyote Run. Chief said he didn't know how I'd stood it this long. Told me to take off. I been carryin' dynamite ever since. Promised myself if'n I ever got in another bind lak 'at 'air, I'd blow myself up. Whut you got in mind, Smoke?"

"One road leading into and out of Bury."

Powder Pete and the other mountain men grinned. They knew then what was rattlin' around in Smoke's head.

"If you men will, find the best spots to block the road to coach and carriage travel. Set your charges. I'm going to give those who want to leave twenty-four hours to do so. I want the kids out of that town. I'd prefer the women to leave as well, but from what I've been able to see and hear, most of the women are just as low-down as their men."

"Simmons's old woman is," Dupre said. "I knowed her afore. Plumb trash."

"I still want to give them a chance to leave," Smoke said. "And I especially want Sally and the women in the Pink House out, along with MacGregor and Little Ben. The rest of the townspeople can go to hell."

Deadlead and Greybull picked up their rifles. Deadlead said, "Us'n and Matt and Tenneysee will block the horse trails out of town. Rest of ya'll git busy."

"Preacher," Powder Pete said, "you take the fur end of town. I'll scout this end. I'll hook up with you in a couple hours and plant the charges."

"Done." Preacher moved out.

"I shall make the announcement to the good citizens of Bury," Audie said. "My articulation is superb and my voice carries quite well."

"Yeah," Phew said. "Like a damned ol' puma with his tail hung up in a b'ar trap. Grates on my nerves when you git to hollerin'."

Audie ignored him. "Considering the mentality of those who inhabit that miserable village, I must keep this as simple as possible. Therefore, the Socratean maieutic method of close and logical reasoning must be immediately discarded."

"Umm," Nighthawk said.

"Whut the hell did you say?" Lobo growled. "Sounded like a drunk Pawnee. Gawdamnit, you dwarf, cain't you speak plain jist once in a while?"

"Rest your gray cells, you hulking oaf," Audie responded. "I'm thinking."

"Wal, thank to yoursalf, you magpie!"

"Silence, you cretin!"

Smoke let them hurl taunts and insults back and forth; they had been doing it for fifty-odd years and were not about to quit at this stage of the game. He turned to face the direction of Bury.

He would give them more of a chance than they had given his brother or father. Ever so much more of a chance than they had given his baby son and his wife, Nicole. Ever so much more.

He let hate consume him as he recalled that awful day. . . .

He had made a wide circle of the cabin, staying in the timber back of the creek, and slipped up to the cabin. Inside the cabin, although Smoke did not as yet know it, the outlaw Canning had taken a blanket and smothered Baby Arthur to death. Nicole had been brutally raped, and then her throat had been crushed. Canning scalped the woman, tying her bloody hair to his belt. He then skinned a breast, thinking he would tan the hide and make himself a nice tobacco pouch.

Kid Austin had gotten sick watching Canning's callousness. He walked outside to vomit.

Another outlaw, Grissom, walked out the front of the cabin. Grissom felt something was wrong. He sensed movement behind him and reached for his gun. Smoke shot him dead.

"Behind the house!" Felter yelled.

Another of the PSR riders had been dumping his bowels in the outhouse. He struggled to pull up his pants and push open the door at the same time. Smoke shot him twice in the belly and left him to die on the craphouse floor.

Kid Austin, caught in the open, ran for the banks of the creek. Just as he jumped, Smoke fired, the lead taking the Kid in the buttocks, entering the right cheek and tearing out the left.

Smoke waited behind a woodpile, the big Sharps buffalo rifle Preacher had given him in his hands. He watched as something came sailing out the open back door. His dead baby son bounced on the earth.

The outlaws inside the cabin taunted Smoke, telling in

great detail of raping Nicole. Smoke lined up the Sharps and pulled the trigger. A PSR rider began screaming in pain.

Canning and Felter ran out of the front of the cabin, hightailing it for the safety of the timber. In the creek, Kid Austin crawled upstream, crying in pain and humiliation.

Another of the PSR riders exited the cabin, leaving one inside. He got careless and Smoke took him alive.

When he came to his senses, Smoke had stripped him, staked him out over an anthill, and poured honey all over him.

It took him a long time to die.

Smoke buried his wife and son amid a colorful profusion of wild flowers, stopping often to wipe away the tears.

16

"What are you thinking, young man?" Audie asked.
"About what Potter and Stratton and Richards ordered done to my wife and son."

"Preacher told us. That was a terrible, terrible thing. But don't allow revenge to destroy you."

"When this is over, Audie, it's over. Not until."

"I understand. I have been where you are. I lost my wife, a Bannock woman, and two children to white trappers. Many many years ago."

"Did you find the men who did it?"

"Oh, yes," Audie smiled grimly. "I found them."

Smoke did not have to ask the outcome.

"There will always be men who rise to power on the blood and pain of others, Smoke," the former school-teacher turned mountain man said. "Unfortunate, certainly, but a fact, perhaps a way, of life."

"The people who run the shops in that town can leave," Smoke said. "Even though I know they are, in their own way, as bad as Potter, Stratton, and Richards. I'll let them go, if they'll just go."

"They won't," Audie prophesied. "For most of them,

this is the end of the trail. Behind them lies their past, filled with crime and pettiness. For most of them, all that waits behind them is prison—or a rope. Theirs is a mean, miserable existence." He waved his hand at the mountain men. "We, all us, remember when that town was built. We sat back and watched those dreary dregs of society arrive. We have all watched good people travel through, look around them, and continue on their journey. I, for one, will be glad to see that village razed and returned to the earth."

Audie walked away. About three and a half feet tall physically, about six and a half feet of man and mind and courage.

Smoke sat back on his bootheels and wondered what razed meant.

He'd have to remember to ask Sally. She'd know. And with that thought, another problem presented itself to Smoke's mind. Sally. He knew he cared a lot for the woman—more than he was willing to admit—but what did he have to offer someone like her? When news of what he planned to do to Bury reached the outside, Smoke Jensen would be the most wanted man in the west. Not necessarily in terms of reward money, for if he had his way, Potter, Stratton, and Richards would be dead and in the ground, but more in terms of reputation. A hundred, five hundred, a thousand gunhawks would be looking for him to make a reputation.

Back to the valley where Nicole and Baby Arthur were buried?

No. No, for even if Sally was willing to come with him, he couldn't go back there. Too many old memories would be in the way. He would return to the valley for his mares; he wanted to do that. Then push on and get the Appaloosa, Seven.

Then . . . ?

He didn't know. He would like to ranch and raise

horses. And farm. Farming was in his blood and he had always loved the land. A combination horse and cattle ranch and farm? Why not? That was very rare in the west—almost unheard of—but why not?

Would Sally be content with that? A woman of class and education and independence and wealth? Well, he'd never know until he asked her. But that would have to wait. He'd ask her later. If he lived, that is.

Deputy Rogers was the first to report back to Potter and Stratton and Sheriff Reese. Josh Richards was still out in the field; he knew nothing of the true identity of Buck West. Not yet.

"North road's blocked 'bout three miles out of town," Rogers reported. "An' I mean blown all to hell. Brought a landslide down four-five-hundred feet long."

Deputy Payton galloped up and dismounted. "South road's blocked by a landslide. A bad one. Ain't nothing gonna get through there for a long time. They's riflemen stuck up all around the town, watchin' the trails. Old mountain men, looks like."

"I should have put it all together," Stratton said with a sigh. "I should have known when that damn Jensen came ridin' in, bold as brass. Should have known that's who it was."

"What are we going to do, Keith?" Wiley Potter asked.

"Wait and find out what Jensen wants. Hell, what else can we do?"

Audie had made himself a megaphone out of carefully peeled bark. He had stationed himself on a ridge overlooking the town of Bury.

"Attention below!" Audie called. "Residents of Bury, Idaho Territory, gather in the street and curb your tongues."

"Do what with a tongue?" Deputy Rogers asked.

"Don't talk," Stratton said.

"Oh."

"Armageddon is nigh," Audie called. "Your penurious and evil practices must cease. *Will* cease—immediately. The women and the children will be allowed to leave. You have twenty-four hours to vacate and walk out with what meager possessions you can carry on your backs. Follow the flats south to Blue Meadows. Where you go from there is your own concern. Twenty-four hours. After that, the town of Bury will be destroyed."

"What's that about arms?" Dan Reese asked.

"Armageddon," Reverend Necker said. "Where the final battle will be fought between good and evil." He looked around him. "Has anybody got a jug? I need a drink."

"I ain't gonna hoof my tootsies nowhere," Louise Rosten said. "They's wild savages out there."

"Just head straight across the flats toward the east," her husband told her. "They's a settlement 'bout thirty miles over yonder. Pack up the kids and git gone. Hell, you can outshoot me."

"Hunts-Long and his Flatheads will escort the women and children to safety," Audie's voice once more rang out over the town. "They'll be waiting on the east side of the creek. You have twenty-four hours. This will be my last warning to you."

"I ain't travelin' with no damned greasy Injuns!" Veronica Morgan said. "I ain't leavin' the hotel."

Her husband looked at her. "Get those snot-nosed brats of yours and get out. I'm tired of looking at your ugly face and listening to those brats squall."

Veronica spat in her husband's face and wheeled about, stalking back to the hotel.

"Potter! Stratton! Richards!" Smoke's voice boomed through the bark-made megaphone. "This is Smoke Jensen. I'm giving you a better chance than you gave my pa, my brother, and my wife and son."

None of the town's residents had to ask what Smoke was talking about. They all, to a person, knew. They knew the town was built on stolen gold and Jensen blood. They all knew the whole bloody, tragic story. And they had consented to live with that knowledge.

Stratton's heavy jowls quivered with rage and fear. He turned his little piggy eyes to Potter. "Now what?" he demanded.

"Just stay calm and keep your senses about you, man," Potter said. "Look at facts. We've a hundred and fifty men in this town. Thirty of them are hardcases drawing fighting pay. Josh is out there," he waved his hand, "with fifteen or twenty other gunhands. We're up against a handful of old men and one smart-aleck gunhawk who is too sure of himself. We've both known Hunts-Long for years. He's a peaceful, trusting Indian and so is his tribe. Send the women and kids out and we'll make ready for a siege. The stage is due in three days. We'll have someone there to meet it, turn it around, and get the Army in here from the fort. Then we'll hang Smoke Jensen and his damned old mountain men and be done with it once and for all."

Stratton and the others visibly relaxed. Sure, they thought. That was a damn good plan. Some of them began to laugh at how easy it would be. Soon all those gathered in the street were laughing and slapping one another on the back. The women were cackling and the men hoo-hawing.

"Sounds lak they havin' a celebration down thar," Lobo said. "Wush they'd let us in on it."

"They're thinking about the stage," Smoke said. "If they could turn it around with a message, they could get the Army in here and chase us all the way to Canada."

"Les' we had someone down thar to meet it with a story," Phew said.

Smoke smiled at that. "That's what we'll do, then."

"Now what?" Dupre said.

"We give them twenty-four hours, just like I promised."

"I can't help but feel sorry for the kids," Smoke said.

"There isn't a child down there under ten or eleven years of age," Audie observed, watching through binoculars. "They are past their formative years; or very close to it. They are just smaller versions of their parents."

The sun had been up for an hour and the women and children of Bury were moving out. On foot. Had Smoke and the mountain men been able to hear the comments of the men, it would have left no doubt in any of their minds.

"I shore am glad to see that bitchin' woman clear out," Hallen said. "Hope I never see her again."

Morgan watched his wife—common law, since each of them was still married, to someone else—and her brats walk out of town. "I hope they're attacked by Indians," was his comment.

Simmons watched his wife trudge up the road. "Old lard-butted thing," he said, under his breath. "God, I hope I never see her again."

Like comments were being shared by all the men as they watched the women and kids move out.

Linda Potter and Lucille Stratton had elected to remain with their men. True to the end. Or 'til the money ran out—whichever came first.

Hunts-Long and his Flatheads were waiting by the creek. They had orders from Preacher to escort the women to the flats and keep them there until the matter was settled in Bury—one way or the other.

"You can't know that for certain," Smoke said, looking at Audie, who had lowered his binoculars from the stream of humanity.

"With very little exception, my young friend. It doesn't hold true always, but water will seek its own level."

"We're gonna have to keep a sharp lookout for Richards's men, boy," Preacher said. "Them fifteen, eighteen riders he's got is all gunhands. Now you listen to me, boy," Preacher spun Smoke around to face him. "Them gold and silver mines that belong to them Big Three assayed out high. One mine, they got the gold assayed out at more than one hundred thousand dollars a ton. You know anything about gold, boy?"

Smoke shook his head.

"Two hundred dollars a ton is a workable mine, Smoke. So them boys ain't gonna just sit back and let you and us'ns destroy a fortune for 'em. We gonna have to be ready for nearabouts anything."

"I done warned them far'ners at the mines to stand clear of Bury," Matt said. "They took it to heart."

"How about the other miners?"

"Some of the miners here now was at the mining camp on the Uncompahgre," Preacher said. "The bettin' is high and fast."

"Who is the favorite?"

"Hell, boy," Preacher grinned. "Us'ns!"

17

According to the calendar, it was still the middle of spring in the mining country of East-Central Idaho. Someone should have told Mr. Summer that. By noon of the day of the pull-out, the temperature had soared and the sun was blisteringly hot. Bury, located in a valley, lay sullen and breezeless, the pocket in which it lay blocking the winds.

And the tempers of those trapped in the town were beginning to rival the thermometer.

One of Richards's men had discovered the blocked road and had hightailed back to the PSR ranch, informing Josh. Janey had just informed him as to Buck's real name. Josh Richards stood in the lushly appointed drawing room of the mansion and stared out at all the PSR holdings. Slowly, very slowly, a smile began playing at the corners of his mouth.

"What do you find so amusing, Josh?" Janey asked, watching the man.

"I will soon be the richest man in all of Idaho Territory," Josh replied. He carefully lit a cigar and inhaled slowly.

"I don't follow you."

"Think about it, Janey. We—you and I—are in the best possible position. Your brother is going to take some losses at Bury. He might even get himself killed. We can hope for that, at least." She shrugged. Whatever happened to Kirby didn't concern her at all. "All we have to do is pull the PSR men off the range, leaving only a skeleton crew with the herds, and station them around the house in armed circles. Let Smoke and his mountain men kill off as many as they can in Bury. For sure, Smoke will kill Stratton and Potter—that's what he came here to do. By the time the siege is over at Bury, Smoke's little army will be shot up and weakened; no way they could successfully attack this place. When they start to pull out, that's when I take my men and wipe them out." He grinned hugely. "Simple."

"So you're tossing Wiley and Keith to the wolves," she said matter-of-factly.

"Sure," he replied cheerfully. "Do you care?"

"Hell, no!" the woman said. "And there's something else, too."

"Oh?"

"You know the Army and the marshals will be in here investigating after it's over."

"Yeah. Sure. What about it?"

"Well, you just tell them some crap about Potter and Stratton. Tell them you found out about some illegal dealings they were involved in; you broke away from them. Tell the investigators you didn't want any part of anything illegal. You can even tell them you and your men joined up with Smoke and the mountain men in the assault on Bury. But," she said, holding up a warning finger, "that means that *everybody* has to die."

"You're a cold-blooded wench, Janey," he said with a great deal of pride and admiration.

"Just like you, love."

"Oh, I like it. I *like* it!" Josh began to pace the floor. He began to think aloud, talking as he paced. "I've got the best of the gunhands out here. Most of these men have been with me for years. They're loyal to me, and to me alone. They'll stand firm. I'll put all the newer men out on the range, looking after the cattle. Put the range-cook out there with them with ten days, two weeks of supplies and tell the boys to stay put." He grinned again, looking at Janey Jensen. "Love, we are going to *rule* Idaho Territory."

"I always wanted to be a queen," Janey said.

Josh and Janey began laughing.

To put a lid on the growing tempers in Bury, Stratton and Potter ordered free drinks at the town's many saloons and hurdy-gurdy houses. Then one drunk cowboy suggested they kick in the doors to the Pink House and have their way with the women barricaded inside.

About fifty men, in various stages of inebriation, marched up the main street and gathered in front of the Pink House. They began hooting and hollering and making all sorts of demands to the ladies. The hooting abruptly dipped into silence when the ladies inside shoved shotguns out through the barricaded windows. The sounds of hammers being jacked back was loud in the hot, still air.

The men took one look at a dozen double-barreled express guns pointing at them and calmed down.

"We are *closed*!" Miss Flora's voice came to the crowd. "You gentlemen have ten seconds to haul your ashes out of here. Aim at their privates, girls!"

A dozen shotguns were lowered, the muzzles aimed crotch-high.

The suddenly sobered crowd hauled their ashes. Promptly.

Preacher watched it all through field glasses. He chuckled. He could not, of course, hear what was going on, but he could guess. "Them gals done read the scriptures to them ol' boys," he said. "I don't think the ladies is gonna be bothered no more after this."

One trapped PSR so-called gunhand emptied his pistol at the ridge overlooking the town. He stood in the center of the street and hurled curses at Smoke and the mountain men. Preacher reached for his Spencer and sighted the gunslick in. He emptied the tube, plowing up the ground around the man's boots. The cowboy shrieked in terror and dropped his pistol, running and falling and crawling for cover. He took refuge in the nearest saloon.

"We havin' fun now, Smoke," Preacher said, reloading. "But it's gonna turn ugly right soon."

"I know."

"You havin' second thoughts 'bout this, boy?"

"Not really. But if those men down there, with the exception of Potter and Stratton, wanted to leave, I wouldn't try to stop them."

"I's a-hopin' you'd say that. Audie! Bring Smoke that there funny-lookin' thang you built."

Smoke took the megaphone and moved down the ridge, being careful not to expose himself. He lifted the megaphone to his lips.

"You men of Bury!" Smoke called. "Listen to me. It's Potter and Stratton and Richards I'm after. Not you. You don't owe them any loyalty. Any of you who wants to toss down his weapons and walk out can do so."

There was no reply of any kind from the town.

Smoke called, "I'm giving you people a chance to save your lives. The men you work for murdered my brother. They shot him in the back and left him to die."

"Rebel scum!" a voice called from the town.

Smoke shook his head. "The men you work for killed my pa."

"Big deal!" another voice shouted.

"Real nice folks down there," Audie muttered.

"The men you work for ordered out the men who raped and tortured and killed my wife, and killed my baby son," Smoke spoke through the megaphone.

Laughter from the town drifted up to Smoke and the mountain men. The laughter was ugly and taunting. "She probably wasn't nothin' but a whore anyways!" a voice shouted.

"I can't believe it," Smoke said, looking at Preacher. "I can't understand those types of people."

"I can," Audie said. "If you were my size, you would know just how cruel many people can be."

"Rider comin'," Tenneysee said.

Sam rode up and dismounted, walking to the edge of the ridge. He waited until Smoke and his friends climbed back up. "Givin' them folks a way out, Smoke?" he asked.

"I tried," Smoke replied.

"They ain't worth no pity," Sam said. "Lord knows I ought to know. I worked for them long enough. I seen them people do things that would chill you to the bone. I ain't never seen a bunch so hard-hearted as them people down there. Lie, steal, cheat, kill—them words don't mean nothing to them people. Simmons at the general store worked his momma to death. And I mean that. Then buried her in an unmarked grave. Cannon at the newspaper is so bad he's barred from the Pink House. Likes to beat women, if you know what I mean. And them ranchers out from town"—he spat on the ground—"hell, they just as bad. They run down and hanged a twelve-year-old boy when they found him leadin' off unbranded stock. He was just tryin' to feed his sick ma. It was pitiful. I seen some sights, but that one made me puke. Don't feel no sorrow for them folks down there, boys. They ain't worth spit."

"Come and get us, gunhawk!" a voice yelled from the town. "We'll give you the same treatment the rest of your family got."

Smoke tossed the homemade megaphone to one side. "I tried," he said. "I tried."

The owners of the three other ranches located near Bury gathered at the home of Josh Richards. The owners had brought their so-called cowboys, many of whom were outlaws and gunfighters. Richards explained the situation at Bury—tactfully and pointedly leaving out that when his partners were dead, he would own it all.

"Well," Marshall of the Crooked Snake spread said, "I can see why we can't rush the town. Them mountain men would pick us off afore we got close enough to do any real damage."

The other two owners, Lansing of the Triangle and Brown of the Double Bar B, nodded their agreement. Lansing looked at Richards and asked, "You got a plan?"

"Not much of one. And my plan is rather self-serving, I'm afraid."

"Self what?" Marshall asked.

"It helps us but doesn't do much for those trapped in Bury," Richards explained.

"Hell with them!" Brown said. "We can always get more shopkeepers to come in."

No one mentioned Stratton or Potter. The men just looked at each other and smiled. Honor among thieves, and all that.

"Let's hear it," Lansing said.

* * *

"I don't understand it," Sam said. "Richards has about twenty gunhands out there at the ranch. And by now he's called in Marshall and Lansing and Brown. Together, the four of them could put together forty or fifty men. That many men could put us in a box. I wonder what they're waiting for?"

Audie was thoughtful for a moment. "Perhaps this Richards person is hoping to gain from all this."

Smoke looked at him. "Sure. If Stratton and Potter get dead, Richards has it all."

"The loyalty of those men is overwhelming," Audie said drily.

"I wanted to burn down the town," Smoke admitted. "And I wanted revenge against those who killed my brother and pa, and who sent those men after me and my family. But as sorry as those people are down there in Bury, I don't want their blood on my hands."

Preacher seemed to breathe a sigh of relief. He knew the young man well, and knew Smoke did not want needless killing on his mind.

"Mayhaps you won't have to kill none of them down there," Preacher said.

"You chewin' 'round on something, Preacher," Beartooth said. "Spit 'er out."

"Well, lets us'ns slip word to Potter and Stratton that Richards is gonna lay out of this here fight. Kinda see what happens after that."

"An' juice it up a mite, too," Tenneysee said with a grin.

"Why, shore!" Preacher returned the grin. "Ain't nothing no better than a good joke." He thought about that for a moment. "At our age, that is."

18

Audie wrote out the first message to be delivered to the citizens of Bury. But it was so filled with big words nobody on the ridge knew what it said.

YOUR SO-CALLED CONFIDANTS HAVE ELECTED NOT TO CROSS THE RUBICON. THEY HAVE NOW SHOWN THEIR TRUE COLORS. THE MOMENT OF TRUTH IS NIGH. TO FIGHT US WOULD BE FOLLY. YOUR TRUE ADVERSARIES ARE YOUR ONETIME INTIMATES.

Tenneysee looked at the note and said, "I et Injun corn and sweet corn and flint corn, but I ain't never et no ruby-corn. Whut the hell does food have to do with this here matter?"

"Imbecile!" Audie snapped at him. He opened his mouth to explain, then closed it, knowing that if he tried to explain about the river it would only confuse matters further.

Audie stood and watched as Smoke laboriously printed another message, pausing often to lick the tip of the pencil stub.

Smoke tied the note to a stick, slipped down the ridge

to within throwing distance, and tossed the message onto the main street.

Then Smoke, Sam, and the mountain men sat back and waited for the fun to begin.

Deputy Rogers had retrieved the stick. Since he couldn't read, he had no idea what was going on. He took the stick to Sheriff Reese. Reese read the message and took off at a run for Stratton and Potter.

"It's a trick!" Stratton said, his fat jowls quivering.

"I don't think so," Potter said. "You know perfectly well that by now all the ranchers know the road is blocked. There isn't a day goes by a dozen or more cowboys don't come into town to raise hell. Janey makes her grand appearance in town every day, weather permitting. No, I think we've been tossed to the lions.

God*damn* Richards!"

"What are we gonna do?" Reese asked.

"I don't know. Give me time to think."

"If they try to send someone out of town, let them," Smoke said. Turning to Sam, he said, "And the one person they're going to meet will be you."

"I don't follow you," the puncher said.

"Your being fired was just a sham. A trick to get you on my side and see who I really was. You make them believe you're still working for Richards. Tell whoever they send out that Richards isn't going to interfere with me— he wants me to destroy the town, and everybody in it. Think you can pull that off?"

Sam grinned in the twilight. "You just watch me."

Sam rode out toward the north, reining up several miles from town. The mountain men built campfires to the south, the west, and the east of Bury. They deliberately left the north dark.

"That damned Jensen is so sure of himself he's not even guarding the north road," Reese said. He cursed under his breath.

"We got to be sure," Potter said. "Reese, send one of your men out to the ranch. Or as close to it as he can get. I've been thinking about something else, too." He looked at Reese. "Who gave the orders to fire Sam?"

"Richards said Mr. Stratton did."

"I never gave any such orders! You're sure Richards said it was my idea?" Stratton demanded.

"Well, yes, sir. But maybe he just used your name and forgot to tell you about it?"

"Why would he do that?"

"Because Sam worked for you, kinda."

But the seeds of suspicion had already been planted and were taking root. "Bull!" Stratton said.

"Looks bad, Keith," Potter said. "I'm beginning to think that just maybe Richards may have sent for Smoke."

"Yeah," his partner replied. "That would fit. That no good—" He bit back the profanity.

"Reese, you go snoop around town while your man is riding out. Go."

"Hold up!" Sam called from the darkness.

Deputy Rogers reined up and tried to peer through the gloom. "Sam? That you, Sam?"

"Yeah. Don't let none of them other riders catch you out here. They'll shoot you on sight."

"What other riders?" Rogers pulled in close to Sam.

"Crooked Snake, Triangle, Double Bar B—and any of Mr. Richards's gunhawks."

Rogers sighed. "Then it's true, Sam?"

"It's true." An idea began to form in Sam's head. He thought Smoke would like it. "I'm ridin' between town and the ranch, carryin' messages back and forth."

"Well, heck!" Rogers took off his hat and scratched his head. "I ain't got no messages to give you. Sorry."

"That's all right." You big dummy! Sam thought. "I got one for you to carry to Potter and Richards."

"They figured it out, Sam."

"Figured what out?"

"That you was all the time not fired and really workin' for Richards."

Sam breathed a bit easier. "I figured they would."

"And Mr. Richards sent for that there Smoke Jensen, didn't he?"

"I think so." This was gettin' better and better, Sam thought. But, he reminded himself, don't drop your guard. Rogers was big and stupid, but still a cold-blooded killer and cat quick.

"What's your message for them in town?"

Sam thought hard. "They're comin' in at noon, tomorrow."

"Well, then, I got a message for you. You tell 'em we'll be a-waitin'."

"No, we won't be waiting!" Stratton said.

"Huh?" Rogers was getting confused.

"Damn right!" Potter said.

"How we gonna get past Smoke and them mountain men?" Reese asked.

"Go holler up the hill," Stratton said. "Tell Smoke I wanna talk to him."

"What do you want?" Smoke called out of the high darkness.

"It was Richards that ordered your brother killed!"

Potter yelled. "Me and Stratton didn't have nothing to do with it."

Smoke knew the man was lying. Knew it because of the dying confession of a TC hand a few years back. Smoke knew Potter had shot his brother. But since Sam had hightailed it back and told them all what he'd done, Smoke had agreed it was a fine idea. He'd play along.

"All right. I never knew who it was. But you was part of it," Smoke returned the darkness-shrouded shout.

"I won't deny that." Stratton's voice. "Neither of us. But what's done is done. I still have nightmares about it, though. If that makes any difference to you."

"That lyin' poke of buffalo chips!" Preacher said. "Only nightmares he ever has is someone stealin' his money."

"Yeah, I know," Smoke told his mentor. Raising his voice, he called, "What'd you want to talk to me about?"

"Ain't no call for us to be fightin' each other, Jensen. We know that Josh sent for you, probably payin' you good money, but whatever he's payin' you, we'll triple it. How about it? You're a hired gun. What difference does it make who pays you?"

"He's payin' me what's on that dodger. All in gold. You want to triple that, I'll take it in greenbacks or double eagles. Send MacGregor up here with the money. Let all the women leave the Pink House. Send them up here with Mac."

"And you'll do what?"

"I'll stand aside and let you three fight it out among you. Deal?"

"Who is Sam working for?" Potter called.

"Richards. But I know where he is, so I can get word to him."

"All right. It'll take us about an hour to get that much money together. We'll have to open the bank."

"I'll be here. In the meantime, you let those women go free. Deal?"

"It's a deal, Jensen."

"Sally?" Smoke called. "You hearin' all this?"

"Yes!" Sally's voice rose faintly from the edge of town.

"Then get some clothes and blankets together and come up here. You won't be harmed."

"We're on our way. And Mister Potter and Mister Stratton?" she yelled.

"We're right here, Miss Sally."

"We'll all be armed!"

No one could hear Stratton or Potter's muttered response. Probably just as well.

19

"Thank Sam for this," Smoke told Sally, as the women scampered up the hill and over the crest of the ridge. "He come up with this idea."

"Came up with," Sally corrected.

"Yes, ma'am," Smoke said.

"Lord have mercy!" Preacher muttered. "Rest of you boys look out now, 'cause them two gonna git to sparkin' and a-moonin' and a-carryin' on like who'd-a-thunk-it."

"Shut up, Preacher," Smoke told him.

"Most unrespectful young'un I ever hepped raise," Preacher said.

"*Dis*respectful," Sally corrected automatically.

"Lord, give this old man strength," Preacher mumbled, walking away.

About forty minutes after the women arrived, MacGregor called up the hill. "Do you actually expect one aging bookkeeper to behave as a pack animal and carry all this money up this mountain?"

"Comin' down," Smoke called.

"Any trouble?" Smoke asked, facing Mac on the hillside.

"Not a bit. Come on, let's walk." He tossed his suit-case to Sam and split the sacks of money between Smoke and himself. When they were out of normal earshot, Mac said, "I told Stratton and Potter I was no gunhand. I wanted out. They dismissed me without a second thought. Tell you the truth, I was relieved to get out. What in the world is going on, Mr. Jensen?"

"Let them destroy each other," Smoke said. "I'll clean up what's left."

"Very good thinking, young man. But what if one side or the other discovers your ruse?"

"My what?"

"Your trickery?"

"I'll worry about that if and when it happens."

"I think I would not like you for an enemy, young man," Mac said.

"When this is over, Mac, you'll probably never see me again. I intend to drop out of sight, change my name, hopefully get married, and settle down."

"I wish you luck, Kirby Jensen."

"Thank you, Mr. MacGregor."

With much good-natured grumbling among the moun-tain men, the ladies were settled in for the night. Guards were posted on the ridges, although none believed they were really necessary. The lights in the town of Bury blazed long into the night as the men prepared for war. Around midnight, very late for a western town, the lan-terns and candles began to go out and the town was a dark shape in a velvet pocket.

The town was stirring before the first silver fingers of dawn began creeping over the mountains, touching the valleys and lighting the new day.

On the ridges, the men and women watched the citi-zens of Bury saddle horses and check out equipment.

"Mines is shut down tight," Dupre told Smoke. The Frenchman had just completed a night-long tour of the country.

"The miners?"

"They around, but they keepin' their heads down and their butts outta sight. They know all hell's about to break loose around here."

"You see any PSR riders?"

"Several. They watchin' the town. Been there all night. I allow as to how they know 'bout the deal you made with Potter and Stratton. Seen one haul his ashes back towards the spread, hell bent for leather.

Smoke's grin was visible on the rim of the tin cup full of scalding black coffee. "Going to be a very interesting day," he said.

"So Wiley and Keith sold out to Smoke Jensen," Josh mused aloud. "Interesting. Thank you for that news." He waved the cowhand away and concentrated on his breakfast, conscious of the eyes on him as he ate.

Marshall and Lansing and Brown sat at the long table in the dining room. Marshall finally said, "They got us outnumbered just a tad."

"Not enough to cause us any concern," Josh replied. "As soon as they start pulling out, my riders will come fogging with the news and we'll have time to get ready. Besides, they're shopkeepers and store owners, not gunfighters."

Brown dashed cold water on that remark. "Josh, there ain't a man among them ain't a veteran of either the Civil War or a dozen Injun fights. They may be scoundrels and the like, but they ain't pilgrims."

Josh laid his knife and fork aside. He patted his mouth with a napkin. "Yes, you're right. They aren't going to just roll over and give up." He was thoughtful for a moment. He picked up a tiny silver bell and rattled it, bringing the houseman to the dining room. The other ranchers hid their amusement at that. "Thomas," Josh said to the black houseman, "tell Wilson and McNeil I wish to see them. Now!"

"Boss," Wilson said, uncomfortable in the lushly appointed dining room with carpet and heavy drapes and expensive chandelier. McNeil stood by his partner's side. The men held their hats in their hands.

"Pick a half-dozen boys from each ranch and take a dozen of our men. Ambush the men from town. To get to here, they've got to come through Levi Pass. Hit them there. Draw enough ammo and food for several days in the field. And, Wilson . . ." He met the man's eyes. "If you fail, don't bother coming back."

"Yes, sir."

Smoke stood on the ridge overlooking the now-deserted town of Bury. His eyes were bleak. Savage-looking. Sally stood by his side, gazing up at him.

"What are you thinking, Smoke?" she asked.

"Take a good look at Bury, Sally."

"I see it. What about it?"

"'Cause this is the last time you'll be able to see it."

"Are we pulling out?"

"No. Not yet."

"Then . . . ?"

"I'm going to burn it to the ground." He checked both his Colts and picked up his Henry repeating rifle. He slowly walked down the hill, Matt, Preacher, Tenneysee, and Greybull following him.

Sally stood on the crest of the ridge, Audie by her

side—standing on a large rock. Little Ben joined them, rubbing sleep from his eyes.

"What are your feelings toward and for that young man?" Audie asked.

"I love him," Sally said quietly.

"It bloomed very quickly between you two. Are you certain of your feelings?"

"Yes."

"When this is over," Audie said, "I believe the burning hate within him will vanish. It's been an all-consuming thing with him for a long time. But hear me out, young woman. No matter where you two go . . ."

"Three," Sally said, putting her arm around Ben's shoulders.

Audie smiled. "No matter where the *three* of you go, Smoke's reputation will follow. No matter how hard he tries, he will never be able to completely shake it. This is wild and savage country, and it will be so for many years to come. If you settle somewhere to ranch, there will be outlaws who will try to take what is yours, and Smoke will stand up to them. Word will get around, and tinhorns and would-be gunhands will follow, the only thing in their minds being the desire to be the man who killed the fastest gun in the west. Then you will have to leave and settle elsewhere, for Smoke is not the type of man to back down. He desperately wants to settle down, live a so-called normal life, but it is going to be extremely difficult. You're going to have to be very strong."

"Yes," Sally said, not taking her eyes from her young man. And she knew he was hers. "I am aware of that. Mr. Audie . . ."

"Just Audie. My last name is no longer important."

"Audie. I am a woman of some means. I recently came into quite a large sum of money. Perhaps Smoke will consent to go back east and live."

Audie smiled. "What would he do, Sally? Can you imagine him in some office, with a tie and starched collar?"

She laughed softly. She could not imagine that.

"He is a man of the west, of the frontier. This is his land. He would not be happy anywhere else."

And I would not be happy anywhere without him, she thought. Odd that I have known him for so brief a time and yet am so certain of my feelings. But I am certain.

Only a few people remained in town, and those looked very suspiciously at Smoke and the mountain men. Their suspicion soon turned to hard reality.

"Pack up and clear out," Smoke informed them. "Get your gear together, and move out!"

"You can't just come in here and force us out!" a man protested.

Smoke looked at the man, open contempt in his eyes. "You did what before you came here?"

The man shuffled his feet and refused to reply. He dropped his eyes.

Smoke looked at the small group left behind in the town. "You all knew you were working for crud and crap. And you didn't care. All you cared about was money. And it didn't make a damn to any of you where that money came from, or how you earned it. I have no sympathy for any of you. Get your gear together and get out of here."

They got.

"Round up all the pack animals you can find," Smoke asked the mountain men. He waved all but four of the men down from the ridge, leaving those as guards. "We're gonna give some of these homesteaders in this area a second chance. Food, clothes, boots, guns, equipment. We'll pass it out later. Let's get to work."

What couldn't be packed out on horses and mules was passed up the hill like a bucket brigade. Soon the stores were emptied. The town was strangely silent and ghost-like. Audie summed it up.

"This town had no heart," the little man said. "One cannot feel sorry for destroying something that never lived."

Smoke tossed the first torch into a building. The dry wood was soon blazing, spreading to the adjoining building. Black greasy smoke began pouring into the sky in spiraling waves. The dry pine began popping like six-guns. Soon the heat was so intense it forced the men back to the coolness of the ridge.

"Soon as them people see this smoke, they'll get the message," Preacher said.

"Those that are left alive," Smoke said softly.

20

Levi Pass lay sullen under the heat of the sun. Bodies littered the pass; men and animals sprawled in soon-to-be bloated death. The first contingent of men, led by Deputy Payton, had been knocked from their saddles in a hard burst of rifle fire from the rocks above the pass. Among the first to die were Rosten, the stable manager; Simmons, who ran the general store; and Deputy Payton. A sheriff back in Iowa would never learn that he could destroy the murder warrant he held for Payton.

Among the gunhands in the rocks, McNeil and a rider from the Crooked Snake and Triangle lay dead. The moaning of the wounded, on both sides, softly drifted out of and above the dust and gunsmoke of the pass.

Then the men saw the smoke belching into the skies.

"What the hell?" Wilson muttered from behind his shoulder on the ridge.

"That bastard Jensen has torched the town!" Potter said.

"Oh, my God!" Stratton said, his face dusty and his elegant clothing torn and dirty. "All our records."

Wilson laughed. "Looks like your boy done turned on you!" he called down into the pass.

"Our boy!" Potter yelled. "He started out workin' for you."

"You lie!" Wilson yelled. "You brung him in!"

"What the hell are you talking about?" Stratton screamed.

Wilson's long-unused gray cells began working. "Now wait just a minute," he called. "You tryin' to claim you didn't hire Jensen?"

"Sure we did," Potter yelled. "But we hired him away from Richards. Last night. Richards brought him in to kill us."

"You're crazy!" Wilson yelled. "Just hold on a second. Everybody stop shootin'. We got to talk about this."

"I don't trust you!" Potter screamed. "You're up to something."

"I ain't up to nothin', you fat hog!" Wilson yelled. "You and Stratton was the ones who wanted it all. Ya'll caused all this trouble."

Wilson stood up from behind the boulder.

Sheriff Reese lifted his rifle and shot the man in the stomach. The .44 round knocked the gunhand backward. He died with a scream on his bloody tongue.

A Crooked Snake rider shot Cannon, the newspaper editor, in the center of his forehead. Cannon was dead before he hit the rocky ground of the pass road.

Levi Pass erupted and rocked with pistol and rifle fire. Britt, a rider for the Crooked Snake, crouched behind his cover and mulled matters over in his mind. He was getting the feeling that that damned Smoke Jensen had set them all up; made fools out of everybody; sitting back and laughing while they were shooting at each other.

He slipped from his cover and inched his way toward the timber, where the horses were tied. He spurred his mount, heading for the PSR spread. He wanted to tell his boss what he'd just heard.

Behind him, the savage gunfight continued, the air filled with shouts and curses and the screaming of the wounded and the silence of the dead.

"Now wait a minute!" Josh said. "Tell me again what you heard back at the pass."

Britt repeated what he'd heard between Wilson, Stratton, and Potter.

Lansing went to a window of the mansion and looked toward the town. Though miles away, he could clearly see the black smoke pouring into the sky. "Shore nuff on fire," he said.

"He played us against each other," Richards said. "And I played right into his hands. He set me up like a kid with a string toy. That damn gunhawk *knew* what I'd do." He sat down heavily. "I don't like being made a fool of. I don't like it worth a damn!"

"He shore done 'er though," Marshall rubbed it in a bit. Marshall and the other ranchers were every bit as tough as Richards, with no back-up in them. They were all thieves and murderers, their pasts as black as midnight.

Richards's gaze was bleak. "Gather up the men. We're ridin'."

"Richards is anything but a fool, Smoke," Sally told him. Standing beside her, Sam solemnly nodded his head. "If he puts all this together, then you've lost your element of surprise."

"I don't think either side wiped the other out in that pass," Preacher opined. "And we ain't heared no gunfire in more'un an hour. I think they got to talkin' and figured things out."

Smoke looked at Tenneysee. "The supplies hidden?"

"B'ar couldn't find 'em."

"We'll get the women over to Becky's place and leave them there. We'll head for the timber and make them come after us."

"The ranches lay in a half circle around Bury," Sam said. "Marshall, Lansing, and Brown will have most of their men out looking for you; only a handful will be at the ranches. The real cowhands and punchers will be with the herds. They're cowboys, not gunslicks."

"Then we'll leave them be," Smoke said. "When we get ready to scatter the herds, we'll tell the punchers to take off for new ground."

"They'll go," Sam said.

"Let's ride."

Leaving what was once the Idaho Territory town of Bury still smoking and burning behind them, the outnumbered band of ancient mountain men, gunhands, and ladies saddled up and drifted into the deep timber, with Sam leading the way. At Becky's small farm, Sam explained the situation to Becky and she agreed to help any way she could. Little Ben introduced the kids to the mountain men. Becky's kids had seen a lot during their time in the west, but absolutely nothing compared with the sight of the old mountain men, all dressed in buckskins and colorful sashes and armed to the teeth. And they certainly had never seen anything to match Audie. No taller than the children, the tiny mountain man captivated the kids. When he jumped up on a stump and began telling fairy tales, the kids sat around him listening, spellbound.

Sally and Smoke walked a short distance from the cabin. "Do we talk now, Smoke?" she asked.

"I reckon so." He waited for her to correct his grammar. She did not.

"Very well. I want to see the west, Smoke. And I want you to show it to me."

"Dangerous, Sally. And not very ladylike. You'd have to ride astride."

She hid her smile. Her father had paddled her behind several times as a child for doing just that. "I'm sure I could cope."

Buck let that alone. "What is it you want to see?"

"The high lonesome," she said without hesitation.

"It's all around you here."

"You know what I mean, Smoke. The real high lonesome. The one you and the other mountain men talk about. When you speak of that, your voice becomes soft and your eyes hold a certain light. That's the high lonesome I would like to see."

"You'll have to learn to shoot," Smoke said dubiously.

"Then I shall."

"Camp and live out in the wilderness."

"All right."

"It won't be easy. Your skin will be tanned and your hands will become hard with calluses."

"I expect that."

Smoke kept his face noncommittal. He had hoped Sally would want to see his world; the world that he knew was slowly vanishing. There would be time.

He hoped.

"All right," he said.

She rose up on her tiptoes and kissed him on the cheek. "You come back to me," she said.

He did not reply. That was something he could not guarantee.

"Nothing left, Boss," Long reported back to Josh Richards. "Jensen burned the whole place to the ground."

Potter and Stratton were now once more joined with

Richards. The opposing sides had ceased fighting in Levi Pass and begun talking. The men were chatting amicably when Richards, Marshall, Lansing, and Brown rode up with their men.

"Nothing?" Burton asked. "My apothecary shop is gone?"

"There ain't nothing left," Long said. "And Jensen and them old bastards is gone. Took the women and left. I cut their sign but lost it in the rocks."

"Sam?" Richards asked.

"No sign of him."

"That was a nice hotel," Morgan said wistfully.

"Beautiful church," Necker said. "Takes a heathen to destroy a house of God."

Simpson spat on the ground. "You damned fake!" he told Necker. "You ain't no more no preacher than I is. I knowed all along I'd seen you 'fore. Now I remember. I knowed you up in Montana Territory. Elkhorn. You was dealing stud and pimpin'. You kilt Jack Harris when he caught you cold-deckin' him."

"You must be mistaken, my good man," Necker said. But his face was flushed. "I came from—"

"Shut up, Necker. Or whatever your name is," Lansing said. "Now I'm gonna tell you all something. Or remind you of it. Remind you all of a lot of things. They ain't none of us clean. We all—*all of us*—got dodgers out on us. Now we can't none of us afford to lose this fight. 'Cause you all know damn well when that stage reports the town is burnt, the Army's gonna come in here and start askin' a bucket full of questions. That means all them pig farmers and nesters in this area's gotta go in the ground. Cain't none of 'em be allowed to live and flap their gums." He glared at Richards. "I tole you time after time that I didn't trust that there Scotsman. He ain't what he appears to be. Bet on it. When the trouble started, he shore wanted to leave in a hurry, didn't he?"

"Yes, he did," Stratton said. "And it appeared that he and Smoke Jensen were friends."

"They got to die," Marshall said. "All of them."

"What about them farmers' kids?" a gunhand asked.

"Them, too," Brown said. "Cain't nobody be left alive to point no finger at us."

"I want Smoke Jensen!" Dickerson gasped from his blankets on the ground. Still gravely wounded, the outlaw had insisted upon coming to the pass rather than leaving with the men Smoke had ordered out before burning the town.

The men ignored him. Dickerson's wounds had reopened, and all those present knew the outlaw and murderer was not long for this world.

"Ya'll hear me?" Dickerson said.

"Aw, shut up and die!" Necker told him. "We're busy."

Dickerson fell back on his dirty blankets and died.

Smoke, Sam, and the mountain men rode west, toward Marshall's Crooked Snake spread. The Frenchman, Dupre, was ranging ahead of the main body of men. About two miles from the ranch, Smoke pulled up, waiting for Dupre to return with a scouting report.

During this quiet, which, all knew, would soon become very rare, Preacher talked with Smoke. "You beginnin' to feel all the hate leave your craw, boy?"

"Yes," Smoke admitted.

"That's good. That's a mighty fine little gal back yonder at that nester place."

"She wants to see the high lonesome."

"Be tough on a woman. You gonna show her?"

Smoke hesitated. "Yes."

Preacher spat a stream of brown tobacco juice on the ground, drowning a bug. "Soon as this here affair is done, you two best git goin'. High lonesome will soon be gone. Civil-lie-say-shon done be takin' over, pilgrims ruinin' everything. Be a fine thing to show that woman, though. She's tough, got lots of spunk. She'll stand by you, I's thinkin'."

"Us, you mean, don't you?"

"You mean the boy?"

Smoke shook his head. "I mean Sally, Little Ben, me, and you."

"No, Smoke," Preacher said. "I'll be leavin' with my pards. They's still some corners of this land that's high and lonesome. No nesters with their gawddamned barbed wire and pigs and plows. Me and Tenneysee and Audie and Nighthawk and all the rest—wal, our time's done past us, boy. Mayhaps you'll see me agin—mayhaps not. But when my time is nigh, I'll be headin' back to that little valley where you hammered my name in that stone. There, I'll jist lay me down and look at the elephant. I'll warn you now, son. This will be the last ride for Deadlead and Matt. They done tole me that. They real sick. Got that disease that eats from the inside out."

"Cancer?"

"That'd be it, I reckon. They gonna go out with the reins in they teeth and they fists full of smokin' iron. They'll know when it's time. You a gunhand, boy; you understand why they want it thataway, don't you?"

"Yes."

"All right. It's all said then. When it's time for me and the boys to leave, I don't want no blubberin', you understand?"

"Have you ever seen me blubber?"

"Damn close to it."

"You tell lies, old man."

Preacher's eyes twinkled. "Mayhaps one or two, from time to time."

"Here comes Dupre."

"We gonna be runnin' and ridin' hard for the next two-three days, son. We'll speak no more of this. When this is over, me and the boys will just fade out. 'Member all I taught you, and you treat that there woman right. You hear?"

"I hear."

"Let's go bring this to an end, boy."

21

"If you're cowboys, turn those ponies' noses west and ride out. If you're gunhands, make your play," Smoke said.

The three riders on the Crooked Snake range slowly turned their horses, being very careful to keep their hands away from six-guns. They sat and stared at the mountain men and at Smoke.

"We're drawin' thirty a month and found," one said. "That ain't exactly fightin' pay."

"You got anything back at the bunkhouse worth dyin' over?"

"Not a thing."

"You boys ride out. If you've a mind to, come back in three, four days. They'll be a lot of cattle wandering around with no owners. You might want to start up some small spreads in this area."

"You be the outlaw, Smoke Jensen?" a cowboy asked.

"I'm Jensen. But I'm no outlaw."

"Mister, if you say you're an African go-riller, you ain't gonna git no argument from me," another cowboy said.

"Fine. You boys head on toward the Salmon. Drift back in three, four days. We'll be gone, and so will the ranches. The homesteaders will still be here, though. Unless you want to see me again, leave them be. Understand?"

"Mr. Jensen, I'll even help 'em *plow*!"

Smoke smiled. "Take off."

The punchers took off.

"Five, maybe six gunnies at the ranch," Beartooth said, riding up.

Smoke looked at Powder Pete. "Got some dynamite with you?"

"You don't have to say no more." Powder Pete wheeled his mustang and took off for the ranch, Smoke and Sam and the mountain men hard after him.

"How do you boys want it?" Smoke called to the deserted-appearing ranch.

A rifle shot was the only reply.

"Hold your fire," Smoke told his people. Raising his voice, he shouted, "Your boss payin' you so much money you'd die for him?"

"Hell with you, Jensen!" the shout drifted to Smoke. "Come git us if you got the sand to do it."

Smoke looked at Powder Pete. "Blow 'em out!"

The old mountain man grinned and slipped silently away. About five minutes later, the bunkhouse exploded, the roof blowing off. A dynamite charge blew the porch off the main house, collapsing one side of the house. Smoke and the mountain men poured a full minute of lead into the house.

"I'm done with it!" a man shouted from the dynamite-ruined and bullet-pocked house. "Lemme ride out and I'm gone."

"Take what's on your back and clear out!" Smoke yelled. "How 'bout you other men?"

"There ain't no other men," the man shouted, a bitter

edge to his voice. "Two was in the bunkhouse. Rafter got another in here. Lead took the others. I'm it!"

"Clear out and don't come back."

"You just watch my dust, Jensen."

They watched it fade out, the gunhand riding toward the west. He did not look back.

"Check the house for wounded, then burn it all," Smoke said.

"You got a mean streak in you," Preacher said. "Shore didn't git it from me."

Smoke grinned at the man who had helped raise him. Preacher was as mean and vindictive as a wounded grizzly.

"I allow as to how we ain't gonna bury them gun-hawks in the house," Preacher said, not putting it in question form.

"Somewhere, sometime, they had a ma," Smoke said. "She'd wanna know her boy was buried proper."

"I'd afraid you say that," Preacher bitched. "I ain't never found no shovel to fit my hand."

"There goes my ranch," Marshall said, looking west into the sky. There was no bitterness in his voice, only a grudging admiration.

The hundred-odd men sat their saddles and stared at the black smoke pluming into the sky.

"We can still save the cattle," one of his men said.

"You want them, you save them," Marshall replied. "I'm headin' out."

"Where the hell you think you goin'?" Lansing asked.

"I'm pullin' out. You boys got any smarts, you'll do the same. I just realized that we ain't gonna stop this Jensen. If'n a man's right, and he jist keeps on comin', ain't nothing or nobody gonna stop him. And you know what, boys? Jensen's right."

"*Right*?" Potter squalled. "He comes in here and ruins everything we worked to build and you sit there and say the man's right?"

Marshall chuckled grimly. "That's it, boys. Everything we got we built on stole money and the blood of others. Hell with it. I'm pullin' out." He wheeled his horse and turned his back to the others.

Josh Richards jerked up his rifle and shot the man in the back. Marshall fell from the saddle, his spine severed. He lay on the ground, looking at the men through pain-filled eyes. "Should have known one of you would do that," he gasped.

Stratton shot the man between the eyes.

Potter looked at what remained of Marshall's men. "Stay with us. All his cattle, his mine holdings—everything is yours if we win this fight."

"We'll stay," one hard-faced Crooked Snake gunnie said. "I never liked Marshall no how."

"Let's ride."

"What do we do with the cattle?" Audie asked.

"Leave them for those cowboys," Smoke said. "They seemed like pretty decent boys to me."

"The cattle on Richards's place?" Tenneysee asked.

"That's another story. We'll give them to the nesters and the miners."

"Seems fair enough," Lobo said. "I damned shore don't want 'um."

"Someone has to meet the stage and turn it around," Smoke said. "Any volunteers?"

"MacGregor said he'd do it," Sam spoke. "But I don't like the idee of one man waitin' out there all alone with a hundred or so gunhands on the prowl."

"You go back and meet the stage with him," Audie suggested. "I should imagine you and your ladyfriend will be settling in this area. So the less you have to do with this matter, the better. Agreed, Smoke?"

"Good idea. Take off, Sam. I'll see you when this is over."

Reluctantly, Sam agreed and rode out, back to Becky's cabin.

"Lansing's Triangle is almost due north from here," Matt said. "We hit there next?"

"That's what they would expect us to do, isn't it?" Smoke asked, a hard grin on his lips.

"Oh, you sneaky, boy!" Preacher said. "You as sneaky as a rattler."

"Whut you two jawin' about?" Phew asked.

"We head straight east," Smoke explained. "For Brown's Double Bar B. I'm betting Richards and all the rest are hightailing right now to set up an ambush around Lansing's spread."

"At's rat good thankin', boy," Beartooth said. "I can tell Preacher hepped raise you."

Preacher stuck out his skinny chest. "Done a damn good job of 'er, too."

"Don't start braggin'," Greybull said. "I been listenin' to you bump them gums of yourn for fifty years. Sickenin'."

"Hush up, you mule-ridin' giant!" Preacher told him.

The other mountain men joined in.

They were still grousing and bitching and hurling insults at one another as they rode off.

"We're spread thin," Brown said to Richards. "Real thin."

"But when they come," Stratton said, "we'll have them in a circle. All we have to do is close up the bottom of the pincers and trap them."

"*If* they come," Lansing said. "I don't trust that damned Jensen. He's a devil."

"He's just a man," Sheriff Reese said sourly.

"A hell of a man," Richards said. "Janey's brother."

"What!" Potter shouted.

"Janey told me before I left the ranch. She knew all along that she'd seen him somewhere, but she didn't put it together until a few days ago."

"What'd she say do with him?" Stratton asked.

Richards shrugged. "Kill him."

Dawn broke hot and red over the valley that Brown called his Double Bar B spread. During the night, Dupre and Deadlead had slipped into the ranch area and found it deserted except for the cook. They had put him on the road after he told them that all the men drawing fighting pay were out with the boss. Just punchers riding herd on the cattle. Give them a chance, and they'd haul their ashes quick.

That was what Smoke was now doing. Alone.

The punchers looked up as the midnight-black stallion with the tall rider approached their meager camp. They all knew, without being told, who they were facing.

"We're cowboys, not gunhawks," one puncher said. "We ain't lookin' for no trouble."

"Then you won't have any," Smoke told him. "Get your gear, pack it up, and ride out." He made them the same offer he had made the Crooked Snake cowboys.

"Sounds good to me," a puncher said. "We gone, Mister Jensen."

Smoke watched them ride out, leaving the herd without a backward glance.

He waved the mountain men in. Lobo inspected the main house.

"Place is a damned pigsty," he reported back.

"Well, let's roast some pigs," Smoke said.

* * *

"That son of a bitch!" Brown shouted, jumping up, his eyes to the east. "He's fired my ranch."

Richards looked at the smoke pouring into the sky. There was a look of grudging admiration on the man's cruel face.

"I've had it!" Morgan said. "Me and Burton and Hallen and some of the others been talkin'. We're pullin' out, headin' west."

The others looked at the rifles in the men's hands. Potter stepped in before gunfire could start.

"All right!" he shouted. "How many of you are leaving?"

Nearly all the men from town were leaving, with the exception of Sheriff Reese and his so-called deputies.

"I gather you're going to join your families?" Richards said with a smile on his face.

"That's crap!" Reverend Necker said. "I don't care if I ever see that old bat again."

"Don't any of you ever set a boot in this part of the country again," Stratton warned.

"Don't you worry," Burton said.

The townspeople rode out without looking back.

Looking around them, the ranchers and gunhands could see where others had deserted them during the night. Quietly slipped away into the darkness. What remained were the hardcases.

"They wasn't much help anyways," a gunnie from the Crooked Snake said. "I never did trust none of them."

"Rider comin' hard," another gunslick said, looking toward the southeast.

Simpson reined up, his horse blowing hard. "Miners quit!" he said. "All of 'em. Said they ain't workin' for none of you no more."

Stratton started cursing. Potter and Richards let him curse until he ran down.

"Where's all them townies goin'?" Simpson asked.

"Turned yeller and run," Long told him.

"Let 'em go. They's only in the way." He looked at Richards. "That smoke back yonderways—that the Double Bar B?"

"Yeah." He twisted in the saddle, the leather creaking. He looked at the men gathered around him. "Any the rest of you boys want to turn tail and run?"

That question was met by silence and hard eyes.

"We gonna make them mountain men and Mister Jensen come to us," Richards declared. "Where's the nearest nester spread from here?" He tossed the question to anyone.

"'Bout ten miles," a gunslick said. "Next one is about four miles from that one."

"Dent," Richards looked at a mean-eyed rider. "Take a couple of boys and go burn them out. Black, you take a couple men and burn out the next pig farmer's family. That ought to bring Mister High-And-Mighty Jensen on the run." Richards started laughing. "And while you're doing that, the rest of us will be setting up an ambush."

"What about the wimmin and kids?" a gunhawk named Cross asked.

"What about them?" Potter asked.

"I thought we agree on that?" Stratton said.

"They have to die," Richards said. "All of them."

22

The homesteader's cabin appeared deserted when Dent and the others galloped into the front yard, the horses' hooves trampling over a flower bed and a newly planted garden. Normally, that action alone would bring the wife on a run, squalling and flapping her apron. It was a game the punchers liked to play with nesters, for few cowboys liked nesters, with their gardens and fences.

This time their destructive actions were met with silence.

Inside the cabin, the man lifted a finger to his lips, telling his wife and kids to be still. The wife nodded and moved to a gun slit in the logs, a .30-30 in her hands. Her husband held a double-barreled shotgun, the express gun loaded with buckshot. That painted lady from town had ridden by the day before, warning them to be on guard. All them ladies from the Pink House was riding around, warning the other homesteaders what was happening. First time he'd ever met a . . . a . . . one of them ladies. Nice-looking woman.

He eased the hammers back on the shotgun.

"Set the damned place on fire!" Dent yelled. "Burn 'em out."

Those were the last words Dent would speak in his life. The homesteader's shotgun roared, the buckshot from both barrels catching Dent in the chest and face. The charge lifted the gunhand from the saddle, tearing off most of his face and flinging him several yards away from his horse.

The homesteader's wife shot the second rider in the chest with her .30-30 just as the oldest boy fired from the hog pen. Three riderless horses stood in the front yard.

The homesteader and his family moved cautiously out of hiding. "Take their guns and stable their horses," the man said. "Mother, you get the Bible. Son, you get a couple shovels. We'll give them a Christian burial."

Black lifted himself up to one elbow. The pain in his chest was fierce. He coughed up blood, pink and frothy. Lung-shot, he thought.

Black looked around him. Douglas and Cross were lying in the front yard of the pig farmer's cabin. They looked dead. *Hell*, they were dead!

Who'd have thought it of a damned nester?

Black looked up at the damned homesteader in those stupid-looking overalls. Man had a Colt in each hand. Damn sure knew how to use them, too.

"Never thought a stinkin' pig farmer would be the one to do me in," Black gasped the words.

"I was a captain in the War Between the States," the man spoke calmly. "First Alabama Cavalry."

"Well, I'll just be damned!" Black said.

"Yes," the farmer agreed. "You probably will."

Black closed his eyes and died.

"No smoke," Lansing observed.

"Thought I heard gunfire, though," Potter said.

"Yeah," Stratton said. "But who is shootin' who?"

Richards's stomach felt sour, like he'd drank a glass of clabbered milk. Sour. Yeah, that was the word for it. Sour. Whole damned business was going sour. And all because of one man. He looked around him. Something was out of whack. Then it came to him. About ten or so men were gone, had slipped quietly away. Hell with them. They still had fifty or sixty hardcases. More than enough to do the job.

Or was it?

He shook that thought away. Can't even think about that. He wondered what that damned Smoke was doing right now.

Janey had never seen a more disreputable-looking bunch of men in all her life. *God!* They looked older than death.

Except for her brother.

Janey looked at the dead gunhands lying in the front yard. The gunhands Josh had left behind to protect her. That was a joke. But there wasn't anything funny about it.

"Hello, brother," she said.

"Sis," Smoke returned the greeting.

"Well, now what?" Her voice was sharp.

"How much money you have in the house, sis?"

"You going to rob me?"

"No."

She shrugged. "Quite a bit, I guess, brother. Yeah. Lots of money in the house."

"Can you ride astride?"

"Kid," she laughed, "I've ridden more things astride than I care to think about."

Smoke knew what his sister meant. He ignored it. "Change your clothes, get what money you can carry, and clear out. I don't care where you go, just go. I don't ever want to see you again."

Her laugh was bitter. "You always could screw up every plan I ever made."

"Don't you care what Richards did to your pa and brother?" he asked.

"Hell, no!"

He remembered his pa's letter. "I guess Pa was right, Janey. He said you were trash."

"Rich trash, baby brother. Doesn't that bother you?"

"Money rich, sis. That's all."

"And you don't think that's sufficient?"

"If you do, I feel sorry for you."

"Then that makes you a fool, Kirby!"

He shrugged. "One hour, Janey. That's all the time I'm giving you. Pack up and clear out."

She nodded and turned her back to him. She stopped and turned around. She gave him an obscene gesture, spat on the porch, and walked into the house.

"You rat sure there wasn't some mixup in babies when she were birthed?" Preacher asked. "You sure she's your sis?"

"I'm sure."

Janey left riding like a man and holding the rope of the pack animal.

"Aren't you the least bit worried about your man?" Smoke had asked her.

"Shoot the son of a bitch as far as I'm concerned," had been her reply. She had spurred her horse and ridden off without looking back.

"What a delightful young woman," Audie said, the crust about an inch thick in his voice.

Smoke watched his only living relative—that he knew of—ride away. He knew he should feel something—but he didn't.

Yes, he did, he corrected.

Relief in the fact that he had found her alive and had offered her a chance to live and she had taken it.

He shook his head.

So he still felt something for her.

But damn little.

"Burn the house to the ground," he said. He looked around him. Deadlead and Matt were gone. His eyes met Preacher's gaze.

"They gone to buy us some time," the mountain man said. "They won't be back."

Smoke nodded his head.

"I tole 'em not to kill Stratton, Potter, or Richards," Preacher said. "You wanted them yourself."

"I do. Thanks."

"Think nuttin' of it. I give 'em to you fer your birthday. Rest of us be takin' off shortly. You know what I mean."

Smoke knew.

Two riders left their saddles before the sounds of the rifle fire reached the column of outlaws. The two men were dead before they hit the ground.

"What the hell?" Reese yelled.

"Ambush!" Stratton screamed.

Two more men were flung backward and to the ground, dead and dying.

"There they are!" Rogers hollered, pointing to a ridge. "Come on, let's get 'em!"

A dozen riders looked at each other, nodded minutely, and slowly wheeled their horses, riding in the opposite direction.

"Come back here, you cowards!" Potter screamed.

"Let them go," Richards said calmly. "Nobody fire at them."

His partners looked at him strangely.

"It's over," Richards said. "We're walking-around dead men and don't even know it."

"What do you mean?" Stratton's scream was tinted with hysteria.

"Look," Richards said, pointing toward his ranch house. A huge cloud of black smoke was filling the air.

"The PSR house!" Reese yelled.

"Yeah," Richards said. He smiled. "And you can bet my darling Janey has taken all the cash in the house—which was considerable; she'd need a pack animal to carry it off—and is gone. Her brother wouldn't kill her."

"Well, you're taking it damned calm," Potter said.

"No reason to get upset. What is done is done."

One of the dying gunhawks on the ground moaned.

"Hosses comin' at us," a gunnie said. "Holy crap!" he yelled. "We're being charged!"

Deadlead and Matt were in the middle of the riders before the gunhands could really believe it was all taking place. With the reins in their teeth and their fists wrapped about the butts of .44s and .45s, the old mountain men emptied their pistols and had shucked their rifles before anyone else could fire a shot. Richards had trotted his horse off a few hundred yards and was sitting quietly, watching it all, Potter and Stratton with him. Stratton's face was ashen, his hands trembled, his once fine clothes were torn and dirty.

Eight more riders had joined the four on the ground before the mountain men were blasted from their saddles. Matt rose to his boots, roaring as his blood poured from his wounds.

"Somebody kill that damned nigger!" a gunslick yelled.

Matt shot the man between the eyes with a pistol he'd grabbed from off the ground.

Deadlead jerked a gunhawk off his horse and snapped his neck as easily as wringing the neck of a chicken.

Twenty guns roared. The riddled bodies of the mountain men fell to the already-blood-soaked dust.

Deadlead lifted his bloody head and looked at Sheriff Dan Reese. "Thank you, boys." He fell to the ground, dead, beside his lifelong friend.

"He *thanked* me!" Reese said, horror in his voice. "Thanked me? For *what*?" he screamed.

"If you don't understand," Richards said, "there is no point in my trying to explain it to you." He looked around him. "Long! Take a couple of boys. Get over to that woman's cabin Sam is sweet on. Kill her and them snot-nosed brats."

"With pleasure," the short, stocky gunhand said with a grin. "I just might get me a taste of that gal 'fore I do."

"Your option," Richards said.

Long took Deputy Weathers and rode toward the nester cabin. They were, despite all that had happened, in high spirits. Becky was a one fine-lookin' piece of woman. They rode arrogantly into the front yard, scattering chickens and trampling the flower garden.

"You in the house!" Long called. "Get your tail out here, woman."

The door opened and Nighthawk stepped out, his big hands wrapped around .44s. He blew Long and Weathers clean out of their saddles. He tied the dead men to the saddles and slapped the horses on the rump, sending them home.

"Those two won't bother me again," Becky said.

"Ummmm," Nighthawk replied.

23

The ever-shrinking band of outlaws and gunhands looked toward the west. Another cloud of black smoke filled the air.

Lansing began cursing. "How in the hell are them old men doin' it?" he yelled. "We're fightin' a damned bunch of ghosts."

"Are you stayin' or leavin'?" Stratton asked.

"Might as well see it through," the man said bitterly. Those were the last words he would speak on this earth. A Sharps barked, the big slug taking the rancher in the center of his chest, knocking him spinning from his saddle.

"I've had it!" a gunhand said. He spun his horse and rode away. A dozen followed him. No one tried to stop them.

"Look all around us," Brown said.

The men looked. A mile away, in a semicircle, ten mountain men sat their ponies. As if on signal, the old mountain men lifted their rifles high above their heads.

Turkel, one of the most feared gunhawks in the territory, looked the situation over through field glasses. "That there's Preacher," he said, pointing. "That'un over yonder is the Frenchman, Dupre. That one ridin' a mule is Greybull. That little bitty shithead is the midget, Audie. Boys, I don't want no truck with them old men. I'm tellin' you all flat-out."

The old men began waving with their rifles.

"What are they tryin' to tell us?" Reese asked.

"That Smoke is waiting in the direction they're pointing," Richards said. "They're telling us to tangle with him—if we've got the sand in us to do so."

Potter did some fast counting. Out of what was once a hundred and fifty men, only nineteen remained, including himself. "Hell, boys! He's only one man. There's nineteen of us!"

"There was about this many over at that minin' camp, too," Britt said. "They couldn't stop him."

"Well," Kelly said. "Way I see it is this: we either fight ten of them ringtailed-tooters, or we fight Smoke."

"I'll take Smoke," Howard said. But he wasn't all that thrilled with the choices offered him.

The mountain men began moving, closing the circle. The gunhands turned their horses and moved out, allowing themselves to be pushed toward the west.

"They're pushing us toward Slate," Williams said. "The ghost town."

Richards smiled at Smoke's choice of a showdown spot.

As the old ghost town appeared on the horizon, located on the flats between the Lemhi River and the Beaverhead Range, Turkel's buddy, Harris, reined up and pointed. "Goddamn place is full of people!"

"Miners," Brown said. "They come to see the show. Drinking and betting. Them old mountain men spread the word."

"Just like it was at the camp on the Uncompahgre," Richards said with a grunt.* "Check your weapons. Stuff your pockets full of extra shells. I'm going back to talk with Preacher. I want to see how this deal is going down."

Richards rode back to the mountain men, riding with one hand in the air.

"That there's far enuff," Lobo said. "Speak your piece."

"We win this fight, do we have to fight you men too?"

"No," Preacher said quickly. "My boy Smoke done laid down the rules."

His *boy*! Richards thought. Jesus God. "We win, do we get to stay in this part of the country?"

"If'n you win," Preacher said, "you leave with what you got on your backs. If'n you win, we pass the word, and here 'tis: if'n you or any of your people ever come west of Kansas, you dead meat. That clear?"

"You're a hard old man, Preacher."

"You wanna see jist how hard?" Preacher challenged.

"No," Richards said, shaking his head. "We'll take our chances with Smoke."

"You would be better off taking your chances with us," Audie suggested.

Richards looked at Nighthawk. "What do you have to say about it?"

"Ummm."

Richards looked pained.

"That means haul your ass back to your friends," Phew said.

Richards trotted his horse back to what was left of his band. He told them the rules.

Britt looked up the hill toward an old falling-down store. "There he is."

The Last Mountain Man.

Smoke stood alone on the old curled-up and rotted boardwalk. The men could see his twin .44s belted around his waist. He held a Henry repeating rifle in his right hand, a double-barreled express gun in his left hand. Smoke ducked into the building, leaving only a slight bit of dust to signal where he once stood.

"Two groups of six," Richards said, "one group of three, one group of four. Britt, take your group in from the rear. Turkel, take your boys in from the east. Reese, take your people in from the west. I'll take my people in from this direction. Move out."

Smoke had removed his spurs, hanging them on the saddlehorn of Drifter. As soon as he ducked out of sight, he had run from the store down the hill, staying in the alley. He stashed the express gun on one side of the street in an old store, his rifle across the street. He met Skinny Davis first, in the gloom of what had once been a saloon.

"Draw!" Davis hissed.

Smoke put two holes in his chest before Davis could cock his .44s.

"In Pat's Saloon!" someone shouted.

Williams jumped through an open glassless window of the saloon. Just as his boots hit the old warped floor, Smoke shot him, the .44 slug knocking the gunslick back out the window to the boardwalk. Williams was hurt, but not out of it yet. He crawled along the side of the building, one arm broken and dangling, useless.

"Smoke Jensen!" Cross called. "You ain't got the sand to face me!"

"That's one way of putting it," Smoke muttered, taking careful aim and shooting the outlaw. The lead struck him in the stomach, doubling him over and dropping him to the weed-grown and dusty street.

The miners had hightailed it to the ridges surrounding the town. There they sat, drinking and betting and cheering. The mountain men stood and squatted and sat on the opposite ridge, watching.

A bullet dug a trench along the wood, sending splinters flying, a few of them striking Smoke's face, stinging and bringing a few drops of blood.

He ran out the back of the saloon and came face-to-face with Simpson, the gunhawk having both hands filled with a .44.

Smoke pulled the trigger on his own .44s, the double hammer-blows of lead taking Simpson in the lower chest, slamming him to the ground, dying.

Quickly reloading, Smoke grabbed up Simpson's guns and tucked them behind his gunbelt. He ran down the alley. The last of Richards's gunslicks stepped out of a gaping doorway just as Smoke cut to his right, jumping through an open window. A bullet burned Smoke's shoulder. Spinning, he fired both Colts, one bullet striking Martin in the throat, the second taking the gunnie just above the nose, almost tearing off the upper part of the man's face.

Smoke caught a glimpse of someone running. He dropped to one knee and fired. His slug shattered the hip of Rogers, sending the big man sprawling in the dirt, howling and cursing. Reese spurred his horse and charged the building where Smoke was crouched. He smashed his horse's shoulder against the old door and thundered in. The horse, wild-eyed and scared witless, lost its footing and fell, pinning Reese to the floor, crushing the man's stomach and chest. Reese howled in agony as blood filled his mouth and darkness clouded his eyes.

Smoke left the dying man and ran out the side door.

"Get him, Turkel!" Brown screamed.

Smoke glanced up. Turkel was on the roof of an old building, a rifle in his hand. Smoke flattened against a building as Turkel pulled the trigger, the slug plowing up dirt at Smoke's feet. Smoke snapped off a shot, getting lucky as the bullet hit the gunhand in the chest. Turkel dropped the rifle and fell to the street, crashing through an awning. He did not move.

A bullet removed a small part of Smoke's right upper ear; blood poured down the side of his face. He ran to where he had hid the shotgun, grabbing it up and cocking it, leveling it just as the doorway filled with men.

Firing both barrels, Smoke cleared the doorway of all living things, including Britt, Harris, and Smith, the buckshot knocking the men clear off the rotting boardwalk, dead and dying in the street.

"Goddamn you, Jensen!" Brown screamed in rage, stepping out into the street.

Smoke dropped the shotgun and picked up a bloody rifle from the doorway. He shot Brown in the stomach. Brown howled and dropped to the street, both hands holding his stomach.

Rogers leveled a pistol and fired, the bullet ricocheting off a support post, part of the lead striking Smoke's left leg, dropping him to the boardwalk. Smoke ended Rogers's career with a single shot to the head.

White-hot pain lanced through Smoke's side as Williams shot him from behind. Smoke fell off the boardwalk, turning as he fell. He fired twice, the lead taking Williams in the neck, almost tearing the man's head off.

Ducking back inside, grabbing up a fallen shotgun with blood on the barrel, Smoke checked the shotgun, then checked his wounds. Bleeding, but not serious. Williams's slug had gone through the fleshy part of the side. Using the point of his knife, Smoke picked out the tiny piece of lead from Rogers's gun and tied a bandana around the slight wound. He slipped further into the darkness of the building as spurs jingled in the alley to the rear of the old store. Smoke jacked back both hammers on the coach gun. He waited.

The spurs jingled once more. Smoke followed the

sound with the twin barrels of the express gun. Carefully, silently, he slipped across the rat-dropping-littered floor to the wall that fronted the alley. He could hear breathing directly in front of him.

He pulled both triggers, the charge blowing a bucket-sized hole in the old pine wall.

The gunslick was blown clear across the alley, hurled against an outhouse. The outhouse collapsed, the gunhand falling into the shit-pit.

Silently, Smoke reloaded the shotgun, then reloaded his own .44s and the ones taken from the dead gunnie. He listened as Fenerty called for his buddies.

There was no reply.

Fenerty was the last gunhawk left.

Smoke located the voice. Just across the street in a falling-down old building. Laying aside the shotgun, he picked up a rifle and emptied the magazine into the store-front. Fenerty came staggering out, shot in the chest and belly. He died facedown in the littered street.

"All right, you bastards!" Smoke yelled to Richards, Potter, and Stratton. "Holster your guns and step out into the street. Face me, if you've got the nerve."

The sharp odor of sweat mingled with blood and gun-smoke filled the still summer air as four men stepped out into the bloody, dusty street.

Richards, Potter, and Stratton stood at one end of the block. A tall, bloody figure stood at the other. All their guns were in leather.

"You son of a bitch!" Stratton screamed, his voice as high-pitched as a woman. "You ruined it all." He clawed at his .44.

Smoke drew and fired before Stratton's pistol could clear leather. Potter grabbed for his pistol. Smoke shot him dead, then holstered his gun, waiting.

Richards had not moved. He stood with a faint smile on his lips, staring at Smoke.

"You ready to die?" Smoke asked the man.

"As ready as I'll ever be, I suppose," Richards replied. There was no fear in his voice. His hands appeared steady. "Janey gone?"

"Took your money and pulled out."

"Been a long run, hasn't it, Jensen?"

"It's just about over."

"What happens to all our holdings?"

"I don't care what happens to the mines. The miners can have them. I'm giving all your stock to decent, honest punchers and homesteaders."

A puzzled look spread over Richards' face. "I don't understand. You did . . . all *this*!" he waved his hand— "for nothing?"

Someone moaned, the sound painfully inching up the street.

"I did it for my pa, my brother, my wife, and my baby son."

"But it won't bring them back!"

"I know."

"I wish I had never heard the name Jensen."

"You'll never hear it again after this day, Richards."

"One way to find out," Richards said with a smile. He drew his Colt and fired. He was snake-quick, but hurried his shot, the lead digging up dirt at Smoke's feet.

Smoke shot him in the right shoulder, spinning the man around. Richards grabbed for his left-hand gun and Smoke fired again, the slug striking the man in the left side of his chest. He struggled to bring up his Colt. He managed to cock it before Smoke's third shot struck him in the belly. Richards sat down hard in the bloody, dusty street.

He opened his mouth to speak. He tasted blood on his tongue. The light began to fade around him. "You'll . . . meet . . ."

Smoke never found out who he was supposed to meet. Richards toppled over on his side and died.

Smoke looked up at the ridge where the mountain men had gathered.

They were gone, leaving as silently as the wind.

24

After MacGregor filed his report with the commanding officer at the fort, the Army made only a cursory inspection of what was left of Bury, Idaho Territory, and the burned ranches around it.

Wanted posters were put out for the outlaw and murderer Buck West. MacGregor wrote the description of the man, thus ensuring he would never be found.

A lot of small ranches sprang up around the area. Very prosperous little farms and ranchers. The ladies from the Pink House stayed. They all got married.

Sam married Becky.

The last anyone ever saw of Smoke Jensen and Sally Reynolds, the two of them were riding toward the mountains, toward the High Lonesome, leading two pack-horses.

"You think we'll ever see them again?" Becky asked Sam.

Sam did not reply.

But as Nighthawk might have said, "Ummm."

Connect with Us

Visit us online at
KensingtonBooks.com
to read more from your favorite authors, see books
by series, view reading group guides, and more.

Join us on social media

for sneak peeks, chances to win books and prize packs,
and to share your thoughts with other readers.

facebook.com/kensingtonpublishing
twitter.com/kensingtonbooks

Tell us what you think!

To share your thoughts, submit a review,
or sign up for our eNewsletters, please visit:
KensingtonBooks.com/TellUs.